N

Praise for
All God's Children
and Thomas Eidson

"In that time and place of the closing of the frontier on the western plains, Thomas Eidson has found an unexplored milieu in which to tell of good and evil. He demonstrates heroism of a kind quite different from the heroics that prevailed preceding that period. Out of the dramatic narration comes Pearl Eddy, a woman determined to endure in a world set against her, and who surely will continue to endure as a literary figure of her time and place."
—Dee Brown, author *Bury My Heart at Wounded Knee*

"Maintains the immediacy of a tale told by firelight."
—*London Times*

"Eidson's novels feature plenty of action but, above all, they are warm tales of morality choices, atonements, and redemptions. Good and evil do battle in people's hearts as well as the OK Corral."
—*Bookseller*

ALL GOD'S CHILDREN

THOMAS EIDSON

A SIGNET BOOK

SIGNET
Published by the Penguin Group
Penguin Putnam Inc., 375 Hudson Street,
New York, New York 10014, U.S.A.
Penguin Books Ltd, 27 Wrights Lane,
London W8 5TZ, England
Penguin Books Australia Ltd,
Ringwood, Victoria, Australia
Penguin Books Canada Ltd, 10 Alcorn Avenue,
Toronto, Ontario, Canada M4V 3B2
Penguin Books (N.Z.) Ltd, 182–190 Wairau Road,
Auckland 10, New Zealand

Penguin Books Ltd, Registered Offices:
Harmondsworth, Middlesex, England

Published by Signet, an imprint of Dutton Signet,
a member of Penguin Putnam Inc.
Previously appeared in a Dutton edition

Originally published in a somewhat different form in Great Britain by
Michael Joseph Ltd.

First Signet Printing, February, 1998
10 9 8 7 6 5 4 3 2 1

 REGISTERED TRADEMARK—MARCA REGISTRADA

Printed in the United States of America

For Sally and Dick . . .
Sisters and brothers don't
get any better

It is dangerous to let man see
too clearly how closely he resembles
the beasts unless, at the same time,
we show him how great he is.

—BLAISE PASCAL

Prologue

Zella, Kansas. December 3, 1891

Like a hand of ice gripping the back of her neck, winter wind blew in across the prairie and into the garden, where they stood staring at the coffin. "Christ, the Way, the Truth, and the Life," she whispered to herself, grasping harder at the hand of her five-year-old son, Zacharias. She could feel the boy heaving in silent sobs. Samuel, her eldest at thirteen, held her arm in support. The twins, Joshua and Luke, ten, clung tightly to each other.

No one had spoken since the elders had carried the box out of the barn and into this frozen place. She knew they might not unless the Spirit moved them.

"Christ, the Way, the Truth," she repeated silently, her thoughts on Matthew and their life together. Fifteen years. Gone so fast?

Low gray fog drifted in over the tops of the towering prairie grasses that surrounded the farm, hovering near the road, sending vinelike fingers probing among the carriages and the legs of the horses, edging across the yard and into the garden where the two groups waited, two distinctly different groups.

Pearl Eddy and her children stood with those who

were bundled in somber black and gray and hatted, twenty members of the Society of Friends. They had driven through fifty miles of cold from the town of Blackwell to be with the Eddys, the only Quakers in Zella. Every so often one of them would trudge off through the snow to break ice from their horses' noses, so the animals could breathe.

"I want to see my father," Zacharias said, staring at two boys standing close to the plank box on the ground before the open grave. They were snickering nervously, each trying to get the other to lift the coffin's lid.

"Thou may not," Pearl whispered, gripping his small hand harder.

"Why?"

"Because thy father is with God," Pearl said, avoiding the truth.

Someone sneezed in the second group of mourners clustered behind the Quakers. These were the towns-people, come to pay their respects. And she could tell from the sounds of clearing throats and quiet cough-ing that they didn't understand the silence, wondering when the service would commence and they could get out of this burning cold.

She was grateful for their presence, knowing how much they had liked Matthew, comforted by the fact that friends, if not relations, were here. She tensed slowly at this last thought. Pearl's parents were dead. She had no other living relatives. On Matthew's side there was his mother, Lillian, and two elderly aunts. None of them had been able to make it in time. She wondered if Lillian would have come even had there been time. She stopped herself. She would not think such thoughts on this day.

She shook her head and braced herself against the cold, her loss, and her fears. She had never understood what had caused Lillian to dislike her, whether it was a mother's natural protectiveness or a feeling of superiority. The Eddys were an old established Rhode Island family—Episcopalian merchants, lawyers, and politicians—while her own parents were immigrant Dutch farmers.

Whatever Lillian's reasons, she had shunned Pearl from the moment she learned of her and Matthew's meeting at Yale. Five generations of Eddys had attended the New Haven college, and Matthew had dutifully gone. But he wanted nothing of commerce, law, or politics. As some men dream of wealth or power, he dreamed of farming.

She smiled through her sadness, remembering the day she had fallen in love with him. Unable to afford college, Pearl assisted the staff of the Yale library, the building some four miles from her family's farm. She cleared her throat and sank deeper into her clothing to avoid the cold, focusing on that wonderful spring morning.

She had been busy opening the reading hall for the day. The room was impressive with its handsome proportions, a large rectangle with towering ceiling and ornate chandeliers. Rows of tall windows were set in the south and north walls, and Pearl was standing near one listening to the beautiful trilling notes of a goldfinch and daydreaming when she heard footsteps behind her.

Turning quickly, she immediately recognized the smiling voice of the young man of twenty-one or twenty-two as Matthew Eddy's. She had spoken to him many times, but only of books. Therefore she was stunned when he asked, "Will you join me at tonight's social?" He had paused grandly. "Perhaps you are not familiar with these?" In response she had stood staring openmouthed at him as if facing a charging lion. Now, fifteen years later, on the saddest day of her life, she was torn not to laugh at what he had later described as the expression of absolute terror on her face.

Never had Pearl been anywhere "socially" unless the few village dinners and gatherings of the Society of Friends, simple family affairs, counted. She knew they did not. But though badly flummoxed, she heard herself saying yes. Then afterward, as she trudged the long road home, she was mortified, swallowing hard bites of air and holding each one as if she might never get another, wondering why in the world she had ever accepted.

All that afternoon she fretted and paced her upstairs bedroom, wringing her hands, dreading the thought of standing beside lovely, bare-shouldered girls in fashionable hairdos and beautiful gowns with well-fitted bodices and flowing skirts, while she wore Quaker gray, her hair pulled back severely in a plain bun. In sheer desperation she had told her mother, Estra, her fears, hoping that when she learned Matthew was not a member of the Society she would forbid it. She had not.

Love had been Estra's greatest talent. The perfect Quaker, she believed in one thing and one thing only: charity toward her fellowman. Pearl recalled their conversation as if it were only yesterday. Estra said, "He is obviously a young man of character to value thy full person regardless of thy dress and mannerisms." Pearl had protested vigorously.

And as the shadows of that bygone day had grown, so grew Pearl's fears. Then, promptly at the appointed hour, Matthew was at the door smelling of cologne and, as her mother described him, dressed in a handsome claw-hammer evening coat, gold studs and matching cuff links on his white shirt, his collar stiff and starched, beaming his bright smile and touching her hand in a marveling way, as if she were God's most beautiful creation. She knew she was not, but his touch was wonderfully convincing.

Even so, she still dreaded the evening. Others, she knew, would not view her in such a kindly fashion. Then something magnificent happened, something that changed her life forever.

After introducing Matthew to Estra, Pearl was starting to the barn for her father when Matthew stopped her, saying it would be his privilege. She and her mother retired to the small parlor to wait. And wait. Fully a fretful hour passed before the two men returned up the walk, their voices raised in earnest debate over various breeds of European poultry. They had stopped along the way, her father explained matter-of-factly, to complete the evening milking. Matthew's fine clothes, her mother whispered, were covered in muck and mud, and he was smiling his wonderful smile and looking as if he had just had the greatest fun a man could have when, suddenly, his collar sprang loose on one side.

When told this, Pearl had successfully suppressed the first titters, then fought off an attack of giggles, turning her head until these passed. Her only mistake had been to listen to Estra's muffled snickering. Once started, neither woman could stop her convulsive laughter. And somewhere in the midst of their heaving peals of mirth, after they had been forced to sit on chairs lest they fall down, tears streaming over their cheeks, Pearl had felt herself deeply moved by this young man who cared not a whit for fine clothes, money, or position, this young man whose simple passion was the earth, plants, and animals.

Giggling at the description of him standing sheepishly in his soiled and fashionable clothes under the yellow light of the parlor's wall lamps, she sensed a goodness about Matthew Eddy and determined, if he would have her, to share life and eternity with him. It had been that simple for her. Never in fifteen years had she been sorry.

For his part, Matthew had fallen just as hard in love with her, having the good common sense to understand that Quakerism was not Pearl's religion but her life. And because he prized her so deeply, Matthew became a soul in the Society of Friends. Or tried. She smiled. He had not been a very good Quaker.

She smiled again before the expression around her eyes and mouth changed to painful contemplation. His decision had been an act of love, but one that had cost him his life. She tensed. She had cost him his life. Her upper lip was trembling hard now, and she reached and touched it with the tips of her fingers.

"Mother?"

"I am fine."

Samuel nodded and returned to staring at the wooden box.

Their decision to move to Kansas had sealed Pearl's fate with her mother-in-law. No matter how many times Matthew had explained that it was he who wanted to move to what easterners called the "grass sea" for free land, Lillian would not believe him, believing instead that Pearl was stealing her boy away.

"I want to see my father," Zacharias moaned. "I have to tell him something."

"Hush," she said softly. "Thy father is gone from this earth." The boy was sobbing hard now.

"We commend our brother to God," Elder Fredrick Gray said in a loud, clear voice that pierced the frigid afternoon air in the same way it did Pearl's heart.

"Take me to him," she whispered to Samuel.

Slowly he guided his mother forward toward the coffin, the two town boys backing awkwardly away.

She knelt and put her hand upon the rough-cut cotton-wood planks. Zacharias stood with his hands on her shoulder, staring down in shock, not willing to believe that his father was inside the wooden box, soon to be in the earth.

Pearl leaned forward and whispered something none of them could hear. She knelt there awhile, then stood. "Zacharias. Thou wanted to say something to thy father."

The boy leaned in tighter against her. "Just that I don't want him to go."

Pearl put a hand on his head and pulled him close. "Zacharias," she said reassuringly, "thy father is with God. That is a glorious thing."

"I want him here!"

"Thou must accept God's will."

The boy stood shaking his head back and forth, tears flowing.

When the townspeople saw Pearl and her boys moving away from the grave, they realized there was to be no more said or done. An audible muttering of surprise rose among them, and then, suddenly, Rose Sherman, an old friend of Pearl's, began singing "Rock of Ages" and slowly people began to join her until all were singing. All but the Quakers. They stood in respectful silence waiting for the song to be over, so they could say their farewells.

They would go as they came, quietly and gently. They would not linger to eat the food that the town women had brought or exchange gossip about the weather and crops, laughing to lighten death the way the others would. No. They would simply go their steady, austere way, love and peace in their hearts. She knew them well. She was one of them. And that scared her.

Matthew had been her bridge to this town, to this

other world. She shuddered, knowing he had died because of it. Now she would have to make it alone. She and her boys. "Follow Christ to find that life which is life," she said quietly, shaking hard.

Then she heard the scream. The two town boys had opened the coffin and stood staring into it as if frozen by the cold. One of the elders hurriedly shut the lid before anyone else could see inside.

Chapter One

Zella, Kansas. April 25, 1893

Someone, she thought, had tried her back door earlier, but the old house remained quiet, and she knew the screen wouldn't open without screeching, so she stopped listening. The early lilacs were in bloom, and she had raised the windows in the parlor where she was sitting for the sweet fragrance. The house was dark. She liked to work this way, comfortable in the peaceful solitude of the night.

Slowly she stiffened, the skin across the nape of her neck tingling with the unnerving sensation that someone was standing behind her. "Yes?" she called softly, expecting one of her boys to respond sleepily from the shadows. But there was no answer. She waited. Still nothing. Gradually the troubling feeling began to dissipate, and she forced it out of her mind.

Pearl Eddy pulled the fabric higher onto her lap and continued making careful stitches around the hemline. And on this night in this darkened and isolated house in the middle of tallgrass prairie, miles from town or the nearest neighbor, she tried to focus on the critical problems in her family's life: how to keep her house and land . . .

Pearl disliked worry. She didn't believe in it. And she was wondering why she couldn't just let go of it when suddenly she was holding her breath and listening once more. Her attention was riveted to the back of the house; a board had creaked as if stepped on. A moment later it creaked again, slowly this time, as though someone were carefully releasing the pressure. The rooms were quiet. Perhaps too quiet, she thought. Her mind began to race with crazy thoughts.

Her heart beat faster. They never locked the doors or windows of the old house. Not when Matthew was alive, not now that he was dead. She was trembling.

"Hello?" she called. There was no response. "I heard thee," she bluffed. The house remained silent. She waited a few minutes. But no other sounds came to her, and she began to feel foolish again, assuring herself the noises were only in her imagination. She returned to her stitching, forcing her thoughts to the house itself.

In her mind it was the perfect home in which to raise children. Its paint and various woods were nicked and marred; the furniture too was worn and comfortable, with a friendly patina of age and happy living. Not stylish, simply practical and durable. While not ramshackle, the substantial old structure was growing a little seedy, needing repairs to windows, the roof, doors, and the like.

In the room's peaceful quietude the clock beside her chimed eleven. She needed sleep, but one of her customers, Mother Rose Sherman, was scheduled for a fitting the next morning. She yawned, cupping her finely shaped hand over her mouth, then sewed on, slowly submerging herself in silence.

She had been making ends meet during the past year and a half from seamstressing and the plants. Barely making ends meet: Things were fraying at the edges. Her throat tightened at the thought, and her mind leaped to the letter. She had received it the week before and repeated it now from memory.

My dear Mrs. Eddy:

Our records show that you have not cleared two loans for farm equipment. We have allowed these debts to remain on our books because of our sympathy during your mourning period. However, we are certain you agree, this matter must be attended to. Therefore, we respectfully request payment in the amount of $500 within sixty days.

I know that I do not need to remind you that under the terms of this obligation these monies must be repaid or your land, buildings, and chattel sold to cover them.

Sincerely,

Alfred Snipes
Manager
The Bank of Kansas

Pearl had not known about the loans. She guessed Matthew had known she would not approve. She bit hard at her lower lip. Five hundred dollars. She did not have it. Her hands were trembling badly now, and she intertwined her fingers and held them in her lap. She had no more than half the needed money.

Pearl jumped. She had felt a slight stirring in the room, a movement of air from behind the chair, as if someone had opened a door somewhere. For a moment she was too afraid to move; then slowly she convinced herself that no one was in the parlor, that the door had been opened in another room. She stood, turning her head back and forth in the shadows, scanning the room with her ears, concentrating hard to pick up any errant sounds in the darkness. Nothing. Nor could she feel the cold draft any longer. But she had felt it. She was certain of that.

The hair rose slightly on her arms. Her thoughts were suddenly no longer on the strange noises or the odd movement of air inside the room but, rather, on something worse, something she couldn't quite grasp.

But it was beginning to frighten her, the nagging sensation that someone was watching her, watching her standing in this darkened room at this very moment. She shivered hard. Quickly she moved through the bottom floor of the house, checking closets and doors and windows.

Fifteen minutes later she had found nothing. Still, she could not shake the alarming feeling that someone was nearby, watching. She tensed. She had not checked her boys.

Once inside the bedroom, she heard the boys' quiet breathing, the sound slowly calming her fears; then she moved along the wall until she came to the window. Shut. She locked it. Pearl stopped beside the twins, Joshua and Luke, touching her fingers softly to both their heads. They were sleeping soundly in a bed that was too small for them, back to back. She rearranged the covers and tucked them in.

Samuel was also in a bed that was too small for him, his bare feet dangling over the end. She wasn't keeping up very well, she chided herself. Couldn't afford to. In Samuel's case it was hard to keep up, the way he was outgrowing things, now even beds.

Big enough to be a man, but still a boy. Pearl placed a hand on his thin back and felt his rapid breath and knew that he was struggling again with his growing worries. Ever since his father's death she had watched him wrestling to figure out who he was and where he was headed in this life. She wished she could be of more help to him.

Pearl kissed the back of Samuel's head and moved on to Zacharias, her youngest. The bedcovers were balled up at his feet, and when she felt his forehead, he was cool. She straightened the blankets over him, then searched until she touched the cold metal of the picture frame. Zacharias was holding it clutched in his arms as if it were valuable treasure. In some ways, she guessed, it was. The frame contained the only photograph they had of Matthew.

"Zacharias," she said softly, pulling gently on the picture. He held on tight.

Zacharias had taken it to bed this night, she knew, as he had every night since his father's death, talking to it—telling it things he wanted his father to know—until he drifted off. Since Matthew's death the boys had been sleeping all crowded together in this one room. For comfort, she guessed. None of them had complained about Zacharias's nightly conversations. It made her want to cry.

"Zacharias, let go of it, child," she said, slowly unbending his small fingers from around the edge until the frame was free of his grasp.

She ran her hand over the fine silver—cold and heavy—a gift from Lillian Eddy, Matthew's mother. The only expensive thing in her entire house. She smiled wearily. Too fine and costly. But since this was their only photograph of Matthew and the boys treasured it, the frame seemed justified.

Pearl was bending to kiss Zacharias when suddenly the house sparrows that made their nightly roost in the wisteria near the boys' window scattered noisily in the darkness. Her mind flew to the earlier noises. "Calm thyself," she whispered under her breath. Possums often climbed the bushes near the house looking for nests. But it was too early for nesting, and possums knew that as well as she did. Pearl trembled.

Her fears focused on the feeling of being watched, wondering if someone outside had tracked her movements through the windows as she walked inside the darkened rooms. Pearl returned to the chair in the parlor and sat tensely holding the frame in her lap.

She sat for a long time to regain some composure, listening for the inner voice of the Spirit. It didn't come to her. But she did hear a sound. She tensed, thinking for a moment that it was a runaway horse outside in the empty darkness of the fields surrounding the lonely farm. But it was something else, something indistinct that seemed to be rushing out of the prairie night toward the parlor. Then she heard the back door squeak and knew. Someone was in the house.

Pearl was backing reflexively toward the parlor wall, listening with her mouth open so that her breathing wouldn't interfere with her hearing, when she heard the cellar door in the hall open, then close, the latch clicking. There were no windows in the cellar. No way out. Would the intruder realize this and suddenly lunge back up the stairs?

She moved quickly across the parlor and into the hallway, hurriedly locking the door. Then she froze, sniffing the air. The odor was at once familiar, but oddly out of place. She bent, searching until her fingers touched it. Blood drops ran in a line across the floor. Whoever this was, he was hurt. Something caught inside her.

Moments later a sudden pounding on the front door of the house caused her to emit a small cry. "Who is it?" She half expected Sheriff Haines to reply, but it was Jake Bidwell who said, "Mrs. Eddy."

Bidwell had once been a hired hand on their farm,

and she had midwifed his second child. She did not care for the way he lived. He worked little, drank hard, and was rough on his wife.

"We're hunting a man," he said, looking boldly past her into the shadows of the darkened house. She recognized the voices of others as workers in the carriage factory south of town or loafers around the saloon and livery.

"Buck nigger," one of them added.

She stiffened.

"Colored," Bidwell corrected, slurring the word. "Robbed Simon James—attacked his three boys."

"Are they alive?"

"The boys are busted up. Simon's with us," he said, nodding his head back toward the yard.

"The sheriff?" Pearl asked, unable to get her thoughts off a young Negro lynched across the Missouri line the year they came out to Kansas. "Cause of death unknown, but severe," the newspaper had cruelly reported.

"Bad nigger," one of the men said. "We'll search your place, then be—"

"Do not use that word, sir."

The man stepped closer. "Like I said, we're going to search this house."

Pearl had opened the door, fully intending to turn the intruder over, but now—without the sheriff present and listening to the drunken sounds of these men—something shifted hard inside her. Whoever he was, whatever he had done, she knew the Negro would not survive the night in their hands. And she could not surrender him to that fate. "Where is the sheriff?"

"Doesn't mat—"

"Yes. It matters," she interrupted.

"We're hunting a gawddamn criminal."

"Perhaps, sir. But not in my house," she said stiffly.

Suddenly the man who had been talking reached out and grabbed Pearl's thin shoulder, studying the handsome lines of her face. "Couple of us could make you feel real safe."

"Pete, let her go," Bidwell muttered. "She ain't that kind."

There was a murmur of agreement.

"Religious truster," another offered.

But the man didn't release her until another said, "We aren't after the Quaker."

Pearl knew the voice was that of Simon James, the owner of a traveling tent show. He and his children lived in Zella during the off-season, and over the years she had helped doctor his daughter, Chrissy, for asthma. Even so, the man had never been passably civil to her.

"We're searching this house," Simon said.

"No, sir. Thou art not."

The men on the porch watched him moving slowly toward Pearl Eddy, their eyes running over his stocky frame. He was maybe five-eight, stout but not soft; his large, fleshy head was wreathed in curly gray locks. This hair, some had noted before, when coupled with his olive complexion, gave him the look of an Italian. It was an observation, they knew, best left unspoken. As leader of the Royal Order of Redmen, a local patriotic organization, Simon James boasted of his "American" blood, and few were inclined to dispute his heritage. His broad face was flat, the nose prominent; the dark eyes were intelligent and hard; the mouth was full. He was not young—perhaps sixty—but even so, he looked to have the strength of a fat bullock.

Simon had a cigar stump wedged in a corner of his mouth, and the smoke billowed around his head, drifting across the darkness in the direction of the gardens. "Get out of my way," he snapped at Pearl.

"Leave my porch, sir," she countered.

"We chased the Negro down your damn road."

"And thou may continue down the road."

Simon James had a loathing for females, and he was breathing hard staring at this defiant one standing in her doorway. In his lifetime women had never done anything but cause him problems. He had been abandoned by both his mother and wife; so much for the motherhood of man, he thought. And as a sailor he had picked up the French pox in a pisspot of a Chinese port, the disease still rotting him in ways he didn't understand but feared. Even as a traveling showman, crusading females—Jills-at-a-pinch—caused him business problems, picketing against scientific exhibits of the human body and curatives he sold, driving him to ruination in many a town. Always the bleeding women. He cleared phlegm from his throat and spit.

"We're going to search this house," he repeated.

"No, thou will not, sir," she said, shutting the door until only a crack remained.

"You hold on—"

"Good night."

When the latch clicked, Pearl slid the dead bolt home. She could hear Simon cursing her, and she waited in the darkness until she was certain they were gone; then she hurried into the kitchen. She forced herself to slow down and braced a chair under the cellar door handle, wondering if it and the lock would hold the man. Probably for a while. Then she remembered what they had said: The man had beaten the three James boys. He didn't sound normal. Perhaps a madman, with a madman's strength.

She leaned close to the door and listened. Nothing. She backed away, then cleared her throat.

"I know thou art down there." She waited for his response. If he heard her, he said nothing. She pulled the door to the parlor shut so that she wouldn't wake the boys.

"Please do not try to fool me," she said, her voice rising. She paused. "I can get a doctor." Still there was no reply, and she stood pondering what else to say.

Some ten minutes later she was sitting on a stool in the hallway facing the cellar door, her troubled thoughts on the man's possible injuries. Was his life ebbing away because she refused to open the door? The image of a Negro in death throes flashed in her mind. Should she not open the door? She hesitated. Was he dangerous? It didn't matter, she couldn't just let him die.

"I am trying to help."

She waited a long time, but no answer came.

"If thou cannot talk, make noise."

Pearl was turning away when she heard a muffled banging from below. She hesitated. Then, with a hand that was shaking so hard she had to hold it by the wrist to steady it, she turned the key in the lock.

He was hiding and shivering in his wet clothes, his throat burning from the leaky stovepipe, his watering eyes searching nervously for whoever had come down the cellar steps moments before. He had been peeking in the darkened windows earlier and thought this house was empty. Obviously not. He heard them coughing from the smoke and kicked himself for having started the stove. But he was freezing and exhausted and fast reaching the point where he didn't care about much. Certainly not Kansas and Kansans. He was hard put to understand why he had ever come here. It made no sense. He went back to searching the darkness.

He knew Negroes who had been taken by mobs. It wasn't going to happen to him. Not while he could still fight. He hefted the sap in his hand. It would work only if he could get close. Except for the weak glow from the stove, there was no light in the cellar. Whoever it was, he had to have a gun. Even so, he was pretty dull-headed, poking around in a dark hole without a light.

Suddenly the fire flared, and he ducked, kicking himself again for starting the stove. But he had run a mile or more in an icy river to escape the town dogs and was near frozen. On top of that he hadn't eaten in two days and was determined to roast the chicken he had pilfered.

"Art thou hurt badly?"

He jumped: a woman's voice.

"I will help thee."

He bit at his lip. The fact that it was a woman didn't make a whole lot of difference; she could still shoot him. Nevertheless, it bothered him. He had never hurt a woman before. He guessed at the distance to the stairs, figuring he could make it in six strides, then forced himself to stop. She would see him as soon as he stood and start firing; then he would be running again. Or dead.

He peeked over the box he was hiding behind, squinting hard. She was white, small, and wearing a long gray dress that swept the floor and blended with the shadows. He guessed she was thirty something.

"Sir? Canst thou hear me?"

He ducked again, feeling stiff and far older than his fifty-some years. It was no use. She knew he was here, and she wasn't going to quit until she found him. Anyhow, things might go better if he just gave himself up. If she got scared and went back upstairs without finding him, knowing that he was down here, she would surely set the mob on him.

When she turned away again, he started for a barrel in front of the stove, stepping as quietly as he could. But he dragged his right foot slightly, the way he did sometimes, not much, but still, it scraped across the cellar floor.

"Sir?" Her voice quivered in the darkness.

Ears like a damn bat, he thought. He sat quickly on the barrel and tried to look nonchalant. Listening to her rapid breathing, he could tell she was frightened. But scared or not, she was scurrying toward him.

He cleared his throat and started easy whistling to warn her. She stopped moving, and he stopped whistling, the notes drifting away ghostlike in the darkness. He squirmed. She was no more than ten feet away, but watching her turning her head back and forth, he knew she hadn't seen him yet.

"I have come to help thee."

He braced. "Pipe needs fixing," he said, as friendly as he could, praying she was a bad shot. Seconds ticked by. He peeked at her. She had hopped back and was staring openmouthed at him, looking small and breathing as if she might be drowning in the shadows.

"How badly art thou hurt?"

"I'm not. Just cold."

She paused. "Thou art not hurt?"

"No, ma'am."

"Thou signaled thou were." There was the slightest change in her tone.

"No, I didn't."

"Yes, thou didst," she said quickly, some of the nervous tension breaking through her voice. "I said make noise if thou art hurt and cannot talk, and thou hit something."

He was surprised. She seemed less concerned about

standing in a dark cellar a few feet from a total stranger—a Negro who had just broken into her house to escape a mob—than whether or not he had humbugged her into coming down the stairs. He hadn't tricked her. The last thing he wanted was a woman down here arguing with him while the whole town was hunting him.

"I didn't signal anything."

"Yes, I heard thee."

He shook his head and started to reply, then decided not to. He glanced at her hands. Empty. No pistol. It must be in her pocket. He was surprised she wasn't waving it around, threatening him. Regardless, since she was agitated about the so-called signal that had caused her to come down, he picked up a hammer and banged the stovepipe a couple of times. She jumped as if she herself had been struck.

"There's your signal. I was trying to get this damn thing to stop smoking."

"Please do not swear."

He nodded at her, embarrassed by his slip, his teeth chattering, and pointed the handle of the hammer at the old stove. "You need a new one."

"Never mind, sir. What art thou doing down here?"

It was a tough question.

"Sir?"

"Fixing dinner."

The absurdity of his reply stopped Pearl for a moment, and she clasped her hands behind her so he wouldn't see them shaking.

"Dinner?"

"Dinner," he repeated. "Chicken."

"Chicken?"

"Yes, ma'am."

She got a funny look on her face. "What kind?"

"Hen."

"But what kind?"

"I don't know." He crossed his arms and rubbed his hands up and down them—hard—then gripped himself, trying to conserve what little body heat he had left.

"Surely thou knowest one from another."

"Red feathers, ma'am," he said, shrugging his shoulders and glancing at the pile of them near his feet. "That's all I know."

"Rhode Island Red," she mumbled. Then the tension building inside her released in a sudden flood of words. "Thou hadst no right to kill my hen, no right to break into my house." She stopped, grappling for words to express her emotions. "Thou—thou ought to be ashamed." She spoke the last of it as if it were the worst thing on earth that could be said about a person.

"I got this chicken down the road."

Her expression didn't change.

"That is my chicken."

He shrugged his shoulders beneath his wet shirt, the cold grabbing him again. Though she was not much bigger than a Russian thistle, she had come down here, without so much as a match, to find somebody who had broken into her house. And now, having found him, she was acting like a Texan at the Alamo. All because of a dead bird.

"That is my chicken," she repeated with growing firmness.

Somehow he had to distract her. "My name's Prophet."

She didn't look the least distracted.

"Not like in money, like prophets in the Bible," he explained.

For a while nothing much happened. Then her stiff expression slowly began to change, the strained look in her eyes relaxing. At last he had said something that had started her thinking. And when she thought, the whole process could be seen on her face. He squinted and tried to make out her features, but in the dark and with his eyes, he couldn't tell much.

"Art thou a minister?"

He shook his head no. Then again. She wasn't six feet away, but she continued to look as if she hadn't seen him. He decided it was best to avoid the question anyhow, so he asked, "What's your name, ma'am?"

"Pearl Eddy."

"Pearl Eddy." He mouthed the words slowly. "Pearl Eddy," he repeated. "Nice. Very nice."

She didn't react. And he knew flattery wasn't going to work on her anytime soon.

"I do not understand thee," she said.

"About?"

"Why thou, a minister, wouldst steal my hen?"

He couldn't believe this woman. . . . She thought he had tricked her because he had banged a hammer on a stovepipe. Now she thought he was a minister because he called himself Prophet. She was definitely missing something vital in her head.

"Ma'am, I'm sorry about the chicken. But it's still just a chicken. From what I saw, there are fifty or sixty others."

"Hardly the point, Mr. Prophet."

"Yes, ma'am." He stood slowly, getting ready to position himself so that he could move between her and the stairs in case she decided to run, but she hopped up onto the first step. Nobody's fool.

"Just saying thou art sorry does not make up for what thou hast done to my hen, sir." She hopped up another step.

She had him now. He might catch her before she reached the top, but she would be screaming all the way. And if this was a trick, there would be men at the top of the stairs. He thought of those dead Negroes. "Just sit," he told himself.

"Yes, ma'am."

"Thou hast no business telling me that my hen was just a chicken." She paused. "Thou knowest nothing about my hen."

It was as if he had strangled her favorite aunt. He settled back down on the keg. "Ma'am, I'll pay for the hen."

The offer didn't appear to appease her much.

The fire cast a wavering glow over her, and he thought she looked pretty, but he wasn't certain in the murky light. Then his stomach grumbled.

"Ma'am?"

"Yes?"

"Do you have any salt?"

She made an awkward little sound. "Mr. Prophet, thou art a bold man. Thou killest my hen, break into my home, then ask for salt to season thy stolen food." She stumbled around on the stairs for a moment, then started up, taking the steps in a careful stride that caught his eye. He stood, and she whirled back.

"Stay where thou art, sir."

He could see she was trembling like a snared sparrow.

"Ma'am, I've done nothing but hide myself from a mob."

That statement was another lie. He had tried to pick a fat man's pocket and been caught. Three other men had jumped him. He had handled them easily enough with the sap, but getting out of town had proved more difficult; the crowd had chased him through yards, up alleys, and over fences, before he had lost them by hiding under a pile of corrugated iron. But then a dog had dug him out, raising a ruckus in the process. After that he had run hard down a river and across fields until he escaped by slipping in here at this lonely farmhouse.

"It is not my place to judge thee, sir." She was halfway up the stairs. "Just stay where thou art."

He watched her slowly climbing, calculating the odds she wouldn't get the mob. Not good. His impulse was to move at once, to rush up the stairs to freedom, but he resisted it. He wouldn't last out in the open. Not with the dogs.

When she was near the top, he called, "If you—"

"Mr. Prophet?"

"If you turn me in."

"I gave thee my word."

"But if you change your mind, I'd be obliged if it was the sheriff." In the hands of the sheriff, he knew, he might have a chance.

"I gave thee my word," she said firmly.

Minutes later she was back on the stairs, tray balanced in her hand, taking her ponderous steps and gripping the banister with her free hand as if she might fall a thousand feet if she let go. She set the tray down on the keg and stood without saying anything. Bread and butter, a glass of milk, pitcher of water, a slice of apple pie, and salt. It looked wonderful. But even better were the two blankets she carried wedged under one arm.

"Thank you, ma'am," Prophet said, hurriedly stepping behind a pile of boxes and pulling off his galluses, his worn and soaking wet flannel shirt and pants, then stopping to look with consternation at his ruined boots, the first new pair he'd had in a long time. He shook his head, then wrapped one blanket around his waist and pulled the other across his shoulders. They were worn. Clean-smelling and neatly patched, but worn. Still, they felt wonderful against his chilled skin.

"Thank you." He was embarrassed standing in front of this tiny woman like some African chieftain in blankets. But she didn't seem to notice or care. Still hitched up over the dead hen, he bet.

"Thou art welcome." There was a cool sound in her voice.

He returned to the meal. He would eat it. Then, if things were still quiet, he would make a break up the stairs and be on his way. He looked at her standing in the deep shadows. She was small but stood up proudly.

"I'm no criminal," he offered, suddenly feeling the need to explain himself. "Just running for my life."

"Though thou stole my hen, sir, I did not say thou wert a criminal."

She kept a bead on the truth, he thought, and she wasn't going to let go of her chicken without a struggle. He had seen bulldogs with less determination. He nodded, watching her between gulps of food.

"Negro," he said, as if she might not be able to tell. "Some men and I disagreed over church money, and they attacked me. Them being white, I ran." He lowered his head and tried to look repentant. "I should not have."

She didn't say anything.

He sat eating and perfecting his tale in his head.

"I was told that thou robbed a man, beating his sons."

"I'm afraid I raised my hands in anger, Mrs. Eddy." He lowered his head and folded the offending objects together at his waist for effect.

"That the men are injured, sir."

Things were getting tight. He bit at the inside of his lip and used the only biblical line he knew: "Wait upon the Lord, and He will strengthen thee." Fortunately it seemed to fit. He glanced back at the woman.

She stood mulling things before she said, "Thou art a minister. I believe thee."

"Thank you, ma'am," he mumbled.

She waited a moment, then said, "Those words are inspiring." She paused. "But the correct phrase is 'strengthen thine heart.' Not 'strengthen thee.' "

"Ma'am?"

"It means, sir, that the Lord will help us master our suffering . . . not help us avenge it. 'Strengthen thine heart' not 'strengthen thee.' "

"Of course," he said, squirming inside and feeling something like guilt. Maybe it was because this young woman seemed ready to swallow seriously everything he fed her. He had been on this earth for quite a while, but he had never experienced the like of it before. Certainly not from a white person. He shrugged it off. Let her believe what she wanted. If she wanted to believe he was the Holy Ghost, it was all right with him. All he wanted was out of this town.

"Your husband upstairs, Mrs. Eddy?"

"He is dead."

That surprised him. Not that her husband was dead, but that she hadn't concocted a tale about one lurking upstairs, waiting to pounce on him. He spread butter on a slice of bread, all the while watching her. The way she stood—staring off into the dusky air, her head canted slightly—seemed peculiar, and he reached into the pocket of his wet shirt and pulled out a pair of rimless glasses, which he shoved onto his nose, squinting hard behind them.

She was small and youthful-looking, her brown hair done up in a neat tuck at the back of her head, her skin the color of flour dumplings. He kept his eyes straining to see her longer than was polite, but she didn't seem to care. She was wearing a long dress that, while well made and of decent material, was dull gray in color and lacking in significant style. And, like the blankets, it had seen far better days.

His overall impression was that she looked drab, though it was too dark to see much beyond that. But even in the dark and with his weak eyes, he could tell the lines of her face were clean and pretty. He wondered again where she was hiding her pistol. It was bothering him. He laid the glasses on the barrel top.

"Mrs. Eddy, where is your gun?"

She turned toward him.

"Being down here in the dark, I was just wondering."

"I do not believe in guns, Mr. Prophet."

Something told him she wasn't lying. "They're very dangerous," he mumbled, knowing he had one in his traveling bag.

"I am here," she continued in the same unhappy tone as earlier, "because I thought thou wert hurt."

"I didn't trick you, ma'am," he said, exasperation rising in his voice.

"I believe thou didst—and thou a minister."

She stared at the dark. He ate.

"I will get the sheriff in the morning so thou canst straighten—"

"I'm leaving when I finish." While she hadn't called the law yet, he wasn't hanging around until she changed her mind.

"Thou cannot."

"I'm going."

"No," she said firmly. He noticed she had this way of pulling up her frame to maximum height whenever she got stiff over something. He figured she had some sand in her craw, but she controlled it well. That was part of what he sensed about her: She was always reining herself in as if she were an unruly colt.

"Yes," he said, just as firmly.

"They are still searching for thee." She paused. "Even if thou got away, it would not be right." She said the words as if he would be committing some awful crime by fleeing.

He didn't respond.

"That is not a proper way to live."

Convinced she was off in the head, he sat looking at her. "Mrs. Eddy, you don't owe me. I don't owe you—excepting for this damn hen."

"I asked thee not to swear. Thou being a man of God, I am surprised."

Again he kept silent.

"I do not believe in people being hurt or killed by other people."

"That's noble."

"Thou hast a responsibility," she continued, ignoring his remark, "to thyself—and to me—to resolve this matter."

"To you?"

"Yes. I am involved in this. I hid thee." She paused. "I do not believe in breaking the law."

She was standing and tapping her foot impatiently. He figured she was doing it to let him know she wasn't happy with him. It was annoying.

"Mrs. Eddy, I'm leaving."

She turned and darted up the stairs, gripping the banister with one hand, then hopped out, shutting the door behind her. He heard the lock turn. Then the chair slid back into place.

"Hey!"

"I will let thee out in the morning, Mr. Prophet," she said, her voice muffled. "Whether thou face thy accusers then or run is thy choice." There was silence for a moment. Then she continued. "But tonight . . . I will not have thee harmed. I'm certain as a minister of the faith thou wilt do the right thing."

"Mrs. Eddy, you don't have any right to lock me up."

"Oh, yes, I do. Thou broke into my house."

"'You're crazy. I can tell things about people," he yelled, "and, Mrs. Eddy, you aren't right in the head."

"In the morning, Mr. Prophet."

Prophet's wet clothes were drying on the cellar line, his pants closest to him, just in case she came back down. He was sitting on the edge of an old bed, thinking. There was no mistaking lunacy in man or beast. And she had it.

He rubbed the last of his Mentholated Liniment for Rheumatic Pains into his sore muscles and stretched out on the mattress. He had been trying to sleep for the past hour but was unable to shake the tenseness. He jumped at a creaking sound in the floor overhead, holding his breath and listening. Nothing. She had kept her word. At least so far. He wondered why. It didn't matter. He was just glad. The men chasing him would likely kill a dog with more tenderness than a Negro.

Months back in Kentucky, an old colored had read him a newspaper story that said there had been a "plague of justice" with 200 Negroes lynched in these United States over the past ten years. He was not keen on becoming 201.

He glanced around him. The room was filled with dusty mounds of old stuff arranged in neat order. Empty boxes, broken chairs, a rusted tub, and jars for canning. Not much else. He wondered about the woman. Odd, was the only conclusion that made any sense. Still, she had hidden him. Nobody had ever done anything like that for him before.

The tightness continued inside him, so he climbed off the mattress, wrapped a blanket around his waist, and began to shadowbox in the darkness, jabbing, feinting left then right, throwing hard body hooks at invisible adversaries. He bobbed and weaved, covered up, and fought out of desperate make-believe situations.

After some five minutes he started to wind badly and bent over, too fast, quickly putting his hands on his knees to catch himself. He could feel the blood and wooziness flooding into his head, and he closed his eyes and locked his legs so he wouldn't fall, gripping harder with his hands.

"I'm not muddleheaded," he said to nobody in particular.

He started to straighten up, but the giddiness was still with him, and he stayed bent over, keeping his eyes closed. "If things get fuzzy, they clear," he said quietly. "And I move as fast as ever." He paused. "I can go forty rounds and take a man out with either hand."

When the light-headedness passed, he lay back down, but his thoughts were still pestering, so he crawled up and shadow-boxed some more as if to prove he still had it, his hamlike fists flying through the air.

"I was no talker. Maybe that's why I haven't had my shot," he huffed, poking his jab at the dark air. "But I'm coming up on it." He stopped punching and began to run in place, bringing his knees up high in a rapid sprint. "All the time someone promising they were going to get me a fight with Paddy Ryan or Bubbles Davis or Joe Godfrey." He stopped talking and just ran. Then he said, "All them years. Just gone."

He was breathing hard now, and he stopped and bent over, carefully, fighting the pains in his lower back, and tried to catch his breath. "But that doesn't make me a chump."

He lay back down on the mattress and stared at the

ceiling, a slight tremor pulling the muscles taut around his mouth. "No criminal either," he mumbled. The tremor passed. "I take things because nobody hires me. But even if they did, I wouldn't be their right kind of nigger. I'm no 'yes, suh' and 'no, suh' boy."

He stared blindly at the shadows above.

Half an hour later Prophet had been peering at the dark ceiling of the cellar for so long he was having a hard time focusing on it. The old feelings were creeping up on him. They came whenever he spent time in a place. They had come fast here. The disappearing woe, he called it.

Everything about him was made up. Birthday. Name. He had changed it three times. It was as if he had just crawled out of the mud to be alive one day. He didn't know much more than that. He hated that feeling of not knowing anything, feeling like somebody else's dream.

He shoved the thought away. He was no dream; he hurt too badly in places to be a dream. And he could remember things; he remembered a few of the folks who had raised him for a while. Mostly he remembered moving on. But at least he remembered; dreams don't remember anything. That made him feel better. If he was a dream, then his children—his girl and boy—were dreams too. And nobody was ever going to convince him of that.

He had spent a whole lot of time keeping his children from being dreams. It was why he followed the route. Hoping for a note with his name—the one the children knew him by—printed across the envelope. That would come one day. He was certain of it. He smiled and shook his head; that would be some day. He tipped his face up and stared at the ceiling boards for a while.

It took ten months, give or take, to walk the route,

taking time out to get fights along the way for spending and saving money. He wasn't certain how many times he had traveled it. Maybe fourteen. He let his mind drift over the familiar terrain. He always started in North Carolina. Sanford. He and Jenny, his wife, had been sharecropping forty acres in Sanford. They had been happy. Or so he had thought. That always confused him: his being happy and thinking she was.

He stood and began to pace, struggling with old remembrances. He had put the children to bed that last night and said his daughter Lacy's and Tyrone's favorite prayer. He closed his eyes now, mouthing the words. Finished, he pressed his lips together. In the morning they were just gone. All three of them, gone. His whole life disappearing like chimney smoke. The only other recollection he had of it was how hard it had been to breathe.

Tyrone had been six. Lacy, eight. He squinted his eyes and tried to remember them. What they looked like. He tried each night so he wouldn't forget. But he couldn't much anymore. He sat and put his hands on his knees and stared at a blank piece of air between his feet and hated the feeling. He cleared his throat and looked back up at the ceiling.

Nobody had a right to take a man's children. Nobody. There wasn't a worse thing in this life. He straightened his back and cleared his throat again. The traveling route ran from Sanford up through Burlington, where Jenny once did waitressing, then Danville, Farmville, and on to Staunton. She had owned a little shop there the year he married her. After Staunton, he walked to Chambersburg, Carlisle, and then Harrisburg, Virginia. Jenny had been raised there. Afterward he headed west into Ohio to Moundsville, Chillicothe, Athens, and Portsmouth, places he had heard her talk about, then into Kentucky to Maysville—because Jenny had been married to another man who lived in Maysville once.

From Maysville he walked to Paris, Frankfort, Elizabethtown, and Mammoth. Her mother was from Mammoth. After that he always cut northeast to Harlan and across the eastern tip of Tennessee through Kingsport and Greeneville and then back into North Carolina through Statesville and Salisbury and finally home again. Only it wasn't home. Some other family was cropping their place, but he always slipped in after dark and stayed a night by the creek where Tyrone and Lacy had played. It made him feel close to them after being on the road.

There were thirty-three towns and smaller places on the route, and he stopped at each post office to see if there was a note. Same thirty-three. Each time, when there was none, he paid the postman to write one—for when the children came looking for him.

Then he wondered again why he was out here in nowhere. He didn't understand it. It had puzzled him for weeks. This was the first time he had ever changed the route, the first time in some thirteen years. He couldn't figure it.

He just woke up one morning in Ohio, a month back, with an urge for walking west. He kept at it until he arrived here. A place he had never been—and wouldn't want to be again. But why? Maybe Jenny and the children were here. It didn't seem likely.

He sat worrying that while he was wasting time in Kansas, perhaps the children were in one of the towns along the route. He shifted anxiously on the mattress. He had to get back. Jerome Prophet looked up into the cellar darkness. "Lacy. Tyrone," he said, projecting his deep voice in a quiet way up through the floorboards and the house above, as if the sound might actually penetrate the roof and soar into the silence of the night sky, drifting until it reached the children. That was all he said.

After he had collected himself, he wondered what it was like living in one place year in and year out, gathering junk, dust settling on you. The only time he had ever stayed put anywhere was on some Frenchman's plantation in Louisiana. He had been kept there until he was maybe eleven and ran off. An old Creole woman had been in charge of him. She had taught him some French and how to sew uniforms for the house Negroes. And she had taught him some respect. Something that he had never forgotten. It served a body well to be respectful. Nothing good was ever gained prompting devilry.

He looked around again, shaking his head. Same house, same smells. Choke a man under layers. The Quaker woman was wrong about staying. Moving kept things balanced. And he had the route to keep.

He stood and pulled out the leather poke he carried inside his pants and sat back down on the mattress, emptying the contents into his lap. Slowly he counted out the money: $261. His providing money for the children. Money he never used. He was proud of that. Keeping it for them made them seem more alive somehow.

After he had put it away, he stared at the boxes around him, cogitating what there might be worth taking in this house. The thought made him feel squeamish, thinking how nobody had never done anything for him like this woman. He wondered what she expected in return.

Chapter Two

After locking the Negro in the cellar for the night, Pearl Eddy had worked late finishing the dress she was making for her customer, Rose Sherman, then overslept, missing her morning meditation. That bothered her. She rarely missed. And the fact that she had simply reinforced her feeling that things weren't going right.

Her thoughts flew to the bank loans, but she forced herself to think about getting the children to school. She was hurrying through the sun-filled parlor, knowing the boys were going to be late and chiding herself, when she heard laughter coming from the kitchen and felt a surge of relief. Her eldest, Samuel, had gotten his brothers up.

As for the Negro, she would give him another chance to speak to the sheriff, would urge him to resolve the matter properly. There was a possibility. He was a minister after all, though he seemed a little gone in the faith. As she moved down the hall, Pearl reached to touch the chair under the cellar doorknob; it wasn't there. Then she heard her six-year-old, Zacharias, say "Tell us about that tiger," and she knew the man was in the kitchen.

"Morning, Mrs. Eddy," Prophet said.

He was cooking what smelled to Pearl like griddle cakes, the boys standing around watching. She sat at the table and didn't utter a word, just tapped the toe of her shoe softly on the floor.

Samuel, the eldest of the Eddy boys at fourteen, took sips of water from the glass he was holding and studied the Negro from the back. Age furrows on the man's neck showed that he was getting long in the tooth. No chicken, the boy figured, but he didn't look decrepit either. While he might be on the shady slope of life, there was something different about him that looked dangerous. He was dressed like a field hand in a worn flannel shirt and duck pants, maybe six-two and 190 pounds, or close to that.

But those things weren't different. What was different were his body parts: They didn't fit, as if he were a collection of lots of people. Thick shoulders spread yokelike over an amazingly thin waist, while arms that were too long for his torso dangled at his sides. His hands too were proportionately far larger than they should have been. Mixed together, these mismatches made the old Negro look powerful.

From the back the rest of him wasn't much. The most interesting thing was that he was bald. Completely so. He didn't look particularly bad this way, just clean like a horse with a butched mane. As Samuel was thinking this, the man turned, and the boy jumped the way he had the first time he saw the harsh, off-kilter visage; somebody had made a butchery of it. The nose had been pushed to one side, scar tissue blanketed the cheeks and webbed the corners of the eyes, and one ear was almost gone, bitten or torn off, Samuel suspected. The boy felt bad for him, but that didn't alter his other definite feelings about this man. And they weren't good feelings.

"Mr. Prophet's an animal wrestler," Zacharias said

excitedly. The boy was small and freckle-faced, his curly hair the color of caramel, his voice squeaky. Prophet smiled at him. The boy smiled back as if they had known each other a long time and were the best of friends; then he struggled to hold on to the red rooster that he had been carrying around all morning.

Now, as Zacharias passed by on his way to the sink, the bird took a calculated sideways peck at Prophet, but the man was ready and dodged. The three younger boys laughed. Prophet didn't see the humor. Nor did Samuel.

"Mr. Prophet is a minister," Pearl corrected Zacharias. "And thou art not supposed to have Hercules inside."

The boy turned and stared him hard in the face, "Thou said thou wert an animal wrestler."

"Both," Prophet mumbled lamely. It was going to do his heart good to even the score with this small woman. Zacharias was squinting at him now. Tyrone had been about his age. Prophet fought the feeling down.

"Samuel," Pearl said.

Tall and thin, with shoulder-length black hair, the eldest had his mother's fine features. Samuel was glancing sideways at him. Prophet had seen that same look ten thousand times before. Fear, distrust, dislike. It didn't matter. The boy gathered up his brothers, herding them toward the back door.

Prophet didn't envy these children with their long hair, old men's clothes, and large black hats. They had to stick out like tulips in rye, red flags for every bully. As bad as being colored children, he figured. Prophet had an eye for spotting fighters, and the twins—Joshua and Luke—appeared to be the right material. They had stopped now and were taking one last look at him; he grinned at them, and they grinned back. Straightforward. Without guile. He liked that.

Even Zacharias looked like a scrapper. But tough as he might be, Prophet could tell the little one missed his father badly. The boy had spent the morning trailing him, hanging on to his hand, and trying to crawl onto his lap. Not even Prophet's frightening features discouraged him.

After putting the bird out, Zacharias darted back and stopped in front of him. "Wilt thou be here when I get home from school?" He leaned over and whispered, "I need thee to do something for my pa."

"Samuel," she said.

"Wilt thou?"

"I'll see." Prophet knew he wouldn't be staying, but for a reason he wasn't sure about, he didn't want to tell the boy.

"Then hold this." Zacharias placed a thin piece of light-colored flint in Prophet's palm.

"What is it?"

"Osage arrowhead. My pa found it." Zacharias leaned closer and whispered, "It's my lucky charm."

Prophet started to give it back to him, then stopped and slipped it into his pack sitting on the floor. No use fussing. He would leave it on the kitchen table.

Zacharias stood and watched him for a moment; then the boy's face broke into a grin, and he darted happily out the door. Prophet told himself that the lad would forget about it by supper. He turned and scanned the room. It was a normal enough farmhouse kitchen: iron sink, kerosene lanterns, iron cookstove, plain white wainscot-paneled walls, and hard-scrubbed wooden floors. She kept a clean house. Almost too clean, he thought. He'd had a rough time trying to prepare the boys' breakfast, the pantries short on salt, coffee, sugar, and most other essentials. He followed her with his eyes as she walked to the old coal burner, watching as she picked up some burned toast, scraping its black surface into the coffeepot with a knife. He was surprised. He had seen poor Negroes make burned-toast coffee before, but never whites. She was definitely stingy, sitting in this big house, keeping her cupboards thin, reusing coffee grinds. But it wasn't any of his affair.

"Nice boys, Mrs. Eddy."

"I locked thee in the cellar."

"And I got out, ma'am."

"It does not matter."

"That's how I saw it."

"I thought thou wert going to run."

"I was leaving"—he emphasized *leaving*—"when I ran into your boys. I didn't want to scare them."

"So thou told them lies instead."

He shook his head, knowing from the night before that if she got wound up on a thing, there was no stopping her. He examined her more closely: small and delicate, but not dainty. Prettier than he had thought, with rich, shiny brown hair, the front of which was carried straight back without a part and tied in a plain bun. Her face was pale, the skin looking as if it had never had artificial color on it, smooth and clean; she had a straight, narrow nose, high cheekbones, and a nicely defined chin. She stood looking alert but with her head canted in that funny way she had.

"It'd go easier on your boys, ma'am, if they didn't have to wear those clothes."

She didn't respond.

He took a sip of coffee, eyeing her over the cup. That was okay. Silence was better than one of her lectures. He took another drink, then noticed that she was slowly pulling herself up straighter.

"Mr. Prophet," she said in a pleasant enough tone, "please do not worry about my children."

He eyed her cautiously.

"Thou art not supposed to be here—or hast thou forgotten?" she continued, speaking carefully. "Thou broke into my home, killed my hen, and involved me in thy unlawfulness." Her volume was rising, the tone not as pleasant as before. "Then thou lied to my children about thy acts and purposes." She stopped and tapped the toe of her shoe.

There was no doubt about it: She was addled. "Your way, Mrs. Eddy," he said, resuming his meal and snatching glimpses of her between bites: pretty but dressed as if she were leading a six-horse funeral.

"I'm going to see the sheriff this morning," she said.

She was at it again. "That would be a waste of time, Mrs. Eddy. I'll be gone before you get back."

"Fine, but it must be done."

"No, it mustn't, but I don't think you see that."

"No, I do not."

"Your choice, ma'am." He pointed at a jar sitting on the kitchen counter. "In the meantime, may I have some of that apple butter?"

Prophet had always known that small things could change a person's life. Later he would remember that this jar had done just that. But he didn't know it now. The only thing he knew was that Mrs. Eddy was blind. Stone blind.

He sat openmouthed, staring at her. Her eyes looked normal enough, a clear, rinsed blue, like sky after rain. He studied them until she said, "Mr. Prophet?" She was gazing into an empty piece of air, holding the jar out a good six feet from where he sat.

Edward Johnson's law office was over Moyer's Cafe, and food odors were rising through the floorboards of the messy little room. Johnson was in a swivel chair behind his desk, watching Pearl pace back and forth in front of the window that faced Main Street, the tapping of her long, thin cane soft on the dusty wooden floor. Moyer's canary was singing downstairs, the notes faint in the morning air.

Tall and lean, with a pleasant face, Johnson wore thick glasses that belied a toughness. At thirty-nine, he still retained a youthful look. He had been the Eddys' lawyer since they arrived in Zella.

"Edward, I have two problems."

Surprised by the words, he looked over his glasses at her. This was a woman who never seemed to have problems. At least not the worldly kind. Certainly none he had ever heard her speak about. "Yes, Pearl?"

"The bank is threatening to call in my mortgage if I do not pay off some loans that Matthew took."

Johnson watched her for a while, waiting for her to continue. When she didn't, he said, "And you don't have the money?"

"Half."

He continued to watch her walking around the office. He had never seen her like this before, her face drawn, her lips moving silently. She turned quickly in his direction.

"I have my seamstressing, the gardens, the new pullets."

Johnson ran a hand through his hair. "How long to raise the rest?"

"Six months."

"Six months," he repeated.

"Yes."

"Long time, Pearl."

"Yes."

Again he was surprised by the worried sound in her voice. But then he thought about her boys and her blindness and—himself the father of six kids—he understood. He did some quick calculating, then worked more slowly through the numbers. "I'll talk to Snipes.

Tell him you'll pay half now. Half in six months. He should accept that."

"Art thou certain?"

"Everybody wants to sell land these days; nobody wants to buy. My guess is Snipes will see that he is better off with part of your money than a farm he can't turn."

The lines around Pearl's eyes relaxed some. "I will bring what I have to the bank."

"Hold it until I work out the details."

She nodded.

"Pearl, I can loan you the money until—"

"Thank thee, Edward. But we do not believe in alms."

"It's not alms. Just a simple loan."

"Thank thee. But no."

Edward Johnson had guessed this answer, the Quaker creed set against borrowing. Funny people, he figured. They thought nothing of giving everything they had to the poor but would starve rather than take charity themselves.

"And the second problem, Pearl?" He glanced at his watch, worrying that court would be opening in thirty minutes and that he needed to read two documents beforehand.

"There is a man in my home."

Some ten minutes later Pearl had almost finished explaining about Prophet, Simon James, the mob, and the dead chicken, and he thought she looked more herself: stubborn and stiff-backed. He was doodling with a pencil, listening to her and thinking about her husband. The man had always been smiling. It made Johnson grin just thinking about him, remembering the day, some fourteen years back, when Matthew Eddy had walked into his office and said he was looking for a lawyer he could buy off; then he had smiled that velvet smile of his. They had become close friends.

During the '85 county elections they had campaigned hard together for two months to defeat the so-called Royal Order of Redmen's efforts to put discriminatory Jim Crow laws on the books. Thinking about it, he knew there was something very right about Pearl Eddy's protecting this colored man, whoever he was. But even so, this was still wild country; Matthew's death was proof of that.

He put the pen down and looked up at the woman. She was handsome enough that he was thankful he was happily married. Blind or not, she would have no trouble finding a new husband, something she and her boys badly needed out here. But he also knew she wouldn't. As the family lawyer he had tactfully put this to her a few months back. In reply she had simply said, "I will not meet Matthew in heaven pledged to another." Impractical, yes. But he liked her for having said it.

He pulled his glasses off and rubbed the bridge of his nose. She had reason enough to worry. Zella's banker, Alfred Snipes, high-strung and unpredictable, might well foreclose, then try to figure out what to do with the land. Johnson shifted uncomfortably on the seat. He could pressure the man for a time. He scratched behind an ear. The Negro was another kind of complication.

Hiding a colored thief—even from the likes of Simon James and his crowd—wasn't apt to sit well with people who normally wouldn't give the old charlatan spit to whistle with. Fortunately, Johnson figured, the Negro was probably exercising the "two-footed solution" down some prairie road.

"He'll run," the attorney said.

"He is a religious man, Edward."

Johnson shook his head. "Preacher or parrot, Pearl, he won't stay around. But if you like, I'll talk to the sheriff."

He locked his fingers together in his lap and began to twiddle his thumbs, leaning back in the chair and stretching his long legs, not wanting to rush her but wishing she would leave so he could finish preparing for court.

"Anything else, Pearl?"

She wasn't hearing him. She had stopped in front of the window and stood listening to the sounds of cat-calls and hollering rising from the street below.

"Edward?"

"Not the Negro," he assured her after he walked over and looked down onto Main Street. "Just a bunch of bums ragging an Oriental family."

"Orientals?"

Johnson cleaned his glasses on the corner of his coat. "Came to claim some fellow's homestead. He had a deal with them: quarter section he owned in Zella for five years of the family's labor in Hawaii. Left it in his will. Legal enough. Unfortunately the land was declared abandoned years ago. But the Oriental woman won't believe it. Judge Wilkins and I showed her the records, but she just shook her head and squatted her family down in front of the hotel." He put his glasses back on his prominent nose. "Doesn't much matter," he added, returning to his desk and stuffing papers into a satchel.

"What doesn't matter?"

"About the land."

"Why?

"They can't legally own it, Pearl."

"Why?"

"Government won't allow it."

"Why not?" she asked quickly.

"Pearl, slow down. The law doesn't matter. Even if these folks could own land, nobody would sell them anything. And eventually that mob would drive them crazy."

Pearl stared down at the street as if she could actually see them. "How long have they been there?"

Johnson glanced at his watch again and thought, Now what, Pearl? He cleared his throat. "Tuesday's train."

"And they cannot buy anything?"

"No."

"Then, Edward, what, pray tell, are they eating?"

Johnson was studying the paper he had just signed and didn't respond.

"Edward?"

"Sorry, Pearl."

"What are these folks eating?" she repeated.

"The judge and I dropped off milk, bread, and eggs last evening."

The catcalls increased.

"And we'll see they get headed wherever they want to go." He glanced at her. "Pearl."

Now it was her turn not to respond.

"Pearl?" His voice firm.

"Edward?"

"Don't get involved."

She nodded. "But thou knowest it is not right, living with children in the dirt of a street."

He glanced at his watch. "Court opens in fifteen minutes."

She was listening to the sounds on the street again.

"Pearl."

"I'm sorry, Edward. What didst thou say?"

"Stay away from the Orientals. That's all I said. People are worked up over them." He was closing his satchel. "And court is opening."

Pearl looked struck by some unseen blow. "What time is it?"

"Nine."

She started moving toward the door, her cane tapping fast. Johnson grabbed quickly at her elbow, guiding her through the maze of papers stacked in little piles on the floor.

"Thou wilt remember to speak to Mr. Snipes?"

"I've written it down."

"And the sheriff about Mr. Prophet?"

"Yes, Pearl."

"And thou wilt not forget to take more food to that family?"

"Yes, Pearl."

Prophet stood in Pearl Eddy's parlor watching the morning sun on the road in front of the farmhouse, checking. It had to be a trick. She had left him alone and gone off in her buggy. But the whole thing smelled. Nobody had ever left him alone in a house before.

His eyes darted over the tallgrasses across the road, searching for bushes moving unnaturally, shadowy forms, the reflection of sunlight off metal, anything that would indicate that people were sneaking around. But there was nothing. All he could see was a massive tangle of redroot, Osage orange, and hundreds of other wild plants. Bobolinks and sparrows were hanging off the tallgrasses, screeching like rusty hinges in the morning air. It was a bleak land by his lights. His eyes snapped back to the road. Still empty. Didn't seem possible.

Squinting at the distant horizon, he thought about his children. They were out there somewhere. Out behind the beyond. He would take a few things and be on his way. She deserved it, bossy and know-it-all. And he needed the money.

Prophet was busy hunting likely hiding places when he heard footsteps coming up the walkway. He had been right. She hadn't left him. She was just testing. He took a quick peek out the curtain and jumped. It wasn't Pearl Eddy.

The woman was yet some distance off—past middle age and heavyset, made up fancy, as if she were headed for church—but that she intended to come through the front door was obvious. And she was coming fast. And there he stood, a Negro in a white woman's house. And the woman gone. He wasn't a genius, but he knew it wouldn't look good. He had no illusions about this.

He turned and started for the kitchen, then halted. If this was a trap, there would likely be a group of men coming that way. There was an open door on one side of the parlor. He took it. In an instant he realized he was in the Quaker woman's small sewing room, the walls lined with shelves heavy with patterns, fabric, and thread. There was a window. He tried it. Jammed. There was a closet. He went for it. Too small to hold him.

Then, to his great consternation, the woman threw the front door open and barged inside, yelling, "Pearl, dearie, I'm here." Worse, she was moving straight for the sewing room. Prophet figured he had many faults, but not being able to make a quick decision wasn't one of them. He had to act. And fast.

Eleven-year-old Chrissy James was wrapped in a blanket and resting in her father's arms, rhythmically opening and shutting her mouth like a baby bird begging for food. Simon James was sitting on the edge of the wooden sidewalk, stroking his child's thin black hair. He said something to her, and she rolled her long, narrow head hard against his chest. Her eyes gazed up, unfocused; then she began to drool in the morning sunlight, blue veins bright under the white skin of her temple.

Simon knew Chrissy would never grow in the ways of women, and she was the only female he cared for. He pulled a handkerchief and wiped her mouth, then looked at the dusty little campsite of the Orientals in front of the hotel. He was studying it when movement across the street caught his eye and he watched Pearl Eddy hurrying down the stairs from the county attorney's office.

He wondered what she had been doing talking to the authorities. They hadn't harmed her place last night. They should have. But they hadn't. He felt his blood rising. If she filed charges ... Simon relit a wet stump of cigar and then spit in her direction. Pearl was too far away to hit, but the row of rough-looking men sitting on chairs behind him appreciated the gesture and laughed. He grinned and chewed on the cigar and continued wondering why she had gone to the county man.

Chrissy's brother, Hector, sixteen, the youngest of Simon's three boys, was standing in the street in front of his father and sister. He made a funny piglike noise with his nose and waited while Chrissy turned her face toward him. His badly poxed face lit up. "Hector pig. Hector pig," he said, grinning and dancing whimsically before her.

Simon continued staring at the Quaker woman. She was obviously in a hurry, stumbling as she quickly put a foot on the running step of her buggy. Once in the vehicle, she let the old horse start on his own down the street. Simon scratched behind an ear. Maybe she had gone to Johnson about the Chinamen. It would be just like her to spill her knitting over them.

He pursed his lips, an idea not quite formed in his mind eluding him. Simon was a man who prided himself on having answers. Letting his mind work the problem, he glanced back at the squatter camp. It was nothing more than a collection of canvas bags, a bunch of Chinamen, an odd-looking pushcart contraption, and some scrawny animals. All of it was shrouded in blue smoke that drifted from a green-wood fire.

The breeze shifted, and he was momentarily caught in the blue haze. He coughed, then wiped at his eyes, the men behind him retreating into the saloon. He sat, determined that no Asiatic was going to force him to do anything. When the smoke finally cleared, he took another look around the site. Things were a mess. The animals were defecating over the family's belongings, and there was mud coated on everything. He spit and shook his head. He had seen hobo warrens that were cleaner.

"Let's get her," he said, nodding his head toward a small black pig.

Simon, his three boys, and some of the Redmen had been stealing from the Asians for the past two hours. Not for gain. Simply to send a message to the Johnny-Johns—as Chinese were known in these parts—to leave town. Half a bag of rice, a pair of sandals, a tattered parasol, all snatched from the edge of the little makeshift campsite whenever the deputy, Elmer Ritter, wasn't looking. None of it was worth a damn. But that wasn't the point.

Penny James tossed a piece of moldy bread to the little pig. "Come on!" he muttered. At twenty-six, the eldest of the James boys, Penny was rather average in height and weight and face but, like his father, barrel-chested. He was Simon's favorite. His ordinary-appearing features were lumpy and bruised from his encounter with the Negro last night. He tossed another chunk of bread to the pig.

Straining against the rope, the sow stretched hard for the tidbit. "Pull, you stupid hog," Penny urged. Runted, swaybacked, and covered with coarse black hair, she was a sorry-looking beast. But they wanted her. There was just one problem: A little Chinese girl of five or six was hanging over the sow's back, watching them and chewing hungrily on each piece of bread they tossed. She darted after this new morsel as if it were gold. "Damn Chinee suckling," Simon muttered.

The men had returned from the saloon, and one of them moved up close and whispered in his ear. Simon's eyes wrinkled at the corners. Dusting the bread off, the girl shared half with the sow; then she went back to her contented wallowing on the animal's back.

"Get," he snapped at her, spittle flying through a gap in his teeth. She laughed, thinking he was playing. Simon was in no mood for this, figuring maybe he ought to take the man's suggestion and let them drop her into one of the wells out on the prairie before she could mature and breed. They had done a Mexican that way once. Simon chortled softly, thinking about the man's frantic hopping and pleading. One hell of a Mexican jumping bean.

Simon yawned, tired from having stayed up most the night chasing the Negro, thinking about the cheekiness of that old man trying to rob him. Simon James was no scholar, but he was shrewd in his way, and as he kept thinking about the colored, the Eddy buggy passed directly in front of him. Suddenly the bits and pieces that had been floating in his head came together in a flash. The woman hadn't gone to the county attorney to charge them with anything. She had been spilling her guts over the Negro.

"That colored and the Quaker spent the night together," he said to the men behind him, his voice implying something darker.

"Go on," one of them said.

"We figure we lost him on the prairie," Simon continued, talking around the cigar in his mouth. "We didn't. She was hiding him." Simon pulled the cigar from his mouth. "I'll bet old Juba is still there."

"Naw."

"Sombitch."

"Damn!"

"We should think about that," Simon said, "the implications." The Redmen should have fixed the Quaker years ago. He would have let them if it hadn't been for Chrissy's asthma. But that wouldn't stop them from picking up the colored. Shielding his eyes against the morning sun with a stubby hand, he let his gaze drift along the wooden sidewalks, the false storefronts. Down near the bank there was a small circle of boys playing mumblety-peg in the dirt, and on the hotel porch some old people reading newspapers. He looked at the business district. Two dozen clapboard buildings faced each other across the expanse of dirt called Main Street, with houses scattered helter-skelter behind. The whole place was broiling in the sun and looked as if it were sitting on the face of the moon. He liked that look.

Simon let his thoughts drift to his traveling show. Next to the Redmen, it was his favorite thing. And for good reason. It had made him a success. As a merchant seaman he had traveled to foreign ports around the globe. And in one, São Paulo of Brazil, on a steamy summer afternoon in 1880, he had witnessed something that had changed his life forever.

For fifty cents Simon had attended a tent show near the pier that advertised an exhibition of cannibals, man-eating snakes, headhunters, and other assorted creatures and horrors of the Amazon. That was all the mental seed he needed, simply to realize that he had paid half a buck to see a bunch of breeds jump around like jackasses on a stage.

Six months later Simon had quit the seas and launched "The Amazing World of Wonders," a bizarre collection of wild natives and other strange oddities, touring his show through the small towns of the Texas Panhandle, Oklahoma, and Kansas.

He saw nothing wrong with the fact that his wild natives were simply dark-skinned Americans costumed to look like fierce desert nomads, Pygmies, Amazonians, and other untamed denizens of the farthest corners of the earth. Nor did it bother him that most of the specimens he exhibited were fakes. "The show's value," he often argued to Angela, his then wife, "is to the human imagination."

It was an impressive caravan and rolling museum of the weird and the grotesque that made its lumbering way each summer from town to town across the boundless stretches of the plains. People, Simon noted with pride, would travel a hundred miles to view his show, lured, often as not, by the heavily promoted "Astounding Marvels."

One of the perennial favorites was "The Heart of Alexander the Great." In reality the heart floating in the green bottle of formaldehyde had once belonged to a Yorkshire pig that Simon had purchased in a Kansas City slaughterhouse, dubbing the enormous beast Alexander just moments before it was sent to the great beyond. "Simply a symbol," Simon had told Angela during one of their many authenticity arguments, "a symbol that thrills men, women, and children, giving them newfound strength and courage." Therefore, he concluded, any minor confusion between Alexander the warrior and Alexander the pig was more than justified.

Simon looked up from the dirt at which he had been idly staring, thinking that as good a draw as Alexander's heart was, it couldn't hold a candle to the old wooden beam that he had salvaged from an Amarillo barn that had been knocked flat by lightning.

In glorious inspiration Simon had seen the true potential of that wood, billing it as part of the very cross used to crucify the Lord of Lords. He had ransomed it—he liked to tell the crowds that gathered in reverent silence outside the tasseled purple and gold exhibition tent where it was housed—at a heavenly price from a wily Arab antiquities dealer who was just about to sell it to wilier Jews.

Simon was always amazed at the boundless joy that simple piece of rotten wood brought people. There was no question in his mind that it had done more good on these lonely prairies than a hundred circuit preachers ever could. "If a man will pay to view this piece of wood," he had once told Angela, "it is because he truly believes he will profit from it. And he will. His faith will profit. As I profit, he profits."

He tensed at the thought of the woman and bit down on his tongue, trying to cool off. But even as he did, another thought forced its way into his head, bringing a new wave of anger. A few months after Chrissy's birth, after a fight when he had slapped her a few times and threatened to put her in a cage with some snakes, Angela had taken off. Simon popped a couple of knuckles. She was always on the rut. He wished he had gotten his hands on her one last time.

Simon forced his thoughts back to the present, glancing across the street at Elmer Ritter, the deputy. The man looked half asleep, and Simon nodded to

Penny, who slid down beneath the rope the lawmen had strung around the camp. If anybody could rid the town of these Asiatics, it would be his eldest boy.

"Hurry up," Penny snapped.

"Hold on," Mike James muttered. Simon's middle son—twenty-two and weighing well over 250 pounds—was on his belly in the street, shoving a long stick with a knife lashed to its end toward the pig. Careful not to cut the animal, Mike slipped the knife blade under the pig's halter and began to saw back and forth. Then the knife slipped under the pressure. He tried again. But again it slipped.

Suddenly Penny was beside him. "Give it to me."

"We ain't going to cut her loose."

"The hell." Penny seemed to hesitate for a moment, gathering himself together; then he thrust the pole forward with a hard lunge, the blade disappearing in the pig's neck, the blow knocking it and the child to the ground. Seconds later the little beast rose squealing and rushing around and around with the spear still stuck in it, blood spraying like a fountain over everything.

"Why'd you do that?" Mike moaned.

"Slipped." Penny chuckled.

Suddenly another Oriental girl stood over them. She was no child this one. A girl, yes, but close to being a young woman and with strong, handsome features. The James boys tensed, expecting her to scream or strike. But she didn't. She just whirled and glared at a place they couldn't see among the large canvas bundles, pointing at the spot and yelling, then kicking dirt.

Penny rose up on his arms and tried to see what she was hollering at but couldn't. Then the screaming girl was joined by an older Oriental woman, who was talking sharply and pulling her away by the arm. After she moved the girl away, the woman shuffled back and bowed twice at the mysterious spot. Penny thought he heard a man's voice say something, but the hog was still squealing, and he couldn't be sure.

He stood on his tiptoes, trying to see what it was among the bundles that had excited these older Orientals. He hadn't spotted anything when his father hollered. Penny and Mike hurried away as Deputy Ritter trotted toward the campsite.

Chapter Three

Pearl let her buggy horse, Jack, slip into a steady single-foot gait on the road west of town, reining the old dappled gray in whenever he broke into a trot. It was habit with her to refuse to draw attention to herself by speeding, even if she was terribly late for a fitting with her best customer, Mother Rose Sherman. While Mother Rose wasn't hot-tempered, Pearl knew she nettled more easily than most.

A wealthy widow at age sixty, Rose Sherman craved fashionable clothes the way some women her age craved chocolate, buying fifteen to twenty new outfits each year. It was a large part of Pearl's income. Pearl also knew that Rose was one of the busiest women in Zella. Therefore she wasn't likely to take kindly to being kept waiting by her seamstress.

Pearl shook her head slowly. How could she have forgotten? The woman was one of the main social pillars in town. No . . . Annoying Rose was not what she needed at this time. If Rose was for thee, she thought, few were against thee. And if she was against thee, look out. Pearl tied Jack to the front fence and tapped up the path to the door.

"Rose?" She tried to sound a cheerful note she didn't feel. No answer. Her heart beat a little faster.

Not finding Pearl at home, Rose must have huffed back into her buggy and headed for town. Pearl stood on the steps and tried to collect herself. The sunlight was warm against her, the morning quiet. "Thou cannot sit idling. Do what thou hast to do," she muttered, remembering her dead mother's words. That thought made her feel better, and she opened the front door and heard laughter.

"Hello?" she called.

"Oh, there you are, dear."

It was Rose Sherman's voice.

"I love it."

"Mother Sherman?"

"Jerome says my new dress fits exquisitely," she bubbled. "And having worked as a fashion designer in Paris, he should know." Rose paused, glancing admiringly at the man. "It has the perfect—what did you call it, Jerome?"

"Silhouette." The accent sounded authentically French.

"That's right, silhouette."

"Who?"

"Jerrroome," the voice with the French accent offered.

"Jerome is your assistant, isn't he?" Rose asked. Then laughed.

"I will explain laaa-tur," Prophet said quickly.

"I must admit," Rose continued, smiling sheepishly at Prophet's fierce features, "I was slightly taken aback when I found this colored gentleman in your sewing room, wrapped head to toe in fabric." She giggled. "But it took me only a second listening to his beautiful French and his exciting talk about the latest European fashions to know he was a genuine Continental and a master designer," Rose warbled enthusiastically. Then she looked at Pearl and clucked her tongue. "Where have you been hiding him, you naughty girl?"

"In the cellar," Pearl said firmly, facing in Prophet's direction.

Rose hooted. "Well, he's certainly a big surprise."

"Yes. He is that."

"Goood morning, Madame Eddieee."

Even with the accent, the voice was unmistakably Prophet's. Pearl felt numb. He had not run. Worse, he was in her house, lying to Mother Sherman and getting away with it. She grappled with the mix of fear and anger.

"I love it," Rose gushed.

"I'm glad," Pearl ventured to say. "As for Jerome, he surprised me by arriving late last night," she said, turning to glare in the direction she had last heard his voice. "But he'll soon be leaving—won't thou, Jerome?"

"Aaaah, Madame, weee can discuss that laay-tuurrr."

Pearl was tapping her foot, a dour expression on her face.

"Ohhh, Pearl, we can't lose him. The two of you must create a dozen outfits for me in Europe's latest styles." She paused and batted her eyes fetchingly at Prophet. "I will pay a premium if they are exclusive."

"Certainly, Madame," Prophet said magnificently.

Pearl was stunned. One dozen exclusive designs. The possibility in the face of her financial need was wonderfully tempting. But no. The man had tricked Rose. He was no more a French designer than she was. She would let Rose down slowly.

"That is always a possibility. But for now let us finish this one."

"Finish? It's finished, my dear. Isn't that right, Jerome?"

"But of course," he said grandly.

"I thought we might add a sash, something in a soft green perhaps," Pearl said.

"Jerome and I discussed that," Mother Sherman said, "but he suggested red."

"Oh?" Pearl tried to locate where Prophet was standing. She was furious—and struggling mightily to control it.

"See what you think." Mother Sherman stood with her heavy arms raised like a large bird in preflight. While she waited, Rose gazed admiringly at the Negro's exotic outfit. He smiled warmly in return.

Earlier that morning, as soon as he had realized he was trapped and that the old woman was headed for the sewing room where he was hiding, Prophet had discarded his worn-out flannel shirt. He stood bare-chested now, a bolt of bright green cloth draped across his shoulders to the floor, robelike. Fortunately the material hid his old pants. To hold it in place, he had tied a dark green cord at his waist and pulled a magenta-colored silk scarf around his neck. Then as a finishing touch he had stuck his glasses on his nose. He smiled again at Rose now, cupping his chin, contemplating his creation, seemingly determined not to look at Mrs. Eddy.

"Here I am, honey." Mother Sherman beamed at Pearl.

Pearl hesitated and then walked over and touched the satin sash, visualizing it with the tips of her fingers. She felt the small stitches in the material. She was surprised. He had actually attached it to the dress. The work was not bad either.

"Isn't it lovely?"

She couldn't lie. "It is nice." Pearl backed up a step, her hands trembling with agitation. "Mr. Prophet, may I consult with thee in the kitchen, please?"

"Prophet?" Mrs. Sherman sounded surprised.

"Jerrrome Prophetttt," he said quickly. "Creole—New Orleans."

"I'll be with thee in a moment," Pearl said to Rose.

The smile returned to Rose Sherman's large and powdery face.

"What art thou doing?" Pearl snapped as soon as she had shut the kitchen door. Then just as quickly, he saw her catching up her anger and boxing it away again. "That is my best customer. I will not let thee toy with her. And thou hast no business—"

"I'm not toying, Mrs. Eddy." He interrupted, his voice low. "That old lady was hammering on your front door."

"Thou had no business opening it," she said quickly. "Thou dost not belong here."

He looked surprised. "At breakfast you were telling me to stay so you could patch things up with the law."

"Be that as it may," she said, straightening her long skirt, "thou shouldst not have opened my front door and then assumed a false relationship with me, involving me in thy trickery and lies. What kind of minister art thou, tricking people?"

"I didn't open your door. That woman walked right into the house." He sounded indignant. "What was I supposed to do: tell her I'd just broken in and was finishing breakfast?"

"At least it would have been the truth."

Both of them stood uncertain of what to say. Pearl was upset at herself for losing her temper, Prophet for letting the little woman boss him again. He watched her struggle with her anger for a moment. Then he turned and walked across the kitchen, putting the silver pillbox that he had stolen from Rose Sherman into his traveling bag.

"Where art thou?" Pearl called.

"Putting my thimble away," he lied.

"Thy thimble?"

"Yes."

She thought about this. "Where didst thou learn to sew and speak French?" She still sounded angry.

Prophet hesitated. He had been taught both skills by the old Creole woman on the Frenchman's plantation. But that didn't sound good enough, so he cleared his throat and lied. "I lived for many years in a French monastery in Louisiana, sewing robes for the monks," he said, sounding heavenly ministerial once again. "And clothes for the poor," he added for extra effect.

This last part of the lie put an immediate brake on Pearl's tongue, and he could see her scurrying around in her head catching up the remnants of her anger. It looked like an opening. He stepped closer. She was breathing hard.

"I was just keeping that woman from getting that mob after me again." Then in a conspiratorial tone he said, "Mrs. Eddy, can't we forget our differences? I didn't have many choices. I just took the one that would work best for both of us."

"I do not view it that way, Mr. Prophet. As I have said, thou art a bold man." She turned to open the hall door. He quickly put a hand on it.

"Oh, Pearl?" Rose called from the parlor.

"Just a moment, Mother Sherman."

"Don't you see?" Prophet continued.

"See what?" Her tone was cool.

"Opportunity."

"What art thou talking about?"

"That woman thinks I'm a French designer. And I do know something about clothes. She'll tell others. Mrs. Eddy, she has offered to pay a premium." He was beginning to pace the room in his enthusiasm, figuring he could make enough off the old lady in a month to cover a couple of years of walking the route.

Pearl was staring blindly at the kitchen stove, as if it were he.

"Just understand, I will not participate in thy lies. Thou art in trouble with the law. I have spoken to the county attorney, and he will bring the sheriff as soon as he returns. Thou canst then straighten out thy legal problems and leave."

"Great, Mrs. Eddy," he mumbled. "I hold on to your best client, I create the business opportunity of your lifetime"—he stopped and looked at the old paint and the cracked window—"and from the looks of things around here, you could use it, and you repay me by running me in to the sheriff."

She turned to his voice. "We just believe different things, that is all."

"We surely do, Mrs. Eddy ... and I'm thinking we should keep it that way." His voice was rising.

"I am sorry thou feelest like that, but that is thy choice."

Prophet watched her for a moment, then turned and picked up his pack and started for the back door. "I'll be going now before your righteous living gets me put in jail." He stopped and looked back at her. "I'll send money for that hen," he snapped.

"Good," she said coolly. "Dost thou need to borrow postage?"

"I'll buy my own."

"Fine," she muttered.

He stepped out into the sunlight and pulled the back door shut with a hard yank that shook the kitchen and made Pearl wince as the dishes rattled.

Five hours later it smelled of rain and evening was casting shadows off the houses and onto the dirt of Main Street when Pearl and Samuel came around the corner from Lincoln Avenue in the family buggy, headed for the center of Zella.

"Is that Negro gone for good?" Samuel asked.

"Yes."

Pearl was dressed in her long gray skirt and blue blouse, a shawl across her small shoulders, a plain black bonnet covering her head. She held a large cooking kettle on her lap.

"How long hast thou known him?"

"Since last night."

"And he is really a minister?"

"He says."

"But thou dost not know."

"Thou meanest, do I have proof?"

"Yes."

"No." She waited a moment. "But I have his word."

Samuel felt like laughing aloud, but he didn't. They rode in silence for a while, Samuel building up arguments against the man, convinced he was a crook.

"Why was he at our house?"

"He had a difficulty with the law."

"Criminal," he said.

"Just a problem."

"I saw him searching over the parlor desk this morning."

"I am sure he was simply curious."

"He didn't look curious to me." He waited a moment, then asked, "What kind of problem?"

"He was accused of robbery."

That did it. "He's bad."

"Thou thinkest he is bad. There is a difference."

Samuel stopped talking and reined Jack in. Staring down Main Street, he saw a crowd in front of the hotel. There was a nastiness about the noise they were making. His mother felt along the buggy seat.

"Thy hat."

He didn't move.

"Samuel."

He put the heavy, black-felted preacher's hat on, then secured Jack to a hitching post, anxiously watching the crowd as he worked. Samuel was a head taller than his mother. He had grown a lot in recent months, and his dark clothes barely fitted him. But he wasn't worrying about his clothes. He was trudging reluctantly forward, carrying the heavy pot, his mother's hand on his arm, his eyes fixed on the people in the road ahead.

As they approached, the men opened a passageway for them that led directly to a little Oriental woman kneeling before a tiny cast-iron stove. Samuel made straight for her, the crowd's noise increasing. He had seen most of these men before—idlers and drunks who hung around the saloons and stables—and he smelled alcohol and old urine in clothes. He knew what these people were after, and he was nervous. Somebody grabbed at his hat, and he dodged, yanking his mother roughly along.

"Crowded," he yelled, not wanting to alarm her.

Pearl knew Samuel was talking to her, but she was too busy arguing with herself to hear him. The county attorney, Edward Johnson, had warned her away from doing this, and she knew instinctively he was correct. But avoiding it didn't make what was happening here decent or right. Her nostrils flared at the stinking smell of steaming mud and rotting manure. These Chinese were human beings living with their children in filth where not even the town's dogs chose to sleep. There was no defending it, she told herself. It was just plain wrong.

Maybe, as Edward said, she had no call getting mixed up with these people. Maybe it would not go down well in town. Maybe she had taken enough of a chance with the Negro. She lifted her chin. None of that mattered. She would do what she had come to do, accepting God's will for the consequences.

As she was thinking this, Penny James suddenly stepped in front of them. "Where you going, boy?"

Samuel stopped abruptly and opened his mouth, but no sound came out, and it was his mother who answered for him. "We are bringing the evening meal to this family, Penny James. Then we will be on our way."

Penny ignored her. "Boy, I asked where you were going."

Samuel stood fighting his rising fear and the awful quivering in his legs.

"Samuel," Pearl said, stepping smartly forward.

Samuel didn't move.

"Let us through, please," she said, putting one hand out as if she might be able to part the seas with it and towing Samuel with the other.

Prophet heard the rising commotion of the crowd and peeked out the door of the boxcar that sat on a siding off the town's business district. He had been hiding inside this sweltering iron cage for the past two hours, whittling on a horse he was carving for Tyrone.

Careful to stay back in the deeper shadows, he wiped his arm across his damp forehead. He didn't need anybody seeing him. As soon as the next east-bound train arrived, he was out of here. Back to the route. Then he spotted the Quaker woman and her boy and shoved his glasses higher up his nose.

They were a matched pair. And right now both looked to be in a pretty pickle. Two men had pinned the boy between them, while a third was hollering at his mother. Prophet recognized the yeller as one who had jumped him in the saloon. He wondered what the heck she was doing in the middle of this mess.

He was starting back to the corner when he saw the hollerer stoop and grasp the bottom of Pearl's long dress. He yanked it up and over her head and tied the gathered top with a string like a bag. The crowd was whistling and hooting, the boy kicking hard to get free, while Pearl Eddy turned in a confused circle, her cotton inexpressibles bright in the sunlight.

Something twisted hard inside Prophet's chest. He had once been shamed in front of his children, made to strip naked by a Charleston crowd and dive in a river for a white man's lost pocket watch. Remembering back, he knew he would have gone down fighting, but they had grabbed Lacy and Tyrone and were threatening to toss them into the water. And neither child could swim. Looking at Pearl Eddy and her boy, he knew some of what they were feeling.

He watched a moment longer until the thing in his chest began rising into his throat, but he swallowed it down. It was the smart thing to do. The crowd outside had wanted to lynch him the night before, and he doubted its sentiments had changed much.

There was no question the woman had saved him. He owed her for that. He just didn't figure he owed her his life. The crowd roared again, and Prophet took to humming quietly to shut the sound out and looked at Tyrone's wooden horse, hoping it would distract him. Instead it caused him to think about the woman's kids. About the teenager out there being disgraced with his mother in the street. Shamed in the town he had to live in. He thought about Lacy and Tyrone looking down at the dirt that day in Charleston, looking as if they would never be able to look up again, and he felt the bad thing rising once more in his throat. "Damn," he said.

Samuel jumped at the sight of him. The Negro was just suddenly there in the middle of them, pulling the string that held his mother's dress, slapping the hands loose that held his own arms, then shoving Penny James backward.

Always before when Samuel had watched him, this man had moved as if he were old and stiff and slow. Not now. Now there was a startlingly quick agility to him, his movements laced with a destructive tension thinly camouflaged beneath a deceptive nonchalance. He seemed suddenly charged with some dangerous energy. It appeared natural enough. But to Samuel it was also scary. It had a similar effect on the men around them, and they backed off.

Caught by surprise, Penny had fallen hard onto the seat of his pants and sat staring up at the Negro until a look of recognition came over his damaged face. "Well, look whose old nigger we got here."

He started up out of the dirt at Prophet, the Negro waiting until he was halfway up before he put a large hand on his head and pushed him back down hard. The mob suddenly quieted.

"Don't get up fast like that again," Prophet said.

Pearl recognized the voice and stopped adjusting her clothing.

"Mr. Prophet?"

"Yes, ma'am."

"What art thou doing here?"

Prophet's eyes were on Penny's angry face. "Nothing much."

"Art thou involved in an altercation?"

"A what?"

"A dispute."

"Not much of one, ma'am."

"But thou art involved in one?"

"You might say."

"Then I want thee please to stop."

Prophet turned and, stunned, studied her face. "Tell him that, ma'am," he said, indignantly nodding in Penny's direction.

"Mr. Prophet, I am telling thee. Thou art a minister of the Lord. Try to remember. The words are 'strengthen thine heart' . . . not . . . 'strengthen thee.' "

Prophet started to answer her, then realized there were more pressing problems. Penny had taken the opportunity of his distraction to scramble to his feet, and now he was crouched and ready to fight. Prophet looked at him and shook his head as if he were tired. "You don't want this," he said in a cold voice. "I guarantee you don't want this." But that Penny James was beyond reason was obvious. Equally obvious was that he intended to kill him.

"Mr. Prophet," Pearl admonished.

"Beat him good! Beat that smart-talking Ethiope!" someone in the crowd yelled. Then Deputy Ritter and two other lawmen were wading through the men with their billies out, and Penny and Prophet and the rest of them were scrambling fast in all directions.

As Prophet ran, someone came up alongside him. It was Penny James. The man lunged and tried to claw his face. He ducked, feeling Penny's fingernails gouging skin back to his ear. Prophet whirled on the run and smashed one of his heavy fists hard into the side of Penny's head. He could tell from the way the barrel-chested man sagged and stumbled that he was going down. He didn't wait to watch it. There was a narrow passage between two buildings. He took it. A train was parked on the track directly in front of him. He leaped through an open boxcar. There was a thick grove of trees down by the river. He went for it.

His feelings all mixed up, Samuel didn't stop watching until the Negro disappeared down beyond the train tracks. The man was a criminal, he was sure of it. But he had also stood up for them against a crowd. It was something Samuel had always wanted to do himself.

"I'll give it to them, Mrs. Eddy," Deputy Ritter said, holding the heavy cooking pot. He nodded toward the Oriental woman. "I'm not supposed to let anyone near. You can see the trouble they cause."

"These people did not cause any trouble, Mr. Ritter."

The lawman just shrugged and turned toward the campsite.

Samuel was now shaking in self-anger, about what he, Samuel, hadn't done. Penny James might beat the stuffing out of him some dark night, but this other thing was gnawing like a rodent at his guts, and he feared it would eat him up inside. The Negro had protected his mother, and he, the eldest son, had done nothing.

He tried to walk it off. Halfway down the street he noticed a small cluster of some of the town's more respectable citizens. They were watching and talking, and though he couldn't be sure, he got the uncomfortable sense they hadn't approved of what they had seen. His lip was trembling, and he tried to fight off another wave of queasiness.

Samuel looked past Deputy Ritter to the Orientals. He was fighting with himself. They had caused all this. They weren't worth it. He looked at the woman with her short hair the color of roof tar, small like his mother and maybe middle thirties. She was dressed in baggy trousers he had never seen a woman wear before and a worn-out green jacket buttoned down both sides. And she was squatting unladylike in front of her little stove. But the thing that surprised him most was that she wasn't wearing any shoes. A grown woman, barefoot. Grown-ups in Zella never went barefoot, unless maybe they were swimming. Their shoes might be near useless, but they wore them.

She looked indecent to Samuel, and he felt embarrassed for her, but she didn't seem to care. She was smiling and keeping up a steady stream of unintelligible conversation with two small girls of five or six, glancing every so often at his mother. A third girl, closer to his age, was kneeling and hand-feeding grain to a bunch of hens as if it were gold. Her head was down, and he couldn't see much of her face.

Trying to keep his mind off what had happened, he scanned the rest of the encampment. Bundles of dirty canvas were stacked in a pile behind the family, and there was a rickety-looking wooden handcart; on top was a large split-bamboo cage with a door in it. It was a strange-looking contraption. Beneath the cart hung a wire chicken pen. He wondered if the chickens were show stock, the way the girl was caring for them. Probably not. He didn't figure these people had anything worth having.

He let his eyes drift over the camp again. There were two pigs. One was dead, stretched out on the cartwheel to cool. The other was a funny swaybacked creature, the hairiest pig he had ever seen. Samuel was turning back to Deputy Ritter when he noticed something else, a small movement among the bundles.

Stretching to his full height, he tried to get a better look. The woman and the little girls ignored him, as though used to the curiosity. He did see the woman staring at his mother again. The shadows of oncoming night were steeping Main Street in darkness, but Samuel thought for a moment that he could see the silhouette of a man's head cast against one of the large canvas bundles. Then it disappeared. Moments later he heard a sharp, chattering voice, a man's voice, coming from the place he had seen the shadow.

He inched closer, pushing against the rope. Nothing. Then he noticed the older girl glaring at him, as if he had done something terribly wrong. Suddenly feeling rude, he started to turn away. But he stopped and glanced back at her.

She was taller than the woman, who was probably her mother, and graceful-looking. The soft contours of her body showed through her worn cotton blouse and pants; her thick black hair bobbed neatly above her shoulders. The eyes were dark and almond-shaped; the mouth was full. She was barefoot as well. But for a reason Samuel couldn't explain it looked okay on the girl.

Samuel turned and walked back to his mother, explaining what he saw, as he always did for her. He looked for the girl again, but she was kneeling behind one of the canvas bundles. "They're poor—like pictures of Chinamen in books."

"Chinese," Pearl corrected.

"Chinese," he repeated.

"And Mr. Prophet?"

"Last time I saw him he was running toward the river. Nobody was chasing him."

She looked relieved.

Samuel thought again about what had just happened. He was still unable to calculate why the Negro had done it. Regardless, it wasn't enough to change his opinion.

They were halfway back to the buggy when the little Oriental woman suddenly jumped in front of them, looking hard at Pearl's face as if searching for something in it.

When he stopped walking, Pearl said, "Samuel?"

"The woman," was all he said.

Before Pearl could respond, the Oriental woman said, "We own land. *Rikuchi.* Here in this place. But they say we don't. They cheat us."

Pearl shook her head. "No. The men who told thee that are honest men. They did not cheat thee. Thy land was declared abandoned. I'm sorry." Pearl waited a moment, then said, "Samuel."

He started to guide his mother around the little woman, but she wouldn't let them pass. "I need your help. *Fujin.* Lady. No one will help me." She paused to study Pearl's face. "Will you help? To you they listen."

There was a strange pleading sound in the voice that Pearl intuitively understood and felt bad about. She listened for a moment to the fast breathing of the woman, thinking again about Edward Johnson's warning and concluding that wrong as it was for these people to be living in the street, there was nothing she could do about it. She had brought them food, and would again if necessary, but there was nothing left for her to reasonably do.

"I'm sorry," she said softly. "Judge Wilkins and Attorney Johnson have promised to help thee on thy way."

"Everybody help us on our way. But no one will help us." The woman stopped talking, and Samuel thought she might cry. But instead she repeated, "We own land. Here." She hesitated only a moment, then quickly asked again, "*Fujin*, will you help? Please."

Pearl took a deep breath. "No," she said slowly. "I cannot. I am sorry."

Curious, Samuel turned on the buggy seat and searched the campsite disappearing in the distance behind them, trying to see the Chinese again. The girl. And whoever had cast the shadow and spoken. But darkness was closing hard, and he couldn't. He did see Simon and Penny James and some other men watching them from the shadows of a nearby side street and squirmed. Then he glanced at his mother. She was sitting motionless, deep in what appeared to be troubling thoughts. Though surprised she had done it, she had been right to turn the Oriental woman away. They didn't need her problems.

"Art thou all right?"

She nodded but didn't look any better.

Though running late, they spent the next two hours delivering eggs, vegetables, and his mother's finished garments to customers in town. And they sold the first of their spring flowers, fewer than the year before. The flower garden was fading. Samuel thought of his father; the gardens had been his love. The familiar hurt filled the boy's chest. It seemed impossible that he was gone.

Samuel forced his thoughts back to their small but thriving business, glancing at the little ledger where he kept track of his mother's receipts and orders. While he and his brothers didn't care much for the work with the plants and the chickens, he knew his father would have been proud. That made him feel better.

Samuel listened to the sound of thunder rolling across the prairie north of town. They were stopped at the house of old man McPherson. Jack began to side-step nervously at the distant rumbling, and Samuel talked quietly to the horse.

Then a bolt of lightning lit the sky, illuminating the little shanty and the scrubby trees around them. Samuel felt a cold swish of wind and shivered, hungry and tired of waiting for his mother to stop talking to Mr. McPherson. He looked down at his worn-out shoes and pants that floated too high up his ankles, thinking about the Oriental girl again. He tried to pull his pants down lower. They moved some but not much, and his shoes were a mess; his little toe had broken through the leather on the right side.

"Mother?"

She didn't respond, just continued talking quietly to the frail old man. Samuel figured they were talking about Mrs. McPherson, about what she had done the month before. He had heard from Billy Jeffers that she had gone into her barn, pulled a sack over her head, lain down, resting her head on a mound of sand, then stuck a pistol in her mouth and pulled the trigger. The sack had kept the splattering down, and the sand had absorbed the blood. He shuddered. His mother had been coming each night since to visit with old man McPherson. Samuel didn't mind that. He just wanted to beat the rain.

Jack was rolling the bit in his mouth, tired and hungry as well. The wind picked up, whipping at the canvas roof of the buggy. Samuel buttoned his jacket against the chill and tried occupying his mind. Once again he thought of his father, and the muscles of his shoulders tightened, as if a cold hand from the shadows had grabbed him. His death still had an awful power over him. He guessed it always would. He wondered if old man McPherson felt the same way.

Then the rain hit, coming in from the north, riding on the wind, angling under the buggy top, and striking his exposed legs. He peered through it until he made out his mother and the old man. Neither of them had moved. They just stood there carrying on their conversation as if it were a lovely night. Samuel shook his head.

Watching her getting soaked, he thought of what an odd mix of things she was, a puzzle. Sometimes he had a time of it trying to get her straight in his head—

who she was and what she believed. But he loved her, he knew that.

"Mother—" he hollered against the downpour.

His stomach grumbled. He wished she would hurry but knew she wouldn't. She had time for people like old man McPherson, who had lost his wife. Where was her business sense, wasting large amounts of time with folks like these? Though she never discussed their finances, he knew things weren't good. He noticed the merchants looking to see if he was bringing money whenever he entered a store now.

He stared down the darkened street at the rough-looking houses. The people in them were all poor. They came here after their regular rounds to drop off extra eggs and vegetables to folks who couldn't buy. Again, Samuel didn't mind. It was just that he was always hungry these days, and his pants were soaked from the knees down and he was beginning to shake with the cold. He wished she weren't so mulish about things. Being Quaker in a mostly Methodist town was enough. The wind came down the darkened street again, and the dripping trees sounded as if they were talking.

Twenty minutes later the rain had stopped, but as the buggy rounded the turn and headed toward the prairie road out of town, Samuel was wet and trembling from the cold. His mother was also soaked, her hair hanging in damp strands, her woolen dress clinging to her.

"Thou needest to dry off," he said.

"Samuel," she said softly, "thou art almost grown." He tensed.

"It is hard growing without thy father." Her teeth chattered.

"I get along," he said, shifting on the seat.

"The world does not hold with much of what we hold with."

"Doesn't matter."

She smiled, but the smile was purely contemplative. Her face looked pale and chilled. He waited, but that was it. She had said all she wanted to say. She had a close understanding with him and his brothers; then every once in a while she would interrupt it with something like this. At least she hadn't spoken about what had happened on Main Street with Penny James.

Half an hour later he stopped Jack in the barn and crawled down and went and stood by the old horse's head. "Mother."

"Yes?"

"In town."

When he didn't continue, Pearl said, "Samuel?"

"I wanted to hit Penny James." He was sweating now in the cool night air. Pigeons were moving in the rafters overhead.

She didn't say anything, and he didn't feel like telling her the rest, but it was bothering him.

"I wanted to hurt him."

She sat for a moment, then said, "But thou didst not."

"But I wanted to. I wanted to do to him what the Negro did."

"But thou resisted," she said, as if he had done a great thing. She paused. "And Mr. Prophet did not."

He felt miserable. He had resisted nothing. He had been afraid. That was the sum of it. She was simply being naive again.

"Samuel," Pearl went on, "thou art old enough now to decide such things for thyself. Thou wilt have to decide many difficult things. But thou must resist violence. What Mr. Prophet did was wrong. Thy father—"

Pearl stopped talking as if the words had been yanked from her.

She gripped the front edge of the buggy seat hard with both her hands, thinking back to that night. To Matthew and what had happened. She was trembling in the barn's darkness when she heard Samuel's voice and forced herself to focus on the words.

"It was just as wrong to let him shame thee," he mumbled.

"We shame only ourselves." Her thoughts were still on Matthew. Samuel was standing at the side of the buggy now. She tensed her arm so that he wouldn't see her shaking and held it out for him.

Her skin felt cool to Samuel, and she climbed down more slowly and stiffly than usual. He wondered if she was sick. Then she oriented herself with her cane and started walking in her brisk way, and he figured she wasn't. She was backlighted by the moonlight falling outside the barn. He kicked at a stone near the carriage wheel. She was at the door now, tapping her long walking stick softly on the ground ahead of her.

"What kind of things?" he asked.

She stopped. "Samuel?"

"Thou said I'd have to decide things. What things?"

She stood for a moment, then said: "What thou wilt believe as a man."

"I'll believe what I believe now," he said quickly, his tone defensive as if someone were trying to take something precious from him.

She turned slowly and faced in his direction; then she pulled her shawl tighter over her shoulders and stood staring as if she might actually be able to see him. Finally she turned away and started toward the house. "It is cool tonight; put the blanket on Jack."

* * *

The first wave of chill night wind blew into Prophet's sweat-covered face from the northeast. He was breathing hard. Five miles, he figured, were what he had run down this lonely road, putting distance between him and the mob in town. He slowed to a limping trot, then a fast, hobbled walk. He didn't know exactly where he was. All he knew was that he was headed east, Missouri somewhere up ahead. Beyond that, Kentucky, Virginia, and North Carolina. It felt good getting back to the route.

Prophet had nothing specific against this barren place. He just didn't know why he was here. It was a waste of time when he needed to be searching for his children. Still, he was glad he had helped the woman and the boy out of their fix back in town. That had cleared his debt with her. He didn't like owing people. Especially somebody who had done something the way she had. Nobody had ever done anything like that for him before.

Prophet wiped an arm across his damp forehead, marveling at what he could still see in the surrounding darkness. Massive walls of plants—sunflowers, coneflowers, wild grape, needlegrass, goldenrods, and hundreds more he didn't know—lined the roadway so thickly that a man would have to hack his way through with a sword, all of it over his head.

But the strangest thing was the fact that there was not one tree around. The place seemed to have suddenly run out of them. That was okay by him. Anything that made lynching a harder act was fine by his thinking. He tipped his head back and stared up at the thick vault of prairie sky floating overhead, strewn with a spray of spring stars, wondering why the woman chose to live out here in this lonely place.

It seemed sorely deprived of the basic comforts. He scanned the surrounding night, the darkness intense.

Not even a neighbor's light to break the loneliness. He had always thought there was a longing in women for the closeness of others and nice things. Maybe that wasn't true with Mrs. Eddy. It didn't matter. It wasn't any of his concern. He was leaving.

As soon as he thought that last thought, he started to feel queasy, as if he were running out on something he shouldn't. The woman was getting to him, he figured. He slid his hand into his backpack, searching for the wooden horse he was making. Sometimes the carving had been a distraction for him. That's when he felt it. Even without looking at it, he knew it was Zacharias's arrowhead. He had forgotten to leave it on the kitchen table.

Chapter Four

Pearl was deep in thought when she entered the house and heard the children in raucous play in the parlor. She stopped, sensing that someone was with them.

"Mr. Prophet?"

"No, Pearl. Edward Johnson."

"Edward," she said with genuine fondness, "it is nice to have thee here."

The twins were howling like attacking Indians, racing around the room, while Johnson sat on the sofa looking comfortable in the midst of the rampage. Zacharias was in the rocker, holding the silver-framed photograph of his father, the frame a gift from his grandmother Lillian.

"Boys," Pearl said, brushing damp hair off her face.

"Looks like Jack took a detour upriver," Johnson joked.

Pearl smiled again, spreading her wet shawl over the back of a chair and unpinning her bonnet. The boys were panting and waiting for a signal that they could resume the battle.

"Excuse me, Edward," she said, moving toward her bedroom.

"Can we, Mother?" Joshua asked.

"Take a lantern and help Samuel with Jack."

"Awwww, Ma," Joshua pleaded.

"Joshua," Pearl said firmly, moving through the bedroom door, "thy brother has been working in the rain all evening. He is cold and tired."

The twins dutifully trooped out the door, but Zacharias continued to sit. Johnson glanced at him.

"I knew your father," he said, reaching his hand out for the photograph.

The boy shook his head.

"I won't hurt it."

Zacharias shook his head again. The two of them sat staring at each other.

"Promise," Johnson tried again.

"No," the boy said, looking away.

"Zacharias," Pearl chided, coming back into the room a few minutes later. She had changed into a black dress and simple white blouse with long sleeves. Like all her things, these had seen better days.

Johnson watched her a moment, then looked back at the boy, who had conceded to turn the photograph slightly so that he could see it. "Your father was a good man," the lawyer said.

Pearl smiled.

Zacharias seemed to be thinking about something else. He looked at his mother. "When did Mr. Prophet say he'd be back?"

"I do not believe he will."

"Yes. He will."

"I do not believe so, Zacharias. I think he had other things that were very important. But thou stop pouting and go help thy brothers."

Zacharias was shaking his head now. "No. He'll be back. He promised."

The boy's tone of absolute certainty stopped her for a moment; she knew how much he missed his father. Then she said, "Hurry now and help thy brothers."

She waited until Zacharias closed the back door, then turned in Johnson's direction. "Edward?" Her voice betrayed her concerns.

"Zacharias seems very fond of the Negro."

"Yes," Pearl said, settling herself in a chair opposite him. "Yes. He is quite fond of him."

Johnson waited for her to say something more. When she didn't, he said, "I spoke to Snipes. He said that the extension is irregular and that he'll have to check the bank's regulations. But that's just Snipes."

"Should I bring the money in?"

"Let me work out an agreement first."

She sat up straighter and smiled. "Thank thee, Edward. When my pullets begin to lay and my seamstressing expands . . . things will be fine."

Johnson walked to the window and stood looking out at the night.

"Coffee, Edward?"

"Yes." He would have a cup and then tell her the rest.

The garden was still dripping from the rain; it looked like a magical, sparkling place in the prairie moonlight. The Eddy boys had not found Samuel in the barn, and they had come searching for him here, laughing and shoving each other into puddles until they approached the fence. This had been their father's garden, the one passion that he had allowed himself in life, and he had shared it with them. Now, whenever they came to this place, they felt close to him.

Joshua led the way under the great arch of climbing roses, a profusion of red and coral blossoms that covered the garden gate, stopping and staring as if seeing the place for the first time, an acre of land lovingly shaped by their father's hand but now hopelessly overgrown and cluttered.

"Sam's not here," Joshua whispered.

"Yes, he is." Luke pointed into the darkness ahead.

Even with the full moon, the shadows were deep, the night seemingly enveloping them like liquid, but still they could make out their older brother standing inside a small picketed enclosure, could see the white cross that marked their father's grave. They had wanted a large stone marker with his name and carvings of angels and some nice words on it, but their mother had forbidden it. They would mark the grave, she had told them, with the simple sign of their Lord and nothing more. It bothered them still.

The night air was chilly, and Zacharias pulled in tightly against Luke. He was carrying Hercules, the rooster, under one arm, the old chicken clucking softly in the cool night air as though he found all this worth serious contemplation.

The four of them stood awhile in the shadowy silence before the grave, sharing something that they felt but had a hard time talking about. They came here almost every day. Alone or together, they watered and did little things with the flowers to keep them growing. But the only real work was on the vegetable garden, the moneymaking plants.

Joshua broke the stillness. "Sam, dost thou remember much about Dad?"

"Sure."

"I get scared I'll forget him. What he looked like, how he talked. And the way I felt about him."

"I just come here and talk to him when I feel like that," Samuel said quietly.

"Does he answer thee?" Zacharias asked.

"I think so."

"Like he used to do when we were working with him? Does he talk to thee like that?"

"No. Not like that."

The little boy looked sad.

His arm around Zacharias's shoulder, Luke tipped his head back and stared up at the stars and the moon drifting peacefully through wisps of white clouds. "Dost thou think he's forgotten us?"

"No," Samuel said quickly. "He would never do that."

Joshua looked skeptical. "Thou said he wouldn't die either."

Samuel bit at the inside of his lip. "I didn't think he would. But he hasn't forgotten us. He never will."

"Why didn't they let us see him before he died? Or in the coffin?" Luke asked. "I wanted to see him."

"It doesn't matter now," Samuel said.

Zacharias was crying without sound. "Mother says Father is happy because he's with God." He snuffed his nose. "But I don't think that's true. I don't think he could be happy without us."

"Just talk to him," Samuel said reassuringly.

"I do. But he never talks to me." Zacharias was crying out loud now.

Samuel put a hand gently on his brother's head.

After a while Joshua said, "Mr. Prophet is gone."

"Good," Samuel said.

"He's not gone," Zacharias snapped in his high-pitched voice.

"Thou art wasting thy time waiting for that Negro," Samuel said.

"He wasn't so bad," Luke said. Joshua nodded in agreement.

"He couldn't be trusted," Samuel said.

"I don't believe that, Sammy," Zacharias screeched

angrily. "I can trust things. Mother says that. And I trust Mr. Prophet."

Samuel didn't want to hurt his brother, so he stopped talking and stared at the moonlight that fell across the grave. He too wished she had let them mark it. It seemed lost and lonely: just the earth and the cross.

The children were outside, and Edward Johnson was standing and looking out the parlor window. He turned, cup and saucer in his hand, and drank some coffee. Pearl was sitting in her chair working on a garment.

"Didst thou happen to speak to the sheriff, Edward?"

He stood fingering the handle of the cup, then set it on the table. "Yes." She looked small—and with her blindness—hopelessly outmatched by all she faced. He picked up his hat. "Yes, I did, Pearl."

"And?"

"Simon claims the Negro tried to steal his wallet."

"They argued over church money."

Johnson raised his eyebrows. "Discussing church funds doesn't sound much like Simon James." He could tell from her expression that his remark had not changed her mind. "Regardless. Everybody agrees that a fight started, that the Negro got the best of it. Simon says he was high on opium from the Chinese."

Pearl stuck her needle into the fabric and looked in his direction. "He was not. And he is not a thief," she said matter-of-factly.

"Others think differently, Pearl."

"He is a Negro minister."

Johnson shook his head in a way he wouldn't have if she could have seen him. "Doesn't matter. The sheriff isn't happy about the mob. He threatened to lock Simon up. Nobody is going to bother the Negro. Least not openly."

Pearl turned her face toward him and smiled and said, "Edward, thank thee."

Johnson didn't return her smile. He walked to the window and stood staring out at the moonlight in the front elm. "Couple of other things about the Negro, Pearl."

"Yes?"

He paused and ran a finger around the inside brim of his hat. "His name isn't Prophet. It's Jerome Gilliam."

She quit sewing for a moment; then she nodded and began again. "Yes. I have heard him use Jerome. I did not know his last name."

"Mr. Gilliam is not a preacher."

She didn't respond.

"He's a bare-knuckle fighter. Or was. He's getting a little long in the trousers, I suppose, to be crawling into boxing rings."

Pearl pressed her lips together and sat contemplating this news.

"Prophet was his fighting name, Prophet of Doom." He hesitated. "He killed a man in an illegal bout in Missouri a few years ago. The court ruled it manslaughter," Johnson continued. "He served a year in the Missouri state penitentiary." He stopped talking and looked at her. She had returned to her sewing.

"Did you hear, Pearl?"

"Yes."

"If he comes back, you should let me know." He watched her a moment to see if what he had said had registered. He wasn't certain. "Pearl?"

He saw a trace of unhappiness around her eyes that lasted only a second. Then she nodded in agreement.

"Good." He felt a little miffed that while he was the

family attorney, Pearl oftentimes didn't listen to his advice. He was feeling this way at the moment, and he turned back to the window and stuffed his badly blocked hat onto the top of his head and sank both his hands in his pants pockets.

"I hear you delivered food to those Chinese." He paused. "And that the Negro got into a fight with Penny James." He waited, then continued. "Over you and Samuel."

"Yes."

"We agreed you wouldn't get involved."

"Yes."

"Yes, we did," he said, sounding like a troubled uncle. "The whole town is talking, Pearl."

"I didn't hold up the bank, Edward," she said with irritation.

"No. But you've got a business. And the boys." He paused. "Pearl, no good will come of your getting involved with that family. Not right after the Negro."

The house was quiet now. Edward Johnson had been gone for two hours, and her boys asleep for close to one. Pearl was still sitting in the parlor and trying to hold her emotions in check. She wasn't succeeding much. Each time she had believed in the Negro, he had deceived her. And now she had learned of the killing. The word made her shudder, her thoughts jumping to Matthew.

She struggled against the painful memory, focusing instead on Jerome Gilliam, gripping her hands, squeezing them as she often did when she was seeking inspiration or guidance. She tried to re-member what he had said about being a preacher but couldn't. He had not told her about the death, but there had been no reason to. But they had talked about his being a preacher. Was that simply a lie? she wondered.

Suddenly a thought flashed into her mind: He could still be a minister. Perhaps the man's death or prison had awakened his spirit. It wouldn't be mankind's first redemption. The world was filled with sinners who had turned to the Lord, far greater sinners than Mr. Prophet. She shifted awkwardly in her chair. Still, from the fight on Main Street, she knew he had not forsaken violence altogether. Even so, her spirits rose. Then she heard a horse running hard toward the farm; moments later someone was banging on the front door.

Hector James glanced worriedly at the face of his father, as he rushed Pearl into Dr. Smith Trotter's office on Elm Street. Simon looked shaken to him, bending and helping the doc hold his sister down on a small cot. Chrissy James's eyes were rolling to white in her panicked struggle for air. The room was hot and humid on Hector's skin and filled with an awful shrieking of a kettle at full boil that made him want to cover his ears. His brothers, Penny and Mike, were standing back watching. Mike was scared, Penny just mad when he saw the Quaker woman.

"Steam isn't working," Trotter said to Pearl over the noise.

Tall and thin, with thick gray hair, the sixty-year-old doctor, even in this emergency, had a genial face. He was the only doctor in the county, and dressed in suspenders and badly pressed trousers that had been pulled over his long underwear, he looked as if he had been asleep. He turned to Pearl, momentarily releasing his grip on the girl long enough for Chrissy to lunge from the cot and scurry crablike to a corner of the room in her desperate hunt for air.

"Take the pot off," Pearl said.

"That's how we've always done it," Simon snapped. Though Pearl had doctored Chrissy numerous times for her attacks, Simon could never quite acknowledge this fact.

Trotter ignored the man and pulled the kettle from the stove. Silence fell over the room, broken only by Chrissy's gasps, the sound wet and thick as she sucked each breath down her swollen throat.

"Gawddamn it, Trotter, she's no doctor!"

"Nor you, Simon," the doctor returned.

If she heard the men, Pearl showed no reaction, bending instead over a large cloth bag, removing various things, and setting them to one side on the examining table. Simon watched her, his fist clenching and unclenching. Meekly Hector said, "Pa, she's helped Chrissy before."

Simon cuffed the boy hard. "Don't lecture me."

"Sit," Trotter ordered, as if the Jameses were children.

Simon lowered his bulk into a chair near the wall, his eyes on Pearl. Moments later Chrissy's panting increased, and he leaped back up. "She can't breathe without the steam!"

Over the years Pearl had battled a dozen or more of Chrissy's attacks, using experience gained helping her own father survive this same frightening disease. She knew firsthand the anguish of watching helplessly as someone you loved strangled, so she ignored Simon's ranting and continued removing things from her bag, humming softly as she worked. The peaceful sound of her voice was a magnet to the child, Chrissy turning on the floor and watching her. Pearl sensed that Chrissy's condition was very severe this night and required another form of treatment. She held a small vial out in the direction of the doctor.

"Eucalyptus essence. Please, a dozen drops in the

pot, bring it back to a boil; then give it and a blanket to me."

Simon watched, listening closely to everything Pearl did and said. She went back to humming and rummaging through her bag while Trotter went for a blanket.

"Chrissy," she called in a pleasant tone, "I'll be with thee in a moment." She paused. "Hector?"

The boy hopped up, nervously eyeing Penny, who sat glaring at him. Chrissy had begun thrashing wildly on the floor again, gasping for air as if each would surely be her last.

"Thou knowest that does not help thee," Pearl called. "Hand on thy stomach. Fill it up with air. Remember?"

"She isn't smart, so quit tormenting her," Simon yelled.

Pearl fought off a moment's anger, then said, "She is the Lord's child, sir. Therefore thou shouldst not presume to judge her intelligence."

Chrissy didn't put her hand on her stomach, but she did stop thrashing. She was staring at Pearl now.

"Hector?"

"Mrs. Eddy?"

She handed him some dried mullein leaves. "Please roll a cigarette from this."

"Pardon?"

"Thou smoke?"

"Yes."

"Then make a cigarette as thou wouldst from tobacco."

The boy hurried across the room, casting worried glances at his oldest brother and father, while Chrissy uttered a deep, gurgling sound that Simon mistook for a death rattle.

"I'm not going to just sit while my girl chokes to

death!" he yelled. Mike James restrained him. Penny didn't move, didn't watch his sister, just kept his eyes locked on Pearl.

Pearl was kneeling now in front of the girl. Chrissy was drenched in sweat and staring wild-eyed at the floor, slobbering and sucking desperately for air.

"Chrissy," Pearl said softly, "Chrissy. Listen. Thou must help." Pearl reached out until her fingers touched the child; then gently she stroked her damp hair. Frantically the girl grabbed for her, as if grasping a log in the middle of a raging sea. The kettle was screeching again.

Pearl sat down beside the child and pulled a blanket over both their heads. Doc Trotter slipped the steaming pot, wrapped in towels, under the edge.

"Is Chrissy going to live?" Simon was torn. He was standing again.

"Pa, let her," Mike said. "For Chrissy."

"I got it," Hector said, rushing back into the room.

"Light it," Pearl said.

As soon as the burning cigarette disappeared under the blanket, Chrissy and Pearl began coughing hard, the woman speaking quietly between gasping spells. Fifteen minutes later it was over. Pearl threw the blanket off and leaned back weakly against the wall, her legs straight out in front of her, Chrissy clinging to her. The two of them looked awful, their eyes bloodshot and tearing badly, mucus draining from their nostrils.

Simon took his daughter. While relieved at her recovery, he showed no gratitude to the woman. Chrissy mumbled something and then stretched a thin arm out for Pearl, the girl's fingers wiggling in the smoky air. She was babbling loudly now, but her father was carrying her toward the door.

"Thou needest thy rest, child," Pearl said. She blew

her nose on a handkerchief, then cleared her throat. "It's thy cat, Mr. James."

Simon ignored her.

"Thy cat," she repeated.

"You're no doctor," Simon snapped.

"Chrissy's attacks come from thy cat," she persisted, wiping perspiration from her face with a wet cloth.

"She's probably right," Trotter added.

"We've been lucky," Pearl continued, sniffing and wiping her eyes on the cloth. "But one of these times we may not."

The James boys were following their father. Hector turned and looked at Pearl for a moment. "Thanks." While he didn't smile, the gratitude was genuine.

"Thou art welcome, Hector."

Mike James nodded shyly in agreement. Then Penny pushed them both out the doorway, stopping to glare back at Pearl. "I'm not done with your nigger."

"That's enough, young man," Trotter said.

"He is not my nigger, sir." She wiped her eyes with the towel. "He is a man. Like thee."

"Nigger."

Pearl pulled herself up straight. "No, sir."

Penny caught up with his father and Chrissy at the Reliable Livery. The night air was cool and moonlit. Simon was standing near the stable door under yellow lantern light, deep in thought, surrounded by fluttering white moths and loud-buzzing June bugs that banged out of control against the wall.

"You got any paper?" Simon asked.

Penny shook his head.

"Get some," he ordered, continuing to look as if he were thinking hard about something.

Penny reached up and pulled a poster down from the livery wall. "Here."

"No," Simon said, handing him a pencil. "You write."

Penny took the pencil and sat down on a bench next to the building. "Write what?"

Simon adjusted the shawl over Chrissy and began to pace up and down the wooden sidewalk. "One blanket," he said. "Write that down. One blanket. Then twelve drops of eucalyptus essence." He thought for a moment. "Put the drops in boiling water. Mullein cigarette." He squinted his eyes. "Plain old dried mullein plant."

Penny was grinning.

With the first sound of sparrows in the wisteria outside her room, Pearl sat up in bed. She was tired and thinking about the things that were bothering her. About her money problems. The Oriental family. Jerome Gilliam and the killing.

She closed her eyes, trying hard to recall the good feelings she had gotten when she chanced upon the idea of his redemption. But now there were unsettling doubts about him—as a minister and, most of all, as an example for Zacharias—and they kept coming back to her. She knew how easily influenced her youngest would be by a man he admired. And Mr. Gilliam was the first man he had admired since his father's death. It was for the best, even though she was concerned about his welfare, that Jerome Gilliam was gone.

The house felt unusually cool as Pearl left the bedroom, headed toward the kitchen. She heard Hercules. "Zacharias, is thy rooster inside?" A strange scraping sound was drifting down the hall. She stopped and listened.

"Hit it!"

"Mr. Gilliam?"

The three younger Eddy boys were helping Prophet take the back door off its hinges, when Pearl entered the kitchen. Samuel was standing off to one side, watching and looking miffed.

Zacharias was puffed up with happiness. "I told thee he would be back." He beamed. "Didn't I tell thee?"

"Yes, thou didst," Pearl said, her voice very quiet.

Prophet, momentarily surprised that she knew his last name, muttered a weak "Morning, Mrs. Eddy."

"Thou hast returned?"

"Paying for that hen, Mrs. Eddy."

Zacharias smiled at the man as if he were the most wonderful thing in the world.

"This door doesn't close right," Prophet said, returning quickly to the hinge and glancing at her periodically. "Figured I'd fix it." The children held their places, but they were watching her as well. All but Zacharias, who seemed mesmerized by the Negro.

"Boys, please feed and water the chickens."

"It's stuck, Mrs. Eddy," Prophet protested, forcing a smile and straining to hold the door by himself. The three boys halted and looked at their mother; Samuel turned and walked outside.

"Help Mr. Gilliam," she relented.

"Who's Mr. Gilliam?" Zacharias asked.

"Mr. Prophet and Mr. Gilliam are one and the same person," she replied. "Is that not correct, sir?"

"Whatever you say, ma'am."

Zacharias shrugged, and Prophet and the boys resumed their efforts. Then suddenly, as if coming to the old door's rescue, Hercules took a hawklike leap at Prophet's ankles. The man hopped wildly to avoid the bird's spurs.

"Call him off!" He was trembling as if the bird were a five-hundred-pound lion.

Pearl stooped and made some clicking sounds, and Hercules broke off the attack and strode over to her. She picked him up and stroked the feathers on his neck. "Good bird," she said gently.

"Dumb bird," Prophet mumbled.

"He is not dumb, Mr. Gilliam."

"Maybe not, but he's trailing way behind smart," he muttered. Minutes later the door was off its hinges and the boys were heading outside.

Pearl waited until she could no longer hear them, then said, "Mr. Gilliam?"

Prophet ignored her, picking up a wood plane and beginning to stroke the tool gracefully over the door edge, wood curls falling. Hercules canted his head and eyed the growing mess on the floor, struggling to get down to investigate. Pearl held him.

"Thou lied to me again."

"Mrs. Eddy?"

"Thou lied to me."

"About?" He frowned.

"Many things."

"Like?"

"Thy name for one. Thou said it was Prophet."

"That's right."

"It is Jerome Gilliam."

"Once—but not now. It's Prophet, Mrs. Eddy, just plain Prophet."

"Not just plain Prophet," she said quickly.

He stopped and looked up at her, sensing she knew still more. How much more he didn't know. He watched her a moment longer, then went back to working.

"Is that not correct?"

"You're the one talking, Mrs. Eddy."

"The Prophet of Doom I believe is thy entire name."

He straightened up slowly. "My, my," he said, after recovering from his surprise. "Along with being righteous, Mrs. Eddy, you're a regular detective."

"Storytellers usually get caught, Mr. Gilliam."

He went back to planing the door edge. "Don't recall I told you stories." That was a lie, and it made him edgy, an unusual reaction for him.

"Oh, yes, thou didst. Thou let me believe thy name had some religious meaning."

"I didn't say a thing, ma'am. If I'd waited long enough, you'd have named me Pope."

She pulled herself up straighter. "Silence that deceives, sir, is lying all the same."

He wondered how much she actually knew.

"Suppose the sheriff told you I boxed."

"Not the sheriff."

He hesitated, guessing she knew most of it. It didn't matter. He had given the boy his arrowhead, and that was why he had come back. He repeated this thought—that he had come back just to drop off the arrowhead—a couple more times but knew inside it wasn't the whole reason. The whole reason had to do with this little woman and what she had done for him. He knew that. He just wasn't willing to admit it to himself. But whether he did or not didn't matter. He could leave now without regrets.

He was studying Pearl Eddy standing with her arms crossed, tapping her foot on the floor and staring righteously into the kitchen wall as if she absolutely knew it was his face, when a sudden rumbling in his stomach reminded him that he was broke. This woman had to have cash somewhere. And she could surely spare him a little. Pearl was smiling smugly at the wall now, looking as innocent as a Sunday school teacher. Crafty like a fox, he figured.

But getting on her bad side—which he knew was easy enough to do—wouldn't help him find her cash. The only way to do that was to stay on her good side, so he could hang around the house. And staying on Pearl Eddy's good side, he figured, meant confessing things of the soul. She had a regular weakness for it. So he did just that.

"Something else you should know, Mrs. Eddy."

She quit staring at the wall as soon as he spoke, taking up a more accurate fix on his position.

"Three years ago." He paused for effect. "I accidentally killed a Negro in a fight. I served time. Just thought you should know." He lowered his eyes, then remembered she was blind and looked to see if she had bought it.

"You killed a human being," she corrected.

Damn, she was an irritant, straightening out every itty-bitty sentence.

"Hast thou sought forgiveness?"

"No, Mrs. Eddy."

"Thou must." She paused. "Thou must step out of life's shadow and live in God's sunlight."

At last something from her that sounded like sympathy.

"I am sorry thou believest in violence, that thou deceivest. But the Lord will forgive thee, Mr. Gilliam."

The lines of a new frown formed on his face.

She continued tapping her foot on the floor.

"Mrs. Eddy, that's annoying."

"No more than thy deceits."

"Ma'am, I came back to pay for the hen," he muttered, exasperated. "Nothing more. I'll fix this door, then be on my way." He squirmed. She was getting to him. Find the money, then hit the road. Not much time. Every man, he knew, had just so much time on this earth to get his things done.

"Fine," she said. "I expect no violence while thou art here."

They didn't say anything else for a while. She just stood holding the rooster while he worked on the door. When she finally set the bird down, it began to scratch in the wood curls. Prophet watched it until he was convinced it had no designs on him; then he scanned the room again. Women mostly kept their money somewhere in the kitchen. But he had been over this one three times. She definitely wasn't like most women. He looked past her into the parlor. Must be in there. Probably in the old desk.

"The county attorney, Edward Johnson, spoke to the sheriff on thy behalf."

He didn't respond.

"Everything is settled, Mr. Gilliam. Thou dost not have to sneak around like a common criminal."

He felt hot on the back of his neck, but he just went back to working. He would find a way into the parlor, he promised himself.

"No one will arrest thee. Those men will leave thee alone." She paused. "Although I would avoid Penny James." Her voice dropped a note, laden with disapproval. "The man thou attacked in the street."

He didn't reply.

"Didst thou hear, Mr. Gilliam?"

"My name's Prophet, Mrs. Eddy. And he attacked you."

"Regardless, as a minister thou knowest better." She waited a moment, then continued. "I have cleared my name," she said, "as well as thine." She hesitated, checking the buttons on her plain blouse. "Whatever thy name is."

"That's nice."

She turned and stared in his direction with an odd

look on her face, staring so long that he got uncomfortable.

"What?" he finally asked.

"Didst thou," she said, rushing her words, "find religion in prison?"

He started to tell her no, then reconsidered. "Yes, Mrs. Eddy," he lied.

"And that is where thou became a minister?"

He didn't even hesitate: "Yes."

Then the boys were trooping back into the kitchen, and she was distracted. Fifteen minutes later the door was back on its hinges and closing properly. Prophet knew about fixing things.

Chapter Five

The hour was late, and Prophet was standing in a pile of fresh wood shavings, bent over a workbench in the tool-shed, squinting hard through his glasses in the harsh light of a kerosene lantern. He swore softly under his breath. This was his fifteenth attempt, and he was ready to call it quits. If he didn't get it done this time, he promised himself, he was going to pack up and hit the road. From that night in Pearl Eddy's cellar till now was only three days, but it felt like a lifetime.

He had only postponed his going because Zacharias had badgered him all day about doing this thing for his pa. Prophet grumbled under his breath. He hadn't had a chance to find the woman's money. But he didn't care anymore. He was beyond caring about money, the woman's baleful stares, or what the boy thought about him. He had to get. His own children were out there.

Prophet looked across the weak light inside the shed at Zacharias, sprawled on his back on some feed sacks, sound asleep. He studied the boy for a time, watching the steady rise and fall of his small chest, recalling that Tyrone had often slept on his back like that. Something pulled in his gut. He shrugged it off. It was too bad the way they had both lost their fathers.

But there was nothing he could do about it. At least not for this boy.

Prophet straightened up and rolled his shoulders to stop their aching; his lower legs were hurting as well, and his hands were tired from all the chiseling. The bad feeling lingered, so he reached into his pants and pulled out the leather poke. He opened it and looked at the money. That always made him feel better, as if there were some future with the children that he was working toward. Moments later he heard a noise from the direction of the barn that caused him to tense, and he stuffed the money away and grabbed a hammer.

"Zacharias," Pearl called.

Prophet put the tool down, then said "shushhhh" out the open door, glancing sideways at the sleeping boy. He hadn't stirred a finger. Prophet smiled. Like Tyrone, he could sleep through the clap of damnation. Prophet wasn't eager to have the woman pestering him. He looked back down at the slab of wood lying on the table.

Zacharias had given him clear instructions about what he wanted done, had watched him work for a time—chattering in his screechy voice about different things, as if the two of them were old friends—then dropped off to sleep, seemingly confident the man was going to produce exactly what he had asked for. Prophet wasn't feeling the same confidence.

He had cut pieces of two-by-sixteen pine planking from a pile behind the barn, planed each piece down to a smooth, fresh surface, then gone at it with chisel and hammer. At first his mistakes had been made early, and he had tossed the ruined boards aside with little concern. But then as he got better at it, his mistakes came later and later into the work, costing him time. This current piece was mistake free and almost done.

He wiped his forehead with a rag as Pearl tapped her way into the room. She looked worried, and Prophet realized he had lost track of time. From the position of the moonlight in the open doorway, the hour was late.

"He's asleep in the corner, ma'am," he said, watching as she worked her way around the table, feeling with her hand for the boy and looking agitated. "To your left," he said. "Figured you knew he was here."

"He climbed out a window," she said coolly.

Prophet grinned.

The night was chilly. She felt Zacharias's forehead and then touched Prophet's jacket, which had been laid over the boy for warmth, nodding at this consideration. She turned and tapped her way back to the workbench. She didn't look agitated any longer, just distant and reserved.

"Mr. Prophet." She stopped suddenly. "Is that what I should call thee?"

"Yes, ma'am."

"All right," she continued. "Mr. Prophet, thou knowest how impressionable Zacharias is."

"He's just a boy."

"Yes. But also he thinks a great deal of thee."

Prophet didn't respond. He just looked uncomfortable and went back to working on the wooden plank.

"I would not want him to get ideas about certain things."

"No, ma'am," he mumbled.

"About violence and swearing." She paused. "Thou understandest."

"Yes, Mrs. Eddy."

"Then thou wilt avoid these things?"

"I plan on moving on. But as long as I'm here, ma'am, you can count on it."

She smiled. "Thank thee." She pulled her shawl tighter around her shoulders. "What does he have thee working on?"

He stiffened. "Nothing," he said, leery about giving away the boy's secret.

She waited a long time before she spoke again. "Mr. Prophet, deceit is also one of the things I would have thee avoid." She stood looking blindly in his direction for a moment before she went on. "We are bound by our thoughts, Mr. Prophet. Surely thou would not want to be bound by deceit."

"Nobody's deceiving, Mrs. Eddy," he said defensively. "I just wondered why you'd think the boy had me working on anything. That's all."

"Because I know Zacharias, Mr. Prophet." She paused. "And because he told me that thou had promised to do something for him."

"Yes, ma'am," he said. "Sign for the garden."

"I smell no paint."

"He wanted it chiseled."

"May I read it?"

"Your garden." He held the board toward her outstretched hand, pushed it forward until the wood just met the tip of her fingers.

She moved them probingly over the grooves of the freshly carved letters. Watching her sightless blue eyes and seeing her lips silently form each letter, he got a feeling for her blindness that he hadn't had before, something of the helplessness and isolation. When she finished reading, he was surprised to see she looked upset.

"Something wrong with it, Mrs. Eddy?"

She didn't answer him. He turned the sign and checked each letter against the ones he had made Zacharias write out for him on a piece of paper. They were all there. And in the right order. He couldn't figure what was bothering her.

THIS IS OUR FATHER'S GRAVE
MATTHEW EDDY
1861 T

"I told the children they could not mark their father's grave with anything but a cross." She seemed to be talking to herself.

"It isn't much of a thing, Mrs. Eddy."

She turned in his direction as if just realizing he was standing beside her. "What is that, Mr. Prophet?"

"The sign. It's not much of a thing—if the boy wants it."

"We don't decorate graves, Mr. Prophet." She paused. "We are dust at the beginning, and we return to dust. My husband is with God. That is enough."

"Maybe not for your boys."

"Please put it outside the garden," she said, turning away.

"It won't be right."

She turned back. "Sir?"

"Outside the garden, Mrs. Eddy, it won't identify the grave. Not the way the boy wants."

She stood still for a few moments, then said, "Mr. Prophet. Outside the garden, please."

He shook his head and wondered if it was her blindness that made her rigid about things. Maybe. Regardless, the boy wanted it on his father's grave.

"It's only a little marker," he persisted.

He saw her skin turning crimson.

"We just believe certain things, Mr. Prophet."

"Your boys, Mrs. Eddy? Or you?"

"We."

"With due respect, I don't see it that way."

"That is thy privilege. But the children are my responsibility." She turned and gathered Zacharias up in her arms. She tripped over a piece of lumber as she started out. Prophet caught her and guided her to the door. Zacharias was breathing softly. Prophet felt sorry for them both and wasn't certain why.

He watched her tapping her way out the door with the sleeping child cradled in her arms, knowing she had never seen his face, never seen him smile or pout. Samuel or the twins either. He let it pass. It didn't give her any right to be stiff about things.

"It isn't a big thing—the sign," he called through the shadows after her.

"Outside the fence, Mr. Prophet."

"It won't work that way, Mrs. Eddy."

She carried Zacharias toward the house without responding.

It was early morning, the day already hot and dry and promising to get even hotter as Prophet stood near the garden gate watching Samuel pull weeds from a clump of sweet rose near his father's grave. He thought of Lacy and her patch of flowers. She had bought the seeds with money she had earned hoeing yams for one of the big farms in Sanford. A whole month's work for a packet of seeds. He blinked hard a couple of times and listened to bobwhite quail calling "sara-lee" in the fields beyond.

Lacy had planted those seeds under the kitchen window of their house, planted them so her mother could see them. Small as she was, she had worked that ground hard. Worked it as if her life had depended on it. "They'll be pretty. I promise it," she said over and over as she watered and fussed at the earth. "And when they blossom, Ma will smile." He cleared his throat. He hadn't understood then. He did now.

Lacy must have sensed what he had not: Jenny's sadness. And she had tried, with her flowers, to bring her mother joy. Tried so hard. Tried to keep her mother from doing what she finally did anyhow. He let out a sigh that was almost a moan, remembering how his little girl had struggled to get those flowers to grow and bloom. The recollection made him want to sit down and cry.

Bloom, they finally did. As beautiful as her promise. Bloomed the week after Lacy and Tyrone were gone. He pulled the poke from his pocket and took out the money and also a folded piece of yellowed paper. Inside was one of Lacy's flowers, faded and stiff with age. But still soft pink in color. "I'm sorry, child," he mumbled.

Prophet turned his shoulders toward the road that ran in front of the Eddys' house, as if turning away from the memory. In his heart he had already begun the journey home. But he knew that home was only where Lacy and Tyrone were. And he had no idea where that was. He took a deep breath and held it, finally letting it go in a long blow.

When he was feeling better, he glanced at the sign, nodding with satisfaction at the simple change he had made. He leaned the wooden plank and its heavy post and another thinner stake against the fence, continuing to watch Samuel. The boy had stopped yanking weeds and was staring at the garden, unaware he was being watched.

"This place is pretty far gone."

Samuel tensed but didn't turn.

"Looks neglected," Prophet continued.

"Not neglected."

"Looks it."

"I thought thou wert a minister, not a gardener." Samuel wiped his face on the back of a sleeve.

"I know something about plants. And something about neglect."

The boy pulled hard at the weeds. "We have no time for it."

"Shame." He paused. "Want some help?"

"No."

Prophet shrugged and picked up a shovel and surveyed an imaginary line between where he stood and the grave. Then he began to dig. Fifteen minutes later the post and sign were set. He checked the angle of the plank face one last time. Satisfied, he picked up the thin stake and walked under the arch of roses and into the garden. Samuel whirled angrily toward him.

"I don't know what thou art up to, but I know it's not good." He hesitated. "And thou shouldst not be here."

"It's just an overgrown garden."

"I don't mean the garden—thou knowest that."

Prophet examined the rocks lining the pathway and selected a heavy one with a flat side. Again he eyed the sign and the grave, surveying the imaginary line between the two; then he carefully placed the point of the thin stake directly behind the little cross.

"What art thou doing?" Samuel challenged.

Prophet ignored him. Satisfied with the stake's positioning, he pounded it deep into the earth, his powerful arm slamming the stone down hard like some mechanical tool. Even Samuel watched this display of strength and was impressed.

Prophet put the rock back, while Samuel squinted his eyes against the sunlight, reading the sign.

"Zacharias wanted it."

Finished, Samuel didn't say anything; he just turned and picked up a board lying in the dirt. From the way he shielded it with his body, Prophet felt he knew what it was.

"What you got?"

"Nothing."

Prophet stepped over and put a hand on the boy's shoulder. "Son, let me see it."

Samuel looked at him a moment, then turned the board over. The crude sign had been painted with red paint.

"Can't see without my glasses," Prophet lied. "What's it say?"

Samuel hesitated.

"Read it," Prophet said more firmly.

"Nigger Town." The boy looked embarrassed.

"Where was it?"

"Front porch."

Samuel started away, then stopped and looked back. "Thou shouldst not be here," he said.

Prophet didn't answer, but he agreed. As soon as he had traveling money. He studied the arrow he had chiseled into the bottom of the sign. It was painted yellow, the plank angled so that the arrow's tip pointed directly at the yellow stake. There would be no mistaking where Matthew Eddy lay. It made him feel good.

When Prophet shut the garden gate minutes later, he caught a glimpse of motion from the corner of his eye. The attacker was hidden behind the roses, and Prophet felt the urge to make a break for it. He fought the sensation. His best chance was to go slowly. He probed the foliage again with his eyes.

The leaves of the bush shook for a moment. Then Hercules strode forward, his beady eyes gleaming with a steely determination that made Prophet's legs weak.

"CCLLUUUUUUUcckkk."

The bird took another step.

"You do anything, dammnnn it," Prophet stammered, "anything at all, and you're going into Sunday's stew! I promise."

Hercules stopped and cocked his head as if considering the seriousness of the threat.

"CCLLUUUUUUcckkk."

"That's right, you coward, just think about it. You and the potatoes and the hot water." Though Prophet had faced hundreds of men in and out of the ring, something about this crazed rooster sent chills down his back. "Just keep thinking."

The sound of Prophet's voice seemed to irritate the bird, his red hackles rising in the morning sunlight.

"Don't you dare!"

Prophet and Hercules were both professional fighters. The difference was that Prophet knew it and did it only for money or a shot at the title. But Hercules seemed to think his was a nobler calling, some sort of strange blood vendetta involving the man.

The bird was standing a couple of yards away, glaring. Then, slowly, he tipped his head forward, stretching his neck out and spreading his wings like a swooping hawk. He held this awkward pose for a moment, teetering; then suddenly he was scurrying forward ready to exact some weird sort of chicken justice.

"Stop right there!" Prophet hollered. "If you do this," he yelled, raising the shovel menacingly over his head, "I'm going to finish your feathered butt once and for all!"

The bird slid to an awkward halt, but his head and wings remained in the attack position, his hackles flaring wildly.

"Oh, Mr. Prophet," Pearl called from somewhere behind him.

"Call your bird off, Mrs. Eddy. Call him off before I kill him!"

"Mr. Prophet, thou hast already killed one of my chickens. And we spoke about violence."

"He started it," Prophet snapped, pointing the shovel at the bird. Hercules was beginning his mad charge again.

"Thou must have annoyed him."

"Annoyed him?" His voice was incredulous. "He attacks me every time he gets a chance."

"Please do not exaggerate." Pearl tapped her cane past him.

"He's crazy, Mrs. Eddy."

"Perhaps he senses thou wisheth him ill," she speculated.

"He's got that straight."

"Thy wrong thinking, Mr. Prophet, brings wrong things to thee. Thou needeth to be more sure of life and God."

She bent and clucked her tongue softly, and Hercules slowly straightened up, then shook his feathers as if he had suffered a great indignity at the man's hands. He strode over to Pearl's waiting arms.

"Good bird," she said softly. "All thou need do is to tell him thou liketh him. Like all of God's children, Mr. Prophet, he responds to love."

"I don't like him. And he hates me."

"He doesn't hate thee. He is only a chicken." She paused. "And thou art a man," she said, emphasizing the last word.

Prophet watched Pearl pull a handful of grain from her pocket and let Hercules peck from her hand. The rooster did this with great care and dignity. "That's how," Prophet said to himself. "She bribes the old murderer."

Pearl stood and held out her hand toward him.

"Just give him some food and get acquainted. I'm certain thou wilt get along fine."

Prophet watched her as she walked toward her chicken pen; then he quickly looked back down at the rooster. He was pecking at a bug in the dirt. Slowly Prophet squatted and cautiously held out his hand.

"Here," he muttered. "Dumb bird."

The rooster stopped chasing the bug and looked up at him, and Prophet had the sinking feeling he could still see hatred in the beady eyes. Then the bird spied the outstretched hand and strode over boldly to investigate. He looked over and under the hand, not trusting the man, then ventured a careful peck. The thumps of the beak seemed harder in his palm than they had appeared with her, but they weren't hostile. So this was the key. They fed the old bird, and he left them alone. Prophet reached out his free hand and cautiously stroked the fine red feathers on the bird's neck.

"CCCLLUUUUcckk."

The food gone, Prophet stood slowly, keeping a wary eye on the chicken. He was feeling better: in control and confident. "Behave yourself, buzzard, and maybe there's more," he said in the sweetest of dulcet tones. "Or maybe I'll slit your gizzard. Understand? Of course not," he continued, crooning gently and smiling down at the rooster, who had returned to pecking the ground. "All you know how to do is pound your ugly mug into the dirt after a bug." Satisfied that he had the bird's number, Prophet turned and studied the house.

It was a grand old structure with soaring gables and majestic lines. The back porch held up a dense mass of ancient wisteria that protruded out from the house like a pouting lip. In the summer it would shroud the porch in cool green shade. He wondered if Samuel was still inside. He wanted another shot at the parlor.

Prophet started walking casually toward the house, wondering how much she had hidden away inside. He had taken three strides when Hercules exploded into him.

"Call him off!" he hollered, running hard for the porch, his right leg dragging slightly. The bird was gaining on him.

Samuel wasn't certain why he had come out into the prairie night. He knew he was still thinking about the grave marker the Negro had put up that morning. The fact that it was there was good. But it was who had done the marking that disturbed him. He turned slowly where he stood, the air still and cool against his skin, the black dome of the sky above fired with countless sparks of light. He usually stopped and marveled at them, but it was late, and he was tired. Something had awakened him. He followed the pathway to the huge barn.

Leaning an ear against the wood, he listened; the only sound was Jack moving in his stall. What was bothering him? It didn't feel like twister weather. He knew he had been dreaming about the Negro. He tensed. About a mob hanging him. He felt guilty, then shivered, remembering that he had done nothing to help the man.

He glanced back at the swell of prairie and the darkened house where his brothers and mother slept, then out across the gardens and beyond to the tallgrass prairie that shouldered the edge of the fields. The grasses were dead silent, swaying and nodding slowly in the night air. He turned in another circle, scanning the horizons for some sound or movement that would tell him what was wrong.

Still nothing. He knew the Negro was sleeping in the barn. Maybe he had banged a door or dropped something, the sound carrying to the house. He leaned close to the wood of the building again and tried to hear the man but couldn't.

Something moved in the dirt near his bare feet, and he tensed. It moved again, and he knew the sound and knelt and picked up a fat Woodhouse's toad, holding it close to his face.

"I surely didn't come out here because of thy ugly puss."

A bright stitch of light darted to the earth in the eastern distance, and moments later the gentle rumble reached him. If it had been westerly, he might have paid attention, but he knew from his father that lightning appearing from any other direction meant a storm that would not reach the farm. He stroked the bony ridges on the toad's head and thought about his father, the memories hurting. He forced himself to stop.

Yawning, he bent and set the little beast free and started walking toward the house. Then he stopped and turned back and studied the darkened barn. Something, a warning of sorts, seemed to move across his shoulders. About what, he had no idea. But he continued to feel it. Instinctively he knew that whatever had awakened him was in the building. He studied the open doorway, waiting for the odd sensation to pass. When it didn't, he started slowly back toward it, his hands trembling.

Coyotes were yipping in the grasses to the west of him, forming up for the night's hunt. He ignored them, squinting hard at the dark square of the huge doorway. Carefully he moved into the blackness of the structure's interior, to stand still, feeling the warmth of Jack and the other animals. A pigeon fluttered in the rafters. There were no other sounds. He waited for his eyes to adjust. He could see Jack's head, his ears pricked, staring at something in the shadows.

Slowly the moon came out from behind a cloud, sending a ray of soft light down into the barn from the hayloft. He froze and felt the blood rise to his scalp. Then he began stumbling backward, gasping for air he didn't need. He hadn't been dreaming. They had hanged the Negro from the rafters.

Samuel whirled and was about to cry out, the sound just beginning to escape his throat, when someone grabbed him from behind and slapped a hand hard over his mouth.

"Hush," the voice hissed in the darkness. Then he was yanked back into an empty stall. Samuel started to struggle to free himself when the voice whispered, "Stop it or I'll kill you."

Something moved off to his right in the shadows, and Samuel saw the shapes of five other men moving, their heads covered in hideously painted masks—weird patterns of red, yellow, green, black, and white—with small slits where the eyes and mouths were, each mask crowned in feathers. The man holding his arms shook him hard.

"Where's the nigger?"

Samuel was confused.

"Boy?"

Samuel motioned with his head toward the rafters, his eyes avoiding the swaying figure.

"That ain't him. Now where is he?" The man cuffed the back of Samuel's head, the blow stinging but nothing more.

His eyes adjusting in the moonlight, Samuel saw the straw man hanging from the rafters. They must have been searching the barn for Prophet when he walked in on them. The Negro didn't sleep directly inside. He made his bed on sacks of grain in a storage room off the back. In the darkness the men hadn't yet found the door. It was hard to see even in daylight, the boards blending into the wall. The Negro, he figured, had already made his escape. As Samuel was thinking this, the man suddenly spun him around and slapped him across the face, the blow hard enough that his legs gave way, and he felt himself going under, feeling dead and slowly falling through heavy air.

Samuel didn't know how long he was gone before they tossed water on him. He came back kicking and sputtering and fell off the barrel they had placed him on; the man holding the rope let go so his neck didn't snap. Then they had him back up on the barrel, soaking wet, his arms tied painfully behind him, the noose tight under his jaw and leading to a long rope tossed over the high rafters of the barn. Somebody began pulling until it started to lift him off the barrel. He was choking and spitting.

"That's enough!"

"Shit, I'd never have believed it!" The man holding him by the knees laughed.

"What?"

"He's a gawddamn genuine Quaker. When he was being hauled up, the sombitch was quaking like a chicken with his head lopped off."

"Sam Eddy."

It was the voice of the man who had hit him. Samuel tried to look down at him, but they had his neck stretched so he couldn't. The blood was roaring loud in his head. But he knew they were going to kill him. He hadn't been able to comprehend it before. But it was true. He was suddenly spitting out vomit and gasping for air.

"Jesssussschrist, he's a stinking mess."

"Boy?"

The rough strands of the rope burned against his

skin, his neck bones hurting as if they were being pulled apart, vertebra by vertebra.

"Where's the nigger?" Then over his shoulder the man said, "Give him some slack before his head pops off!"

Samuel took a loud gasp of air when the noose slackened, then another. He'd had it. He was graying out, his eyes blurring, his body covered in sweat. He tried to motion toward the dark corner where the small door stood hidden in shadows, telling himself the Negro had already fled. But he couldn't get his body to move right. Then he tried to speak, but like that evening on Main Street, he was too scared.

"I'm going to let them," the man warned. He turned toward the shadows and said, "Haul him up some." Then to someone else, he said, "Come over and feel him quake. Watch the puke."

Suddenly the man who had been talking took a shot from a board across the back of the skull, collapsing where he stood; the others scattered. Then the barrel was tipping, and Samuel clamped his eyes shut, waiting for the sharp yank that would break his neck. It didn't come. He hit the ground and rolled, the rope singing over the rafters after him. Then somebody grabbed the collar of his jacket and dragged him into the deeper shadows. Samuel caught a whiff of liniment. The Negro hadn't run.

In various places in the darkness there were the ominous sounds of pistols being cocked. Prophet had Samuel down behind a stack of lumber at one end of the barn.

A voice in the darkness said, "Where the hell are they?"

"How do I know?"

"Light a match."

"You light one."

"I ain't got one."

"Too bad. I ain't lighting a match so that nigger can shoot me."

They could hear the injured man moaning.

"Grab him and let's get out of here!"

"What about the nigger?"

"He's all yours."

"Bullshit."

The barn had been quiet for over an hour, and Samuel was trying to feel relief. But it wasn't working. Even in the cool of the night he was drenched with sweat, and every few minutes he would start to shake and couldn't stop. The Negro was sitting on the ground in the shadows, watching him.

"Are they still out there?" Samuel asked.

Prophet shook his head. "But let's wait."

"Would they have hung me?"

Prophet didn't say anything.

"Would they?"

"No."

"How dost thou know?"

"They were trying to scare you."

Samuel stiffened at the words, staring hard at the Negro's face. "Because of thee!" he cried, lunging at the man and hitting him hard in the face. "Damn thee to hell!"

Prophet didn't move, didn't speak.

Prophet squatted in the bright afternoon sunlight, two stories above the earth, surveying the roof of the house and thinking about what had happened last night. From the look of him, he figured Samuel was still in shock. He wouldn't talk about it, didn't want his mother to know, and didn't want the sheriff involved. He was trying to act as if it hadn't happened. But it had. Prophet was more certain than ever that he had to go now. Even though he was convinced that the men were just trying to frighten the boy into telling them where he was, it still wasn't any good.

Suddenly little Zacharias appeared on the ground below. The boy had liked the sign and the yellow stake and had followed Prophet closely throughout the morning, keeping up his constant chatter as if he were catching up on a lot of things that he had wanted to say to someone for a long time. Prophet guessed that someone was his pa, so he let him talk. Now the boy stood squinting at him as if he were a hero of sorts. While Prophet was glad the boy liked the sign, all this attention made him uncomfortable.

"Can I come up?" Zacharias hollered.

"Nope, too high."

"Then thou must come down. To dinner. Ma says so."

"Not ready."

Prophet was tired of her orders. He pulled off a faded blue bandanna tied over the top of his head and wiped his face with it. Finished, he took another look around. Once again the same sense of awe came over him as he faced the ancient, silent enormity of these plains. It was unsettling.

When viewed from the vantage of the roof, the grasses surrounding the farm flowed seemingly forever in great undulating waves to far horizons. The Eddys' fallow fields had gone back to prairie, leaving the yard and gardens besieged on every side by walls of wild plants. How this woman could live out here escaped him completely. Thinking about her again—about her stubborn self-righteousness—he spit defiantly, careful not to hit the boy. Then the boy spit.

"Knock that off," Prophet said.

"Thou did it."

"You aren't old enough."

Prophet went back to thinking. She wasn't going to cow him. Nope. He was a free man. And determined to stay that way. Pridefully so. He looked back down at the broken shingles and ripped tar paper off the roof.

"Zack," he called down, "ask if your mother has shingles."

The boy disappeared, returning a few moments later. "She says come to dinner. We're waiting on thee."

"Does she have shingles?"

The boy dutifully disappeared again, then reappeared moments later. "No."

"Tell her I'll eat later. On the porch."

The little boy looked up at him as if he had just burned a stack of Bibles, hesitating until Prophet said, "Go on." Then he darted back inside the house. Prophet spit again. He would eat where and when he wanted. He didn't work for her. And he wasn't going to be bossed anymore. He took a deep breath, feeling better at having finally declared his independence from the small woman. He scanned the roof again. The closer he looked, the more he saw that the grand old house was in sorry shape. She was tighter with her cash than he had suspected.

When he glanced down, she was standing with her head tilted up, her eyes fixed blindly on the chimney as if she knew for certain it was him. "Mr. Prophet, we are waiting." She was still acting coolly toward him.

"I'll eat later."

"Thou wilt eat now." She disappeared into the house.

"Hey! Mrs. Eddy!" He craned his neck, searching for her. But if she heard him, she wasn't coming back outside. He kicked at a piece of loose shingle, slipped, and almost fell. "Damn," he mumbled. Then he shrugged and started slowly down. It wasn't worth fighting over. He was hungry, and she was just ornery enough not to let him eat if he didn't do it now.

He took his time washing up on the porch. Even so, when he entered the kitchen, they were still waiting for him, seated around the kitchen table, their hands folded neatly in their laps, looking like mourners. Pearl was at the head of the table. Zacharias was missing.

Prophet took the chair opposite her. She sat staring at him in her blind way. It was unsettling. He wondered if she could see anything at all—shadows and such. He nodded at Samuel. The boy shut his eyes. Prophet could see the rope burn on his neck, and from the dark circles under his eyes it looked as though he hadn't slept all night. He didn't blame him.

Prophet glanced at the food: jackrabbit browned and served with gravy, corn bread, and greens. Toothsome. The woman, with the boys' help, could cook, and he was starved. He picked up his fork and then saw Joshua slowly shaking his head, the movement a warning. Prophet lowered his hand back to the table.

Moments later Zacharias darted into the room carrying what looked like part of King Solomon's treasure. The boy struggled into his chair and leaned over to him.

"This is my pa," he said in solemn tones, holding up a photograph framed in silver.

Samuel's eyes popped open.

Pearl half raised her head. "Zacharias."

"Sorry," the boy muttered.

He had been right: There was money in this house.

"Mother, my shoes are hurting," Luke complained.

"Mine too," Joshua added.

"This is not the time," Pearl said, tipping her head back down as if she were drifting into a deep sleep.

Ignoring Samuel's glare, Zacharias again mouthed the words, "This is my pa."

Prophet put his finger to his lips, then held out a hand for the magnificent frame. Solid silver.

Zacharias looked ready to burst with pride. Prophet pretended to admire the smiling, square-jawed man in the photograph, while gauging the metal. Top quality.

"Where do you keep this?" he whispered.

"Where it's safe," Samuel interrupted, taking the frame and starting for the parlor.

"Handsome photograph."

"Samuel and Mr. Prophet. Please. We are about to receive the Lord's bounty."

Prophet ducked a slow-buzzing horsefly. He hated Kansas flies. Three were pestering him now. The infernal creatures thought they had teeth. He waited until they were crawling around a spot of breakfast on his pants leg; then he moved a hand so quickly that it blurred before Zacharias's eyes.

Prophet dashed the insects down on the floor and stepped on them before they could recover. Zacharias's eyes widened. Two squished flies. The boy grinned. Prophet frowned. He was slowing up . . . should have caught all three. It didn't matter. Savvy stood for something in the fight game. He went back to waiting.

Finally curiosity overcame him, and he dropped his napkin and peered quickly under the table. The boys were wearing high-button shoes. Zacharias's right sole was hanging, while Joshua's toes looked ready to burst forth at any moment. The laces on all three pairs were spliced with knots, the leather cracked and hard. No wonder they hurt. He was shaking his head and sitting up when he noticed her own sticking out from under the long gray dress: as badly worn as the boys'.

There was no figuring it. Miser maybe. He had heard of folks like that. He watched as Zacharias took a wild swing at a fly, missing. Prophet narrowed his eyes at the boy and shook his head. Zacharias settled down. Prophet's stomach was growling, and he took a deep breath and resumed listening to the maddening tick of the parlor clock. "Need shingles, Mrs. Eddy."

The boys giggled.

"Children," she said, her eyes still clamped tight.

Unable to tell what was so funny and not wanting to trigger another round of merriment, he didn't say anything for a while after that. But then he was growing ravenous, so he cleared his throat and said, "Mrs. Eddy, shall I speak over the food?"

"If thou art moved to, Mr. Prophet. Otherwise it is not necessary."

"No, ma'am," he said quickly.

Minutes later—when he was just about to ask why she had bothered to call them to dinner—Pearl raised her head and smiled that smile of hers that spoke of heaven's light. Then she picked up a bowl and began serving. "Praise the Lord," he muttered under his breath.

"Buy shingles. I'll patch the roof, Mrs. Eddy," he said between bites.

"I do not have the money, Mr. Prophet."

He stopped chewing. Her expression was serene enough. Nevertheless, she had just told a lie. He was certain of it. He had seen the frame. She had money. He squirmed, not caring for the thought of her telling tales. Still, he knew people did strange things over money. Lying was just one of a long list.

"That's okay. Other things need fixing."

"Thou hast done enough. I consider the hen paid for."

"Fine, Mrs. Eddy." He wasn't going to beg her.

They went back to their respective silences, with Prophet thinking about the route and his children.

There were training camps in the Carolina woods where he could get a sparring job. It was an idea that had been kicking around in his head for some time. Didn't matter what they paid. When he got in the ring with one of those name fighters, he would knock Satan's horns off him. Then they would see just how good he was, get his picture in the papers so that Lacy and Tyrone could spot him. The more he thought about it, the more he liked the idea. "It just might work," he mumbled.

"I am sorry, Mr. Prophet. What did thou say?"

"I'll be on my way this afternoon."

Zacharias looked as if he had been gut-kicked by a mule. "We were going to talk," he said quietly.

"We still can. After lunch."

Zacharias darted out of the back door.

"Zacharias?" Pearl called.

"He just wants Mr. Prophet to stay," Joshua said.

"Thou couldst help us build a sod house behind the barn," Luke added.

"Boys, Mr. Gilliam has things he must do. So do all of thee."

"Prophet," he corrected.

She hesitated, then said, "Mr. Prophet."

Then the back door slammed again, and Zacharias ran panting into the room. "People are coming down the road!"

"Please go to the cellar, Mr. Prophet."

"He's not our problem," Samuel objected.

"Samuel," she said firmly, "lock Mr. Prophet in the cellar."

"I can't."

"Why not?"

"He's gone."

Pearl Eddy opened the front door and listened anxiously to the sounds of a crowd milling around her front yard. Someone was walking across her porch. She raised a hand and touched the high collar of her blouse. "Yes?"

"It's the Chinese woman," Samuel said.

Pearl forced a smile and nodded. Though relieved a mob hadn't come for the Negro, she was uncomfortable facing this woman again. "Hello," she said.

The woman didn't respond; she just stood looking at Pearl's face in the same curious way she had the evening in front of the hotel, as surprised as Pearl that she had chanced upon her here on this lonely road.

"I'm sorry," Pearl continued, "but I cannot help." The words seemed to take something out of her, and she sucked in a deep breath, letting it out slowly.

"Mizu. Water. That is all I want from you." The woman held a large ceramic jar in her arms as if it were a heavy baby. "The town help us on our way." Her eyes were fixed hard on Pearl's face.

Watching his mother, Samuel began to worry that she might get involved. They already had the Negro hiding somewhere. They didn't need this Asian family. He turned and looked past the woman to the girl standing behind the old cart with its towering cage, holding her little brother gracefully on her hip. He watched her until he heard his mother's voice.

"Where?"

"Out of town."

"There's just prairie."

"To rikuchi. To our land."

Pearl looked surprised. "Thou dost not have any land."

"They ask me where we want to go. I say: to our land."

Samuel ran his gaze over the thirty or so men standing in their yard, wondering if any of them had been the ones in the barn last night. Probably. He shivered. "I'll get the water," he said, reaching quickly for the jar.

"Yes," Pearl said absently. Finally she collected herself. "Joshua and Luke, gather all the eggs thou canst find." She paused. "And bring that sack of cornmeal off the back porch."

The boys darted away.

"Thy land doesn't exist," Pearl began again.

The woman just stood staring into her face as if she were disappointed with her. Pearl cleared her throat. "The men—the judge and Attorney Johnson—they did not steal thy land. They are honest men." She paused. "And they say that thy land has been lost."

"Not lost. We are going to it. To rikuchi."

"But it doesn't exist."

"Land always exists."

"Yes, but the county took it," Pearl explained. "For back taxes." She paused. "Even if it had not gone to taxes, thou couldst not legally own it. Thou art not a citizen."

The woman shrugged her shoulders and took the jar of water from Samuel. Small though she was, she held it without any apparent strain. "It does not matter. These men take us to it."

The woman turned away, and Pearl could hear her moving down the steps. "Thy land is gone," Pearl repeated firmly. "All these men are going to do is abandon thee and thy children out on the prairie."

"Land is never gone."

"It is gone," Pearl said, sounding frustrated. "I would help thee if I thought I could. I would." She hesitated a moment. The words seemed to stick in her throat, and she had to force them out. "But I cannot."

The woman studied Pearl's face a moment longer; then she blew out her nose in a disdainful way and continued down the steps. "Land is never gone," she said again. The twins followed with the eggs and the sack of meal. The crowd cheered as the woman approached, the noise brutally festive-sounding.

Pearl started to take a step out onto the porch, then stopped herself and leaned into the side of the doorway. Concerned that she might fall, Samuel watched her. Then she pushed away, orienting herself, and walked quickly toward her bedroom.

Prophet had remained hidden in the tallgrass behind the barn until the crowd had moved off down the road; then he had gone hunting Zacharias. He found him down by the creek, lying on his stomach in the coarse white sand near the edge of the clear water. His big hat was next to him. Sunlight was falling through the overhanging leaves of an old cottonwood, making thin yellow blotches that moved constantly over the boy and the creek. Save for the choppy sound of shallow water over rocks, it was quiet here until a blue jay spotted them and took to scolding from the high limbs of a tamarisk bush.

Prophet waved a hand at it, and the bird wheeled away into the sky and silence fell over the place. He sat down hard next to the boy. Zacharias didn't look at him, but Prophet could tell he had been crying.

"Sometimes we just got to do things," he said.

Zacharias didn't respond.

"Even if it's a hard thing."

Zacharias turned his body away some, as if he were avoiding the words, and looked to be studying the grains of sand under his nose.

"Your pa would have understood." He waited.

Zacharias shook his head hard. "There's no good reason. Not for leaving people behind. None." He hesitated. "My pa shouldn't have done it either."

"That's not fair, boy. Your pa didn't have a choice."

"Maybe he didn't. But thou dost."

Prophet leaned his hands back in the sand and sat looking up at the leaves of the cottonwood moving slowly in the breeze, thinking how this child reminded him of Tyrone. He cleared his throat. "I'm not leaving you. Not that way. I've just got to find something I lost."

Zacharias snuffed. "Sammy said I couldn't trust thee."

"You believe that?"

Zacharias didn't answer.

The blue jay had returned and was hopping from branch to branch, eyeing these intruders warily. Prophet watched it for a while, then reached into his pocket.

"I'll make a promise."

If Zacharias heard, he didn't let on.

"Once I find what I'm looking for, I'll come back."

Zacharias ignored him. Prophet thought about Tyrone and Lacy, about how badly it hurts to lose people you love.

"Here," he said, setting the little wooden horse on the sand in front of the boy. "Carved it from spellbound wood." He would make Tyrone another.

"That's just basswood." The boy didn't pick it up.

"Things aren't always plain to see," Prophet said. "Anyhow, you keep it. Until I get back."

"Just basswood," Zacharias repeated. "And I don't want it."

"It's magical. You want something, you just rub it and presto!"

"I got my arrowhead."

"Maybe. But your arrowhead won't bring me back."

"I don't believe thee."

They sat there in the kaleidoscope of shadows and

sunlight for a long time, the grasses seeming to sing faint songs in the breeze, sounding the way Lacy had. Zacharias wasn't looking at Prophet or the horse.

"What do you want to talk about?"

"Nothing," Zacharias said fast.

"Your pa?"

"No."

"What then?"

Zacharias didn't answer him.

Prophet watched him for a while; then he reached out and patted the back of his head. Zacharias twisted away, and Prophet could see he was crying without sound. The man stood and headed back toward the farm to get his things.

Pearl was still feeling sick over the Orientals when an hour later she opened her front door to the sound of hard knocking and was immediately swamped by a wave of thick perfume. The smell was unmistakable.

"Rose?"

"Shhhhh," the woman cautioned.

Sheriff Haines, a short, thick-bodied man with a kindly, froglike face, was standing beside her. He tipped his head of prematurely white hair in a gallant way. "Mrs. Eddy."

"Sheriff?"

"Is he still here?" Rose whispered, her eyes searching the shadows behind Pearl.

"Who?"

"That Negro."

"Rose?"

"Pearl," Rose hissed, "his name isn't Jerome Prophet. And he's no French designer." Rose stepped closer and took hold of Pearl's hand as if the news she was about to impart might cause paralysis. "He's a killer."

"Rose—" She looked suddenly embarrassed and turned in the sheriff's direction. "Edward Johnson spoke to thee about him."

"That he broke into your house, but you didn't want him arrested."

Rose Sherman raised a liver-spotted hand to her throat. "Pearl Eddy? You let a killer touch me but didn't want him arrested?" She patted her powdered face with a lace handkerchief.

"Rose, the death was accidental." Pearl gripped her hands together. "But thou art right. I should have told thee he was not my assistant."

Rose made a little harrumphing sound deep in her fleshy throat and looked indignant.

"Mrs. Eddy, the Negro isn't holding you against your will?"

"He is not dangerous, Sheriff—"

"I beg your pardon," Rose cut in. "My pillbox. That man stole it."

"That couldn't be, Rose," Pearl said.

"Pearl Eddy! How dare you call me a liar!"

"All I mean, Rose, is that Mr. Prophet is not a thief."

The sheriff cleared his throat before Mrs. Sherman could respond. "Is he here?"

"Yes." Prophet's voice came from the hallway. Samuel and the smaller boys were standing behind him.

"What's the matter?" Zacharias asked.

"Nothing," Prophet said.

Sheriff Haines put his hand on his pistol grip when he saw Prophet's face. "Out on the walkway," he said.

Prophet moved ahead of the man into the front yard, where two deputies waited; one immediately began to pat him down. He looked back at the house, embarrassed the boys were seeing this, feeling the way he had that day at the Charleston docks.

"Have you arrested him, Sheriff?" Rose called.

Suddenly Zacharias darted forward and delivered a couple of well-placed kicks to Rose Sherman's heavy ankles, then shot away before his brothers could grab him, down the stairs and across the yard to attack Sheriff Haines in the same way. "Run, Mr. Prophet! Run!"

"Zacharias!" Pearl gasped.

Prophet grabbed the boy up in his arms. "Zach, settle down. There are times to fight, times not to."

Pearl tensed. "Mr. Prophet."

He looked at her for a moment, then said, "Sorry."

Rose was moaning. "Oooooh, my ankles."

Pearl looked confused. "Thy ankles, Rose?"

The ashen hue of Rose's skin slowly turned crimson. "Never you mind, Pearl Eddy!"

After the men and boys had gone into the house to look inside Prophet's pack, Pearl turned toward the woman's heavy breathing. "Rose, I should have told thee. But to accuse him of stealing is wrong."

"Shelter a murderer with your children if you wish, Pearl Eddy. But I will not give him comfort. You see the ill effects. That young one is dangerously violent."

Pearl crossed her arms and began to tap her foot.

Minutes later the men returned.

"Where is it?" Rose demanded.

"He doesn't have it," the sheriff said.

Rose Sherman looked indignant. "He's obviously hidden it."

"Maybe. But I can't arrest him on maybes."

"You have my word," Rose snapped.

"But you didn't actually see him steal it."

"That is beside the point. He's a murderer and a liar."

"Rose." Pearl interrupted. "Mr. Prophet stole nothing. He is a minister."

Rose laughed derisively.

Prophet turned and studied the side of Pearl's flushed face as if she had suddenly risen to a new level of daftness. No one had ever taken his part before. And strangely, now that it had happened, he didn't like it. Especially since he was guilty.

He watched Pearl clasp her hands behind her back, noticing she looked suddenly worn-out, her contentiousness seemingly drained away. He hoped so. For a woman who didn't like warring she had a special talent for it. He was waiting for her to give up and go back into the house when in a quiet voice she put things in dispute again.

"Mrs. Sherman is mistaken, Sheriff. Mr. Prophet stole nothing."

"That's right!" Zacharias yelled.

"Zacharias. For the last time," she warned. Joshua and Luke grabbed their little brother.

The sheriff looked at Prophet. "You keep your skirts clean." Prophet nodded and then went back to staring at Pearl.

"He is still a vagrant," Rose said.

"How much cash you have?" the sheriff asked.

He wasn't about to venture Lacy and Tyrone's money. "Dollar maybe."

The sheriff looked disappointed. "Need ten."

Rose appeared instantly delighted by her small victory, unaware it was to be fleeting. Pearl had started her foot tapping again in that steady, determined drumming way she had. Prophet sensed she was girding herself for round two. Like all good fighters, she could take a devastating punch and still get up. Pure guts and reflex. He was wishing she would stay down.

"I'll just be moving on—"

"No, he will not," Rose snapped. "This Negro is a vagrant, and I demand his arrest."

Sheriff Haines frowned. "Let the man leave town, Rose."

"You arrest him," she said, a warning in her voice. "I'll not be humiliated by the likes of a thieving murderer. I don't care what Mrs. Eddy's odd feelings are toward this Negro," she hissed, the words carrying an unseemly implication. "That's something she will have to answer for."

The sheriff looked at Prophet. "Get your bag."

Zacharias had squinted his eyes and was winding up to have another go at Rose, but Luke and Joshua held him.

Prophet was starting for the doorway when Pearl said, "Stay where thou art, Mr. Prophet."

Her hands were on her small hips, and she looked ready for some action that he was certain would be unwise. Slowly she turned in the direction of Mrs. Sherman. He could see she was shaking. "Rose, surely thou dost not mean to have this man arrested because he has no money?"

"Absolutely," Rose replied, tossing her gray-haired head.

"Rose, thou art too good a person."

"Apparently not as good as you," she said, insinuating something else again.

Pearl waited a few moments before she spoke, snippets of Edward Johnson's warning about getting involved and Mr. Snipes's letter flashing through her thoughts. But these things could not stop her rising anger. "Then, Rose," she said, "we can no longer be friends."

Prophet closed his eyes and shook his head.

"There's no question of that!" Rose Sherman snapped.

Pearl nodded. "I simply wanted thee to understand." Her voice trailed away uncertainly.

Pearl's eyes were shining with a strange expression, and Prophet knew that she was about to cry. He had the urge to grab her by the shoulders and shake her and tell her to stop.

"Sheriff, a man is not a vagrant if he is working."

"Yes."

"Then Mr. Prophet is not a vagrant. He has been working for me. And I will vouch for him while he is in town." She pulled herself up straight again, seemingly having regained her strength. "Is there anything else?"

The sheriff smiled and shook his head. "No, ma'am."

Zacharias started to holler and hop, but Luke clamped a hand over his mouth, and Joshua grabbed his shoulders.

Rose Sherman looked stunned for a moment; then she started limping off the porch. Halfway down the stairs she stopped to rub her swollen ankles and gave Pearl a cold, penetrating stare. "Pearl Eddy, you'll account for this!"

"Good-bye, Rose," Pearl said very quietly.

Samuel had been standing on the back porch since Rose Sherman and the sheriff had gone, watching the open window of his mother's room and listening to her pacing to and fro over the hardwood floor. She had been doing it steadily for two hours. The relentless footfalls were making him tense. He wanted to go inside and say something that would make her feel better, but he didn't know what was wrong or what to say.

Earlier the Negro had headed east down the road toward the railroad tracks, Zacharias crying after him until the twins had caught up with their little brother and held him back. Samuel had watched the three of them shouting good-byes to the man. For his part, he was glad the man was gone. Perhaps now the strangers in the masks would leave them alone. He didn't care if they were just trying to scare him. They had done too good a job of it.

He was thinking these thoughts when he looked up and saw his mother standing in the doorway of the kitchen. He waited for her to say something, but she just stood staring off toward the barn as if she were listening to some sound.

"Art thou ill?"

"No," she said, her voice sounding faraway.

"Dost thou want a glass of water?"

"No."

Neither of them spoke for a while. Then Pearl said, "Samuel, take Jack and bring the sheriff, Judge Wilkins, and Attorney Johnson."

"Why?"

"Just do what I ask, please."

Chapter Six

Daylight was fading over the prairie, shading the grasses pink, bird sounds dying in the last breeze of evening. The wheels of the Eddys' buggy were moving slowly in the sands of the road as it headed back toward the farm, a crowd of ruffians following. Edward Johnson and Judge Hyram Wilkins, a smaller, considerably older man, walked alongside, leading their saddle horses.

"If that is the law, then they will stay at my home," Pearl said firmly. She was seated beside Samuel, the boy guiding Jack down the deeply rutted road. Small groups of townspeople were waiting in buggies or on horseback along the route, watching as they passed, no one saying anything. Then Samuel saw Rose Sherman with three women in her large double trace surrey; they too had stopped to stare as the buggy moved by. Something in their collective look made Samuel want to crawl under the seat.

He glanced past his mother at Johnson and the judge. He knew they had his family's interest at heart. He also knew that what his mother was doing was decent enough. But it was foolhardy. Nobody wanted these people around.

"Not a smart idea, Pearl," Judge Wilkins warned.

The judge wore a long, heavy raccoon coat that made him seem even thinner than he was. He wore that coat all year long. Past eighty, he was puffing hard to keep up in the sand.

"Sam, slow that horse before I drop dead in the road," he snapped.

"Pearl, it's not a good idea," Johnson said, agreeing with the judge.

The crowd, trailing a dozen yards behind the buggy, kept back by Sheriff Haines and two deputies, was in a sullen mood. Having just walked the Asiatics miles out onto the hot prairies, they didn't cotton to the fact that Pearl Eddy was bringing them back again like an old broody hen.

"It is a far better idea, gentlemen, than that law," Pearl said, turning toward where she had heard their voices. "Thou art certain?"

"Pearl Eddy," the old man squawked, "this is the third time." He opened a small book and pushed a pair of metal-rimmed glasses up the bridge of his nose, stopping while he hunted up the correct passage. "No persons of color shall be on the streets of Zella after sunset." He cleared his throat and hurried after the buggy; his pretty chestnut mare with four white socks trotted after him. "Unless in the employ of white residents and on a specific errand for said whites." He pulled his glasses off and looked up at her. "Just rarely enforced."

"Outrageous, sir," she muttered.

"It's silly," he admitted, "but folks signed the complaint."

She didn't respond. The setting sun had turned the prairie from pink to orange and seemed, to Edward Johnson, to have ignited Pearl's face with its light. Dressed all in black, with no makeup, no jewelry, her handsome features firmly set, Pearl Eddy looked to the lawyer like an avenging angel. He reached a hand up and touched her forearm. She stiffened, and he quickly withdrew it. "They can camp on the edge of town, while we raise money for their passage home."

"The woman does not want to leave, Edward. Thou heard her. And there are little children. They do not have proper things to camp out on the plains."

"They'll be fine for a night or two, and in a few days she'll see that this isn't going to work."

Samuel knew that Johnson and the judge were going to lose this argument, so he quit listening and looked over his shoulder at the Chinese struggling behind the buggy. All their belongings had been precariously loaded onto the rickety handcart, the old vehicle swaying back and forth on its large wheels, as if it might collapse at any moment. The mother, with her infant harnessed to her back and the older girl beside her, was pushing hard behind it, the two smaller children grasping the woman's baggy pants, as if they would be cast into hellfire if they dared let go. The family's hairy pig trotted alongside, tied to the axle. Every once in a while the little animal dug his hooves in, forcing the women to pull him like a plow through the deep sand.

Pearl and Samuel had found them that afternoon in a flimsy tent that had been pegged down in the middle of a desolate strip of land known as the sandhills, some three miles west of their farm. They were a sorry-looking lot, sorrier even than when he had first seen them squatting on Main Street. After a couple of hours or so of hard talking, his mother had convinced the woman, Eiko Kishimoto, to come back to their farm.

Samuel had sat sweating on the buggy seat, surrounded by the jeering crowd of men and boys, while the two women argued their points back and forth like big-time debaters.

"Thou canst pursue thy claim to this land just as easily from our farm," his mother had said.

"I can pursue it from here," countered the woman, a grim smile frozen on her features.

"Thou cannot survive here."

"We can."

"There is no water."

"We will dig for it."

"Maybe one hundred feet down."

"Maybe."

"Thy children."

"What about them?"

"They cannot live out here."

"Why?"

Back and forth they tugged, through the hot afternoon. The turning point finally came when his mother openly questioned whether or not the land they stood arguing over was indeed the same piece of land described on the woman's deed. That did it. Not right away but slowly. It eroded Eiko's determination to live or die on this particular spot of earth. She had no intention of giving her life for a piece of land that might not be hers. She was a very practical individual.

He looked at her now, a short, small, shapeless woman, somewhere in her late thirties, he guessed. She was still wearing a fixed smile on her face. But her eldest daughter was not smiling. She was tense and seemed ready to fight at any moment. Even so, Samuel had to admit, scowling or not, she had an attractive face. It was unlike any Chinese he had ever seen in photographs. He continued watching her. Then suddenly she looked up at him, her eyes flashing, and he quickly shifted his gaze to the top of the canvas bundles, stopping at the bamboo cage. It was a strange contraption, four feet tall and some three square, secured to the cart by leather thongs. Stranger still was the fact that he could make out a shadowy form through the cage's thin slats. To his surprise, the girl lifted her head and yelled at the cage. The woman spoke sharply, and the girl quieted.

Unable to figure what was inside the odd container and uncomfortable with the girl's hostile stares, Samuel looked back at his mother. She was sitting very straight with her arms folded across her breasts, gazing sightlessly over Jack's head. The judge and Mr. Johnson had stopped walking and now stood watching the buggy moving away down the road. Samuel took a good grip on Jack's reins, as if what he was about to say would cause the old horse to lunge out of control across the prairies.

"Thou hast always told us to avoid ill-considered things."

Pearl didn't respond.

"Judge Wilkins and Mr. Johnson say this is ill considered."

"These people have no place, nothing to eat."

"Thou told the Negro we cannot even repair our roof." He paused. "We've got Zacharias and Joshua and Luke. I worry about them, not these strangers."

She waited a moment before she spoke. "I will decide this matter." She stopped talking and put her hands in her lap, rubbing them slowly together.

Samuel stiffened. "We cannot do it."

"Thou art not my husband. Thou art my son."

The boy's face reddened, and he shook his head obstinately; then he turned back just as a tomato arched through the air and splattered against the back of the girl's head. He winced for her. But it was as if the tomato had not even touched her. She didn't flinch or react in any way, just continued shoving the little cart, staring ahead as if at some invisible enemy, tomato juice dripping from her hair. The crowd roared in approval. Jack picked up his pace.

"I'm going to help with the cart," Samuel hollered over the yelling. Pearl nodded and took the reins.

Prophet had been steadily searching for most of an hour. Instinctively he sensed time running out. From long experience he knew it was never safe to be inside a house longer than thirty minutes. On his knees in Pearl Eddy's bedroom, his hands running expertly around the bottom of the dresser, he was hoping he would find money hidden there. But there was nothing.

Half listening to the ticking of the mantel clock in the parlor, he rocked back onto his feet and surveyed the room carefully one more time. It was plain and neat and empty of anything valuable, plain and neat like the woman herself. A white porcelain bowl and pitcher sat on the bedside table; a four-poster bed stood against the far wall. The floors were hard-swept, barren wood.

He ran his hand over his smooth head, wiping it clean of perspiration, his eyes coming to rest on a neatly sewn sampler hanging on a wall. "Charity," it read. That's all he wanted. But he sensed he wasn't going to find any. Not in this woman's house.

After pretending to leave earlier that day, Prophet had slipped back and hidden in the gully down the road, watching until he had seen the Eddys leave. He thought about Zacharias, remembering how the boy had cried and pleaded when he left, how he had attacked the old lady and the sheriff, and he didn't like the sour feeling it gave him in his gut. He swallowed it down. It was time the boy learned some hard facts. He shouldn't be trotting around believing in every Tom, Dick and Harry, who dropped out of the sky. This thought—that he was teaching the boy a valuable lesson about life—made him feel better.

As soon as he had seen Mrs. Eddy and Samuel leave the farm, Prophet had let himself into the house. Fat lot of good that had done. The only things of worth that he had found so far were the books on the shelves. Dozens of them. For a blind woman, she surely liked her books. But he couldn't cart them off across the prairie. He shook his head. Even her thimbles were brass, when silver and gold were all the rage.

He moved into the parlor, a nerve exploding somewhere in his head urging him to be off. But she had to have valuables somewhere. He had seen the silver frame. Suddenly, off in the distance, he heard a faint sound that was very familiar, the noise of a crowd, an angry crowd . . . and it was growing louder. Damn this place. Three mobs in two days. For a lonely road this one was getting a mess of traffic.

He was starting for the door when he spotted a corner of the silver frame sticking out from behind a sofa pillow. He disliked doing it. This was the boys' father. But he also disliked not eating. He stared at the photograph, thinking.

He wasn't certain how long he had stood there cogitating about the boy, the woman, and his own children, thinking how they were somehow tied together, whether he liked it or not, before he started to remove the photograph. He would leave it on the table. He stopped and listened again; then he ran to the window, his right leg dragging badly now, and looked out.

Dust was rising a hundred yards down the road. They were coming fast, and he wasn't waiting around until they arrived. He flew out through the kitchen.

Half a mile from the house, Joshua, Luke, and Zacharias darted out of the wall of roadside weeds and up beside the buggy, their clothes torn and dirty. The road was steeper here, and the two Asian women, the mother and her daughter, were having a hard time getting the cart to roll. They were taking deep breaths, and Samuel realized he had set too fast a pace.

"Get Zach into the buggy and take over from Mother!" he hollered at the twins. Then he turned back to the cart.

"Is Mr. Prophet back there?" Zacharias asked, glancing back over the seat at the crowd.

"I am afraid not," Pearl said, a slight smile set firmly on her face.

"Take Jack in through the back," Samuel called. "And when we get inside, get the barn door and shutters closed down fast."

"No," Pearl said. "We will not barricade ourselves inside our home. These are our neighbors."

Samuel glanced at his brothers and rolled his eyes, then started again for the Chinese. The woman, Eiko, stopped smiling and studied him closely; then she nodded and made room on the cart handle. He glanced sideways at her. She was smiling again. He wondered what she found to be happy about. They would be lucky if they didn't get stoned. He started shoving. The rickety contraption moved slowly forward. Samuel struggled to squeeze between the woman and the girl. The woman gave way for him. But the girl wasn't budging.

"I need room," he growled. She ignored him.

He started to say something more, then figured she wouldn't understand anyway, so instead he pressed his shoulder against hers and began to apply steady pressure. He could feel her shoving back. She was strong. He pushed harder. She did the same. And suddenly the cart and its towering cargo was surging forward.

"Josh, get Jack moving!"

Samuel held his breath for a moment, thinking that he was hearing a tapping sound coming from the bamboo cage that rose above him. But then the noise of the crowd and the pounding in his ears of his own blood drowned it out. The girl was pushing harder. He strained to stay up with her.

The eastbound freight train was slowing as it climbed the hill, a cold southerly wind blowing. He waited for the brakeman to pull his head back in the caboose. When he did, Prophet went for the boxcar without hesitation, throwing in his bag, then lunging. Inside he checked to see he hadn't lost anything. The train was rocking steadily now and picking up speed; he hadn't been spotted. He glanced through the open door into the evening light settling over the town. Zella, Kansas, wasn't a bad-looking place. It just wasn't for him.

His thoughts drifted back to Pearl Eddy. She was crazy. But she had kept her word. He opened his traveling bag and pulled out the silver frame, examining it closely. It was a beauty. He was sorry he had taken the photo, but he'd had no choice. He ran his fingers over the smooth, cold metal, his eyes studying the features of the man in the picture. He was young and happy-looking, handsome with dark eyes and hair, nice features—a good match for the woman. But the thing that got Prophet was how joyful he looked.

Prophet was still staring at him when his fingers felt something under the cloth behind the photograph. He unsnapped the back and sucked in his breath. He felt he could go without breathing for a long time.

He had been right all along. She had money hidden away. And he had just found some. Slowly he forced his hands to count it: $250. He wanted to cry out in joy. But he couldn't. He felt funny. As if he hadn't just found something valuable but, rather, had lost something.

"Thank you," the Oriental woman said, smiling and nodding up and down. Her two young daughters had quit clinging to her legs, but they still looked frightened.

"Everything is okay." Samuel grinned. They hid from him behind their mother. Amazingly the baby had slept through.

"Thank you, boy," the woman said again. "What is your name?"

"Samuel." He smiled at her. "And thou art welcome."

Putting a finger to her breast, she said what he already knew, "Eiko Kishimoto." Noticing him looking at her daughter, she pointed the same finger at the girl. "Fumiko."

It was his turn to nod. He was breathing hard and watching the girl. She was standing next to the cart, also catching her breath. She studiously ignored him. Tomato still dripped from her hair. Samuel put his hands in his pockets and wiggled his pants down so they covered more of his ankles; then he rolled his right shoe over so she couldn't see his little toe through the break in the leather. But she wasn't watching.

They had just entered the barn, and Samuel could hear the sheriff ordering the crowd off their property.

He walked outside and dunked a rag in the rain barrel and returned. He held it for a minute, then walked over and offered it to the girl, Fumiko. She didn't even look at it. She just turned and walked away into the barn's shadows. His face was hot from embarrassment, and he quickly laid the rag on the wheel of the handcart, as if he had no idea why he was carrying it.

That was when Samuel heard it again, a series of rapid tappings from inside the little bamboo cage. He stopped and listened. It sounded like a woodpecker knocking impatiently against a tree limb. Seemingly in response to this noise, Fumiko directed an unfriendly remark at the cage that needed no translation.

The woman barked a few coarse-sounding words of her own at the girl, and Fumiko turned and began to untie the bundles on the cart. The woman continued to stare at her, the impatient tapping continuing, until Fumiko relented and hopped up on the cart and unlatched the small door to the cage. Samuel followed her with his eyes. She was tall and slender with a nice profile and long eyelashes. Finished with the door, she jumped back to the ground and returned to the small mountain of canvas bundles.

Samuel's gaze didn't follow her. He couldn't take his eyes off the tiny door of the cage. His mother and brothers were coming toward him.

"Samuel."

"One moment, Mother."

Pearl stopped beside him. "What is it?"

"Just something odd."

"What kind of odd?"

The sound of the boys' breath being sucked in was loud in the barn. They stood trembling. Something or someone had shoved the cage door open from the inside.

"Boys?"

"In a moment, Mother," Samuel answered, his eyes glued on the shadowy opening.

The Oriental woman was keeping up a stream of what sounded to Samuel like apologies. His eyes moved slowly over the dark figure inside the cage, and he quickly changed his assessment. It wasn't a cage at all; it was more like a tiny throne room of varnished bamboo, complete with a high-backed chair padded in a rich green velvetlike material.

"Samuel."

He was staring at the strange sight. "There's a little Oriental man," he said, his voice reflecting his confusion. "He's sitting in a tiny bamboo room that rides on top of the cart."

"Who is he?"

"I don't know."

Samuel's gaze still hadn't moved off the man. He was maybe in his seventies, small and trim-looking, but not frail or weak. Nor did he look sick or so old that he couldn't have helped with the cart. But from the way he sat staring haughtily over the heads of everyone in the barn, he looked as if work of any kind were beneath his dignity.

He reminded Samuel of a little king, arrogant in his beautiful mahogany chair, wrapped in fine red robes of silk, gazing out imperiously with his small dark eyes as if none of the rest of them existed. Samuel studied his face closely. The skin was oily and deeply lined, monkeylike in some respects, but the fierce features commanded attention and respect. His silver-colored hair was pulled back into a bun that would have looked feminine on most men. It didn't on him.

The woman hurriedly shoved the small cart deeper into the barn, the tiny man swaying expertly with the movements of the wheels and the woman's shoving. Samuel wondered how many hundreds of miles they had pushed him over the years.

With the cart in a quiet corner of the barn, the woman barked another order at the girl. It had no effect on her.

Suddenly the old man rapped a bamboo staff he was holding hard against the cage, and the girl moved, retrieving a small stool from the cart. Then, with a movement so fast and ominous that it caused Samuel and his brothers to hop backward, the old man leaped from his chair, grunting and brandishing the bamboo rod in his hands. He stood bent-kneed, his sandaled feet spread wide, a fierce scowl across his face.

In the lantern light, his skin glistened as if waxed. He looked ready for mortal combat. Then, with his banty, roosterlike legs still bent, he took a great exaggerated high step on the cart top, turning for the first time to glare at the boys.

They held their collective breath.

"I wish Mr. Prophet were here," Zacharias whispered.

"Samuel, what is going on?" Pearl demanded.

"It's the old man," he whispered.

"Yes?"

"He looks dangerous."

"Don't be silly. These are our guests. I want to meet them."

As if their voices had triggered it, the woman and the two small girls bent over at the waist; the older girl did not move until the woman grabbed her arm and yanked her forward. Even so, her bow was not obedient.

When the old man finally reached the ground in his funny half-squatting way, the woman and the two little girls scurried ahead of him, rolling out a large reed mat. With deliberate and posturing movements, he settled himself into a cross-legged position, his back to them, staff across his knees.

"Samuel," Pearl said.

He didn't respond. He was studying the back of the tiny man sitting in the darker shadows.

"Samuel," she said again.

The tone of her voice caused him to sense that she had something serious on her mind. "Yes?"

"I want thee to collect as many eggs as thou canst find." She paused. "Then cull two pullets and get them ready."

Samuel looked stunned. "Kill them?"

"Yes."

Slowly his expression changed from surprise to anger, the skin on his neck reddening. "That's our egg business," he said firmly.

"It will not harm us to cull two of the least likely layers."

"We've already done that."

"We do not have enough for dinner," she said quietly.

"I told thee we could not care for them," he said, his voice rising.

The younger boys looked shocked at the boldness of their brother, their eyes on their mother's face. She stood motionless for a moment, then reached out to search with her hand until she found him. She set her hand softly on his shoulder. "And I told thee that thou wert my son, not my husband. Dost thou remember?"

Samuel looked down at his feet. "Yes. But I do not agree with what thou art asking."

"Perhaps. But I still have asked thee."

Samuel waited a moment longer, then started toward the barn's back door and the henhouse.

"Hello?"

Samuel turned to see the Oriental woman struggling to hold a dead pig up by its hind feet. The two little girls were crying again and reaching out to touch the carcass.

"Hello, Samuel," the woman said in an oddly cadenced voice. Her smile had turned into a grimace at the strain of holding up the dead animal. She shoved it out toward him. The girls screamed.

"Samuel?" Pearl called, confused by the sounds.

"The woman wants me to take her dead pig."

"Samuel," Eiko coaxed.

Samuel scrunched up his face and didn't move. Eiko struggled forward.

"Cook the pig," she said.

Pearl nodded in the woman's direction. "Yes. Thank thee," she said smiling.

The woman smiled back.

"Samuel, take the pig, please."

He looked as stunned by this directive as he had been by the order to kill the pullets. "It was hanging on their cart."

"Gutted and bled?"

"Yes."

"Then she was cooling the carcass."

"There's no telling what it died from," he protested. "It's got stiff black hair all over it."

"Samuel, we know how to clean pigs."

"Yes. But we don't know the meat is good."

"I'm certain it is."

"Samuel. Salted. No rot." The woman was nodding vigorously.

"Thank thee, Eiko. That's very generous," Pearl said.

Samuel still hadn't moved. He was trying to think of another argument when he noticed the girl watching him with a sullen look. He felt suddenly uncomfortable.

"Josh and Luke, get a fire going," he said, grabbing

the pig's hind legs, then glanced back at the girl. "We'll burn the hair off." She was moving forward, and he thought for a moment that she was coming to help, but she turned and collected the crying children. He noticed that her hair looked damp and clean. He looked but couldn't see the rag. He suddenly felt warm all over.

Chapter Seven

There was brisk activity in the barn following the meal of pork and fried vegetables that Pearl and Eiko had made. They all had enjoyed it—all but the old man, who continued to sit in the shadows, his back to everyone. It was late evening now, and Fumiko was unloading the family's parcels. Eiko, the mother, was busy setting up their tiny charcoal stove, the baby bellowing and the two girls darting giggling through the barn, chased by the three younger Eddy boys. Though he was playing the game, Samuel could tell that Zacharias was still sad about the Negro.

Pearl stepped before the woman now, a shawl across her shoulders. She hadn't said anything in a while; she had just stood there letting the family get settled. Her three youngest sons joined her, sweating and panting, while the two little girls talked to their mother, pointing every so often at the Eddy boys and laughing.

Samuel was oiling the hinge on the buggy door and watching. He had oiled the same hinge three times. He wasn't certain what he was feeling; he was just worried about his mother's decision to bring these people here. He was certain it would bring the town down on their heads and the men in the masks back. He wondered again if he should tell her what had happened that night.

He decided not to. She would not do anything practical like put padlocks on the doors, certainly not buy a gun, or even talk to the sheriff. She would just continue trusting in the Lord. That wasn't a bad thing, just impractical. He felt a chill across his shoulders. The Negro had started it all. But his mother had capped it off bringing these people here.

"Samuel?" she called. He joined her, and she put a hand on his shoulder and said, "Eiko?"

The woman looked toward them. She was smiling, and the little girls were grinning. Fumiko just stood watching. The Orientals had been so hungry that Pearl had made only basic introductions earlier. She was about to remedy that, Samuel knew, and he felt uneasy.

"Eiko, these are my four boys. Samuel, you have met." She put both hands on his shoulders. "And Joshua," she said, running her fingers lightly over his cheek. She brought her hand back and touched gently at a scrape on his skin. The smile left her face for a moment; then she continued, introducing Luke and Zacharias. Samuel knew she had spotted the bruise.

Eiko listened carefully. She seemed to understand English very well, Samuel thought. That was something anyhow. The two little girls, and even the baby, paid attention. But not the older girl, who was poking at the ground with a stick. And certainly not the old man. Samuel had noticed that once she had gotten him seated on his mat, the Oriental woman ignored the old man, as though well used to his ways. He just sat, his back to them, staring at a corner of the barn, all this beneath him.

"So very nice," Eiko said, standing up quickly and

bowing slightly at the waist. "So nice to meet you," she said in her awkward cadence, smiling enthusiastically.

"Boys," Pearl said quietly.

"Pleased to meet you, ma'am," the boys chorused.

The woman said something Samuel couldn't understand, and the little girls moved closer to her, the taller of the two carrying the baby. The baby looked nice and chubby. From the thin look of the little girls and the rest of them, Samuel was sure they were keeping him fed at their expense. Both girls were dressed in shabby pajamalike clothes. He felt bad for them.

He looked away to the oldest girl, who continued to unpack things from the bag. Eiko was watching her as well, the smile leaving the woman's face as she spoke stiffly to the girl. Reluctantly, the scowl still on her, Fumiko came and stood beside her siblings.

"And these are my children," Eiko said proudly.

"Samuel, take me to them."

This was the part he hated. It always embarrassed him. And this time, with the girl, it would be even worse. But there was no escaping it, so he took his mother's arm and guided her forward, stopping in front of the woman.

"May I touch thy face?" Pearl asked.

"Yes, yes." The woman nodded enthusiastically, sticking her head forward. She looked serious, as if this were a tremendous honor.

At least she was good-natured, Samuel thought, as he guided his mother. Suddenly the woman reached up and took Pearl's hands and brought them quickly to her face as if she were being blessed by the pope.

Pearl's fingertips moved carefully over her smooth features, across the round and pudgy cheeks, the heavy lips, the curve of flat nose. She was no beauty, Samuel figured; she just had a pleasant face that had a certain strength to it.

"Eiko." The woman beamed.

"Eiko," Pearl repeated.

Pearl was concentrating hard, her expression focused. The woman frowned momentarily, as if this were a very solemn occasion. Then, after Pearl had finished examining every bit of the woman's visage, she brought her fingers back to the mouth. The woman smiled, and Pearl slowly traced her lips with the tips of her fingers. Then the woman touched her fingers to Pearl's lips, and she too smiled. Then Eiko's eyes began to tear through her smile. Then Pearl's eyes were tearing as well. Samuel didn't understand.

The two little girls giggled and squirmed but seemed to enjoy having Pearl touch them. Samuel watched as his mother's fingers moved through their snarled and dirty hair, over the grimy little cheeks. He knew that she was cataloging everything, missing nothing. Not the hollowness of their cheeks. Not the dirt. Nothing. Her hands went back a couple of times to their hair. He didn't need to look at her face to know that bothered her. She was big on cleanliness. She took a deep breath. One of the little girls was tall and narrow-faced: Tamoko. Her sister, Isi, was small and narrow-boned with a bright oval face.

The baby, Ituro, sucked Pearl's fingers enthusiastically. She laughed and let him. Samuel looked to see the oldest girl standing a few feet away, staring sullenly at the ground. The woman said something to her. Reluctantly she stepped forward and raised her head. Samuel started to say something to restrain his mother, but the Oriental woman shook her head at him and nodded, and he brought his mother's hands to the girl's face. She frowned as the hands touched her, stiffening as if she deeply resented this.

"Fumiko," her mother said.

"Fumiko," Pearl said, as if the name were a delicious

taste to be savored. She held the young girl's head firmly between her hands for a long time, the way Samuel had seen the town's Baptist minister do at healings down by the creek. He wished his mother would let go. The girl gazed into the material of Pearl's dress as if she too were blind. But she didn't try to pull away. Then Pearl's hands moved down and touched at the tattered fabric of the girl's clothing, moving expertly along her shoulders, down her arms. Samuel knew she was taking her full measure.

"Thou art a beautiful young woman, Fumiko," Pearl said. Then the girl stepped back into line. She didn't look quite as angry.

"Thy father?" Pearl asked, waiting for the old man.

The woman frowned. "Father-in-law. Shincho Kishimoto," she said with great dignity, as if the name might mean something to Pearl. "My father-in-law," she repeated.

Pearl reached her hands out, waiting for the old man. The woman shook her head hard. "He will not allow you to touch him."

The old man barked something in his language.

Eiko looked uncomfortable.

From the shadows where Shincho Kishimoto sat came an additional few sharp words, cutting through the air. The woman looked at him, then back at Pearl. She was plainly respectful of the old man but disturbed by what he had said. He barked at her again. She looked reluctantly at Pearl.

"He believes white people are inferior," she said. "I do not," she added quickly, clearly embarrassed.

Pearl turned in the direction of the grunt and said, "It is a pleasure to meet thee, Mr. Kishimoto," her voice friendly.

The old man didn't move or grunt again.

"Boys," she said brightly.

"Good evening," they said in rough unison.

In the kitchen Pearl and Eiko were washing the last of the evening dishes. Except for Fumiko and Samuel, the children were all playing stick-can in the backyard. The older children and the old man were still in the barn. Mr. Kishimoto had not touched Pearl's meal, behaving as if it were carrion or poison. Eiko had scolded, but to no avail.

Pearl was bending over a large copper basin filled with soapy water, her sleeves rolled up. She held out a wet plate, and Eiko took it and began to dry it with a towel.

"The judge offered to help thee start on thy way to China."

Eiko looked confused. "China?"

"He thought thou might want to go back to thy country."

"We are not Chinese," she said. "Nipponese— Japanese."

Pearl smiled at the mistake. "Then Japan. Or perhaps Hawaii."

Eiko suddenly looked serious. "Here," she said firmly, pointing at the floor with the dripping plate. "We own land—deed." She pulled a paper from a cloth bundle that hung from a cord around her neck.

"Eiko, thy land no longer belongs to thee. It was lost to taxes." Pearl tensed as she said the words, then shook it off. She wouldn't lose the house. She wouldn't, she assured herself.

The woman's smile seemed to freeze. She continued drying the plate for a moment longer than necessary. "We stay. We farm." She paused. "For my children."

The last words brought a feeling of sadness to Pearl.

"Thou wouldst need money to do such a thing. A

great amount of money. Enough for land, animals, equipment, and seed. I know."

The woman looked surprised. "You are a farmer?"

"Not a good one." Pearl laughed.

"I am a good one," Eiko said confidently.

"I'm certain thou art, but without money—"

"What is enough?" the woman interrupted.

Pearl shook her head. "I don't know—hundreds of dollars."

The woman shook her head, indicating she didn't have that much, then realized Pearl couldn't see her and said, "I don't have."

Pearl nodded. "Nor I."

Eiko watched her for a while. Then suddenly her face brightened. "Fumiko and I can work for you— clean and cook until we have enough."

"I do my own housework."

"You are blind," the woman said bluntly.

"I am able to work. But even if I wanted to, I could not pay thee."

"I am a good worker," she said with pride.

"I am certain," Pearl said, submerging a dish into the sudsy water. They worked quietly for a while, each concentrating on her own thoughts. Then Pearl said, "I will try to find thee a job in town. It will help until thou decidest certain things."

Eiko beamed. "I work hard. We farm."

Pearl smiled slowly and then reached out her dripping hands, waiting until Eiko grasped them in her own. She liked this woman, who had dug in her bare feet against the town's pushing—to make a place for her children. Pearl understood that.

Zacharias darted past them into the parlor, the screen door banging behind him, and the mothers let go of their hands and went back to the dishes. Eiko was humming a happy little song in the quiet of the room.

* * *

Samuel was lying on his back, half under the buggy, applying grease to the axle of the carriage. He hadn't heard it squeaking, but it was wise to keep it greased. Every so often he would turn his head so that he could see the girl, Fumiko. She was busily rummaging through the various bags, pulling out matting and blankets for the night.

He had furiously mixed feelings about her. His first impression had been correct: She was better-looking than he thought Oriental girls could be. In fact, she was prettier than a lot of girls in Zella. But she was too surly to be nice, acting as though she were better than anybody else.

He crawled out from under the carriage and wiped his hands on a rag, then went over to the barn window and looked out toward the road. All was quiet now. Thank goodness. He looked back and watched Fumiko again.

She was trying to manhandle a large canvas bundle down from the wooden cart; her grandfather, sitting on his mat a few yards away, did nothing to help. He was the laziest man Samuel had ever seen. Pulling his pants lower, Samuel hurried across the stable, taking a path close by the little man. As he passed, he thought for a second that the fierce old geezer had moved slightly. But he paid him no mind and reached up and took hold of the bundle. The girl stopped and watched him for a moment; then together they pulled the heavy canvas to the ground.

"There," Samuel said, dusting off his hands. He didn't know what to say now. "Any more?"

She didn't respond, just loosened the straps. But then, he figured, she probably didn't know how to speak English. He felt better, just having helped. He

watched her for a while; then he started back toward
the buggy.

He wasn't certain what happened next. The little
man was sitting cross-legged, a shawl of some sort
drawn over his thin shoulders. He looked half asleep.
But as Samuel passed, he suddenly let out a sharp
yelp—*ei!*—and swung his stick, catching Samuel
across the ankles and dropping him in a heap. Then
the old man hopped up in his half squat, looking as if
he were going to wallop him again. Samuel rolled
away, clutching at his head to keep it from getting
split like a melon.

Satisfied, the old man sat on his mat again, settling
down as if nothing had happened. Fumiko looked at
Samuel for a moment, giving away nothing with her
expression, then went back to the bundle she was
working on.

Samuel was stunned, his eyes tearing from the pain
and embarrassment. There were no broken bones, but
the blow had numbed his lower legs. He struggled to
his feet and glared across the shadows at the old man,
about to blurt out something in his anger. Then he
caught himself and turned and hobbled out.

The old man waited silently in the shadows for a
few moments; then he stirred slightly, saying something in a childish-sounding falsetto to the girl. She
grew red in the face and shook her head. The old man
said it again. And made an odd little noise that might
have been a laugh.

Pearl and Eiko continued to stand at the copper
basin, washing and drying the remaining dishes, perfectly at ease with each other's company. Pearl could
hear her youngest rummaging through the house,
opening closets and moving books. He had been
doing it for the past fifteen minutes.

"Zacharias, what art thou doing?"

There was no response. Then she heard a door slam shut and the sound of running feet. "Zacharias," she called, raising her voice to the level she used to discipline.

Still, no response came. Pearl waited, then straightened up and dried her hands on a towel. "Zacharias?" she called one last time, then turned and walked into the darkened parlor. She stopped and listened. She could hear the soft sound of crying.

"Zacharias?"

"Father's gone," the boy sobbed.

Late that night Pearl sat facing Samuel in the small parlor. The Kishimito family had settled down in the stable, and Pearl's younger boys had been asleep for an hour. The house was quiet. Samuel was bent at the waist, working under lamplight at a long table. The only sound was that of his scissors as he cut blue cloth from a heavy bolt. Neither he nor his mother had spoken in a while when he finally cleared his throat, the noise loud in the stillness.

"He did it," Samuel repeated.

Pearl didn't respond, but Samuel thought he had seen her wince. He didn't care. He had moved beyond anger to a kind of certainty. Now she knew that the Negro was a thief.

Finished cutting the cloth free of the bolt, Samuel took the pattern for a pair of children's pants that his mother had told him to use and pinned it into place on the fabric. He glanced at her in the hard yellow light as he worked, wondering what she was thinking. He hoped to Hades that she wasn't feeling sorry for the Negro again, but there was no telling with her.

Samuel doubled the blue material and quickly

snipped around the pattern's edges with an experienced eye developed over three years of pattern cutting. His father had cut them before that. But when Samuel had turned eleven, the task had been passed to him. He didn't mind.

"I knew he was a thief the moment I saw him," he said.

She was dressed in her long flannel nightgown, which fell in graceful folds to her cloth slippers, her brown hair brushed out and hanging over her shoulders. Her gentle face looked paler and more reserved than he had seen it since the day they buried his father. And she looked tired. He glanced at the clock standing in the corner: one o'clock. He felt the fatigue himself.

"Thank thee, Samuel," she said in a soft voice that he had to strain to hear above the hiss of the lamp. "Thou canst put out the light and go to bed." She paused. "I feel like working some," she added, pulling the cloth for one of the children's outfits onto her lap and beginning to thread a needle.

There was a sad, lost sound in her voice that scared him and suddenly made him feel bad for what he had said. "It's late," he said quietly. "Thou shouldst get some sleep as well."

Pearl smiled and nodded. "In a little while."

She had begun to sew. Samuel reached and turned the wick down into the kerosene until the flame sputtered out. Slowly his eyes adjusted to the dark, and he stood watching her as she sat sewing inside a soft ray of moonlight from the window, looking like an apparition in the darkness. He shivered at the thought. He loved her and felt a surge of admiration for her.

"I'm sorry," he said, the apology seemingly fitting many things: his badgering attacks on the Negro, his protests over the Orientals, the shared sadness they felt over the loss of the photograph, even their current circumstances—all of it.

She smiled again and continued to sew. "Get thee to bed," she said softly. Samuel watched her a moment longer, then left, quietly shutting the door behind him to keep the room from getting drafty. When she was certain he was gone, Pearl stopped sewing and sat thinking. She sat long enough for the moon's light to move off her and onto the worktable. She was breathing hard, in short gasps, a searing pain in her chest as though her heart were breaking up inside her.

She began to shake her head back and forth, slowly at first, then increasing until her hair was flying over her thin shoulders. Then she collapsed in sobs in the chair. The money was gone. And while she had fought the thought for most of the night, she knew that Samuel was right. Jerome Prophet had stolen it.

She bit at her lip until she tasted blood, fighting off the tears and a rising sense of desperation. She was swamped by the sensation that she was losing everything she had been trying so desperately to hold on to for her boys: their home, a decent living, a future. All of it was slipping through her fingers. And all of it was happening because of her own acts. She shook hard, then fought to calm herself. She had sheltered the man and defended him. A shudder went through her as if an invisible hand were shaking her.

The house would be auctioned now. As soon as he learned that she had no money, Mr. Snipes would proceed with the foreclosure. She didn't blame him. He had no choice. He had already given her one extension.

She felt her heart contract, her breath quickening. Could she hold the family together? Her hands were trembling hard, and she clutched them together in a tight ball. She was heaving for breath, panic over-taking her once more. Then she stopped and sat up straight, a deep anger—stronger than she had ever felt—seizing her, shoving the panic aside.

"How couldst thou?" she snapped. "I believed in thee, I sheltered thee, I gave thee food and my protection." She fought down the angry sobs welling up inside her breast. Never in her life had she felt so betrayed.

She struggled against her emotions, desperately seeking some inner peace. It was no use. She sagged back into the chair. "Jerome Prophet, how couldst thou?" she cried.

It was shocking but undeniable. They were right there in his hand, his eyes glued to them under the harsh lantern light. After a moment of casual contem-plation Prophet cradled the cards and glanced toward the bar. Best hand of his life and he had to draw it in a seven-by-nine east Kansas town called Moonlight.

"What you looking for?" The dealer squinted at Prophet. "Gawd, you're an ugly bastard." That was maybe the twelfth time he had said it. The man was tall and heavy, drunk and humorless.

"Not fit to be seen," Prophet agreed.

"I asked what you were looking for, old man?" the dealer grumbled.

"That girl selling beer."

Prophet counted the dealer not much more than a drifter, certainly no gambler. They had lost almost identical amounts. The difference was that the dealer was getting disagreeable over his misfortune, while Prophet was getting grouchy over the man. He rabbit-hunted after every hand, searching through the undealt cards to see what he might have drawn, and he was shy in the pot too many times.

A movement caused Prophet to glance at the age, the player directly to the dealer's left. He was small and weasel-faced, with nervous eyes that had suddenly started jumping to every hand around the table. Prophet watched him arranging four cards facedown, side by side in close order, the fifth off to the right. Working a straight. Sweet dreams.

The two other players just looked tired. The one to the dealer's right was late forties or thereabouts, thinning yellow hair and a puffy face, dressed in a worn suit; road drummer was Prophet's guess. Something lumpy under his vest looked like a parlor gun.

The dealer was wearing a small silver pistol on his hip, and weasel-face was probably carrying as well. Friendly little trio. Only the young farmer to Prophet's right looked as if he weren't in the Mexican militia. Prophet too was clean.

The dealer straightened a stack of coins in front of him, creating a sound of metallic clicks as he let them drop back into place on the table. Prophet reached and picked up his cards as if he had just remembered they were there. Four kings. An Immortal, an unbeatable hand. The first time ever he had drawn four honest sovereigns.

"Forget the beer," the dealer advised.

"Why?" Prophet wasn't interested, but he asked. It was about manners. About respect. The old Creole woman that he had lived with in Louisiana had taught him certain things to do and certain things not to do in life. Being polite in conversation was one of those things you did. So he asked.

"You want me to tell you about things like this, for Christ sake? It'll make you wanta cry." The dealer waited and then grinned and said, "I guess so."

"Sure," Prophet said.

"This is a clean establishment."

"Right."

"Therefore they don't serve gawddamn niggers."

The words drifted slowly through the room as if they were a bad smell. Prophet felt the muscles of his shoulders and neck bunching. Instinctively he calculated the distance between himself and the man, guessing his weight, height of the table, and the quickest route to the back door. He hoped it was unlocked.

He cleared his throat, jiggered his cards, and looked up at the man. "Hell of a smart rule."

Nobody moved or spoke for a moment; then somebody at the bar laughed, and others joined in.

"Smart nigger," the dealer said.

"We playing?" the weasel whined. "It's my bet. Five dollars."

Prophet shoved the money forward.

"Ten," the dealer snapped.

Prophet looked up at the man, at the meanness in the dark eyes, at the ears that stuck out perpendicular to his head. Bat ears. No respect for others. Betting out of turn. The weasel backed down and said, "Ten."

Prophet glanced at the small man. "You want five? It's your bet. If you want five, it's five."

"I said ten," the dealer snapped.

Prophet looked at him. "And you said it out of turn."

"Ten," the small man said.

"You want ten?" Prophet asked.

"Yes."

"Ten," Prophet echoed, adding the coin. The dealer was glaring at him, but Prophet ignored him.

It was simple five-card draw with jokers a bug and no pot limit, and the second round of betting drove the pile of money and chips past a hundred dollars. The farmer and the drummer folded. Then the dealer was reaching into his coat, and Prophet was rising from his chair until he saw the hand holding a roll of bills.

"Fifty dollars," the dealer said, counting the money out. The saloon was quiet now. The drummer and the farmer had dropped out with hardly a whimper between them. The little man wasn't going to be bullied.

Prophet returned to studying the dealer's face, deciding he didn't have a hand, just a feeling of superiority that he could run the little man and a colored man out of a high-stakes game.

Then a voice came to him. He had just reached into his pocket and grabbed Pearl Eddy's money—his hand and fifty dollars headed for the betting pile—when the voice exploded inside his head: "Jerome Prophet, how couldst thou!" He froze. There was no mistaking it.

The Quaker woman had lectured him enough so that he recognized her voice when he heard it . . . and he had heard it. There was no doubt in his mind. He glanced quickly around the room. She wasn't to be seen. He looked again. Nowhere.

He trembled as if he had been touched by a phantom, echoes of the voice still ringing inside his head as he lowered his hand and the money to the betting pile. He had never been a believer in much beyond this life, but at this moment—in this dusty saloon a hundred miles from the town of Zella—he knew he had heard Mrs. Eddy admonish him when he touched her money. She might as well have been sitting right beside him.

Then someone grabbed his hand, and Prophet turned, staring into the face of the dealer. The man had half risen from his chair and was squeezing Prophet's fingers, trying to force him to release the money.

If he had been sober or smarter, the dealer would have sensed something that wasn't safe in the Negro and backed away, but the alcohol had fuzzed his thinking. That, plus the fact that he was younger and outweighed Prophet by maybe fifty pounds; he figured the Negro wouldn't want any part of him. Niggers had no guts, he told himself. Those were the reassuring thoughts going through his mind when he smashed Prophet's hand down onto the table.

"Let go of me," Prophet said in an icy voice.

Prophet had been applying pressure against the man's hand to hold it above the table. Now he relaxed, and the man must have figured he had won. He hadn't. In a movement so fast no one knew exactly what had happened, Prophet jerked his hand free and grabbed the dealer before the man could react.

"Don't cuss me," Prophet said.

The man tried to pull away, prying at Prophet's huge fingers with his other hand. Prophet was slow to anger, but he had arrived, clamping harder. The man went for his pistol. Using the mental notes he had been making all night, Prophet brought his left across the table in an arcing collision with the bearded face, the impact producing a popping sound like a cork out of a bottle. Then blood and a tooth were on the table. Not a knockout punch, nor meant to be. He had simply intended to slam a little sense into the man. But perhaps, he figured, staring at the splattered blood and tooth, he had been too enthusiastic.

The dealer was screaming and groping blindly for the gun when Prophet hit him a second time. No sooner had he done this than he heard the voice again. "Jerome Prophet." That was all he heard, but it sounded like damnation. He froze, then slowly released the man's limp hand and stood, turning and staring past the crowd of men. They backed away. Sweat broke over his body. She wasn't there.

Was he going crazy? He picked up the money that had fallen from his hand, then looked across the table at the dealer slumped in his chair, drooling blood down his shirtfront. The rest of the table was wanting no part of this.

He calculated he had about thirty-five dollars in the pot. "We'll play this one, okay?"

The weasel-faced man nodded.

Prophet turned his kings, then nodded at the drummer. The man turned the dealer's hand: little bobtail, three jacks. Prophet smiled. The little man still hadn't moved.

"Turn them."

The man reached a shaking hand and flipped his cards: straight flush.

"Son of a—" Prophet muttered. The man had filled the damn thing. Prophet was shaking his head now and moving toward the door, trying to calculate the odds.

He stood in the deep shadows near the livery watching the back of the saloon to see if anyone was going to follow him, his thoughts on the scream in his head. It had unnerved him in a way he definitely didn't like. It was as if she had been standing right behind his ear. He had never heard her yell before. Never heard her speak in more than a stiff tone. But now she sounded like the wrath of God. He shivered in the cool night air and started walking toward the railroad tracks and the place where he had hidden his bag and bedroll.

In the darkness of an alley he picked up his belongings, stopping only long enough to gaze up at the sky. The moon looked like a yellow plate floating over the buildings. "How the heck did you find me, Mrs.

Eddy?" he mumbled. The answer came in a burst of wind that kicked dirt and leaves down the alley. He turned and started slowly for the railroad tracks, clutching what was left of her money.

Chapter Eight

Barn swallows were darting every which way, chasing insects in the early-morning air, and Samuel and his brothers were hauling hot water from the cauldron they had hung over a wood fire in the backyard, rushing the steaming buckets into the kitchen, where their mother had ordered the copper tub placed after breakfast. Zacharias was holding Hercules under one arm and trailing along behind them, still sobbing over the loss of the picture. For the past two nights he had cried himself to sleep because he would never see his father again.

Samuel wanted to cheer up the boy, but he had no comfort to offer him. He himself had thought the photograph would always be among those things in his life that would last forever. It stunned him to think that it was gone. The moment he had heard he knew it was the Negro and said so. But Zacharias refused to believe it.

He was feeling embarrassed and faintly annoyed as he entered the kitchen. Fumiko was there, but she seemed either not to notice or not to care about his presence. Despite himself, he had thought about her during the night. He figured it was just that she was around his age and foreign. He was just curious, he told himself.

His mother was bent over the bath, testing the temperature of the water. Fumiko was eyeing her cautiously. He wanted to laugh. There would be no escape. He could have warned them of that after she had run her fingers through Tamoko's and Isi's dirty hair and touched their soiled clothing. She was death on dirt. Therefore he hadn't been surprised by the order to set up the bath, even though it wasn't Sunday. But two things had surprised him.

The first was the three outfits on the table. She had to have sewn all night. The second surprise was that she had regained her normal bouncing spirit. He was relieved, amazed at how she always seemed able to bounce back. He watched as she left the kitchen, heading for the parlor, talking happily over her back to Eiko, who nodded enthusiastically.

Samuel lingered, pouring the last pail of water slowly, listening to the happy talk, observing the little girls' excitement over the new clothes. That was one of the good things about his mother, she could make any chore seem a picnic. Except it wasn't working with Fumiko. She was leaning against the counter with her arms crossed over her breast, looking sullen. Even knowing his mother's persuasive powers, he still wondered how she was going to get this girl into the bath. Then his mother returned.

"Eiko?"

"Yes?"

Pearl was holding out a cotton dress and a pair of shoes. Samuel looked back down at the tub, fighting his feelings. It was a wonder they had anything, the way she behaved. Maybe she had four dresses to her name and two pairs of shoes, and here she was giving these away. He looked back up. Eiko was crying.

His mother looked equally touched, but when the woman reached for the dress, she sensed it and held up her hand. "Not until thou hast bathed."

The woman started to protest.

"Not until thou hast bathed," Pearl repeated firmly.

Amazingly, he had caught a glimpse of Fumiko almost smiling, apparently pleased that the tables had been turned on her mother.

"Certainly not until thou hast had thy bath," Pearl said once more for emphasis, hanging the dress on the kitchen door. Then she picked up the splashing Ituro from his bath in a smaller copper tub on the kitchen counter, turning toward the girl. Samuel smiled to himself; she had good timing.

"Fumiko, please dry brother while thy mother bathes."

The girl stepped forward quickly, looking almost helpful and certainly enjoying her mother's consternation, and wrapped the pudgy, dripping Ituro in a towel. These people had been living in the middle of roads and barns so long, Samuel thought, that they were out of the bathing habit.

"Thank thee," Pearl said brightly. Then she turned back toward Eiko, who continued to look like a cat cornered by dogs. "The water is cooling."

For the first time since he had seen her, Fumiko was enjoying herself. She almost smiled. And it made him feel good. His mother had this way with people.

"Samuel, put the blanket over the window; then thou and thy brothers start another kettle. I'll call when we are ready. We'll need three more tubs," she said, calculating. "Tamoko and Isi together ... Fumiko ... and Mr. Kishimoto."

Eiko drew her breath in hard at the naming of her father-in-law, while Fumiko clapped her hands together in glee.

"No. No wash Mr. Kishimoto," Eiko warned in a trembling voice.

Pearl laughed. "I have no intention of washing Mr. Kishimoto. He will have to do that himself. I will simply provide the facility to accomplish it."

Fumiko was standing in a peculiar way now, feet together, bouncing up and down, her hands clasped gleefully over her mouth as if she were attempting to contain a massive explosion of mirth.

"I won't tell him." Eiko shook.

"I'll be happy to," Pearl said, holding out a bar of soap and a washrag toward the woman, who still looked in a state of shock. "Hurry," she coaxed, while Samuel made a quick exit.

Later the same day Samuel was still gleeful over the memory of what happened. He was in the buggy now, waiting for his mother to finish her conversation with the widow Wendell. The two women were standing in the early twilight on the widow's front porch. Jack stamped a foreleg and shook his head, trying to lose a horsefly. Samuel crawled down and chased it for him, rubbing the old gray's forehead and remembering.

After the females had finished their baths, Pearl had marched out of the house, across the yard, and into the dim light of the barn, looking as if she were heading to Sunday tea. Samuel and his brothers trailed behind at a distance, knowing that if she caught them, she would send them on some unpleasant errand. Eiko and the two smaller girls remained inside the house, as if seeking physical protection from the wrath of the old man's coming rage. But not Fumiko. She had strolled along behind them, pretending she was on other business.

Samuel had watched her, surprised at the freshness of her look. He glanced back up now at his mother draped in her dull gray dress. She held a basket in her arms and was patiently listening to widow Wendell gabbing. He was filled with a sense of admiration for her. While she studiously avoided style herself, she had an uncanny sense of it for others. Blind she might be, but she could imagine what looked good. It was an amazing gift, Samuel thought.

There was nothing dowdy about the clothes she made; her designs were always sophisticated and freshly modern. Never extravagant, her creations nevertheless had a pleasing flair and worked to the physical advantage of the wearer. They certainly did for Fumiko, he recalled. That morning his eyes had moved slowly over this changed person as she hung back to look at the hollyhocks near the well.

It wasn't just the dress. It was as if the dress highlighted her beauty, her cheeks smooth like polished stone, her brown eyes dark and deep. He was equally amazed that his mother—blind, who had done nothing but run her hands quickly over a face and body— could create such an impression. She had stressed the girl's height at the same time that she emphasized her strong shoulders. His mother's needlework had made Fumiko as pretty as any girl in Zella.

"Come on, Sam," Joshua had complained in a whisper.

At his brother's call he had turned toward the barn just as his mother said, "Good morning, Mr. Kishimoto." There was no reply. Nor did the old man move in any physical way.

Inside the barn the boys' eyes slowly adjusted to the weak light. Mr. Kishimoto had his beautiful red robe draped over his thin shoulders. Then as if to underscore the fact that he didn't want to be disturbed, he had executed his amazing half rise from his squatting position, rudely turned his back to Pearl and settled down cross-legged on the mat with little physical effort. He was certainly agile for an old man.

"I don't like him," Luke had mumbled.

The others had nodded.

"Mr. Kishimoto," his mother had said, "my boys are preparing thy bath. Please follow me to the kitchen." Pearl had turned as if there were no doubt that he would follow and started tapping her cane back toward the large doors.

Halfway across the barn she had stopped and turned, listening for the old man. "Mr. Kishimoto, I know that thou understand English."

Still, there was no reply.

"I assume thou hast not bathed in a period of time. I also assume from thy clothing and manner that thou art a man of education and refinement. Therefore it must be distasteful to thee to go without cleaning thyself." She paused. "Thy bath will be ready in ten minutes. All the women and children will leave the house until thou art completed."

No sound or movement stirred the cool air inside the barn.

"I will clean thy garments. If thou hast replacements, fine. If not, I have a suitable robe for thee to wear until thine is dry."

"No." The harsh word had shot through the air like a bullet.

Then his mother was pulling herself up straight the way she did when she got heated over something, and she began tapping her foot, a small cloud of dust rising from the dirt.

It was at that moment—watching her stiff frame and that familiar tapping foot—that the boys had begun to sense that perhaps old Mr. Kishimoto was in for a fight. The old man may have sensed this as well because without moving a muscle anyone could see, he said, "Put it in barn." Then, as if to clearly show who was boss, he barked, "Now!"

She had nodded and said, "Of course." Then just as firmly, she added, "It will now take longer than ten minutes."

Samuel remembered Fumiko's mumbling something in Japanese and looking shocked. They had all been, but the boys knew their mother well enough to keep deathly still about it.

"Quiet," he had whispered. Too late.

"And ye children with the large ears, I want Jack's stall and corral cleaned before lunch. Also his water tank."

Fumiko had started to walk away when Pearl said, "Fumiko, that includes thee, child."

They had moaned, but the punishment had been worth the spectacle. The girl had done her share, ignoring the lot of them throughout. But for some reason Samuel didn't understand, it didn't matter how rudely she acted. She just seemed to make the work go better.

Night had fallen over the town, and Pearl was crawling back onto the buggy seat, Samuel guiding her with a hand. She looked tired. They had made their regular deliveries, but each had taken longer than normal, as Pearl sought work for Eiko and Fumiko. So far she had found nothing.

Her expression was one of deep contemplation. He picked up Jack's reins, the old carriage horse automatically turning away from the hitching post toward home. "Thou couldst use some dinner," he said, trying to sound cheerful.

She straightened and placed her hands in her lap. "First I want to speak with Mrs. Randolph."

His heart sank. He was hungry and tired. Her care

for poor folks was going to make his life a misery. It would be another hour before they started home, he was thinking, when she said, "Drive me there. Then borrow a livery horse from Mr. Syth and go home."

He started to protest, but she looked too worn. Jack would bring her home whenever she gave him his head; he had been doing that for more than twelve years. Still, Samuel felt bad about leaving her. He looked at her face again, at the profile even a son could admire, but in the waxing moonlight she looked lost in a way that scared him.

"I don't mind waiting."

She smiled. "I thank thee. But thou need to make certain the others have eaten."

He hesitated, ready again to protest, but something in the lines around her eyes said it wouldn't be fair to continue arguing. "Only if thou promise to hurry."

"I promise."

The bell in the steeple of the Methodist church was ringing nine when Pearl let Jack have his head. She was exhausted, having just left Sarah Randolph's with no more success than any other attempt to find the Kishimotos jobs. Everyone seemed to know she was looking for work for the women, and everyone was at once helpful and not helpful at all, offering up the names of neighbors and relatives who might need a cook or cleaning woman, but never needing one themselves.

She paid no attention to the horse as he threaded his way through the alleys and side streets of the livery and saloon district, heading steadily toward Lincoln Avenue. The old animal would take Lincoln north until it ran into the road that cut west across the prairie. He would follow that for three miles, turning in at their gate.

If the boys didn't hear the buggy, Jack would gauge the door and make his final turn into the barn. Amazingly he rarely bumped the carriage into anything. Once inside he would stand quietly until unharnessed. Familiar with all this, Pearl paid him no mind as they moved along.

Zella was no more than three thousand people, and at this hour the streets were empty and quiet. But it wouldn't have mattered if she had been in the middle of New York City, so deeply was she submerged in her worries. Somewhere nearby a door slammed, and a dog barked in response, but Pearl paid no mind to the disturbance, her thoughts on the missing money, her boys, her failure to find work for Eiko and her daughter. Nothing seemed to be going right. She tried to probe the silence of her mind, searching for the familiar inner peace, the inner light that would speak to her. It didn't work. Her thoughts traveled back to the evening's efforts.

She had made calls on six families, folks she knew used hired help. Their reactions had all been different but surprisingly similar: Each had seemed sympathetic to the plight of the woman and her children, but none was willing to do anything about it. What bothered her most were the lurid tales of Asians kidnapping children, poisoning employers, stealing fortunes, and selling teenage girls as slaves. Sarah Randolph had told her that they ground up children to make strange potions . . . and stole like Hindus.

She had tried to argue, but the more she did, the more exaggerated the stories became. She stretched her tired body on the buggy seat and shook her head, then breathed in deeply, trying to let the cool air of the plains clear her mind. Spring was coming hard on the land, and she could smell the weed growth by the side of the road. She heard an owl make a low pass over the roof of the buggy, its wings swishing in the night like those of an avenging spirit.

Jack's hoofbeats were steady and soothing. The old horse seemed to know that Pearl wouldn't want him rushing, and he obligingly took his time heading out to the cross-prairie road. Pearl let her shoulders sag, feeling like crying but knowing that was wrong. She had to stand up to her troubles; a struggle in a good cause, she told herself, would turn out all right. And the Kishimotos were a good cause. Every bit as good as holding on to the farm.

Pearl forced herself to relax and leaned back onto the seat, listening to the last faint sounds of the town slipping away behind her. Then, suddenly, Jack shied at something, and Pearl gripped the side of the buggy, talking gently to him. Probably a possum scurrying on the side of the road, she thought, picking up the reins.

"Settle down," she said softly to the old horse. But Jack wasn't ready to settle down, and she sensed that he was about to break into a trot. She pulled him in, uncertain what had spooked him. "Jack."

The horse was turning his head to watch both sides of the road. Then he snorted, the buggy rounding the turn onto the cross-prairie road too quickly, the animal stepping hurriedly into a single-foot, causing the carriage to bounce over the ruts. Finally, the wheels straightened out, and the buggy headed down the road, into the night and the tallgrass plains. But something was bothering the horse. She listened but couldn't hear anything unusual.

Pearl knew the few lights of town were slowly being left behind, floating like a small island of stars on a great sea of black, as Matthew had once described it. Her thoughts drifted to him. They had made this same ride together hundreds of times, Matthew talking about plants, animals, the weather, politics, everything. She chewed at her lip, realizing, as she did a dozen times a day, how much she missed him. She wondered whether the hurt would ever go.

Matthew had died a painful death. But he had never surrendered to the pain, never lost his dignity or serenity. Or his beliefs. She caught herself. His? Or simply hers? She shuddered at the possibility.

For a moment she had a passing sensation of unease, sensing something nearby that made her want to wrap her arms around herself. Again Jack broke into a trot, and Pearl reined him in, uncertain still what was bothering the animal. She sat with a good grip on the lines in case he suddenly got it into his head to bolt; then she tensed, thinking she had heard something trip over a rock to the rear of the buggy.

"Hello?" she called.

No response. Jack was still nervous. Pearl listened hard again, a vague feeling growing in her that something was near the buggy. They hadn't seen a wolf in years. Maybe it was a loose horse. More likely it was a stray dog.

She forced herself to relax, trying to decide what she was going to tell banker Snipes about the money. It would take a year to save the amount she needed, and by that time she would be facing new debts. The dark mood seemed to come at her like a wave out of the darkness. She struggled against it. She wouldn't give in. God wasn't indifferent.

All she had to do was let the Spirit work. Her throat tightened. But what if this—the loss of the money, the loss of the house—was part of His plan for her? Could she surrender to that? She felt the pressure and indecision tearing at her like some ravenous creature. Pearl jumped as the buggy bounced over the center rise in the road, heading in a direction she sensed wasn't right.

"Jack, where art thou going?" she called, trying to bring the animal back to where she believed the road ran. But strangely he would not respond.

Pearl braced her feet against the front of the buggy. "Whoa, Jack," she called firmly, pulling harder on the reins. But this didn't stop the horse, who continued moving in the new direction. Pearl was confused.

In all these years Jack had never made a wrong turn on the route home, and he had never failed to stop when reined in. She relaxed her grip on the leather lines for a moment, then pulled them back firmly. "Jack, stop!" she called.

It had no effect. She couldn't grasp the meaning. She could hear that they were on a road, the wheels of the buggy turning in sandy ruts. But which road? And why had Jack turned? Was there fire ahead? She felt the panic rising in her throat and stopped it; the prairie grasses would be too green for fire for another month. She focused again on her problem.

There were a number of small roads that intersected the cross-prairie road. Could the old horse have taken one by accident? Not by accident. Had something in his head snapped? Had he gotten into locoweed? She doubted it. He had been behaving normally enough, and his hoofbeats sounded normal. It seemed impossible. Jack knew the road home even in a hard snow. Something would have had to prevent him from taking it. That last thought hit her like a physical blow.

Pearl's heart began to race. That was why he wasn't responding. That explained the noise she had heard and the feeling she had gotten: Someone was leading him, holding the reins beneath the bit so that when she yanked, the horse didn't feel the pressure and didn't respond in any way.

She was certain of it; she could sense their presence and knew there was more than one walking silently alongside the buggy. She sat up straighter. "What dost thou want?"

The silence held, and then she went on, speaking more quickly. "Thou hast no right to deter me."

When Pearl felt Jack start down the incline, she knew where they were taking her. They had turned off the cross-prairie road onto the old south trail that dead-ended at Simpson's Creek. It was a lonely spot a good mile out of town, surrounded by cottonwood trees and sandhills and nothing else; the closest farm was miles off. No one came here unless he wanted to load water or swim, and no one would be coming at night. She fought a shiver.

"If thou art trying to frighten me, it will—" she said in a rush, then halted. They had already frightened her.

When Jack stopped, the quiet of the prairie fell down hard on the place, and Pearl said, "I expect thee to take me home now." She fought the fear building in her breast, clasping her hands together to control their shaking, trying to escape by letting her thoughts travel back in time.

In her mind she was walking down the hallway of her childhood home, climbing the stairs to her room, and curling up on her bed, listening to the ticking of the mantel clock and the steady purring of her cat— forgetting this night, this cold place.

But she could not forget. She was here in this desolate spot, and she sensed them closing in on her, and there was nothing she could do. Her muscles contracted as someone climbed onto the seat beside her. She could hear his breathing, smelled liquor and tobacco, then felt a callused hand rough against her cheek. She reached to remove it, but the man grabbed her wrist hard and held it pinned back against the seat while he ran his hand slowly down her front. Someone else grabbed her left arm.

"Ye should be ashamed. Ye have mothers and sisters." She was trembling but also sensed a numbness spreading slowly through her until she no longer felt as if she were pinned against the seat while they pawed at her. In her mind she was standing away from all this, would always be separate from it.

"If ye violate me, ye violate them."

They were tugging at the bodice of her dress. She did not try to strike them. Even if she could have, she would not. Someone kissed her, hurting her mouth. They were ripping at her clothes now.

Then the flutelike notes of a meadowlark drifted through the darkness toward her. She focused her mind on the sound. It came again, sharply and clearly through the shadows, the familiar "seee youuu" strange-sounding in the quiet of the night.

In all her years on the prairies she had never heard one singing after sundown. The muscles of her back tensed. It had been Matthew's favorite bird. He used to whistle the call when he was coming in from the fields at day's end. And she chose now to believe that he was whistling again, telling her he was with her, would always be with her. She was concentrating hard on this thought when suddenly the man holding her wrist yelped like an injured dog and slumped into her lap.

"What the hell?" the man to her left said, letting go of her arm as if she were leprous.

Pearl pressed her fingers against the neck of the unconscious man, feeling for his pulse, and used her free hand to search for his wound. Eventually she found a large lump on the back of his skull. As she was struggling to pull a blanket over him, fighting broke out behind the buggy. Somebody was yelling, and she could hear moaning.

"Stop that!" she shouted, as if she were breaking up

a fight among schoolboys. But this struggle was deadly serious and not among boys, and they did not stop, the blows coming faster and accompanied by groans. Then someone splashed wildly through the creek. Jack bolted, dragging the buggy up to the wheel hubs into the water, and then stopped.

Moments later another man broke and ran, trying to escape through the grasses to the right of the wash, but she heard someone pursuing and then a crashing sound. "Stop!" she yelled. Again they paid her no mind.

Pearl Eddy wasn't certain what it was that led her to the conclusion. It just seemed to suddenly be there in her mind, and she was certain she was right. She turned in the direction of the struggle.

"Mr. Prophet."

Silence.

"Mr. Prophet, I know thou art there," she scolded.

There was no response save the noise of the continuing struggle. Pearl pulled herself up straighter on the seat, cradling the head of the unconscious man in her lap.

"Mr. Prophet . . . thou stop . . . this instant."

The sounds of fighting did seem to her to slow for a moment, then resumed full force. She was certain that she had been correct.

"Mr. Prophet!"

"Can't," he panted.

"Thou certainly can."

"No," the voice rasped.

"And why not?"

The fight continued for a moment; then the same winded voice gasped, "Not winning."

"All of ye, stop!"

But they did not.

"Mr. Prophet, I expect thee to set the example."

Someone groaned and seemingly let out his life's breath, the silence of the prairie flooding in on the place, and she shivered and clutched at the limp body beside her. "Thou seekest trouble." Pearl was suddenly fighting back tears. "Mr. Prophet, how many men hast thou hurt here?"

No response came to her.

"Mr. Prophet?" she called, wiping at her cheeks with the tips of her fingers, then searching for Jack's reins but not finding them. The man on the seat moaned, and she shook again in the cold night air. "Mr. Prophet?" she called, slightly more worried-sounding this time.

When no answer broke the silence, when the frigid prairie wind whipped down into the sandy gully, bringing a deepening chill to her—a chill that would kill a person lying hurt and unconscious on the cold ground for any time—Pearl Eddy started to climb down into the creek waters to search for the injured. She suddenly halted.

The buggy had tipped with the weight of someone stepping up on the far running board. He was breathing hard. Light flurries of late spring snow blew in from across the river, and Pearl felt these stinging against her face. Then abruptly the unconscious man was being pulled across the seat.

"No. No," she pleaded, grabbing the man's shoulders and hanging on. "He will die if he gets chilled."

The pulling stopped.

"Thank thee."

Seconds later the buggy swayed as the man stepped back down into the stream. She heard him splashing through the water. Then she felt Jack turning back toward the shore.

"Are others hurt?"

There was a muffled answer, drowned in the rushing noise of the stream.

"I did not hear thee," she sniffed.

"Not badly," Prophet said louder, still breathing in heaves.

"Are they conscious?"

"Ran off. Like street dogs."

"Or harmed men."

"Whatever, Mrs. Eddy."

The man on her lap moaned long and slow.

"What did you do to him?"

"Hit him with a sap."

"I see," she said reproachfully.

"Better than what he had planned for you, Mrs. Eddy."

"Please do not talk, Mr. Prophet."

"Why, Mrs. Eddy?"

"Because I am terribly cross with thee."

She sat staring forward into the night as if she were watching something far away in the darkness, something that hurt her to look at. After Prophet had led the horse back up the rise, she crawled down and stumbled into the bushes. He could hear her retching, then gagging hard. He went and wet a rag at the river.

"Here," he said.

She was wobbly as if she were sick or freezing, and he had to help her back into the buggy.

"You okay, ma'am?"

She took a hard breath and stiffened up. "Yes." Her voice sounded normal, but she was shivering hard, and he pulled a second blanket out of the buggy's boot and draped it over her shoulders. She looked small and childlike, he thought, sitting under the blanket.

She had mostly recovered by the time the man on the buggy seat sat up and groaned. He was young, most probably a drifter, with filthy clothes and ragged, dirty hair. Prophet grabbed him by the lapels of his jacket and yanked him bodily out of the vehicle.

"Mr. Prophet," Pearl said stiffly.

Prophet had his massive arm cocked.

"Mr. Prophet," she repeated.

"Fine," he mumbled, lowering the arm. "Let them hang him."

The man began to blubber.

"Violation of a white woman," Prophet said, "is a hanging offense."

"I was not violated."

"That's where it was headed, Mrs. Eddy," Prophet snapped. "Rape. Plain and simple." His eyes were locked on the man's terrified face.

"There is no need to be vulgar, sir." She paused and then turned in the direction of the man's sobbing. "What is thy name?"

He didn't respond until Prophet shook him again.

"Hank. Hank Meyers." The man was moaning piti-fully. "I'm sorry. I have a mother."

"So do worms," Prophet hissed, yanking him close with a force that left no doubt of harm if he resisted.

"Mr. Prophet, that is no way to talk," Pearl said coolly.

The men were face-to-face, not paying attention to her.

"M-m-man paid us," Meyers stammered.

Prophet grabbed bigger handfuls of Hank Meyers's tattered jacket. "Who?"

"Mr. Prophet," she said again.

"Never saw him. He paid my friend ten dollars." The man's eyes were pleading, and he was writhing in Prophet's grasp. "Mister, don't let them hang me."

Prophet shook him again, angry that these men would harm Mrs. Eddy for any amount.

She heard the sound of Meyers being shaken. "Mr. Prophet!"

Prophet was seized with the desire to drive his fists into the man, and no smack-bang act of repentance was going to change his mind.

"Don't let them hang me, please," Meyers sniveled.

"No one is going to harm thee," Pearl said quickly.

"Maybe thirty years," Prophet snarled. "I've been there. Isn't pretty. Maggots crawling—"

"Mr. Prophet, art thou quite finished with thy little dramatization?"

He didn't say anything for a while, just scowled at the man. Then he let his breath out and said, "Fine."

"Thank thee."

She waited a moment to make certain that Prophet had calmed down, then turned her head in the direction where she thought the young man was standing, missing him by a couple of feet. "Mr. Meyers?"

"Yes?"

"Thou hast learned an important lesson this night, have thou not?"

"I have!" He was sobbing like a child.

"Then go and find God in thy heart." She paused. "Thou art His own."

Prophet was staring in disbelief at her.

"Thank you! Thank you!" Meyers blubbered, wiping his eyes on his sleeve. "What can I do to repay you?"

"Repay the Lord."

"I promise."

A minute later she sensed him still standing there. "Thou may go."

"I can't."

"Why not?"

"The Negro won't let me."

"Mr. Prophet," she said in her disappointed way.

198 ⁓ Thomas Eidson

Prophet stood for a moment holding on to the man's lapels, still staring at her, not ready to let him go.

"Didst thou hear, sir?" she asked.

Reluctantly he shoved Meyers away, gave him a hard kick on the rump, then climbed up into the buggy.

Chapter Nine

It seemed to Prophet a strange thing to behold. He had knocked men cold, threatened them with death, beaten them into submission, but looking back at this man, standing in the road gazing after the buggy in a trancelike way, he realized he had never brought another human being to this level. Never. Hank Meyers just stood there staring, his lips moving silently. Staring as if he wanted to follow.

It was peculiar and unsettling in a way Prophet didn't fully comprehend. It said something about this tiny woman, something he sensed but didn't understand and certainly didn't want any part of. "You should have let me get it out of him, Mrs. Eddy; then we should have turned him over to the sheriff."

"He renounced his sins."

"You don't believe that, ma'am."

"I do. But even if I did not, I do not believe in violence or vengeance. Only God has the right to punish." Almost as an afterthought she said, "As a minister thou knowest that."

Prophet flinched. "He knows who paid him."

The snow was falling now. "He said he did not."

"That was a lie."

"Mr. Prophet, we witnessed his repentance."

"That was a lie too, ma'am," he said, marveling at her naiveté.

Pearl pulled herself up straighter on the seat but didn't respond. She was trembling again. "There is a part of God in every man, sir, whether thou choosest to believe it or not."

He ran a hand over the top of his bare scalp to wipe the melting snow off, watching a star shoot across the heavens and wondering why anyone would want to harm this tiny, gullible woman. It didn't make sense.

That old lady Rose Sherman might have stirred folks up some, but at most they would have just stopped doing business with Mrs. Eddy. That would have been punishment enough. No. It was something else. He was sure of it. Prophet gripped the reins and clucked the horse into a trot.

"Please slow down," she said quietly.

He reined the horse back.

"Thou wert headed somewhere, I recall."

"Yes, ma'am."

"And?"

He had been asking himself this same question. He thought about the voice in the saloon. He should have just mailed her the money and the photograph. But he hadn't. He had hopped a train back, built a fire by the side of the tracks and made a cup of coffee he didn't want, then started toward the farm, running into the buggy and the men. He had found her by pure chance. Or, as she liked to calculate everything, by ordained Providence.

"Mr. Prophet?"

"I just came back, Mrs. Eddy." He pulled up the collar of his coat.

"The hen is paid for."

"Not the hen."

"What then?"

Prophet waited, listening to the sound of the horse's hooves and watching the snow drifting down. "Maybe what you said to that Mrs. Sherman." That was part of it, he knew. The other part he wasn't sure about.

"I spoke for myself. Thou wert innocent."

Prophet squirmed on the seat, then started whistling softly.

Pearl listened to the notes, thinking about the photograph and the money until a sense of shame came over her. The idea that he was a thief had pestered her for the past two days, and she had given in to it. She had condemned an innocent man in the worst of all possible places: her heart.

"There was something thou had to do. Thou said that."

"Yes, ma'am."

"And?"

"I just came back," he repeated.

"Because of what I said to Mrs. Sherman?"

"Maybe."

She sat for a while, thinking that there was more to it. He seemed lost and confused. She had never before sensed that about him. Some sad, disorienting pursuit seemed to be driving him in circles. Aside from his random acts of violence, Jerome Prophet was a good and caring man. Until this moment she had thought of him as brimming with purposeful, though often ill-conceived, action.

"Thou could settle down."

"Yes," he said but not really listening to her. He was thinking instead about Lacy and Tyrone.

"Thou never didst?"

"Ma'am?"

"Never stayed in one place?"

"Not long."

"Thou couldst start a business."

She heard him blow a little air out his nose as if what she had said were crazy. "Thou art good with tools. Zella has few tradesmen."

"Build my own coffin, Mrs. Eddy."

She ignored the comment. "Thou would be accepted."

He glanced at the side of her graceful face and started to say something, then didn't, figuring she had been through enough this night.

"Thou could raise a family."

"I have one, ma'am."

Pearl smiled and waited for him to continue. When he didn't, she said, "How many children?"

"Girl and boy. Eight and six—when I last saw them."

"Thou couldst bring them here," she said with a bright note.

He watched the dark heavens for a while. "I don't know where they are, ma'am."

"Thy children are lost?"

"From me."

"Mr. Prophet?"

"Their mother took them."

They didn't talk for a time after that. He sat watching a spot of black air over Jack's steadily bobbing head, while she sat peering down at a place on the floor of the buggy. About a mile from the farm she raised her head. "Hast thou looked for them?"

"Yes, ma'am."

"Where?"

"Towns we lived. Or where Jenny, my wife, lived or talked about. I walk a regular route, Mrs. Eddy, checking the post offices to see if the children have asked for me, looking in the Negro hotels, on the streets, and in the colored sections. Just asking around."

"Thy wife's parents or kin?"

"The ones I knew, dead."

"These towns, Mr. Prophet, where are they?"

"North Carolina, Kentucky, Ohio. Places like that."

Pearl tensed, her mouth open slightly. "How long hast thou been doing this?"

"For a while." He didn't want to tell her how long. It made it seem hopeless, and he didn't feel that way about it.

"There must be a better way," she said quietly.

He started to tell her about the training camp idea, then stopped. She wouldn't like it. Moments later the lights of the Eddy house came into view down the road, and Jack picked up some speed. Pearl felt this in the spin of the wheels and sensed they were nearing the farm.

"Mr. Prophet."

"Ma'am?"

"I am sorry."

"About the children?"

"Yes."

"Yes, ma'am."

"There must be a better way to search for them."

"Yes, ma'am."

"I just don't know what it is."

"Yes, ma'am."

She returned to her thinking again, and a cast of the moon's soft light over her face made her look momentarily like a painting of the Madonna that he had once seen in a store window in St. Louis. But she was flesh and blood, not some Bible story.

"Thou understandest, thou owest me nothing. I will not accept almsgiving."

"Yes, Mrs. Eddy. I'll just see your boys and then be on my way." He was thinking about how he could best get the picture and the last of her money back in the house. He wouldn't care if she was a millionaire, he didn't want anything of hers anymore.

"That is fine," she said, "as long as we have an understanding."

"About almsgiving, Mrs. Eddy."

"And violence." She spoke the word as if it were damnation itself.

"Yes. Violence too," he added. He glanced at her and cleared his throat. Then he cleared it again.

She heard him the second time. "Sir?"

"Any chance, ma'am, you were north of here last night in a little town called Moonlight?"

"No."

"No. Of course not," he said.

The mystery was gone. Prophet stood staring at the gaggle of Asians in the barn, a strange look in his eyes. They were the same ones he had seen hunkered down on the street in town. He put his tongue between his teeth and bit down, as if trying to keep himself from saying something he knew he would regret.

"These are the Kishimotos—"

Pearl was introducing him, but Prophet wasn't paying any attention. The little Oriental woman had hopped up and was smiling at him as if they were long-lost cousins or something. He nodded at her in reflex and then turned and started for the back porch, his large pack swung over his back. He knew now why the men had been hired to harm Mrs. Eddy. He also knew she wasn't crazy; she was suicidal.

"Mr. Prophet," Pearl called. He stopped and waited for her to catch up. "Thou may use Zacharias's bedroom."

"When's the funeral, Mrs. Eddy?"

"I beg thy pardon?"

"The funeral. For you and your boys, ma'am?"

"I do not understand."

He just shook his head. He was certain she didn't understand, and that was something he couldn't believe. Kids had more sense. "I'll sleep in the cellar. Look better."

"What do thou mean?"

"You don't need a Negro sleeping in your house, ma'am," he snapped, surprised at his own anger. "And Chinamen in your barn."

"They are Japanese, Mr. Prophet."

They walked on in silence until they reached the back steps. Chinese or Japanese—didn't matter. He wondered how she had gotten this far in life without knowing any of the rules. He looked back toward the barn. He didn't care if she called them Japanese or Jack-be-nimbles; they were still Chinamen. Negroes could make it in this world if they knew the rules. Not Chinamen. Maybe that was where the saying "Not a Chinaman's chance in hell" came from.

Wasn't fair. Wasn't foul. It just was. That was what bothered him. This woman never saw things the way they were. Just her way. Period. And her way was mostly wide of the mark.

She had grasped the railing now and was slowly climbing the steps, as he followed. "They had no place," she said softly as if she had read his thoughts. She sounded tired.

He swung the pack off and looked up at her. "They don't belong here, Mrs. Eddy."

"That's not thy decision."

"Still the right one."

"They had no place," she said again.

"They're the reason those men grabbed you."

"Thou dost not know that," she said quietly.

"Yes, I do. You can't bring folks like them into a

town like this." He paused. "They've got strange habits, ma'am. They aren't like normal people."

Moments before she had looked too exhausted to stand, but now she straightened ramrod stiff, and Prophet could see the fight in her eyes. "That is enough, Mr. Prophet. Though thou may wish to believe differently," she stammered, "none is greatest in the kingdom of heaven."

She turned and walked to the edge of the porch and stood facing the dark gardens, continuing to fight her emotions. "We are all equal in the eyes of the Lord, Mr. Prophet."

"Not where I'm from."

When she finally spoke again, her voice was filled with an odd mixture of anger, frustration, and fatigue. "Dost thou understand me?"

"I understand you've got trouble, Mrs. Eddy." He paused. "You ought to cogitate on that."

"Thank thee for thy concern," she said, tapping her way into the house. "I will bring thee blankets." She hesitated. "Thou rememberest how to find the cellar?"

He didn't care for the way she had asked that, but he shrugged it off and headed for the cellar.

Alfred Snipes's office in the bank was cramped and dusty and smelled of stale fish and other things that he fed to Queenie, his large gray cat. The animal was sitting on his messy desk, Snipes petting it while his eyes moved over Pearl. She was standing in the morning sunlight that flowed in a bright beam through the window. He was busy making a hungry survey of the contours of her body under her heavy gray dress. She was clutching her small purse and cane together in both hands and looking uncomfortable.

Snipes continued to contemplate Pearl's figure with a half smile behind his rimless glasses, his hand steadily stroking the back of the cat as if he might be stroking Pearl. Seemingly lost in a daydream, he licked his lips. Small and thin, with a large nose that stuck out like a rock formation from his narrow face, Alfred Snipes had been a bachelor all his life. But that had not kept him from thinking hard and often about women and what it would be like to be with one. He stroked the cat faster.

"Mr. Snipes?"

He sat up awkwardly, as if caught doing something he shouldn't have been. "Well, yes. There is the possibility of a loan. But without a husband it would be highly irregular." He looked her over again. "And there is the matter of the other loans." He stood and picked up his heavy cat, the animal struggling to free itself. "You understand."

"We have always paid our bills, Mr. Snipes."

"Until now," he reminded her. "And then you had a husband."

"We still pay our debts, sir." Her manner was stiff and a bit awkward. She was well aware that Mr. Snipes was not immune to the attractions of women, and she was working hard to make certain that she neither said nor did anything to mislead him.

"I understand you have a Negro male with you." He watched her face closely, as if searching for a sign of something in it.

"At our farm," she corrected, "staying at our farm."

He smiled. "Of course." He ran his fingers slowly over the cat. "I would have to come out and inspect the premises," he said, turning to look out the window, developing his idea. "It would have to be after regular work. Perhaps tonight. You understand that."

"To inspect the farm. Yes. I understand that."

"Fine. Let me think about it." He was rubbing his hand over the cat in a nervous way.

Prophet was sitting on the ground in the Eddy garden, watching birds and ground squirrels and prairie chickens feeding along the edges of the cultivated land, his eyes roaming slowly over the place, feeling as if he were alone on the earth and it were the first day of creation.

Mrs. Eddy had called him to the back porch earlier to recite the names of the places on his traveling route, so Samuel could copy them down. Neither he nor the boy had felt comfortable doing it. But they didn't argue. He continued moving his gaze slowly over the garden.

Two gardens, really. One was a rectangular two acres of carefully tended vegetables, the early-spring growth marking the neatly ordered rows. The other, identical in shape but half the size, was filled with flowers of differing hues and forms.

The flowering plants were nicely mixed with fig trees, peaches, and pomegranates, the ground covered with thyme, rosemary, and boxwood. Around the edges were arbors for grapes, boysenberries, and raspberries. There was no question of the talent of the mind that had shaped all this. The garden had been cleverly designed to take advantage of layered plantings that filtered or captured the prairie light and warmth, depending on season and need.

Prophet balled a handful of rich loam, admiring the tattered remnants of the man's work. But talent didn't matter now. The garden was returning to nature, unruly and chaotic. Once the plants had been keeping happy company, but now they warred for crucial space and light, crowding and choking in a struggle to survive.

Prophet was eyeing this when he heard a shuffling sound on the garden path and turned to see the older Asian woman hurrying along carrying a basket, obviously intent on the early-season produce. She stopped and smiled at him, raising both her arms and flexing them like a circus strongman, then making a throaty laugh. She had done this same pantomime the night before when Pearl Eddy had introduced them. It embarrassed him, and he looked away. Then he heard the woman clucking her tongue in disapproval, and he glanced back at her. She was frowning at the wild masses of flowers.

"No good," she said. "Too nice. You are strong. We fix."

He nodded, but he had no interest in working with this little woman. He worked alone. He tossed the ball of dirt down and walked over to look at the garden's little graveyard.

"Thou shouldst not be in here."

Prophet looked back over his shoulder at Samuel's angry face. The boy was outside the garden, his hands gripping the top rail of the fence.

"The garden doesn't belong to either of thee, and thou shouldst leave it alone."

"Samuel," Pearl said in a firm voice. Earlier Prophet had seen her tossing corn to the hens, but he was surprised by her sudden appearance. She had a knack for being places—at the right and wrong times. "Mrs. Kishimoto and Mr. Prophet are guests."

Samuel stood his ground for a moment, slinging his schoolbooks in their leather strap over one shoulder and staring sullenly at Prophet; then he started for the road in his long stride. "Thy guests," he said, loud enough to hear.

"If thou wishest it, my guests. In my house. In my husband's garden. And thou wilt respect that."

For certain, she didn't accept much sass. But Prophet could tell she viewed discipline as a responsibility rather than something she enjoyed. Just when he thought she was done, she called, "Samuel," in a voice loud enough to ensure the boy heard.

Samuel stopped, his back turned to her. "Yes?"

"Dost thou understand?"

The boy hesitated, and Prophet wanted to crawl under the nearest bush. Even Mrs. Kishimoto had turned away, politely pretending she couldn't hear a word. That surprised him. He would have guessed she would be ogling the whole thing. Instead she was busying herself with garden matters.

"Yes."

"Good. When thou gettest home from school, thou canst assist Mrs. Kishimoto. She has some ideas for the garden."

The boy had started walking again.

"Samuel?"

"I heard thee."

"Good."

Suddenly the back door of the house burst open, and Zacharias popped out like a dark seed from an overripe melon. "Father's back! Father's back!" The boy was screaming and running toward his mother.

Prophet quickly busied himself with a small patch of weeds, glancing out the side of his eye at Samuel; the boy glared in his direction. Then the garden gate opened, and Zacharias jumped onto his back.

"Mr. Prophet's back too!"

Prophet stood and spun in circles, the boy clinging to his neck and laughing, Mrs. Kishimoto smiling happily. Prophet was careful not to look at Pearl.

"It's a miracle!" Zacharias yelled.

"Not a miracle, but certainly a wonder," Pearl said. Something in her voice made Prophet spin harder.

Though she undoubtedly knew for certain that he had stolen and then returned the photograph and what was left of the money, Pearl made no mention of it throughout the morning. He had planned to be impudent if she hit him with it, but she hadn't, and he doubted he could now because he had been put off by how politely she was behaving.

The day was warm and he was sweating as he worked at resetting some sagging posts in the garden fence. Mrs. Kishimoto had been hanging clothes on the line when she made a side trip to inspect his work, staring solemnly at the line of posts, nodding with satisfaction. It was easy to see she appreciated his labor. He liked that. But then she started teasing him again about his muscles, and he retreated toward the barn to search for roofing nails.

The woman rejoined Mrs. Eddy on the back porch, where they were washing clothes in a big kettle. She was talking fast and laughing. It was a pleasing sound. The little girls were playing with the baby in the dirt nearby; the Eddy boys were in school.

Prophet stepped inside the barn and let his eyes adjust to the dim shadows. He could hear the old horse moving in his stall and pigeons in the cool darkness of the rafters. The place smelled of hay and oats and leather. It was a good smell.

Moments later he saw the teenage girl looking for something in one of the big canvas bundles the family used to transport its belongings. He had met her the night before and nodded at her now. "Looking for nails," he said.

If she understood English, she made no attempt to respond. She just returned to her searching, the same sullen look on her face, snatching furtive glances at him as if she didn't trust him. Prophet ignored her, moving quickly toward some dusty shelves on the back wall where dirty jars and cans stood in rows. More than likely the nails he needed would be in one of them, he figured.

Prophet glanced briefly at the tiny old man, who was sitting cross-legged on a straw mat, his eyes closed. Prophet was getting on in years himself, but this old man looked ancient. A beautiful red robe was draped across his thin shoulders. Prophet was tiptoeing quietly so he wouldn't disturb him when somewhere outside he heard Hercules crow. He tensed and turned back to see if the rooster was following. That was what saved him.

The old man looked asleep, but Prophet caught a slight movement of his yellow hands. It telegraphed. He couldn't believe it. The little Chinaman had positioned his grip on the wooden staff. And Prophet knew instinctively what was coming.

Incredible as it seemed—even though he was expecting it—the blow took all his agility and quickness to avoid. It came at him so fast that Prophet sensed rather than actually saw the swing slashing ankle-high. The back cut was just as quick, and it too would have caught him had he not already leaped to safety. Then, with a final movement as rapidly deceptive as a magician's, the old man had the staff lying harmlessly in his lap.

"What the hell was that for?" Prophet hollered.

Kishimoto didn't move a muscle. Didn't even twitch. He looked like a sleeping lizard again—as if he had been asleep the entire morning. But Prophet figured he was squinting at him through his eyelashes. And he could tell something else. It wasn't a physical thing, but he was certain he saw it: The old man was stunned, stunned that he had missed at close range and with the advantage of surprise. It was apparent he wasn't used to missing. This made Prophet feel better. Even so, the attack confirmed what he already thought: These Chinamen were strange.

"Damn Chink," he mumbled under his breath.

When he looked up, he saw the girl watching him. She was surprised as well. The little man, he figured, must have been a big ankle slapper in the old country. And he had to admit if he hadn't read the movement of the hands correctly, he would have been nursing banged-up shins. But he had, and the crotchety old man was troubled by that fact. Prophet smiled.

He found the nails he wanted in an old coffee can, watching Kishimoto from the side of his eyes as he searched. This place was getting on his nerves. The Quaker woman was crazy enough to get them all killed, her son wanted him lynched, the rooster was determined to destroy him, and now this old man wanted to bust his legs with a damn stick.

He glared at Kishimoto. He'd had about enough. He would repair the roof, then be on his way. He started to walk way around the old man. Then he stopped. He would be damned if he would avoid a little Chinaman with a stick.

"You try that pole trick again I'll break it over your head."

The old man didn't respond.

"Understand? *Comprende?*"

Kishimoto looked dead.

"You've had fair warning," Prophet said sternly.

He took his time moving by the little man, just to let him know he wasn't afraid of him or his stick. He was feeling good, certain the old man had learned who was fastest.

Prophet froze.

The noise was familiar, and he was seized with the

214 _ THOMAS EIDSON

desire to flee, but before he could, he caught the full brunt of Hercules on his lower legs.

Prophet hollered, then broke for the door. The rooster was making good time behind him.

"Get him off. Get your damn bird off!"

"Mr. Prophet, I've asked thee not to swear," Pearl called from the porch.

"Call him off, Mrs. Eddy, or I'll wring his neck!"

Prophet leaned against the well house, his eyes fixed on old man Kishimoto. The little Japanese had been sitting next to the barn like a stone statuette for the past hour, close to the building but not touching it, as if simply using it to protect his backside from a surprise attack. "Lunatic," Prophet muttered.

The tiny man was cross-legged and stiff-backed on his little reed mat, his hands gripping his ever-present stick, his eyes closed. He looked like a desiccated mummy trying to ambush flies.

"Crackpot," Prophet mumbled.

Pearl and the woman were in the kitchen cooking, the sounds and smells drifting across the yard, while Hercules lounged in the shade of a large bush with his harem. Prophet shook his head. They all were crazy.

But he was crazier for having come back when Lacy and Tyrone needed him. He promised himself he would remedy that after the evening meal. He straightened up and stretched, concerned that he was getting out of shape. Then he heard a noise and turned to see Joshua shoot through the garden hedge, running as if the devil were a half step behind and gaining.

"Josh?" Prophet called. The boy didn't break stride as he disappeared around the corner of the house.

Prophet was just turning back when Luke broke through the leaves, emitting low cries of terror. He followed his brother, dodging Prophet's arms.

The bushes trembled again, and Samuel's head appeared, followed by Zacharias's, the boy clinging to his brother's neck. Samuel tried to dodge around Prophet, but the man was having none of it. He grabbed Samuel by the shoulders and forced him to stop.

"Let go!"

"What's wrong?"

Samuel was just getting ready to answer when the bushes trembled yet again. The lad wasn't the ugliest boy Prophet had ever seen, but he could have been runner-up, with dirty yellow hair and pocked skin. He was thick and coarse-looking. He came to a quick halt when he saw Prophet's hard features and was quickly joined by three others, all about sixteen and tough-looking. From their clothes, Prophet guessed town kids.

"Help you boys?"

Hector James took a moment to reply. "Watch who you're calling boy," he snapped, trying to screw up some courage. "My pa and brothers don't tolerate niggers smart-talking me."

"Unless you've got proper business, son, get off the Eddy property."

Hector squinted hard at Samuel. "We got business, don't we, Sammy-girl? But it can wait." The squint turned into a grin that wasn't friendly.

Samuel didn't say anything. Though scared, Zacharias stuck his tongue out at them. Prophet liked him for that.

"You brave boys run along now." He took a step forward, and the four of them hopped back as if they thought he might be contaminated with some deadly virus.

"Don't threaten me, old blackie," Hector shot back.

Prophet didn't answer right away. He just stood

looking at the boy. Finally, he said, "Son, my name's Prophet. I'm not one for ceremony, but you call me mister from now on. That clear?" He stared hard at the boy's face for a moment, then continued. "One more thing. You gang up on these boys I'll be as hard as goose crap to get off. You tell your pa and brothers that."

Hector started to lip something, then looked at the scars, the mangled ear, the hard eyes and thought better of it and ducked out through the hedge. His friends followed.

Prophet swung Zacharias up onto his back. He could feel him trembling. Samuel was watching the hedge as if he expected a buffalo to charge through at any moment.

"What happened?"

"Nothing," Samuel said, turning and heading for the garden gate.

"Something did."

Samuel whirled around. "We don't need thy help. What thou didst is just going to cause more trouble." He started back toward the house. "Thou dost not belong here."

Prophet set Zacharias on the ground.

"I want thee to stay," the boy said, looking up at him. "I rubbed that horse—and thou came back."

Prophet nodded. "Go tell Josh and Luke I want to see them."

"Keep it up—up, up!" Prophet was saying some fifteen minutes later. "Keep poking it out. Keep it in his face. Jab and jab and jab."

He was behind Joshua, holding the boy's arms up in a boxer's stance, then shoving his left forward hard and sharp. Luke and Zacharias were watching and practicing their own jabs, while Samuel was sitting on

Jack's corral watching. The twins had been through the mill: black eyes, lips split and bruised.

"That ain't going to stop anyone," Joshua said, carefully moving his swollen lips. "Just sticking my arm out like that ain't going to stop anybody."

"No. But it'll drive them to distraction." Prophet straightened up and let go of Joshua's arms, then wiped the sweat from his bald head with a rag.

They were behind the barn, the three boys stripped to the waist, their skin white like toad bellies. Their mother kept a tight rein on them. It was a shame. They weren't sissies, just made to look that way.

"I don't see how distraction is going to save me," Joshua protested. "Just get them madder."

"Like a fly keeps bothering you," Prophet said, moving his left hand around and over, behind and under Joshua's face, the boy's eyes following it.

"That fly gets you distracted," he continued, bringing a slow, soft left toward Joshua's chin. The boy moved to block it. "And you forget certain other things," Prophet said.

"Like?"

"Like," he said, bringing his second huge fist over Joshua's dropped guard to the boy's exposed chin and tapping it gently, "where that fly's right is."

Joshua grinned and Zacharias laughed with glee, and they went back to practicing their lefts with more vigor. Everybody but Prophet noticed Mr. Kishimoto. He was standing behind the Negro, holding his shiny stick, watching intently.

Strangest of all, Samuel thought, the old man seemed genuinely interested in the boxing lesson. Every once in a while he would raise one of his legs in a high step, then put it back down, as if he were limbering up. There was a glint in his sharp eyes, and he was obviously enjoying himself.

Then Prophet stepped backward and said, "Okay, let's try—" He hadn't finished the sentence when Kishimoto took a couple of quick hopping steps and let him have it with the stick across the back of his shoulders.

The sheer force of the blow knocked Prophet forward, and he bellowed and rolled in a somersault across the ground. Rapidly he was up and facing Kishimoto—ready to fight. The boys scattered.

The old man was taking his giant, high steps, moving back and forth, positioning himself against Prophet, looking for an opening, his stick held menacingly in his hands.

"You old fool bastard," Prophet hollered. "You're loony, but I'm going to give it to you anyway!"

Prophet began to circle the little man, forcing him to turn, feinting rushes and then continuing to circle. They were like two oddly matched gladiators, carefully taking each other's measure. The yard was quiet. Hercules stood at the corner of the barn watching, as if he might try to catch the Negro off guard himself.

Prophet was just about to lunge when he heard, "Mr. Prophet! What is going on?"

"Ask him!"

Pearl Eddy was tapping her cane fast and looking as upset as Prophet had ever seen her. He figured the old man saw this as well since he wasn't pursuing his attack any longer.

Pearl was moving her hands quickly over the boys' faces and bare upper bodies. Her fingertips carefully noted swollen eyes and puffed lips.

"When did this happen?"

"After school," Joshua said.

She paused. "Ye were attacked?"

"Yes," the three of them said in rough unison.

"And ye fought back?"

The boys looked sick. "Yes. Zach, Josh, and I did," Luke said.

Prophet waited for her to console them. She didn't.

"Get your clothes on. And since ye have such abundant energy, ye can clean the chicken shed before dinner." She paused. "And after dinner I will have other more constructive things for ye to use thy energy on."

The boys trudged off around the corner of the barn. Samuel hopped down from the fence and started after them. His mother heard him.

"Samuel."

"I wasn't involved," he said quickly, raising his hands as if in surrender.

"Thou allowed whatever was going on here to happen. And thou art the eldest."

Samuel stopped and looked at her, his face turning red. "And Mr. Prophet is thy guest. I figured thou wouldst let him do whatever he wished."

Pearl stood still, her face dead white in the evening light. The boy scuffed at the dirt with the toe of his shoe.

"I shall talk with thee in the house," she said quietly.

Samuel looked sick.

She turned back to face Prophet, but in her anger she had forgotten where he was standing and stood talking to the open prairie. "What wert thou doing with the children?"

"Talking about boxing, ma'am."

She corrected her stance so she was pointed toward him. "Talk is not what I heard."

"You mean when you walked around the barn?"

"Yes."

He fidgeted.

"Mr. Prophet."

"The old man jumped me with his stick, Mrs. Eddy."

Pearl stood contemplating what he had just said. Then she straightened up some. "Thou wouldst have me believe that Mr. Kishimoto attacked thee?"

"Yes." Prophet looked for him, but the little man was gone. Smart little bastard.

"Why would he do that?"

"I don't know why—just that he's crazy."

She stood thinking. "That is what thou said about Hercules—that thou did not know why he attacked thee and that he was crazy. Is that not right?"

"They're both crazy."

Pearl crossed her arms and shook her head slowly as if he were a hopeless soul. Prophet didn't care for her look of weary authority.

"It's the truth, ma'am," he said.

"And thou wert teaching the children to fight? What possesses thee to do such things?"

"To defend themselves," he said, thinking that sounded better.

Pearl took a deep breath. "To harm others."

"That's one way to put it."

"Is there really another, Mr. Prophet?"

"Like I said, ma'am, to defend themselves."

"It is the same. Absolutely the same. And I will not have it."

He shrugged. "Suit yourself, Mrs. Eddy."

When she next spoke, her voice was quiet, but there was no mistaking her resolve. "Thou wilt not teach my children violence, Mr. Prophet. Is that perfectly clear?"

"Ma'am, what do you think happens to them out there?"

"Nothing that justifies violence." She hesitated. "Is what I have said clear to thee?"

"You felt their faces; they've got black eyes, scrapes, and busted lips."

"I know the problems of my children," she said. "Now please answer my question. Is what I have said clear to thee?"

"With respect, ma'am, it's balderdash."

"Mr. Prophet, I know what it means to be different."

"This isn't about being different. I'm different. This is about being bullied and beaten."

"Do we understand each other, sir?"

He watched her for a moment, letting his anger cool. "They're your boys. But it's a shame."

"Thank thee for thy concern, but it is what we believe." She paused. "I have spoken to their teacher many times. But it has done no good. I shall try again."

"That'll just make it worse."

"Thou meanest well, Mr. Prophet. But it is what we believe."

"What you believe, Mrs. Eddy."

"I am the children's mother, sir." She paused. "I have a responsibility for their upbringing."

"Yes," he muttered, implying something else.

The argument had taken more out of her than Prophet had figured, and she turned now, disoriented, and started to walk into the side of the barn. He grabbed her arm and guided her around the corner. When he got her repositioned, he released her elbow but stood ready to grab her again in case she started to walk into something else. She didn't.

She moved out into the evening sunshine, her face empty of emotion, but appearing deep in what looked to be a worrying thought. Probably trying to figure some way to make certain her boys couldn't protect themselves. He wanted to say "handcuffs," but something in her unsteady stride kept him from it.

* * *

Pearl knew that Jerome Prophet was right. The belief was her own. She had forced her will on the children, allowed them to be harmed because she believed as she did. She climbed the steps of the back porch slowly, her mind mulling this troubling matter. Then she stopped. No. It was not just her belief. It was the will and the word of God. She was simply a tool. She would not turn her back on that. Matthew had not. And she would not, even though the pain of her boys tore at her heart.

Prophet kicked at a stone, his mind worrying the thing he hadn't admitted to the woman. Not fighting back caused the boys to be bullied, but there was more. He and the Asiatics had made them bigger targets. It was that simple. Samuel was right.

He was just deciding he would hang around no more than another day or two to see that the boys weren't ganged up on when he caught a blurring motion out of the side of his eye. He grabbed instinctively at the movement and caught the old man's staff in the middle. He yanked. Then yanked again, surprised by the force it took to wrench it from the little man.

Stripped of his weapon, Kishimoto went into a strange fighting crouch, his hands open and stiff like little meat cleavers. Prophet glared into his wrinkled face. If the tiny man had been surprised the night before when he missed hitting him, he was stunned now that Prophet had disarmed him, his beady eyes focusing with a slightly confused expression.

"I warned you," Prophet bellowed.

Kishimoto seemed beyond speech.

"Didn't I warn you?"

The old man was moving his hands and arms in a

strange flowing motion that looked graceful and yet funny, as if he were playacting.

"Knock it off or I'll break your damn stick," Prophet yelled.

Still, the old man continued his strange pantomime of movements.

"Okay. You asked for it!" Prophet brought his knee up and the stick down with a powerful jerk, then tossed the broken pieces at the man's feet.

"There! Now don't ever hit me with a stick again, don't even look at me, or next time I'll break it over your skull. Understand?"

Kishimoto's eyes were glued on Prophet, his hands and arms moving in their strange gyrations. Then suddenly he yelled, "Ei!" and flew forward with a kick of his sandaled feet that just missed Prophet's chin.

"You crazy old bastard!" Prophet yelled, surprised by the accuracy and height of the kick.

Kishimoto was back in his silly crouch again; then suddenly, in a move that Prophet hadn't even remotely anticipated, this tiny warrior sprang through the air, feet first, with another savage thrust at his bald head.

Though caught off guard, Prophet was still on the defense and managed to catch him in midair, feeling at once that he was all bone, tendon, and hard muscle and realizing that he had the quick reflexes of youth.

At least twenty years his junior and a good hundred pounds heavier, Prophet was still struggling to subdue him, the man squirming wildly out of one hold after another. Each time he freed an arm or a leg, Kishimoto thumped him a blow to the neck or the head, the last one a blast that caused Prophet to see sparks and the sky to go suddenly dark.

The Negro shook it off, shocked the old man had the power to stun him. Then he put a headlock on the wild little Japanese, dragged him to a nearby water trough, and tripped him so that he fell inside. He disappeared under the water. But in a flash he was up and sputtering; then he gave Prophet a hard smash to the nose with the palm of his hand that started blood flowing.

Until now Prophet had been trying not to hurt him. But he was hurriedly rethinking his options.

"That's enough gawddamn it!" he bellowed, diving in on top of the little warrior, who at the moment looked like a half-dead rodent. The weight of Prophet's body carried both of them under the water.

Ten minutes later it was over. Prophet almost had to drown the old Japanese into submission. Even then Kishimoto hadn't surrendered. He had just flopped to the side of the water trough, vomited, and then tried to get into his fighting stance and slipped on the algae, falling back under the water.

Afraid that he might really drown and that Pearl Eddy would blame him, Prophet yanked the old man up and tossed him out onto the dirt, then crawled out himself and limped off, gasping for breath and amazed at what it had taken to subdue this tiny man. He was crazy. But he was also a fighter. But what was he fighting for? Prophet had no answers. All he knew was that at an earlier time he must have been a holy terror.

As he rounded the corner of the barn, Prophet heard squishing behind him, and he whirled back, fists clenched, ready for round three. But there wasn't to be a third round.

When he saw Prophet, the old man stopped trotting and looked at him with his fierce countenance, then bowed. It was a deep bow that carried respect and obedience. Prophet didn't know what to do, wondering if it was a trick. He didn't trust anything about this man.

"Leave me alone," he said, speaking slowly so the man would understand. Kishimoto bowed again. "Good," Prophet said. "Just leave me alone."

Night was falling, and rain was coming. Prophet was on a ladder trimming the wisteria on the front porch and figuring he would leave—the urge growing in him to get back to hunting for Lacy and Tyrone—when a carriage he didn't recognize drove in behind the house. Five minutes later the front door swung open, and he ducked forward into the wisteria. The way things had been going in this town, he figured hiding in bushes was smart.

He could hear Mrs. Eddy. Carefully he parted the plants and peeked. She was on the porch not five feet away, while a pinched-faced little man stood rubbing his hands and ogling her.

"Yes. The loans are past due, Mr. Snipes. And yes, Matthew used the farm to secure them. But I must tell thee again. I do not have the money." She paused. "We are having some difficulties."

Blood was suddenly pounding hard in Prophet's head, surging through his body until he was hot and sweaty. He was a fool. Things he should have understood he hadn't. The leaky roof. The banged-up windows and doors. The lack of food. The bad shoes. Clothes too old and sizes too small. All were there like righteous testimony. The woman wasn't a miser or a liar. She was broke.

"As Mr. Johnson told thee, I had half the money last week, but much of that has been lost."

The man asked how much she had.

"One hundred and one dollars and twenty cents."

Prophet pressed his eyes and lips closed. "I had

half, but much of that has been lost." The words hammered on his skull. The $101.20 was, to the penny, the amount he had returned with the picture. The rest he had lost in the poker game. He felt sick.

She was talking again. "Yes, I am a widow, sir. But married in my heart."

Prophet's eyes jumped to Snipes. The man continued to examine Pearl in the same hungry way. Then with a jack-in-the-box motion, he sprang forward on his toes, pushed his pouty lips out, and kissed Pearl's forehead. Caught by surprise, she turned away. The man scurried after her.

"Mr. Snipes, please." Pearl frowned. "Thou must control thyself. Or I must ask thee to leave."

"You don't think I'd suit you?" he whined. "I don't see why not. You need to remember. There is a limit to the number of men who want a blind woman. Caring for them is too great."

"I'm certain I would be a tremendous burden, sir," Pearl said, steadily tapping her foot on the porch boards. "But that is of no concern since I have no intention of marrying."

"Marrying doesn't have to be a consideration," he said, licking his lips, "as long as certain wifely duties are discharged." He stepped up close behind her and put his small, bony hands on her shoulders. He was sucking in little gasps of air. "Nothing would give me greater pleasure than granting you the loan . . . if you could see your way clear to—"

Pearl stepped away from Snipes's grasp.

Seeing the extreme discomfort on her face, Prophet moved his hands in front of him like a swimmer, sweeping the green tangles aside until his head and shoulders were suddenly, ominously visible in the flickering lamplight of the porch.

So amorously intent was Snipes on Pearl he didn't

see the Negro right away, but then something in the shadows caught his eye, and he glanced up into the forbidding face, Prophet glaring down like some mad demon out of hell. Seemingly as an alternative to fainting, Snipes uttered a shrill, unnatural sound and stumbled backward through the doorway and into the house. The porch was suddenly silent.

"Mr. Snipes?" Pearl called, turning slowly and listening for the man. "Mr. Snipes? Art thou all right?"

Prophet heard the back door slam and then the carriage rattling out of the yard. He let the vines close over his face, glad he had sent Snipes packing but upset about the stolen money and what he had done to this woman.

For a moment he thought about making up her loss with Lacy and Tyrone's providing money. But he forced himself to stop thinking like that. He was willing to do a lot of things in this life, but that wasn't one of them.

Prophet was slowly crawling down the ladder, step by careful step, deep in thought about these matters, when Pearl Eddy whirled toward him.

"Hello?" she called.

He froze, trying not to jiggle the vines.

"Mr. Snipes?"

He was becoming an expert on Pearl Eddy, and he knew that once having heard him, she wasn't going to quit. She knew somebody was in the wisteria, and she would probably guess who in a moment. He didn't know how she did such things; she just did. He shrugged his shoulders.

"Just me, Mrs. Eddy. Coming to prune the vines." He stepped down off the last step of the ladder. "But I can see it's a bad time. I'll do it in the morning." He was quickly folding up the ladder.

"Mr. Prophet, is Mr. Snipes with thee?"

"No, ma'am. I think he had to go back to town."

"Really? How strange."

He watched her tapping down the front steps. Damn.

"Mr. Prophet," she called at the bottom of the stairs, stopping and turning her head to listen for him. "Mr. Prophet?"

He wanted to slip away, but she had him in earshot, and that meant she had him. "Yes, Mrs. Eddy?" He stuffed his hands in his pockets, looking down at the ground, and rocked back and forth over his large feet.

She tapped over to him.

"Evening, ma'am."

"Mr. Prophet, I have the solution." The words sounded as if she were holding some holy revelation in her hands.

"Mrs. Eddy?"

"Thy children. I was certain there had to be a better way."

"Ma'am?"

"I've determined a way thou canst search without having to walk such distances."

He straightened up, interested.

"It is not efficient," she continued, "the way thou art doing it, no. But this new way will reach the towns . . . and do so every day." She bit at her lower lip, struggling to control her enthusiasm.

"It will greatly increase thy chances of finding thy children." She hesitated. He knew she wasn't comfortable with exaggeration of any kind, and she stood for a moment lost in thought, weighing, he guessed, what she had just said for its truthfulness. "Yes. I'm certain of it," she said finally.

He was listening closely now, studying her face to see if she was simply gathering moonbeams again. She didn't look it.

"How, ma'am?"

"Thou walked in the past because thou weren't settled."

"Ma'am?"

"Thou had no permanent address."

"I just walked."

"Yes," she said, focused hard on her idea. "But now thou dost."

"Mrs. Eddy?"

"Our farm. Thou canst use our farm as thy address." She was looking pleased as if this simple thing, an address, were somehow the one and only barrier to finding the children.

He didn't see it that way and frowned. "Thank you, ma'am," he said, still feeling bad about her lost money and not wanting to hurt her feelings on top of it.

She crossed her arms over her breasts, obviously well satisfied with her idea. "We will write to each town on thy route. We will contact the postmaster, the sheriff, the newspaper editor and tell them about thy children, providing their full names, nicknames, giving physical descriptions, and anything else thou believest is important."

He frowned again, filled with disappointment. "Why would they care?"

"Sir?"

"Those white folks, Mrs. Eddy. Negro kids, that's what they'd say." He wiped sweat off his upper lip. "Excusing the liberty, ma'am, they aren't likely to do much."

She surprised him with a small smile. "They will, sir."

He shook his head, not agreeing. "Why?"

She looked serious again. "First, because we are on God's own mission."

Prophet scratched his head. "God's mission? Two black children?"

"Absolutely, Mr. Prophet. God wants thee reunited with thy children." She had pursed her lips and was nodding up and down in a purposeful way. "Thou must believe that."

He rubbed a finger up and down the side of his nose, growing concerned over the practicality of her mind. He should have figured that was predictable. "Any other reason you can think of that they might help?"

"Yes."

"Which is?"

"We will offer recompense."

"Recompense?"

"Yes."

"Recompense?"

"Yes. Money. This afternoon in town I was told by Sheriff Haines and the county attorney, Mr. Johnson, that one hundred dollars are standard payment in such matters."

He looked shocked. "One hundred dollars? For what?"

"As payment to whoever helps us find the children. And another fifty dollars to the sheriff, postmaster, or newspaper person who passes the information to us."

His look of shock had not diminished. "Let me get this straight, Mrs. Eddy. We're going to shell out one hundred and fifty bucks to some white folks who send us a telegram or letter and tell us they've seen a couple of black kids, about the look and age of Lacy and Tyrone, running around down South. Is that the deal?"

"No. We will release the money when we and the bank are satisfied that we have found thy children."

"The bank?"

Pearl waited a moment before she said, "The First American Bank of Kansas City. Mr. Johnson, the county attorney, has suggested that it is nationally known and can serve as the bonding institution."

"Bonding institution?"

"I have been told that we cannot simply send a notice out, that it would not be taken with the degree of seriousness required. We must demonstrate that our offer of a reward is guaranteed by a legitimate financial institution." She looked as if she might stop; then she said in a quieter voice, "We will post fifty dollars with the bank and sign a promissory note for the remainder."

She waited a moment; then, as if she were telling him some great secret of the evolving universe, said, "Mr. Prophet, walking isn't effective. Dost thou not agree?" She had lost where he was standing and was staring off intently into the dark tangles of the wisteria, waiting for his answer. "Mr. Prophet?"

He didn't respond.

"Time passes as thou walkest. People forget. It is just too chancy."

She was maybe more practical than he had at first thought. But he didn't like this idea of hers any better for it. It wouldn't work. And she didn't have the money. And what he had—Lacy and Tyrone's providing money—he wasn't about to risk like this. Some smart white folks would just figure a way to fleece him, never helping find the children.

He shook his head. White people—whether sheriffs, newspapermen, or postmen—weren't going to set off searching the South for two colored kids. Not for a hundred dollars, or two hundred. He was convinced of it. His training camp idea was still the best way to find them.

"I don't have the recompense," he mumbled. "You don't either, ma'am."

Pearl looked up in his direction, pressed her lips together in a tight smile, and then said, "Whatever we must do, Mr. Prophet, we must do." Her expression was rapt. "After that we will trust in the Lord." She paused. "He will provide. I promise thee."

Prophet wasn't hearing her anymore, and he scarcely saw her. He was remembering another promise, the one about Lacy's flowers, and hurting. As he looked now at Pearl and thought about the past, a trick of the light in his tired old eyes reminded him of Lacy and the way she looked that last night.

Chapter Ten

It was pitch-dark in the messy bedroom when Alfred Snipes rolled over and opened his eyes, the fire having died in the corner stove, the air cold to a point where he could see his own breath. From the heavy silence, he could tell it wasn't more then two or three in the morning, and he wondered what had awakened him. He was trembling but knew it wasn't from the cold. He just didn't know why. Perhaps it was a result of his frightening encounter with the Negro the evening before.

The deep purring of his cat on the pillow next to him was at once both comforting and sedating. Slowly the fear ebbed, and he yawned and rolled onto his side, draping a thin forearm across the animal.

Suddenly something rewoke Alfred Snipes. He sat bolt upright in bed, his eyes probing the darkness surrounding him, his heart lunging in his chest. He had been dreaming about Mrs. Eddy's Negro. He was certain of it, the man leaping at him beastlike out of half-closed doors, alleyways, dark corners, the bank vault, everywhere. He rubbed his eyes. Nothing but shadows. But something had awakened him.

Still groggy, he wondered if he was continuing to dream, and he reached blindly for the candle on the nightstand. His hand submerged in a bowl of cold water. He jerked it away, the bowl rocking precariously.

"Don't spill it," a man's voice warned.

He began to shake harder. His first thought, one that worried him almost every night, was that someone had come to rob the bank, to murder him for his keys to the cash boxes.

"Who is it?" His voice broke from the fear.

Silence.

"What do you want?"

Still no response. But he did hear a chair scrape on the floor. Snipes shoved his bare legs out of the covers and sat up on the edge of the bed. "I'll holler," he threatened.

"And I'll cut your throat."

Snipes froze, then fumbled with a match, the small flare briefly illuminating three shadowy, masked shapes before his trembling fingers dropped the flame and darkness flooded back into the room.

"Don't light another match."

Snipes tried to control his fear. "What do you want?"

"You hear? Not stupid things like lighting matches."

Snipes didn't respond, just wet the sheets. Then he began to whine, a low, shrill cry that was building slowly into a scream for help.

The man's fist caught the little banker high on the forehead, slamming his skull back hard into the wall. Snipes was on his back, propped up on his elbows, and looking in a dazed way at the man who had hit him. He had quit whining.

"Let me explain the rules, cousin. You say anything other than answer what you're asked, anything, and I'm going to give you to these men to kill. They're eager to do it. I'm not. That's my promise. I'm like your guardian angel. But if you light another match, I'll put

it out in your eyes. Or if you holler, I give you to them."
The man waited a few moments, listening to Snipes's
frightened breathing, then asked, "Understand?"

"Don't hurt me," Snipes pleaded. "I'll give you the
keys to the safe. Just don't hurt me."

The hand came swinging out of the darkness again
and slapped him hard across the face, his hair flying
from the blow.

"Listen. I'm going to explain it to you once more.
This is between you and me. So listen carefully. If you
don't get it, they're going to kill you." There was a
shocked silence for a few moments; then the man went
on. "You say anything other than answer me, these
two guys are going to stick things in you until every
porcupine in a hundred miles will be making eyes at
you."

"The safe—" Snipes sputtered.

The hand came out of the darkness and slapped
him, harder this time, loosening a tooth and causing
his mouth to fill with blood.

"You're dense as a doorstop. We aren't interested."

"What then?"

The hand slapped him again. "What's it going to
take to get you to shut your gawddamn trap."

Snipes was sniveling hard. But he kept his mouth
shut.

"Smart fella. You got any more brilliant things to
say?"

He didn't answer.

"Shit!" the man said, then slapped him again.
"Smart guy. I asked you a question."

Snipes was moaning and crying and spitting out
blood. "What—what?"

"You got any more brilliant things to say?"

"No!"

"Good. Now sit up and put your finger in the water."

"Huh?"

"Shit! You hit him," the man said to one of the two men behind him. "My hand's starting to hurt."

"No!" Snipes pleaded, raising an arm to protect his face, and sitting up and jabbing an index finger into the bowl of water.

"Maybe not dumb like a doorstop. Maybe like a toad."

The men laughed. Then the one talking continued. "Now this is real simple, cuz. It's a test. Just to check things you tell us. It's smart to pass it. I'm telling you that 'cause, like I said, I'm your angel. You with me?"

"Yes!" Snipes squealed.

"Brilliant," the man said. "Now here's how it works. You hold your finger straight up and down in the water. Don't let the tip touch the bottom. If we catch you touching the bottom, we'll just chop off a little so you won't have that nasty problem of it being too long. Got it?"

"Yes!" Snipes said quickly.

"You're getting smarter. Now shut your eyes. I'm going to strike a light." He watched Snipes jerk his head to the side and snap his eyes shut.

"I guess I don't have to tell you what will happen if you peek."

Snipes shook his head hard.

"Good."

The man put a match to the wick of a candle, the glow casting a small circle of wavering light, illuminating three men wearing Indian headgear over painted leather masks. The one who had been talking stood looking down at Snipes's hand. Then he glanced over at the little man's head; one of his eyes was puffing, and blood was running in a trickle from the corner of his mouth.

"This ain't going to work if you shake all the time. That's the whole damn point of this. You ain't supposed to shake."

"Okay! Okay!" Snipes sniveled.

"Tut-tut. Cuz. I didn't ask you any question. Shit. I ought to punish you, but I'll let it slide."

Snipes strained to control the quivering of his arm. The three men crowded around and stared at the water in the bowl. Finally, the talker said, "Okay. First question. Easy one. You ever heard of the Royal Order of Redmen?"

Snipes nodded hard.

"You got to answer with your mouth and keep your arm still."

"Yes!"

The three men bent over the water, studying the ripples.

"Was he lying?"

"Yeah."

"No! No!" Snipes cried.

The man slapped him hard on the top of his head. "Only when we ask a question, dumb shit." He looked back at the water's surface. "I'm not certain. I think he was telling the truth. He's just scared shitless. Water didn't move much. We'll use that as the test."

"I think he was lying."

"Okay. Let's ask him something else. Is this town called Zella?"

"Yes!"

"See," the man said. "I've done this before. It's about the same amount of ripples. Good."

The man glanced to see Snipes wasn't peeking. "Remember, finger off the bottom. Okay. The woman who came into the bank this morning."

"What woman?"

"Tut-tut, cuz. Only when I ask a question. Otherwise you mess up the water and get blood all over. The Quaker. Remember?"

"Yes."

"Why was she there?"

"Loan. She came for a loan."

The men watched the water and nodded to one another.

"And that's why you went out to her farm?"

"Yes. To inspect it."

"Did you?"

"What? Did I what?"

"Inspect the farm?"

Snipes hesitated, then said, "Yes!"

"Whooops," the man said, leaning closer over the bowl. "Let me ask that again, bright boy. Did you inspect the farm?"

"No!" Snipes snapped. "I went to, but I got run off."

"She wants a loan but runs you off her property?"

"Not her. Her Negro."

The man nodded. "So the old black massa is still there, huh? Armed?"

"I didn't see."

"What's the woman buying that she needs a loan?"

"Nothing."

"Nothing? She just borrows money. What is she, a collector?" The men laughed.

"She's near bankrupt," he moaned. "Past due on two loans. Bank holds the paper. She wants a new loan to pay off the old ones. To buy time."

"You lying?"

"No!"

The man bent down close over the water, looking at it from the side. "You jiggled some."

"I'm telling you the truth! She's out of money."

"You give her the loan?"

"No."

"Smart." He nodded a few times before asking, "How long before you foreclose?"

Snipes shrugged his shoulders and got slapped again.

"Listen, smart boy. Talk, don't shake your head. Now try again. When do you foreclose?"

"I could now, but the county attorney is all over me not to. And he's on the bank's board."

"Foreclose on her."

"What if she pays off the loans?"

The man lunged forward and grabbed Snipes by the throat and squeezed hard on his trachea. "Listen, I'm tired of standing in this room smelling your piss and dancing with you. Foreclose on the woman. How long will it take?"

Snipes sat drooling blood and gasping for breath.

"I asked a question."

"I've got to file with the county." He gagged and then quickly said, "Post her property."

"How long?"

"Thirty to forty days."

"Get it done."

One of the two men standing behind the talker said, "Go ahead, ask him." He was chortling about something.

The three of them laughed together. Then the talker said, "Oh, yeah. One more. Your finger touching?"

"No," Snipes said quickly.

"Good, cuz. Here it is. What are you going to do with your cat?"

Not understanding, Snipes started to shake his head, then caught himself and said, "What do you mean?"

"What are you going to do with your cat? Simple question."

"Feed her?" Snipes ventured.

The man slapped him again. "That's a lie. Answer me."

"I don't know—walk her, let her outside! What kind of a question is that?"

The men were laughing and moving toward the bedroom door. "The right answer, Mr. Banker, is bury it."

The three of them stood in the deep shadows next to the side of Snipes's small white house, doubled up with laughter, listening to the man inside crying over his dead cat. Then the talker pulled his leather mask off and slipped it beneath his shirt. "Let's get out of here," Penny James said.

Mr. Kishimoto was grating on Prophet's nerves, following him everywhere, even to the outhouse. He would shuffle along in his baggy robes and sandals as if he were on some important mission, as if he and Prophet were a team. Nothing Prophet did seemed to discourage him.

At the moment Kishimoto was sitting on the ground, dozing as Prophet dug the earth. He was digging where Eiko had told him to. The day was warm, and Prophet was sweating and thinking that it had been three days since he had run the little banker off. He hoped he hadn't ruined the deal for Mrs. Eddy.

Eiko hurried down the garden path carrying a wooden bucket of "manure tea" that Prophet had made under her careful instruction. She had been fussing over the plants all morning long. Inside this garden world she was boss; she knew about growing things. She was a barefoot despot ordering him,

Fumiko, her girls, and the Eddy boys back and forth as she organized the work. The only one she left alone was her arrogant father-in-law.

Prophet actually liked what Eiko was making him do. He was learning some new things, like how to make liquid fertilizer by filling burlap bags with one part chicken manure, one part horse manure, one part rotting compost, and, finally, some ground-up dry fish that Eiko carried in a bag. They soaked the mixture in a large trough of water overnight, and in the morning there was a nice yellow fertilizer for the young plants.

He had also learned to build slug traps by cutting openings in old coffee cans whose bottoms had been filled with a solution of jelly and water. Once they were ready, the two of them sank the cans up to the opening in the ground. The next morning they found dozens of dead slugs inside each can. She knew some things. He liked that. He liked to learn. Especially practical tasks.

Eiko was hurrying by him again. He had stopped digging and stood leaning against his shovel, catching his breath.

"Not difficult. Not difficult." She smiled at him.

He ignored her. That was her answer to everything. But this was his fourth bed of mounded earth, and he was beginning to tire. He watched Fumiko trotting by with two buckets suspended from the ends of a pole she carried over her shoulder. She reminded him of a young river oak, tall and straight and strong. Though a girl, she would soon enough be a handsome woman. She had been moving back and forth like this for a couple of hours. Like her mother, she was a work-horse, though unlike her mother, she never smiled. He was still leaning against his shovel as Eiko moved by him again.

"You not lazy, earth not lazy," she said in a bright voice.

"Thanks," he said. "But I'm tired of digging."

"We want a happy garden."

"Sure. Sure."

"The earth is hard. Water stands, roots drown. Need home where roots grow deep and plants are strong like you. So work." She beamed at him. "Sky, earth, and people—everyone *hataraku*. Work."

He ignored her, putting his foot on the blade of the shovel and pushing it deep into the soil. He motioned with his head toward the old man. "Why does he follow me around like a dog?"

She just giggled.

"Great," Prophet said. "Tell him to leave me alone."

"You tell him. He doesn't listen to me."

"I tried."

She shrugged as if she had lost interest in this brief conversation about her father-in-law and pointed to the mound of freshly turned earth. "Not difficult. Not difficult."

He went back to digging. They had been working steadily since sunup. Pearl had brought them cool drinks and a noon meal. She was still acting coldly reserved around him. He guessed it was over the boxing lessons.

He didn't agree with her. The world was a dangerous place, where a man had to watch out and protect what was his. But she was flexible as an anvil. It seemed a heavy burden on these boys. Proof of just how heavy came an hour later, when the four of them trudged into the yard after school.

Joshua had a cut cheek, and Luke had a large mouse puffing under an eye. Zacharias was limping. Even Samuel was sporting a bruised lip. They were standing near their father's grave, glancing from it to the vegetable garden. There was a lost look about them as they stood, bruised and battered, in the tangle of weeds and flowering plants.

"Going to work the flowers for a while," he called to the woman.

"Not difficult. Not difficult," she said. "Strong man. When you are done, you come back. *Isogu*. Hurry."

As soon as he started down the path toward the boys, the old man hopped up and trotted after him like an obedient terrier.

He looked at the battered kids. "Rough day?"

The three younger boys nodded.

"What do you say we clean this place up?"

Samuel turned and walked away.

"Sam?" Prophet called.

The boy didn't answer.

Zacharias came over, and Prophet picked him up in his arms. "Sammy's got to take Ma on her rounds. That's how we make our living."

"I see."

"But," Zacharias confided, "I don't think we can fix the garden. Sam says it's too late."

Prophet eyed him for a moment, then said, "Nothing is ever too late." He ruffled the boy's curly hair. "What happened to your leg?"

The boy looked away. "Nothing."

"Maybe that's what you tell your mother—but not me."

He looked back into Prophet's face. "Harry Adams kicked me."

"Why?"

The boy looked past him to Mr. Kishimoto; the old man was standing with his bandy legs spread and his hands on his hips, looking like some sort of toy soldier on guard duty. Zacharias leaned close to Prophet's ear and whispered, "What's he doing?"

"I don't know. I'm not even certain he knows."

Zacharias thought that was funny, and he grinned.

"Why did Harry kick you?"

"He called thee a bad name, and I called him the same."

Prophet pulled him close until their foreheads were touching. "You listening?"

The boy nodded, grinning, his head rubbing up and down against Prophet's.

"Never, never defend me," he said, suddenly turning the boy upside down and holding him by his ankles. Zacharias was screaming with peals of laughter. "Understand?"

"No," Zacharias yelled, giggling.

Prophet pretended to drop him, and the boy squealed again.

"Understand?"

"Zacharias, what art thou doing?" Pearl Eddy was tapping her way over the yard toward them.

"Just playing," Prophet answered for the boy, smiling and setting Zacharias down on the ground.

Pearl was not smiling. "Zacharias, thou hast chores."

"Yes, Mother," he said, looking over his shoulder and giggling at Prophet, then trotting off toward the henhouse.

Pearl let him get out of earshot. Prophet could tell she was fighting her anger.

"We spoke about thy influence on Zacharias."

"Yes, it would be bad if he laughed a bit, Mrs. Eddy," he muttered, feeling prickly over the boys' being beaten again.

She started walking back toward the house. "We do not believe in idleness, Mr. Prophet."

"Fun, you mean."

"As thou once said, sir, we see things differently."

"That we do, Mrs. Eddy."

He turned and was walking back along the path toward the vegetable garden when Pearl called to him. "Mr. Prophet."

"Yes?"

"Samuel mailed the notices this morning."

"Notices?"

"For thy children."

He didn't speak for a few moments; then he said, "It won't work, ma'am."

"It will, sir," she said resolutely.

Prophet dug at the earth with the toe of his boot for a while; then he looked back up at her and asked, "The money. Did you send it?"

"Yes."

"Fifty dollars?"

"Yes."

"Where'd it come from?"

"The silver frame, Mr. Prophet." She no longer looked upset; her expression was one of peaceful rapture. "Once it was lost completely. I believe it was brought back to us for a good and holy cause. So I sold it." She turned toward the house, probing with her cane for landmarks.

Prophet fixed the woman in his eyes and stared hard at her. She was risking everything on bleary-eyed mysticism and a bad idea, risking everything on strangers. It made no sense, throwing money away that she desperately needed.

"It won't work," he said quietly, then louder: "It won't work. And you shouldn't have done it."

"Thy children need thee."

"But it won't work for them."

"It will, sir." She spoke as if she had already seen the future, and it was a sure thing. "And we have our eggs, garden, and sewing. More, we have our belief in the Almighty."

"You have nothing, ma'am. Don't you see that?" He was sorry as soon as he said the words.

She didn't answer, just continued walking.

Samuel pulled steadily on the reins, backing Jack out of the Carlsons' darkened yard. He glanced at his mother sitting in the shadows on the seat beside him, looking small and clutching a new dress in her lap, worried about something.

He didn't know what had happened on the Carlsons' front porch minutes before, only that she had returned to the buggy carrying the new dress she had made for Ellen Carlson.

"Was it the wrong material?" he asked. That was what she had been told when a blouse she had delivered to Mrs. Jennings had been rejected. This had never happened in the four years that he had been driving her. He turned onto the road. "Mother?"

She looked toward him as if just realizing he was there.

"I'm sorry, Samuel."

"Was it the wrong material?" he repeated.

Pearl waited a moment longer, then said, "No." Her voice sounded distant. "Mrs. Carlson said she hadn't ordered any dress."

"That's a lie," Samuel said.

"Samuel."

"I was there when thou talked about the color with Ellen," he continued, a worried sound in his voice. "She wanted red, just like thou made."

Pearl turned back in her seat, clutching the new dress as though it were a dead child. Quickly she went over what had happened this evening, stunned by the enormity of the events.

None of the five women she had spoken to about work for Eiko and Fumiko had been interested. It was a repeat of the night before. Each had a story about Orientals who had worked for a relative or friend and who had done something awful. Again and again Pearl had tried to talk their concerns away. It hadn't worked. She shifted uncomfortably on the buggy seat, running the tips of her fingers over the soft material of the new dress.

While those turndowns had hurt, she had been prepared for them; over the past few days she had come to the realization people weren't having the Kishimoto women in their houses, around their food, their valuables, their children.

What she had not been prepared for was the fact that in one evening's time four of her seamstressing customers had not only refused to accept their orders, but told her they didn't need anything new. She gripped the dress in her lap. She had lost four customers.

She bit her lip, recalling Rose Sherman's warning: "You'll account for this!" She desperately needed the money for these clothes.

She had accepted the staples Prophet had brought in his large pack in exchange for his room in the cellar. Even so, the food was running out. There were twelve people. The thought numbed her. She had been struggling just to keep her boys going, and that was when she had had all her customers. Panic rose in her throat.

The food wouldn't last, and she had no idea where she would get more. The eggs and the garden helped, but these things were sold to pay bills. And now there was the new promissory note. Thankfully, her garden business was flourishing. And Eiko had ideas for getting more production from the plants. But how much more? And how quickly? Her sewing had always been the real moneymaker. Now it had all changed.

Pearl was counting on the loan. That was what she and Mr. Snipes had discussed, a one-year loan that would clear the equipment loans and her other bills, providing time for the gardens and hens to come into full production and to rebuild her seamstressing business.

She shivered as if cold. The thought of her rising debts, the loss of the house descended on her again. Yes, she had to borrow from the bank. Alms from friends like Edward Johnson she could never accept, knowing it was nothing more than charity, but this loan from the bank she would try. She was wondering why Mr. Snipes had left so abruptly the other night and why he had not been back since when Samuel stirred beside her.

"It's because of them."

"Samuel?"

"Folks are turning their orders down because of the Negro and the Japanese."

The words clamped on to the back of her neck like a cold hand. She hesitated a moment, then said, "Yes." She wouldn't lie to him. "Wouldst thou have me turn them out?"

"Why are they our problem?"

"Because God gave them to us."

"I don't believe that." He slapped the reins on Jack's rump, and the horse began to trot.

"Samuel."

He reined the horse in. "The Negro could survive," he snapped. "He's done it before; he's nothing but a thief. Thou know he stole Father's picture." He paused. "I don't know why he brought it back. But he's looking out for nobody but himself."

"And who art thou looking out for, Samuel?"

The boy didn't answer.

Pearl folded the red dress neatly in her lap. Then she said, in a quiet voice, "Please take me to the Phillipses."

Old Rake Phillips was a giant of a man. The boys at school said he had the body of a Greek statue and a statue's brains. He cleaned out the slaughterhouse waste at night and mucked the town liveries during the day, and all he had for it was a tiny income and a constant bad smell about him. His wife had been dead for a long time, and he lived in a run-down house with his seventeen-year-old daughter, Sarah. Samuel glanced at the red dress and knew why they were headed to the Phillipses.

He let his thoughts drift to Ellen Carlson and Fumiko. While Ellen was a beauty, he thought, Fumiko was somehow lovelier. He wasn't certain what made her so. He just wished she were friendlier. She was anything but. Still, she was pretty. He wished he were brave enough to say something to her directly, though he wasn't certain what it was he would say.

He moved uncomfortably on the seat, thinking that he wasn't brave enough to talk to a girl. He watched a possum scurrying along a nearby fence. It was true—and further proof of his deficiencies as a man. He clenched harder at the reins as they pulled up in front of the Phillips house.

After he had helped his mother down from the buggy, he crawled back in and sat watching her and Sarah Phillips talking out front of the old shanty. While Sarah wasn't ugly, he thought of her as homely.

"I couldn't, Mrs. Eddy."

"Thou certainly can, Sarah."

"I haven't money, and I've got no use for it."

Samuel sat in the buggy listening. Evening had turned to night, the air was cold and still, and their words drifted clearly across the poorly kept yard. The possum was climbing the trunk of an old apple tree. At least Sarah had some common sense, he thought.

She and the dress didn't go together. It would just hang in a closet. She would look silly wearing it to school. The dress wasn't practical for her.

"Sarah, thou wilt graduate in two months," Pearl continued. "I have heard that thou art good with numbers. Like thy mother."

He had forgotten that Mrs. Phillips had been a bookkeeper in town. He shook his head. His mother kept facts about folks cataloged in her mind. Not bad facts or mean ones, just facts that often came in handy.

He glanced at Sarah's tall, awkward frame as she stood bending to talk with his mother. Those must have been better years for her, he thought, having a mother at home and probably some money flowing in. Her father wasn't a bad man; he was just a slow thinker and worked so hard that Samuel thought he looked more like a beast of burden—filthy and wheelbarrowing loads of offal around town—than he did a man. He wondered what it smelled like in their little house.

"I'm fair with numbers." Sarah's voice had dropped some. Samuel knew she was shy.

Pearl paused. "Stand up and let me see how this fits."

Sarah straightened up while Pearl held the dress against her. Even at a distance Samuel could tell it wasn't a bad fit.

"It is right for thee, Sarah Phillips," Pearl said. "I want to take it in slightly at the waist and let down the hem some. And I think thou couldst use a little more shoulder."

"I can't afford it," Sarah said, sounding as if she wanted to flee back inside the little house.

"Thou dost not have to afford it, it is thy graduation present. I want thee to wear it to graduation." She paused. "Then I want thee to wear it on thy job interviews."

"Job interviews?" Sarah sounded as if she had been slapped.

"Yes. This town has not had a bookkeeper since thy mother died."

"My father is going to get me a job."

"Where, child?"

"I don't know."

Samuel could tell she was being evasive. And he knew that wouldn't do with his mother. Pearl stood a good two heads shorter than the girl, and Samuel watched now as she raised her arms and felt the girl's face and hair, which hung down in shapeless strands. He squirmed as he always did when she touched people. It seemed so intimate, yet it was the only way she could tell what they looked like. Still, it bothered him.

"When thou goest for thy interviews, wear thy hair up in a bun. Thou hast a strong, handsome face. Do not hide it."

"I don't know how," Sarah said shyly.

"I will put it up for thee," she said. "It is Friday. I will have the dress back by Wednesday. In the meantime, thou wilt go to the library and get a volume on bookkeeping. Promise?"

"Father has already gotten me a job." Then quickly she added, "I think."

"In Granger's slaughterhouse?"

"Maybe."

"Thou canst do so much better, Sarah."

The girl didn't answer.

"I'll talk to thy father," Pearl said firmly. "I will also talk to Mr. Snipes at the bank and other business-people in town. I am certain thou canst build a nice business." She paused and reached her hands out to the girl. "Sarah, thou must do this. For thyself."

The girl looked uncomfortable again. But she didn't respond.

"Good," Pearl said, as if through her silence Sarah had agreed with her.

It was Saturday noon, market day in town, and Main Street was crowded with rumbling wagons, bellowing oxen, and shouting men, the sidewalks filled with women in sunbonnets and children having fun. The air was bright with sunlight and hurt the eyes. Prophet trailed behind the three younger Eddy boys, as they headed for the general store, old Kishimoto trotting behind him. My faithful servant, Prophet thought. Sure.

Prophet looked at the aged warrior from the corner of his eye. He was dressed in a crazy yellow outfit with long sleeves, tied like a woman's skirt around the waist. His legs were bare. He carried a new stick that he had carved from white ash tied across his back. He looked ridiculous, but worst of all, he bowed like a cowed dog whenever Prophet happened to look his way. So Prophet had taken to avoiding a direct glance.

The old man had attracted a crowd of gawkers, and they were trailing along, making insulting comments about how sweet his legs looked and whistling at him. Mr. Kishimoto, as haughty as ever, simply ignored them. Prophet tried to.

The Eddy boys had disappeared inside the general store, Prophet following. The Japanese warlord stopped on the sidewalk, taking up his wide-legged stance, a fierce scowl on his face, looking as if he were guarding the door to a king's palace.

"Get that Chinaman out of there!" the man behind

the counter yelled to no one in particular; then he went back to a pile of paperwork.

"He's not a Chinaman, Mr. Curtis. He's a Japanese," Zacharias said proudly.

"I don't care if he's an Israelite—get him out of my doorway."

Prophet walked out and motioned the old man over to one side. "Stay here," he said gruffly, as if addressing a dog. The onlookers were watching closely, a few of them pointing openly at Prophet's scarred face. He paid no attention.

The old man bowed.

"And stop that," he hissed.

Mr. Kishimoto bowed again.

"Lookee there, the nigger has got himself a nigger. And she's wearing a skirt," somebody yelled from the back of the crowd. The whole lot of them roared.

Prophet ignored them. It wasn't the place to start a riot. Especially with Mrs. Eddy around. He went back inside and stood for a moment watching the boys, looking at their worn-out clothes; then he pulled the leather poke out of his pants and put it quickly on the counter. Looking at it made him squirm.

"Like to see what you have in shoes," he said. He would replace the money as soon as he got another fight. Something told him that Lacy and Tyrone would want him to do this.

The salesman looked up from his paperwork and visibly drew in his breath. Prophet was used to the reaction.

The man squinted at him a moment, then asked, "What size you wear?"

"For the boys."

An hour later he had the three little Eddys situated at a table near the front window of a dingy saloon called the Lantern House. They all were wearing new straw hats and shoes, and Prophet was feeling good about things. Some men were shooting pool in the back; another group was playing cards. He watched the woman bring the boys their lunch, and he could tell from their excitement that they weren't used to buying meals out. It made him feel even better.

He leaned back against the bar and took a long drink of beer, letting his eyes drift over the table of men playing poker, then out the front window at the gawkers eyeing the old man.

Prophet thought for a moment that he saw Pearl Eddy across the crowded street, then he wasn't certain. But the boys were certain, and they darted out of the place like frightened cats. Zacharias left so quickly he forgot his new hat on the chair. Prophet shook his head and turned back to the bar to take a long pull on his beer. She was good at spoiling fun.

Prophet stretched his sore muscles, realizing how hard he had been working for the little Oriental woman and determined to have his beer and to enjoy himself in the sanctuary of the saloon. Then he heard Pearl Eddy's voice through the open door.

"Where is Mr. Prophet?"

She didn't sound happy.

"In there," Joshua said meekly.

"Mr. Prophet."

He was facing the bar, determined to ignore her.

"Mr. Prophet, I know thou art in there."

"Another beer," he said, smiling at the bartender.

The man tipped his head in the direction of the door. "Mrs. Eddy wants you."

"She can wait."

The man shrugged and started to pull the beer.

"Mr. Prophet."

"I'm busy," he called over his shoulder.

The bartender was knocking the head off the second beer when the saloon's doors screeched and the tapping of Pearl Eddy's cane started across the floor. Prophet turned, unable to believe what he saw. She was standing inside the saloon, a deep scowl on her ordinarily placid face. Angry or not, no self-respecting woman entered this kind of establishment.

"Mr. Prophet," she repeated, turning her head to try to locate the sound of him, her lips pressed hard together.

"Damn," he said, slamming some coins down on the counter and grabbing a paper bag off the floor. He took her by the elbow and hurried her out onto the sidewalk. The crowd backed away.

"You can't go in a place like that," he growled.

"And why not?" she snapped. "Thou took my children in there!"

"That's different."

"It certainly is not. That is a house for gambling and liquor." She paused. "Thy inclination to blasphemous living will not be visited on my children, sir. I have told thee."

He watched her for a few moments, the crowd pressing in around them. Then he said, "Zach, here's thy hat." He held it out to the boy, but Pearl reached and took it, feeling the new straw material. He could see her stiffen.

"What else did thou buy?"

"Shoes." He paused. "They needed them."

"I will not accept thy charity."

"They need shoes," he said stiffly.

"These don't hurt my feet," Zacharias said.

This seemed to stop her, and she waited a moment, then continued. "We will discuss it later."

Prophet started toward the buggy.

"Mr. Prophet, I asked thee a question."

"About?"

"Why thou would take my boys into a saloon."

He shifted awkwardly. "It's the only place in town where a Negro can order a meal, and I wanted to treat the boys," he said.

Pearl looked stunned, her face turning red. She held her cane in both hands, and for once in her life she seemed not to know what to say. Then, in a quiet voice, she said, "I see. I'm certain the food is good."

"It's decent," he said.

"Yes, I'm certain it is," she said quickly. "Let's go home."

As they started down the steps, old man Kishimoto darted ahead of them, his stick held diagonally across his body like a soldier clearing a path for officers. The crowd backed away.

"Quit that," Prophet snapped.

The old man stopped and bowed, then fell in behind them. They were nearing the buggy now, passing a small collection of loiterers who were hooting and whistling, when Prophet saw him. Hank Meyers didn't look much different from that night on the prairie road. "Here he is," Prophet muttered to himself, "the instant repenter. Damn fake." Prophet studied the man's face. He didn't look right in the eyes, dazed or in a trance. Meyers had stepped out of the crowd and was staring hard at Pearl as she passed. Prophet moved toward him in case he made a grab for her.

"What do you want?" Prophet snarled.

The man didn't answer. He just continued to gaze at the side of Pearl's face as if he had something urgent to say to her but couldn't bring himself to.

"Mr. Prophet?" Pearl called over the noise of the crowd. Joshua and Luke each took hold of one of her elbows and guided her around the pools of mud and filthy water, steering her toward their buggy.

Then, suddenly, Penny James and three other men had pushed their way through the onlookers. "I guess old niggers are slow to learn," Penny said.

Prophet didn't say anything, but he slipped a rag out of his back pocket and wrapped it around the bruised knuckles of his right hand, while Penny tugged on a pair of work gloves. Over his shoulder, Prophet said to the Eddy boys, "Take your mother home."

Luke and Joshua tried, but Pearl wasn't budging. Kishimoto had hopped alongside Prophet and stood staring at the men with narrowed eyes, his stick at the ready, while Zacharias took a place on the other side and tried to look mean.

"What is Mr. Prophet doing?" Pearl asked the twins.

The boys hesitated.

"Luke, Joshua?"

"Penny James and some other men are causing him some trouble," Joshua said.

Prophet and Penny were slowly circling and measuring each other in the middle of the street when Pearl stepped up, canting her head and listening for Prophet among the growing crowd noise. His arms up in good bare-knuckle style, he glanced down at her, "Go to the buggy, Mrs. Eddy," he said, "before you get hurt."

"I will not. And thou wilt not fight like a dog in the middle of a street. Dost thou hear?"

He was still looking at her when Zacharias yelled, "Mr. Prophet!"

Prophet turned his head back toward Penny in time to catch a hard punch square on his nose. He staggered back a step but didn't go down, and this surprised

Penny, who prided himself on the power of his right hand. He had just never fought somebody like Jerome Prophet.

"Hit him back, Mr. Prophet!" Zacharias screamed, losing control of himself in the excitement of the moment. "Stick thy left out!"

"Zacharias Eddy!" Pearl snapped. "Get thee to the buggy this instant!"

Zacharias took a few steps, then stopped and shook his head and turned back, unable to leave, his little fists clenched tight, his lips trembling. His brothers were coming fast to retrieve him. Kishimoto had his stick at the diagonal, waiting for somebody to make a wrong move. Prophet was still staggering, his legs buckling some, and Penny was closing in when Sheriff Haines and two deputies broke through the onlookers and pushed Penny and the crowd back.

"Mrs. Eddy," the sheriff said, "get these men out of town or I'll throw them both in jail." He turned to Prophet. "I told you stay out of trouble. I won't again." He looked at the blood flow from Prophet's nose, and asked, "Broken?"

"No," Prophet said, tipping his head back to try to stop the bleeding.

"Is what broken?" Pearl asked.

"Nothing," Prophet said.

Before Prophet knew what she was doing, Pearl had reached her hands up to his face, touching his lips and feeling the blood streaming from his nose.

"Get your hands off," he snarled. "People are watching." The noise of the crowd had stopped as if someone had pointed a loaded cannon at them, the silence sudden and unnerving.

"And thou art bleeding."

"It doesn't matter."

Prophet tossed the paper bag in the back and hurried Pearl and the boys into the buggy, trying to act like a hired hand. But it was too late. Pearl Eddy had already made the mistake.

The church bell tolled eleven o'clock, the sound drifting across the prairie stillness like something lost. Everyone but Prophet was asleep or headed there. It had been a long day. Both he and Zacharias had been in serious disgrace with Mrs. Eddy since the affair that afternoon with Penny James. The boy had been on forced duty cleaning out chicken pens until a couple of hours ago. Prophet had helped him whenever he could slip in undetected.

He brought out his bottle of Mentholated Liniment and rubbed some over his bare shoulders and neck, the odor pungent in the air. Then he capped the bottle and stood and pulled his shirt back on. Finished, he picked up the paper bag beside him and climbed the steps to where the boys had lined their new shoes against the wall, still worrying about what Mrs. Eddy had done, touching his face like that in front of that crowd.

Samuel's shoes were in their accustomed place at the head of the line. Prophet opened the bag and pulled out a new black pair. Unlike the old high-tops, these were for a man, plain-toed, low-cut, and laced. He set them down and went back to his seat on the steps.

He was cold now and told himself so, but he didn't move. He had been sitting on the back steps of the house for the past hour, wondering where everything was headed. No place good, he figured. He tipped his head back and watched an almost full moon riding high over the darkened prairie landscape, seemingly escorted by bright white clouds. The dark, flickering shapes of bats stitched through the air above.

The surrounding yard was still, almost too still, the silence broken only by the soft snoring of the old Japanese sitting in the dirt a few feet away. Perhaps it was this sound that tugged him from his thoughts, focusing his mind on a new and distant sound, slight but urgent. He stood slowly, but it was gone. He took a step down, then waited.

He was starting to turn back to the house, convinced that he had been mistaken, when the tiny noise came to him once more. It was sharper and more desperate-sounding this time, coming from the direction of the barn and sheds.

Prophet grabbed the hammer he had been working with earlier and jumped down off the steps. He broke into a run, followed just as quickly by Mr. Kishimoto, brandishing his stick.

Prophet was out of breath and dragging his foot badly when he reached the corner of the barn, kicking himself for not keeping his roadwork up. He stopped, peering at the surrounding shadows and standing absolutely still, ears straining to hear. Nothing. One of the little girls coughed inside the barn, the sound at once peaceful and disarming. He relaxed some, wondering if he had simply heard some creature taken by an owl. He didn't think so but wasn't certain why he felt this way. Then he noticed the old man sniffing him and the smell of mentholatum.

"What the hell are you doing?" he hissed.

The old man just went back to staring at the shadows. Prophet saw him wrinkle his nose and take another whiff of air.

"Quit that! You don't smell so good yourself."

He moved his gaze over the shadowy shapes of the sheds, peering carefully into the darker openings of the doorways. Nothing seemed out of place. He was moving slowly along the side of the barn—the old man following annoyingly close behind—when he heard it again, a shrill cry that raised goose bumps on the back of his neck. It had come from one of the sheds behind the barn. Somebody or something was hurt. The old man mumbled a few words in the darkness.

"Hush," Prophet said, turning his head to catch any new sounds that would explain what was happening. But the cry was gone, as if snatched from the night sky by some invisible hand. Then he thought he heard a stirring in the smallest of the three sheds and faced toward it, taking a better grip on the hammer. The old Japanese said something else.

Prophet turned to reprimand him and saw him pointing at the largest of the three sheds. Prophet shook his head and pointed his own finger at the smallest. The old man shook his head vigorously. Prophet was just starting to tell him he was wrong as hell when something banged hard against the wall of the bigger building. Kishimoto bowed.

"Okay, okay," Prophet whispered, irritated that the old man had been right. "Just keep your mouth shut."

He moved forward carefully, stopping outside the door and waiting. It sounded quiet enough inside, maybe too quiet, maybe quiet like a trap. He took a couple of deep breaths and saw the little man doing the same. The old fellow was a fighter, pure and simple, Prophet would give him that.

He gave Kishimoto the professional courtesy of nodding when he was ready to move; the old Japanese nodded back. Prophet drew another breath, then put his hand on the door, shoved it open, and went in fast. He swept the black air in front of him with a hard swing of the hammer, then backed quickly against the closest wall, ready for anything that might come at him.

The old one had followed fast behind him—he was

sure of that—but he couldn't locate him anywhere in the dark air surrounding him. The tiny man was waiting silently in the same way he was.

He held his breath, probing the darkness for sound. Nothing. He could sense something in the room besides the two of them, but there was still no noise or movement. A few seconds later Prophet heard Kishimoto yell, "Ei!" and the swishing of his stick, these sounds followed by a loud, snapping noise and a yelp. Then it was silent again.

Prophet pulled a match from his pocket and struck it. They were standing in the chicken shed surrounded by piles of dead and injured hens, feathers floating everywhere. Kishimoto was off to his right, crouched and looking ready to take on the Mexican army if need be, something lying motionless at his feet. The match burned his finger, and he blew it out.

He struck another. In its light he saw that the old man had killed a dog coyote with a blow from his stick. How, Prophet wondered, had he done that in the pitch-black interior of the shed?

Before the third match had expired, Prophet had counted thirty-two dead or injured hens, and that was just the beginning. The coyote had gone on a killing frenzy. The old man was dispatching the worst of the injured birds with his hands. Then Prophet saw the rooster, Hercules, wedged defiantly in the corner and the old Jap grabbing at him. The third match went out.

"No!" Prophet yelled, hurrying to strike another. "Don't!" In the light of the next match Prophet saw the little man looking at him with a puzzled expression, his small hand grasping Hercules's bloody neck. Prophet held up his hand. "Don't," he said again. He lit the lantern that was hanging near the shed door.

The old rooster was in bad shape. The coyote had taken a bite out of his side, and one wing was hanging broken and useless. Prophet took him from Kishimoto and examined him closely in the lantern's blaze. Nothing else seemed broken, and the bleeding had stopped. Still, he looked half dead. He didn't relish telling Zacharias.

While he was running his hands over the bird, the rooster raised his head and took an exhausted peck at his hand.

"I should have let him finish you, you ungrateful bastard."

The old bird's hackles rose defiantly.

"Don't start with me!" Prophet snapped. "You're in no condition to start anything."

The Jameses' home was not what a person would expect after meeting the Jameses. Expensive English and American furniture was grouped comfortably around a handsome stone fireplace, and there were other soft touches of refinement: light lace on a pillow in a wing chair, wintry needlepoint designs, pink ruffles, Brussels rugs. Faint remembrances of Simon James's wife, Angela.

The men trooped quietly in through the foyer. They regularly held the Royal Order of Redmen's council of chiefs meetings here in the musty-smelling parlor, perfecting their plans to build a lodge bigger than the new Masonic Temple, discussing local political candidates and town issues, planning events and money raisers.

And when necessary, the group determined the disciplines and punishments for certain people. It had been formed nine years ago by Simon, believing that decadence was rampant in the growing town and the resulting criminal punishments not hardly severe enough. The Redmen had pledged themselves to purge Zella. Within two years they had fifty warriors and many more sympathizers.

Patriots, the Redmen were dedicated to shared ideals of American democracy and the Protestant religion, each man sworn to take care of his fellow tribesmen in time of need, to protect their town and institutions.

The seven council chiefs had just finished the ritual smoking of the ceremonial pipe. Simon was sitting on the sofa gently stroking the cheek of his sleeping daughter, Chrissy. The man rarely went anywhere without the child; this night was no exception.

Cleopatra, Chrissy's big yellow cat, dropped off the top of the sofa and curled up on the girl's chest. Chrissy's breath stirred the yellow fur. The secret oaths and fellowship signs having been exchanged, the men seated themselves on the lodge's sacred circle of chairs, a quiet falling over the parlor.

In the soft yellow lamplight Simon studied the demonic faces painted on the leather masks worn by each council member, his thoughts drifting back to their ten-dollar collection to buy the Quaker woman trouble the other night. Unfortunately they had hired tramps who had been bested by the colored. And now things had gotten worse.

Simon cleared his throat and said, "Thank you, red brothers, for coming so quickly." He walked to the window and looking out at the clear night sky for a few minutes, studied the moon through the trees, the men's eyes on him. He turned back. "Some of you witnessed the filth on Main Street today, a white woman fondling a Negro male." He paused. "Proverbs says: Where there is no vision, the people perish!" he roared.

There was a murmur of agreement.

If Simon James was nothing else, he was a showman

and a fair orator given to exhortation. "Our beloved Washington had a vision for America. Andrew Jackson had this same vision. George Custer had it. And we have it! It does not include misbegotten whites fondling coloreds. The fancy word for such ill unions is miscegenation. But I call it the touch of the tar brush!" Simon slammed his hand down so hard on the end table that the flame jumped out of the top of the kerosene lamp.

There was loud muttering of support.

"America's glorious vision rides with each of us. It came here on foot, in wagons, on horses or mules. It came inside each of you . . . in your hearts. And we've sworn to keep it flourishing. At any cost." He paused and let his eyes sweep slowly over each masked face. "Right is right. It always was. It always will be."

"Hear. Hear."

"Yes."

"Amen."

Simon stood and walked back to the window and let the men think over what he had said. "We have taken steps with the banker Snipes to see that the woman and the Asiatics will be driven from Zella. That's half the nest of vipers. The other half, the Negro, we will handle ourselves."

Simon still had his back to them when Penny said, "Pa, Chrissy doesn't look good."

Hector's bawling cry, when he hit the front porch of the Eddys' farmhouse on a dead run, had not been an exaggeration. Chrissy was barely breathing by the time Pearl was brought into the Jameses' dining room. Eiko followed a moment later, carrying a basket. Simon was sitting in a chair beside the child, holding his head between his hands, while Mike and Dr.

Trotter tried desperately to give Chrissy a mixture of whiskey and tea.

Pearl sensed death in the room and battled her emotions, trying to hear the girl's breathing. Doc Trotter and Mike James stepped back as Pearl approached. She put her ear to the girl's heart and listened to her choking slowly. She pressed her fingers to the carotid artery and felt the pulse fading. Eiko moved alongside Chrissy as well now. She had stubbornly refused to let Pearl come into town without her, concerned about her after the attack at the river.

"Doctor?" Pearl said.

"No use, Pearl." Trotter sighed, turning his head away from the table where Chrissy lay gurgling her last. "They tried to handle it themselves."

Pearl could smell the mullein smoke and the sharper odor of eucalyptus oil in the hot, humid air of the room. "Ohhh, Chrissy," Pearl moaned. She leaned over and held the child's head in her hands. "God loves thee."

Simon hollered, "She's not dead!" Then he saw Eiko. The woman was kneeling and searching through her basket.

"What is that Chinese whore doing in my house? Get her out!" Penny started for Eiko.

Doc Trotter whirled and faced the two men. "In God's name, have the decency to let Chrissy pass in peace."

"She's not dying!" Simon moaned.

Eiko had found what she was looking for. In her hands she held a long bamboo box. She moved Pearl back. Then she leaned over the girl and straightened out Chrissy's limp body. Chrissy was making a rattling sound deep in her chest. Eiko hurried around the dining room table until she was standing at the top of the girl's head, checked her alignment, squinting and shoving one of her shoulders until the body was where she thought it should be.

Suddenly Simon lunged and grabbed her by the arm. "I'll kill you if you touch her again, you damn yellow bitch!"

Eiko wrestled free of Simon's grasp. "Leave me alone, man. She is not dead yet. Leave me alone."

Hector, Mike, and Dr. Trotter succeeded in pulling Simon back across the room, forcing him into a chair. Then they heard Penny's voice behind them.

"Get away." Penny was standing to one side of the table, pointing a heavy revolver at Eiko.

Pearl turned and stepped in the direction of the man's voice, guessing that she was stepping between Eiko and Penny. "Thy sister is still alive. The woman is helping her."

"She's a gawddamn conjurer," Penny snapped, moving the pistol so that he had a clear shot at Eiko.

Eiko was ignoring the threats, concentrating hard on Chrissy's prostrate form, as if visualizing something that none of the rest of them could see. Then she removed a small three-inch-long needle from the bamboo box and bent over the girl.

"I'll kill you before I'll let you work your damn voodoo on her," Penny shouted.

"You kill, go ahead. You kill." Eiko challenged him, leaning closer over the girl and rechecking the body's alignment. Chrissy's face was turning blue now. Eiko took a deep breath and inserted the needle in her neck. Then she moved down to the girl's waist, pulled out another needle, and stuck it into her hand. Everyone was watching, not certain what the woman was doing.

"Eiko?" Pearl asked.

"I am working. Do not bother now." Eiko was busy sticking pins in various locations around the girl's torso.

The noise of the pistol's hammer locking in the stillness of the room made everyone jump—everyone but Eiko. The woman continued to stick needles into the girl as if she were oblivious of everything else around her.

"Don't do it, Pen—"

Doc Trotter's voice was cut off by another sound, a piercing "Eiii!" Suddenly Penny James was crumpling unconscious to the floor, the pistol sliding harmlessly over the carpet.

Mr. Kishimoto was standing in his squat-legged stance, brandishing his shiny staff in a menacing way at the rest of the Jameses. He had been followed into the room by Prophet, who stooped now and picked up the pistol, which he stuck in his waistband. Prophet had watched the two women leave the farm in the buggy earlier that night and decided it might be wise to trot along behind, and from the look of things he had been right. As always, the old man had tagged along, amazingly keeping up stride for stride for the entire three miles into town. He was indeed a tough little bastard.

"You boys sit tight," Prophet said, enjoying himself for the first time in a while. "Or Mighty Mite here will part your hair down to your navels."

"Mr. Prophet!" Pearl snapped. "What art thou doing?"

"Just checking in on you."

"That is not what I mean. What art thou doing to these men?"

"Wasn't me," he said quickly. "It was the old man."

"Must thou always try to shift the blame to others?"

"Fine, Mrs. Eddy," he mumbled as if it weren't worth arguing with her about. "I just came to see if you needed any help, and the old man followed along."

"We do not need thy violence."

"I can see that," Prophet said, shaking his head and looking around the room at the sweating fat man being restrained by his sons and Trotter, then at the unconscious form of Penny James and the heavy pistol he had been threatening to use to blow Eiko's head off. He shook his head, repeating, "I can see that."

"Nor do we need thy sarcasm, Mr. Prophet."

"Yes, ma'am."

"My God," Trotter gasped, "what did you do?"

Prophet turned to see the James girl struggling to sit up and gasping for breath. She looked awful, like somebody rising from the dead, needles sticking out of her in a dozen places.

Eiko clapped her hands together like a mechanical monkey. "Good girl. Good girl. Big breathe. Big breathe."

When Prophet saw that Pearl was preoccupied, he bent over and pulled Penny James up bodily by his coat front and threw him hard into a large chair, causing it to slide backward over the floor and into the wall. Mr. Kishimoto was after Penny in a flash, his stick at the ready in front of the man.

Trotter couldn't take his eyes off the needles. He looked dazed, as if he had witnessed the raising of Lazarus.

"What are those things?"

"Those *hari*." Eiko grinned. "Needles."

"But what did you do?"

"I poke yin-yang line. Arm sunlight yang. So the girl breathe. It makes good sense, yes?" Eiko was nodding up and down vigorously as if consulting with a fellow physician. "Make good sense, no?"

Trotter could not stop shaking his head. Simon had tears running down his cheeks, looking at his daughter, who had come back from the dead. Pearl also sobbed, while Eiko babbled on about yin and yang. Old man Kishimoto just stood waiting for Penny James to make a wrong move. And Prophet could do nothing but scratch his head at how Mrs. Eddy never believed him about the rooster and this old man.

Chapter Eleven

Even after a week of hard thinking about it, Pearl was still amazed that Eiko had saved Chrissy's life. The child's recovery was as close to a miracle as anything she had ever witnessed. She knew the smell of death, and Chrissy James had been oozing the foul effluvium. She shivered. God had been in that room. Pearl was certain of it.

Pearl was holding a bucket and leaning against the well, contemplating this, the late-afternoon air warm upon her skin, her free hand rubbing idly over the woolen fabric of her long skirt. Eiko had made light of what she had done. Neither Pearl nor Smith Trotter had.

Simon James, however, was not impressed. Joyful, yes, that Chrissy had survived but crediting none of it to Eiko. That same night he had ordered all of them, Dr. Trotter included, from his house. Given what had just happened, it was a breach of good taste of the first water in these parts. Worse, he had followed them out into the yard, threatening Prophet and Mr. Kishimoto. Thankfully, Prophet had restrained himself.

Pearl forced herself to think good thoughts about Simon James; then she let her mind drift. The yard was filled with late spring sunlight, birdsong, and swarms of insects. She was thinking back to the loss of

272 ☙ THOMAS EIDSON

her hens. She had counted on the sale of the eggs for months until it had become a mental insurance policy, one she had often dreamed would ultimately save her and the boys. Now with half the hens gone, that dream had evaporated. There was no question left, she had to borrow from the bank. She wondered again why Mr. Snipes had not sent word when he was coming back.

Pearl turned and lowered the bucket into the well, her thoughts drifting again. Things hadn't been all bad. Hercules had survived. The old bird hobbled around now with a permanently crippled wing that dragged pathetically along the ground, but his fierce pride remained unbroken. And the garden had exploded in new growth, spurred by the weather and Mrs. Kishimoto's care—growth so luxuriant that it promised to replace the lost revenues of the dead hens.

But it couldn't compensate for her lost seamstressing clients. She had only three steady customers left. Still, there had been other gifts. After posting the reward for Mr. Prophet's children, ten dollars had remained from the sale of the frame, and at Eiko's urging she had purchased seven young shoats to be fattened on the surrounding prairies. Eiko claimed she was good with pigs, and Pearl believed her.

As she cranked a bucket of water out of the well, she reminded herself that God had seen fit to take, but He had also given. Prophet and the Kishimotos were part of His gift—even if Samuel and the town did not believe so.

"Get away, both of you!" Pearl heard Prophet order.

She smiled and picked up the bucket and started back toward the house.

"I'm warning you both, I'm sick of this," Prophet continued. "Don't make me get after you."

The man was magical in his way, Pearl thought. Zacharias and the other younger children followed him, Mr. Kishimoto followed him, and now, after his recovery, so did Hercules. She didn't understand it. The man certainly didn't encourage it. He threatened and complained, but it didn't seem to matter. Her only concern was the influence he was having on Zacharias. The man could do no wrong in the boy's eyes.

"Why don't you follow each other, you enjoy it so?" Prophet grumbled, stepping over the rooster and heading for the barn. Undaunted, the bird and the little man trailed faithfully along.

Prophet squatted and began to rifle through a box of tools, pulling things out and setting them aside, until he found what he was looking for. He started to shut the lid on the box, but Hercules had stuck his head inside and was carefully examining its contents.

"Do you mind?"

The old bird pulled his head out to stand with his legs spread and his head tipped, eyeing the man. His broken wing was hanging limply on the ground, and Prophet noticed that all the dragging had rubbed the edge raw. He was going to ignore it but couldn't. He stooped, and before the bird knew what had happened, Prophet had grabbed him up, holding him tightly against his chest, as the bird struggled.

"Stop it," Prophet warned, disappearing into the tack room next to the barn. Mr. Kishimoto took up guard duty at the door.

Daylight was fading when Prophet finally came out of the shed, still holding the squawking rooster tight in his arms. He squatted. Mr. Kishimoto squatted.

"Behave yourself," Prophet ordered.

He held the rooster out at arm's length as if he were

a lit stick of dynamite, then let him go. While Hercules hadn't attacked him since he had saved him, Prophet didn't trust him. The old bird didn't move for a moment. Then he tried to flap his wings. Only one came up; the other was held neatly against his body by a new leather harness that Prophet had fashioned for him.

"How's that?"

The bird turned his head and pecked at the leather a couple of times, then began to stride around with some of his old arrogance.

"Good," Prophet said, heading back toward the barn. "I did you a favor; now do me one. Get away from me."

Old Mr. Kishimoto trotted behind him in his odd quickstep, followed by Hercules. Prophet just shook his head.

"That's silly, Truella." Pearl was dumbfounded. She was standing in the softening light of late afternoon on the woman's front porch.

"It's what I've heard." The town woman, Truella Parker, paused. "You have them tending your vegetables."

"Mrs. Kishimoto is a wonder in the garden," Pearl said.

"I don't doubt it."

Something in the woman's tone snagged at Pearl. "Truella?"

"I wouldn't say anything excepting I'm worried for you and your boys."

Pearl held her breath and waited.

"You know why those vegetables grow so fast, don't you, Pearl?"

She shook her head no, sensing from Truella's tone that she didn't want to hear either.

"They fertilize them," the woman whispered, as if she had just let Pearl in on some black secret of life.

"We all do."

"Not their way."

"Truella?"

"With human droppings."

"Truella!"

Two hours later the sun was colliding with the wide horizon and casting a deep blue haze over the land, as Prophet and Zacharias stood in the field beyond the gardens looking at the strange plants. Eiko's rangy black shoats were rooting among them. Mr. Kishimoto was squatting nonchalantly a few yards behind, picking his yellowed teeth with a small stick, while Hercules scratched busily in the dirt nearby. Prophet knelt and took a closer look at the plants, Zacharias standing by his shoulder.

"What are they?" Prophet asked.

"I don't know. I just know my pa ordered them from somewhere far away, and when they arrived, we planted them. Took us almost a month there were so many. That was a couple years ago."

"Need to work, need to work," Mrs. Kishimoto called impatiently to him from the vegetable garden. When Prophet didn't acknowledge her, she trotted over as if to roust him out of his idleness. She spied the little withered plants and squatted beside him, squinting. A moment later she looked up, and her face broke into a smile.

"What?"

"Hayberries," she said.

"Huh?"

"Right—that's what Pa said." Zacharias smiled. "Strawberries and good to eat." Then the boy frowned.

"But we never got but a few scrawny ones. They didn't come to nothing."

Prophet ran his fingers over one of the desiccated-looking tendrils. The little plants were putting out runners in all directions, and small buds were forming on the stems. He ran his eyes over the field, row after row of them.

Eiko was sucking her teeth as if she had just had a sumptuous meal, a habit he had come to learn meant she was thinking about something. Prophet turned his attention to the woman.

"If they weren't half dead, would they be any good?"

Eiko sucked her teeth again and said something in Japanese. The old man answered her as if he could care less. She began pulling the straw off one plant, then the next. "Oishii berry. Good berry."

"These?" His voice was skeptical.

"Waking up," she said as if talking to herself. "Need water and seed of cotton," she mumbled, continuing to uncover the rows. "Get!" she hollered at a shoat digging his nose among the little plants. She darted after him, giving him a hard kick on the rump and driving the lot of them squealing from the field. She trotted back and hunched down again.

Prophet made some quick calculations. There were some four acres of them, and from their spacing he guessed they had a few thousand plants.

"Valuable?"

She held up her thumb and said, "Grow two times bigger." She smacked her lips, then asked the little man something.

"Cashee," he muttered, as if the effort were too much for him.

She nodded vigorously, "Hai—cashee crop."

"That's what Pa said. That they'd bring us cash. But they never did much."

Eiko ignored the comment, clucking to herself in a satisfied way.

"They don't look so hot to me," Prophet said.

"They have just left winter." She sucked her teeth some more. "Good plants." Then she was scurrying along the rows and pulling the rotting mulch off plant after plant. He had been right, there were thousands of them.

Prophet was helping now, his enthusiasm growing. "How much do these produce?"

"Much." She knelt and stuck a finger into the dirt near one of the plants, frowning when she pulled it out. "But they need water."

They watered until Prophet was about to drop and it was too dark to see and they were in danger of trampling the plants' weedlike creepers. Finally, Eiko called a halt to the work. Prophet hung back, waiting until she and the children had left. He stood in the darkness staring at the field of strawberries and thinking. The old Japanese squatted patiently behind him, as if he had nothing in the world he would rather be doing.

Pearl looked different to Prophet as he helped her down from the buggy. Smaller maybe. Or maybe it was the vastness of the dark sky. Samuel was holding Jack's reins and staring angrily at the barn. The cool night air drifting across the yard was rich with the scent of new roses and honeysuckle, but Prophet was paying no attention. He began to lift the unsold baskets of vegetables from the buggy, his gaze on the woman.

"What happened?"

Pearl bent and picked up a heavy basket of early squash and turned toward the back porch, but Prophet took it from her. She looked weak and disoriented, as if she didn't know what to do next.

"Sam, what happened?" Prophet asked again, his voice insistent.

The boy whirled toward him in anger. "Thou wantest to know what happened?"

"Samuel," Pearl said.

"The man asked."

"Samuel," she repeated, sounding stronger.

"No," Prophet said. "Let him tell me."

"As long as it is done respectfully."

"Oh, I will. I wouldn't want to upset Mr. Prophet with the truth of what he and that family are doing to us."

"Samuel, I will not remind thee again." She sounded more like her old self now, and the boy was backing down.

"People are saying our produce is spoiled," he muttered, his voice more subdued.

"With what?"

The boy looked back over Jack's head. "Waste. Urine and feces. From the Asians."

"The Kishimotos," Pearl said stiffly.

"Fine. Urine and feces from the Kishimotos."

Pearl stared into the shadows.

Prophet cleared this throat. "That's crazy."

Samuel clucked to the horse, the animal starting slowly through the darkness toward the barn. "Maybe," he mumbled. "But if folks believe it, they won't buy."

"Thou must have more faith in people, Samuel," Pearl said.

The boy didn't answer. Prophet stood looking at

Pearl in the shadowy light, unable to believe this young woman's luck. She had lost her sight. She had lost her husband. He had watched her take one tumble after another trying to help people. Even so, she had always bounced back up. But looking at her from the side now, he doubted she would again. Given enough punishment, even fighters with heart caved in.

Then she turned and looked in his direction, and the expression on that blind and beautiful face, calm and dignified and unlined with deceit or pride or greed, told him better than words that he had underestimated her yet again.

"God will solve our problems, Mr. Prophet."

"Will he now?"

"Yes."

He shook his head. "Of course, Mrs. Eddy. What a lucky break losing your vegetable business. God stepped in just in time."

She started for the porch. "Don't be cynical, Mr. Prophet."

"I wasn't. I was being practical."

"It sounded like the same thing," she said, locating the stairs with the tip of her cane and starting up.

Prophet watched her as she turned at the top of the steps and stood breathing in the sweet smells of the garden. So typical of her, he thought. Treading water at the bottom of a cesspool, but smelling flowers in the air and thinking she was standing in a beautiful meadow.

"What are you going to do?" he asked.

"Make dinner."

He frowned. "That's not what I meant."

She held out her hands, and he passed her a basket filled with chard. "Life works out," she said, confirming once again her impracticality in Prophet's mind.

"How?"

She walked slowly toward the back door. "That is not our concern." She paused. "It just does in right causes."

"Me and a bunch of Chinamen aren't some right cause. I'll be going soon. They ought to as well."

He could see that her temper had flared again. It made him feel better.

"The Kishimotos are Japanese, not a bunch of Chinamen. And while thou canst leave if thou wishest, they do not have thy abundant choices."

"They've got enough." He stopped talking and listened to the tapping of her small foot. Then he said, "If I was you, I'd watch attaching a moral to everything."

"Thou art not me, sir. And I am surprised at what thou as a minister preach."

"This isn't about me," he said quickly. "This is about you. You've got no call doing these things."

"Thou art wrong."

"About?"

"My having no call, as thou put it."

"Meaning?"

"We are called." She emphasized the word we. "Each one of us—to establish God's kingdom," she said with an edge to her voice. Then she turned, the basket on her hip, and tapped her way into the kitchen.

"Like I said, you got to stop with the morals," he called after her. She didn't respond.

He stood watching her through the open door a moment, then spun around and ran into Mr. Kishimoto. "I thought we had an understanding! You were going to keep out of my way, wasn't that our deal?"

"Hai!" the old man said, bowing hard.

"Then do it! Just do it," he ordered, stomping off toward the strawberry field.

The old man shuffled along behind him, trying to maintain a three-pace distance as they headed for the strawberry field. Prophet was working hard at ignoring Kishimoto when he heard the sound of a buggy coming down the road. He trotted back and hid in the shadows at the side of the house, the old man following behind.

Prophet peeked around a corner and squinted at two men climbing down from a red Cumberland buckboard pulled by a pair of matched bays with white patches on their foreheads. One of the men was tall and not too old, the county attorney, Prophet knew, and the other, much older, perhaps older even than Kishimoto.

From Pearl's back porch Judge Wilkins and Edward Johnson could see the lanterns moving in the distant darkness, and they watched the shadows cast by the Oriental woman and her eldest girl as they worked building a fence. From their expressions the men might have been staring at lepers. Pearl was standing on the porch next to them. The Eddy boys were out back feeding and watering Jack and the pigs.

A gust of night wind rose and whipped Pearl's long gray dress around her legs. The air was cool and smelling now of the verdant growth of the prairie. Summer had almost arrived. Pearl sensed something wrong in the men's silence, something more than their belief that she was stubborn to have done what she had done. Steamy smells of cooking wafted out onto the porch. "Gentlemen, I have fresh vegetable soup."

Neither man answered.

"Judge?"

"No, thank you, Pearl," the judge said, taking a long draw on the cigarette he held in his bony hand.

Pearl didn't care for the tone of his voice.

"Edward?"

The attorney looked away from the moving lights and studied her features for a moment. "Pearl, you've got the problem the judge told you you'd get when you took these people in."

"And what problem is that, Edward?"

"There's talk your place has been turned into—" He stopped and looked at the old man, as if hoping he would pick up the conversation for him. Judge Wilkins let out the smoke he was holding in a long breath, watching the wind moving through the trees at the far end of the garden. He made no move to assist the younger man.

"Into what, Edward?"

"An opium parlor. That the Asian women are for—" He stopped again.

"Yes?" Her tone shifted.

"Sale." He shuffled his feet uncomfortably, then rushed ahead. "That you've taken up with a black man, intimate with him in public. That you're unfit as a mother."

"None of those things is true," she said.

"No. And people in town who are your friends don't believe it. But still, it's a problem."

"For others perhaps," she said stiffly.

"No," Judge Wilkins said quickly. "For you and your boys." He tossed his cigarette out onto the dirt behind the porch and turned toward her, pulling his large coat tightly around him. "It's essential that you get rid of these people, Pearl Eddy. And quickly." He had a gruff way about him normally, but now his tone was almost commanding.

Having known Pearl for more than a decade, the men were not surprised when they heard the small, steady sound of her foot tapping against the boards of the porch.

"Being stubborn won't work this time, Pearl," the judge said. "It's essential."

She was silent for a moment. "Judge, there are only two things essential in this world: God and the human heart."

"Don't start your religious palaver, young woman. You're just being stubborn, and you must not be." He stopped and struck a match to a second cigarette, hacking as he drew the smoke into his lungs. "People are at risk because of what you're doing."

Pearl didn't respond, just continued tapping her foot.

"Don't ignore me, Pearl Eddy. You've put people at risk. Your boys, these people, Edward."

"Edward?"

The attorney looked uncomfortable to be included.

"He stands for reelection in less than one hundred days. What do you think his chances will be if he's suspected of supporting this kind of nonsense?" he said, pointing off toward the field. "The sheriff, the town council, all of them are facing the voters. Doc Trotter is running for county coroner. Every one of these men is afraid to get mixed up with riffraff like that," he said, nodding his narrow head toward the moving lanterns and blowing smoke out his nose.

A nerve had begun to twitch under Pearl's eye, and she reached up a hand and touched it. It wouldn't stop. "Judge Wilkins," she said slowly, her voice lowered, "thou and I are friends; therefore, I excuse thy choice of words."

"Of course, Pearl. I apologize. What we're talking about isn't riffraff"—he hesitated—"it's outrageous behavior, young woman. If you were my grand-daughter, I wouldn't tolerate—"

"Judge," Edward intervened. "Pearl, all we're trying to say is that this problem isn't going away on its own."

Pearl was still tapping her foot. "Edward, let me repeat: I don't have a problem. The problem is elsewhere."

"Nevertheless, it's a problem."

"For others perhaps."

"No, for you and your boys," Edward emphasized.

"That's crazy reasoning," the judge snapped. "It's absolutely essential you get rid of these people, Pearl Eddy." His tone sounded more frustrated than before. He pursed his thin lips and looked her up and down for a few moments, his small gray eyes squinting to slits in exasperation. Then he seemed to seize upon an idea that would surely convince her. He hacked a cigarette cough, clearing his throat. "Pearl, listen. A murderer comes into your house and threatens to kill you. Understand?"

She nodded, still tapping her foot.

"It's a problem, correct? A problem whether you invited him in or he broke in, correct? It's a problem whether you admit it or not, correct? No matter what you do or think, it's still a problem. So you deal with it. You escape. You shoot him. You knock him over the head. It doesn't matter. The point is you deal with the problem."

"No," was all she said.

"Yes! Yes! Yes! It's a problem."

"Only if I accept it as a problem."

Squinting harder and looking as if he were going to burst, the judge stared at her gentle face in the weak light of the moon. "I'm going to use those words silliness and riffraff again, Pearl, so I'd best be going. Edward."

The men stopped at the bottom of the stairs. "The town is against this, Pearl," the judge said, looking up at her. "Maybe a few agree with you, but I suspect those brave souls haven't beaten a path to your house to help out. And I promise you they won't." He paused. "You're standing alone." The gruffness was gone from his voice, replaced by a tone of concern. "You think about what we've said. Edward and I came as old friends. But you've got to save yourself. We can't do it for you." He paused and looked around at the house and barn as if he were looking at the inside of Satan's living room. "Edward is taking a chance coming out here to warn you. He's got kids of his own."

The judge started for the buggy; then he turned back. He looked hot again. "When they come for you, lassie, I won't stand up for you. No one else will either. And, Pearl, they'll come for you. Make no mistake."

He turned back to the buckboard. Edward waited until the judge was climbing up into the vehicle; then he turned and looked at Pearl, who was staring off into the lonely night.

"Pearl," he said finally, "Snipes came to me a few days ago and tried to get a foreclosure order on your farm." He paused. "I told him that the judge and I wouldn't go along, that you would pay half the loan money and would raise the rest within six months."

Pearl looked stunned. She collected her thoughts, then said, "Mr. Snipes and I had discussed a loan."

"Why?"

"Most of the money I had is gone."

"Gone?"

"Yes. I need a loan now."

Edward shook his head. "It isn't going to happen."

"Why?"

"He says this place isn't worth six hundred dollars." Edward waited a few moments, then said, "I don't believe that. But it shows just what the judge and I have been saying. Snipes doesn't want trouble."

The judge called impatiently from the darkness.

"I'll talk to Snipes again," Johnson said.

Pearl listened as the bays put their shoulders into the harnesses and pulled the buckboard out of the yard; then she sat down on the top step and rested her head on her hands. "People are at risk. Foreclosure." She was having a hard time breathing. Then she tensed and slowly sat up straighter, sensing someone had joined her on the steps.

"Mrs. Kishimoto?"

"Just me," Prophet said. The old Japanese settled down into his cross-legged position on the ground near the bottom of the steps.

The three of them sat for a while without saying anything. Prophet watched the moon rise over the trees beyond the garden and thought about her troubles: the town turning on her, her desperate need for cash, and the threatened foreclosure. Her own thoughts stayed focused on the judge's warning that people were being hurt because of her. Even as she had tried to prevent it, people were being hurt.

"They're right," he said.

"About?"

"The need for us to leave."

"No."

"Yes."

Prophet turned his head toward her. Sitting in the shadows with her arms wrapped tightly around her knees, she looked like a small child.

"What are you going to do?" Prophet asked.

"Listen."

"What?"

"I'm going to listen to the Holy Spirit, Mr. Prophet."

He closed his eyes, finding it hard to believe this woman. "You need money, but you can't earn it because of me and those Chinamen." He saw her tense and corrected himself: "Japanese. And now the bank isn't going to give you any. They'll call your mortgage . . . and you signed that note for my children. I'm obliged, but there's no future in what you're doing."

Pearl folded her hands in her lap and asked, "Why hast thou stayed, Mr. Prophet? Under thy logic, there's no future for thee either."

He cleared his throat. "I don't know."

"I don't believe that."

He shrugged.

"Thou art a man who knows why he does things."

He ignored her, tipping his head back and examining the wide spray of stars in the black sky. When he had Jenny and the children, he had known why he did things. But the logic of his life had been sundered by their loss.

He could hear the sound of his heart beating in his ears, but it was also the sound of Lacy's and Tyrone's hearts. An echoing sound that seemed to spread in gentle waves out into the night, into the dark immensity of time and space. Where were they?

"So why hast thou stayed?" she started again.

He kept his mouth shut. They sat for a time in the shadows. Prophet cleared his throat. "Your problem is that you believe in people too much. It's going to get you hurt."

Pearl stood and straightened the pleats of her long dress.

"I mean it. You believe in people too much."

She turned in his direction. "There's nothing better in this world to believe in, Mr. Prophet."

"They'll break your heart."

She smiled, looking as though she had nearly recovered from her talk with Edward Johnson and Judge Wilkins. "Thou art wrong, sir. They will renew my soul."

He shook his head; there was no reasoning with her, so he changed direction. "After I'm gone and the Japanese are gone, you could start over in another town."

"Art thou saying good-bye, Mr. Prophet?"

He ignored the question.

"We've sent the posters to the towns, Mr. Prophet. Thou dost not need to go."

"Begging your pardon, ma'am, I'm not the believer you are in those posters." He paused. "When I get some money, I'll pay you for what you sent to that bank." He stopped talking and looked into her face for a time, as if he were memorizing it, wanting to remember what she looked like when he was no longer here.

"Anyway," he said, looking quickly to where Mr. Kishimoto sat sleeping on the ground, "there's no hope for it here."

"There is always hope."

He started up the stairs, moving stiffly. "I'm going to catch some sleep. That old woman works me hard."

"Mr. Prophet?"

"Yes?"

She reached her hands out toward him. He felt the blood rushing to his face and wanted to turn and flee, but couldn't. He knew things like this meant everything to her, so he filled his lungs full of air, shut his eyes, and stepped forward.

Pearl Eddy's hands moved slowly over his face as if she too were memorizing him for when he was gone. He stood bent over slightly at the waist so she could reach him, his arms dangling limply at his sides. He felt foolish, but he also felt something that he had felt only once before in his life: that he was part of a family and that this woman, and most of her children, cared for him.

Finally, she let go of him, and when he opened his eyes, he thought he could see hers filling with water. He turned away and tipped his head back and looked up at the night sky and blinked a couple of times.

"Mr. Prophet, I thank thee."

He swallowed and then cleared his throat. "For killing your hen?" He tried to joke.

"For all thou hast done." She turned toward the kitchen, stopping only to say, "But thy violence. It must be denied, Mr. Prophet." She hurried into the house.

Prophet heard the first summer crickets beginning to chirp in the night.

Neither Pearl nor her boys heard him climb the cellar steps late that same night, letting himself out of the kitchen. He stopped for a moment, swinging the door open and shut to test it, pleased with his repairs. Then he hoisted his pack onto his back and tiptoed away from the house, careful not to wake Mr. Kishimoto, who sat rigidly upright, but asleep, at the bottom of the steps.

When Prophet reached the little rise of ground and the trail that led through the tallgrass prairie to the railroad tracks, he stopped and looked back. The outline of the house was visible in the moonlight, duncolored, its clapboard covered with ivy and wisteria. Something about it—the way it sat like some forlorn creature adrift in an endless void of black—bothered him, and for a moment he had the desire to retrace his steps. But he heard the faint train whistle and started away at a limping trot. He didn't look back again.

Chapter Twelve

This morning was another hot day filled with a profusion of brilliant sunlight, small puffs of white clouds chasing pools of shadows across the prairie. Eiko was kneeling and pulling weeds from the vegetables while Pearl stood holding Ituro in her arms. Zacharias was sitting on the ground a few feet away, rubbing the back of the small wooden horse and watching vesper sparrows running through the grass like mice.

"Mr. Prophet has left," Pearl said quietly.

Eiko looked up at the woman, at what she perceived to be melancholy in her expression, then beyond her to the thin blue sky, her thoughts on the Negro. Eiko had known since sunrise—when she saw her father-in-law searching frantically through the farm buildings and pens—that he was gone.

"Good worker," Eiko said, returning to the weeds, not giving away anything about how she felt about him or his leaving. Still, Pearl thought she could detect a sadness in the woman's voice.

"Yes. And a good person." Pearl paused, listening to the grasses that seemed to be whispering faintly in the sunlight. After all the times that he had threatened it, she had not really believed he would actually leave. But he had now, and Pearl knew that she would miss him. Miss his gruff good-naturedness, the joy he had brought, his candor, his wonderful capacity for life. Yes, though she was relieved that he would no longer lure the boys, Zacharias especially, with his spell-binding acts of violence, still, she knew, losing this man was a stiff price to pay. Pearl stood up straighter. "He has things he must accomplish."

"Yes," Eiko said, digging hard at a stubborn colony of redroot that had sprouted among the cabbages. "Strong man," she said, stopping for a moment to make her familiar pantomime for Zacharias to see, but without the smile that usually accompanied it. Zacharias, straight-faced as well, flexed his own arms, as if in honor of the Negro, and then went back to rubbing the little horse.

Eiko was thinking now about the big, rough-faced, dark-skinned man, remembering things she had liked about him, but unable to stop thinking about this other thing that made her uncomfortable. "Strong man and smart," she finally said.

Pearl nodded, shifting Ituro to her hip.

"Smart to go."

Zacharias was standing beside his mother looking solemn but contemplative. "He isn't gone. Not for good." The boy was holding the small wooden horse in both his hands now.

"I don't believe that is correct, Zacharias. But Mrs. Kishimoto and I are having a talk now. Go help thy brothers collect the eggs."

"Okay," he said, sounding matter-of-fact and slipping the horse into his coat pocket. "But he isn't gone."

Pearl adjusted the baby on her hip and turned to where she could hear Mrs. Kishimoto working. "Eiko?"

"Because of the trouble he and we cause you. Smart to go."

"That is not true," Pearl said quickly. "He was not smart to leave because some people are against things."

"Not things. Us." She tugged hard at a stubborn piece of redroot.

According to the marks Prophet had penciled on a piece of paper, it had been twelve days since he had started for home, and his efforts to get back into fighting shape were on schedule. He took hold of the top rope on the ring and squatted and pulled backward, stretching out the muscles of his arms and shoulders. He had been averaging some eight miles of roadwork a day since Zella, running along the train tracks until he was too exhausted to go anymore, then waiting for the next freight.

Prophet stood up and ran in place; then he began a fast flurry with his hands. A group of hecklers high up on the wooden bleachers inside the barn began to whistle and taunt him. He ignored them. He was standing in a beam of sunlight that shone down from a hole high up in the barn's roof, his sweat sparkling like diamond dust. The ring looked permanent, so he figured the fight business was legal in these parts. Either way it was no concern of his.

All he wanted was to win enough to send Mrs. Eddy what he owed her with enough left over to make it back to those training camps. He was halfway home. The thought made him feel good, and he went back to throwing fast combinations at imaginary opponents. The only other thing he needed besides money was a good fight to put an edge to his punches.

His thoughts drifted to Mrs. Eddy and her boys.

They were probably out working in the heat of the garden, pulling weeds and watering under that slave driver Mrs. Kishimoto. She and the Quaker woman made some team. He admitted to himself that he missed them. Then somebody tested the bell at ringside, and Prophet jumped.

The barn was filling with spectators, the crowd cheering for somebody called White Lightning. Prophet hoped he was good enough to let him work up a decent sweat. His plan was to carry him for half an hour, to get in some heavy work and to please the locals, then to dump him. Not humiliate him, but he needed a knockout. The agreement was an extra $75 if he dropped him.

That money, plus the winner's purse of $150, would give him what he needed. As he was thinking this, a sudden roar erupted from the crowd, and Prophet knew without looking that his opponent had arrived. Before he turned, he bet himself that the man would be a giant with a hideous face. That was standard for small towns: faces ugly enough to peel paint from houses. He turned and stared.

His first thought was that this was either a contestant for another bout or a joke to work up the crowd. But the longer he stared, the less it looked like either. The man had been greased to keep cuts down, and he wore black shorts tied around the middle with a nice satin sash and light kidskin shoes like the kind Prophet had seen on bicyclists. In fact, that is what Prophet thought he looked like: a cyclist, with his thick brown hair parted neatly in the middle.

Pale and mild-featured, he couldn't have weighed more then 170 pounds. He wasn't particularly weak or poorly built. The problem, Prophet saw immediately, was that there just wasn't enough of him—not enough weight, not enough muscle, not enough reach on his arms.

Staring into his quiet gray eyes and feeling sorry for him, Prophet guessed he needed money worse than he did. It was a shame. Under different circumstances, Prophet might have even let him have it. But the circumstances weren't different.

"I don't allow dancers in my ring, Negro," the brute of a man who was doing the refereeing said to Prophet. "You fight or I'll throw you out."

Prophet nodded, his eyes on his opponent. The man was staring at Prophet's chest and blowing out his nose in short, rapid bursts. Prophet shook his head. He sounded like a fighter; he just didn't look much like one.

Just as Prophet was thinking he would tell the man during their first clinch not to worry, if he cooperated, he would put him on the canvas easy, the referee was shoving them together.

Prophet moved in fast to tie the man up so they could exchange views, but the Sunday school teacher hopped back and popped him hard on the forehead with two quick successive left jabs that stung. Prophet was surprised, and he put his hands out to measure the man. But as he was doing this, a fast arcing left hook to the side of his temple caused him to take a quick couple of faltering steps to catch himself. That did it. No more messing around. This fella might be on the small side and look harmless, but this definitely wasn't his first day at the rodeo.

They exchanged a couple of meaningless shots to each other's ribs, the crowd roaring as the white fighter waltzed out of harm's way. Then the man was back at it again, a busy bee, delivering a series of quick blows to Prophet's middle and then dancing away again without Prophet giving him anything more than a glancing blow to the shoulder.

"Just warm up," he told himself. "Just warm up."

Prophet could feel his right leg dragging some, but that didn't matter. It did that sometimes. They fought without any real damage for another fifteen minutes. Then, after a brief exchange that Prophet thought he had gotten the best of, the man telegraphed a right cross, and Prophet slid right, slipping it, realizing too late that the man had meant him to do that very thing. The left that Prophet ran into was a straight snapping punch from the man's shoulder, a short punch. But when it connected with Prophet's face, it felt as if it had been thrown from somewhere down near the Gulf of Mexico.

Prophet recognized all the symptoms: surprise, silence, no pain, no feeling, no sense of anything but a body that wouldn't move right and weighed too much.

He was going down, and all he could do was gasp a little air and realize somewhere deep inside the black mass of nothingness that was now his brain that he had waited too long. His day in the ring had passed.

"Of course I'll buy the asparagus, Mrs. Eddy," the barber, William Smith, said. He sounded slightly uncomfortable. "Deal is a deal," he continued. He was standing on the sidewalk outside his barbershop under a large yellow canvas banner that read: RE-ELECT GEORGE HAINES COUNTY SHERIFF. Smith's partner, Henry Fegan, and two other men stood watching them through the window.

Pearl looked relieved. She continued to sit on the buggy seat while Samuel handed her Jack's reins and started to get out. But before the boy could reach the ground, Eiko had hopped down to carry the basket of asparagus to the old man.

Smith took a step backward as the woman approached. "Right there," he said, pointing at the sidewalk. He was counting money in his wallet and watching Eiko as if she might snatch it.

"Mr. Smith, I would like to introduce Mrs. Eiko Kishimoto," Pearl said brightly.

"Sure," the old man grumbled.

"Mrs. Kishimoto and her family are staying with us," she added.

"I've heard," he said, handing Pearl the money.

"Thank thee. I'll deliver again next Monday."

Smith said quietly, "Mrs. Eddy, may I speak with you a moment?"

The old man took Pearl by the elbow, guiding her down the sidewalk in a gentlemanly way, out of earshot of the barbershop and the buggy.

"We've been friends for a time."

"Yes."

"What I've got to say now has nothing to do with that."

Pearl just listened.

"The way folks are feeling, Mrs. Eddy, it would be good if that woman didn't come to the shop."

She and William Smith and Hank Fegan had been friends for a dozen years. She drew a breath and said, "Mr. Smith, whatever thou wishest."

"Just until this blows over."

"Yes." Pearl cleared her throat. "And next week's delivery?"

He hesitated, then said, "Let us see how we like this one, and then we'll decide."

"I understand." She started tapping her way back toward the buggy, the barber hurrying alongside her.

"We're just trying to stay in business."

Pearl stopped and turned in his direction. "Mr. Smith," she said quietly, "thou and Mr. Fegan and I have been friends for many years. I have always cherished our friendship." She paused. "I see no reason not to continue to cherish it now. My best to Mr. Fegan."

William Smith swallowed hard as he watched the small buggy moving slowly away toward Main Street.

From her seat among the vegetable baskets, Eiko watched the figure of the little barber receding behind the buggy and asked, "What was wrong with him?"

"Nothing," Pearl said.

"You lose another customer?"

"Mr. Smith just wants to try this asparagus before ordering more. That is certainly fair."

Samuel shook his head. William Smith and Hank Fegan had been two of their most dependable customers. He wanted to say, yes, we've lost customers because of you and your brood. But she beat him to it.

"Because of us," Eiko said firmly.

Samuel suddenly felt a smidgen of respect for her. She had more horse sense than he had thought possible in an Asian.

"We cannot stay."

Edward Johnson and Judge Wilkins had been right, Samuel thought. Eventually Mrs. Kishimoto would figure out this wasn't going to work and decide to leave. Only his mother was too naive to see it for herself.

"Thou canst stay. The people in Zella are just not used to Orientals."

"We cannot," the woman repeated.

Samuel didn't hear her. His thoughts were on Fumiko.

It was warm in the sunlight and cool in the shade, the way late spring was in these parts. The sun, halfway to noon, burned out of a thin blue sky and hit Samuel in the eyes, partially blinding him. He was squinting hard and focused so intently on Fumiko that when they turned onto Main Street, he almost drove Jack into the middle of the accident.

It was a bad one, and it had happened only moments before. Bystanders seemed frozen in different positions, staring at the tangled wreckage of the two drays that had collided, one tipped on its side and pinning the arm of a young man of around eighteen underneath. Samuel reined Jack in hard, causing his mother to tip forward on the seat.

"Samuel?"

Samuel was about to answer when the young man writhing in the street let out a scream and sat up, his sleeve empty. Still, nobody moved as the boy staggered to his feet, his sleeve seeming to explode with a spray of blood.

"Samuel?"

"It's Ernie Sherman," Samuel stammered.

Suddenly the injured boy was staggering toward the crowd, holding his hand out. The people backed away as if he were threatening them with a weapon.

"What's happened?" Pearl asked.

"He's lost an arm." He sounded stunned.

His mother's sudden rush to get out of the buggy freed Samuel from his paralysis, and he leaped down to help her. Ernie Sherman continued to stagger after the crowd, which backed away.

"Hurry," Pearl said.

Samuel had just grabbed his mother's elbow when he saw Eiko tackle the Sherman boy from behind and pull him to the sidewalk. By the time Samuel and his mother got there, the woman had a thong of cloth wrapped around what was left of Ernie Sherman's arm.

Eiko, drenched in blood, was straddling the boy's chest. Ernie was opening and shutting his mouth as if he were trying to say something. Eiko snatched a paintbrush from a man standing nearby and stuck it into the thong and began to twist it. But the blood was still flowing. "Sammy. My *fukuro*! My *fukuro*!"

"What?"

"Bag. Bag!"

Samuel rushed her old green bag to her, and she pulled something out he couldn't see and began to work over the injured boy. She yelled loudly in Japanese at him, then slapped his face—Samuel figured to keep him from dying.

Slowly the flow of blood stopped.

Pearl was on her knees beside Eiko, and the injured boy, checking the bloody stump with her hands to see that the flow had stopped.

"Has it?" Eiko asked, straining hard to hold the knot tight.

"Yes. We need blankets!" Pearl called. The boy was unconscious and looked ghostly pale. "Blankets, please!"

One of the men rushed across the street to Collier's store, hollering for blankets.

They were rolling Ernie over, Pearl cradling the young man's head and Eiko holding tightly to the paintbrush and the twisted knot, when the boy's grandmother, Rose Sherman, arrived. Seeing the blood-spattered Oriental woman bending over her injured grandson, she began to strike at Eiko with her purse.

"Get her off! Get her off him!" she screamed hysterically, seeing her grandson like that.

"Rose! Stop it!" Pearl yelled.

But Rose wouldn't stop. She continued to strike at Eiko's back with her purse until two men stepped forward and grabbed Eiko's shoulders, pulling her back. She fought them, struggling to hold the brush in the knot.

"Get away, leave her alone, you damn fools!" Dr. Smith Trotter hollered as he reached the scene. "She lets go and Ernie is dead. Now get away!"

Night had fallen hard over Main Street when Dr. Trotter and Rose Sherman walked out of his office. They both looked spent. Ernie was inside with his parents and a nurse. The doctor untied Rose's black Morgans from the hitching post and then helped the heavy woman into her surrey. She had been crying hard, creating streaks that looked like stream beds in the thick white powder on her cheeks.

"Rose," Dr. Trotter said, patting her thick hand, "Ernie lost an arm, but he'll live. We all need to go to church and thank God for that." He stopped and looked into the old woman's face. "He should have died."

"Smith Trotter!" she said, shocked.

"He should have, Rose. That injury was massive." He stopped talking and seemed to be thinking about something. "Massive," he muttered again.

"Yes," she said, dabbing at her eyes with a handkerchief. "I can't thank you enough. Bless you."

Dr. Trotter put his hands in his pockets. "Don't thank me."

"You're too modest, Smith Trotter."

"No. I didn't save Ernie. That Oriental woman saved him, Rose."

Rose Sherman didn't say anything.

"Your grandson should have bled to death amputated like that. That woman saved him."

"Anyone could have done it," Rose countered.

"That woman and Pearl Eddy, Rose. They saved young Ernie. Nobody else." He patted her hand again. "I've got to get back to him. Good night."

Rose didn't answer. And when he turned to shut the door of his office, he saw that she was still sitting in her surrey as if lost in some deep and troubling thought.

Pearl stood in the barn that night praying for Ernie Sherman and listening to the sounds of supplies and clothes being gathered. The little girls, Tamoko and Isi, were sitting on a bale of hay watching their mother and Fumiko load the family's belongings onto the cart and looking as if they were about to cry. The younger Eddy boys were behind their mother, watching with faces just as sad.

Samuel was standing in the deeper shadows of the barn, staring at Fumiko and feeling a vague sense of loss, as if he were slipping over the edge of some dark abyss he hadn't even known existed. She was leaving just when he had begun to understand things. He was coming to terms with his family and was admitting to himself that he had feelings for her. Still, he didn't have the courage to talk to her. A cold breeze was blowing in through the barn door, striking him full in the back and heightening his sense of discomfort and loss.

The old man was a bundle of nerves, sitting in his accustomed corner, his eyes darting anxiously from the barn door to the windows. Every few minutes he would trot outside to look for the Negro. He had been doing this in the same worried way for the better part of two weeks now. From the strained look on his worn face it was apparent he was deeply depressed that he

had let the man get away without him. Shincho Kishimoto would have followed Jerome Prophet anywhere.

Pearl had continued to miss the Negro as well.
When she thought about it, she realized how that
night he had formally said his good-bye. Prophet she
knew was searching for his children, but she also
thought he was searching for something else, for
something of himself that seemed to be lost. She
prayed he would find both.

Pearl forced herself to stand up straighter. Zacharias
had been too attached to him. She tried to find the
small boy in the mix of sounds inside the barn but
couldn't. Since his departure Zacharias had faithfully
maintained his belief that the man would return. She
felt sad for him. Love could be such a hurtful thing.
Pearl heard the woman and the girl moving nearby.

"Eiko, we will be fine. Thou dost not have to do
this." She paused. "Mrs. Sherman and others will be
grateful to thee for saving Ernie's life."

Eiko stared at her across the dim light that sepa-
rated them, looking as if she thought Pearl Eddy was
momentarily daft. "You will lose everything." She
paused. "We go to claim *rikuchi*. Our land."

"It isn't thine any longer," Pearl said, raising the old
argument.

"It is abandoned. We will claim it," she said in her
matter-of-fact way.

Pearl waited a moment, then said, "Thou cannot.
Thou must be a citizen." She paused. "I am sorry."

Eiko thought about this for a moment but seemed
undaunted. "We will go. You will not make money if
we stay. And lose everything," she said flatly. Eiko
heaved a large canvas bundle up on the cart. "No
make money. Lose everything," she repeated.

Slowly Pearl began to walk toward the huge door,
her cane tapping quietly against the dirt floor, the

noise an intrusion on the silence that she was seeking in her mind. Outside, she stopped and stood in the breezy darkness, hardly breathing, waiting for some message of hope or direction, anything. But nothing came to her. Nothing at all. She was losing so much that seemed important, and she was unable to do anything about it.

Pearl was fighting the tenseness that ran across her shoulders when a line from the Bible came to her: "Beareth all things, believeth all things, hopeth all things, endureth all things." She could feel the relief flooding through her.

Moments later, as if she sensed someone's presence in the night, she turned swiftly, her ears probing the sounds of the barnyard for movement.

"Yes?" she said to the darkness.

"Just me, Mrs. Eddy," Prophet said.

Pearl stood very still for a long time, blinking as if she were having trouble with her eyes. She was smiling in a funny way when she finally said, "Mr. Prophet, thou hast returned."

He didn't say anything.

"I am glad," she said, smiling broadly now. "Come inside. The children and the others will be thrilled."

"No, Mrs. Eddy. I've been waiting so I could talk to you alone. To bring you something."

"Mr. Prophet?"

"I've got some money for you."

Pearl stiffened, her smile changing to a frown. "We have talked about alms before, Mr. Prophet." She paused, then smiled again. "It is enough that thou hast returned."

"This isn't alms, Mrs. Eddy. I owe you that fifty dollars for the reward. And the rest I want to talk about."

Pearl didn't respond.

"There's a man in Kansas City who buys fruits and vegetables. He sells to stores and restaurants." Prophet paused and took a long look at her.

"Those strawberries of yours are worth money. He'll pay cash for your crop." He hesitated, then plunged his hands into his pants and pulled out the small leather poke that contained Lacy and Tyrone's providing money. He held it as if it were something alive that would die in the air.

He didn't know when he had made the decision to give it to her. He just knew when he woke up after the fight, realizing that he couldn't whip anybody good anymore, he also realized he couldn't let this woman and her children lose everything. Not after what she had done for him. And tried to do for Lacy and Tyrone. He had to settle up with her.

"You take this, ma'am. And hold on to your farm. And raise those plants."

Pearl was shaking her head slowly back and forth in the cool night air. "Mr. Prophet, I can—"

"This isn't charity," he snapped. "I owe it, and you gotta take it." He stopped, wanting to confess that he had stolen her money but not able to do it. "Lacy and Tyrone would want it."

Pearl raised her head to him. "Thou art going back to search for them. Keep the money, Mr. Prophet. Find thy children, and then bring them back here."

"Don't start dreaming. There won't be anything here if I do that. And it will be as much my fault as yours. You take this."

"It wouldn't be thy fault."

He reached out and thrust the leather poke into her hands and was turning away into the darkness when Zacharias caught a glimpse of him and burst out of the barn door on a dead run.

"I told thee! I told thee! I told thee—"

Prophet bent and caught a shrieking Zacharias in midair, as the others crowded around him. The boy suddenly stopped and leaned back in the man's strong arms, peering up at his face. "Mr. Prophet?" he said, his eyes wide. "Art thou okay?"

"I'm fine."

The old Japanese scurried around behind him and took up his accustomed rearguard position. Prophet started to say something to him, then shrugged as if he knew the words would be wasted. He turned away so that no one would see his good eye filling with water.

"What happened to thy face?" Zacharias asked.

"Nothing," Prophet snapped, glancing nervously at Pearl. "I just stopped to talk to your mother. Now I got to be—"

"Mr. Prophet, hast thou been fighting?"

"Some."

"Thou promised thou wouldn't."

"Yes, Mrs. Eddy. I'll be going now."

Zacharias and Pearl said the word almost in unison: "No!"

Prophet, looking half starved like some homeless cur off the streets, his normally thin face gaunt and covered with fresh cuts and festering scabs, his clothes filthy and torn, was leaning weakly against a stack of grain sacks inside the barn now. After the white fighter had knocked him out in the ring, a crowd of unhappy bettors had dragged him out behind the barn and worked him over good.

One of his eyes was badly swollen and bloodshot and draining a puslike mucus over the edge of the lower lid, and he was trying to keep Eiko from touching it. The woman had been fussing over him for some time now, administering her collection of salves and medications and warmed-over verbal bromides.

"No move. No move. You are heck of a strongman."
She laughed, her hands moving tenderly over his
wounds. "You come back, Mrs. Eddy will lose everything. Did you know that?"

Pearl was standing off to one side, cradling the
small leather poke in her hands. Samuel stood farther
back in the shadows, watching the man and feeling
the familiar anger pulsing through him, while
Zacharias and the old man studied the Negro as if he
were some great personage. Even Hercules had come
down off his roost to cluck and drag his one good
wing over the ground in his scurrying sidestep
around Prophet's legs, as if he might restart the wars.
Nothing much had changed.

"Nobody is losing anything," Prophet said to Eiko.
"Mrs. Eddy has the money." Noticing that Pearl
looked as if she were wavering again, he quickly said,
"We are partners. I've invested in this thing."

Always interested in making money, Eiko asked,
"What thing, strongman?" She walked around behind
him and inspected a deep gash in the top of his scalp
that she had cleaned earlier by pouring in some
yellow liquid that foamed and made Prophet holler.
She was threading a needle and waiting for him to
answer.

"What thing?" she prompted.

"Strawberries. There are two yields, right?" he
asked.

She licked the thread to get it to go through the eye
of the needle and nodded. "Cashee crop. Grow *futatsu*.
Twice grow berries."

"Good," he said, loosening up some and beginning
to enjoy the fact that he was back with these people.
"Because that's what I said we'd deliver."

While she didn't say anything, Prophet could tell
Pearl Eddy was thinking. It made him feel good.

"Say what to who?" Eiko asked.

Five minutes later Prophet had finished telling her about the produce man in Kansas City and she had finished stitching the cut. She put her needle away, closed her medicine bag, and turned and walked back toward the cart and her eldest girl. "Good luck, strongman. We are going."

Prophet looked stunned. "You can't do that. I don't know anything about these plants. I wasn't even going to stay! You're part of the deal. You got to stay."

Eiko heaved another canvas bag up onto the cart and shook her head. "We go."

"You can't do that!"

"We go to our land," she said stubbornly.

"None of the rest of us know anything about growing these damn plants!"

"Mr. Prophet, thy language, please," Pearl said.

"I'll watch my language, but you tell her running isn't allowed," he said. "Tell her, Mrs. Eddy. Running isn't allowed." He walked over to the cart and returned the bag to the ground. The old man trotted along behind. "Don't you know about running?" Prophet asked Eiko, sounding tutorial.

The little Oriental woman squinted at him for a moment as if he were a lunatic, then snatched the canvas bag off the ground and stuck it back on the cart. "We go," she barked.

Prophet whirled toward Pearl. "Tell her about running."

"Mrs. Kishimoto has her family to think about."

Prophet looked as if he had been shot. "Let me get this straight. You preach to me that running is never right. But that's just because I'm alone. If you've got a family with you, it's okay to hightail it any time you see fit."

"It is not the same," Pearl said quietly. "Mrs. Kishimoto is not running away."

"Running is running, Mrs. Eddy," he snapped.

No one spoke or moved for a moment. "Those strawberries are worth money. Shipping costs are paid by the purchaser. All we have to do is pick them, pack them in boxes, ice them down, put them on the train, and deliver them to Kansas City."

His eyes darted from Pearl to the Oriental woman. "But it isn't going to happen unless she stays," he continued, staring hard into Eiko's face. The woman betrayed no emotion.

"Mr. Prophet, that isn't fair."

Mr. Kishimoto barked something in Japanese.

Mrs. Kishimoto thought about what the old man said, studied Pearl for a moment, then looked back at Prophet and began to suck on her teeth. "Big money, strongman?"

"Big."

"How much?"

"Nine hundred dollars is what I calculate. Four-fifty each crop."

She sucked harder on her teeth and thought about things for a moment longer, then raised her arms in her familiar strongman pose and said, "You are strongman. Unload the cart." And to Pearl: "You not lose everything. We will stay. You not lose. Everybody will be rich."

Samuel stared at the Negro. As relieved as he was that Fumiko was staying, he was utterly convinced that nothing tied to this man would turn out right.

There was much progress made in the gardens during the next ten days. The fence to keep the pigs out was finished, the thousands of strawberry plants

were carefully cleared of weeds, and the soil was cultivated; then every plant was fertilized with ground-up
cottonseed. After they had completed these projects,
Prophet dug irrigation ditches down each of the long
rows. Everything was done under the watchful eye of
Mrs. Kishimoto. And as the spring moved toward
summer the berries came fully to life and began to
grow and flower in earnest.

Things were good, Prophet felt. Mrs. Eddy had
finally resigned herself to taking the money as his
share in the strawberries. And while giving it up still
bothered him, he felt good that he had paid her back.
Lacy and Tyrone would understand. Prophet stood
straddling a row of strawberries and itched at the
stitches in his scalp and watched Pearl Eddy talking to
Mrs. Kishimoto. She had given the cash to the attorney,
Edward Johnson, who had, along with the old judge,
negotiated a sixty-day grace period for the remainder
of the money. That was plenty of time to bring in the
first of the two harvests of berries, Eiko said.

Eavesdropping around the front porch one evening,
Prophet had heard Edward Johnson tell Pearl how
Snipes had acted like a poisoned man when they told
him that they—the attorney and the judge—would
fight the foreclosure. The little banker, Johnson said,
had been determined to go ahead with the proceed-
ings. In response Edward and the old man had talked
to some others on the bank's board and voted Snipes
down. Nope, things weren't half bad.

In addition to work in the gardens, Prophet spent
nights constructing a watering sluice from old rain
gutters he found behind the barn. He sloped the
trough down a wooden trellis that he built, the device
serpentining from the well to the edge of the field. The
contraption saved hours of backbreaking labor, and

Mrs. Kishimoto and Mrs. Eddy behaved as if he were some engineering genius, embarrassing him with their lavish praise.

"Brilliant," Mrs. Eddy would say whenever she heard water coursing down the sluice. And if Mrs. Kishimoto heard her, she would say, *"Hai! Saino ni michita!,"* which he figured meant something similar in Japanese.

Along with their hard work on the strawberries, they maintained the vegetable garden and even found time to put the flowers right. This latter effort was led by Prophet. All the boys helped, though Samuel did so reluctantly when Prophet was around.

Samuel's level of output rose significantly whenever Fumiko was in sight. Prophet knew the boy had thoughts about her; he just wasn't certain about Fumiko's feelings. She was tough to get a bead on. She never spoke and didn't smile unless playing with the little children. She was carrying a bucket of water across the garden now. He watched her turning her head slightly to follow the boy.

Fumiko watched Samuel as he stood bent over, hoeing madly at a row of vegetables. She smiled inside, knowing he did this for her benefit. Though thin, he had a nice face and hair. She had not learned much else about him in the weeks since they had arrived here, and what little she did know had been gleaned from various things she had witnessed him doing. There were things she liked: his face, his eyes, his thoughtfulness, the way he took care of his little brothers, the sound of his voice. And things she didn't: his shyness, his anger at the Negro. Now, staring at him, she realized she was glad that they had not left. Fumiko walked on. They might never own their own land. Maybe the woman was right. But even if that was so, they had found something here that she and her mother and sisters, and even her grandfather, had somehow lost over the thousands of miles they had traveled since Japan. They had found their dignity again. That was better than land, she knew.

The afternoon sun was burning Prophet's back as he bent over the plants, carefully spreading the heavy roll of netting that they had ordered from a company in Minneapolis. While the plants were showing only flowers, and therefore were of no interest yet to the birds, Prophet was taking no chance that there might be a flock of crazed flower eaters out there somewhere.

He stood and stretched, looking out at the massive barrier of grass beyond the fence. The few times he had tried to penetrate it made him leery of ever doing it again. It was an awesome thing. He had become lost in it that morning while trying to take a shortcut from the field to the barn. He didn't like the feeling. It made him sweat. The thick grass scratched his face and tore at his clothes; the masses of waving plants were filled with millions of creeping and crawling things he couldn't see and the screeching of nesting birds.

Prophet arched his back, feeling better and stronger than he had in the weeks since the fight. He looked at Samuel, the boy standing only a few feet away clearing piles of dead weeds from between the rows with a rake. He could work hard, Prophet knew, and he wasn't mean-spirited. But Prophet also knew that he didn't like or trust him. Most likely he never would.

"How's it going, Sam?" Prophet said, trying to make polite conversation.

"Fine," the boy said curtly.

"You've done a good job clearing the rows."

The boy didn't answer him, and Prophet knew that

would be the extent of their conversation. He bent over his work, pulling back a thick matting of strawberry vine and finding himself staring straight at the blunt head of a coiled massasauga rattlesnake. Thick as Prophet's wrist, the heavy-bodied reptile lay no more than a foot from his face. He froze. Smaller than the diamondback, the massasauga was a lot more aggressive and just as deadly. The fields around the farm crawled with these fierce gray rattlers.

He had killed a five-footer earlier this week in the rhubarb patch, and he had seen the young pigs eating another out behind the barn. They were easy enough to kill if you saw them first, but now the tables were turned in a deadly fashion.

Prophet was off-balance, and the snake had obviously heard him coming and coiled and was poised to explode. Anything might trigger the strike. Prophet fought the trembling in his body. He hated snakes of all kinds, but this was the worst kind, and it was right in his face, its forked tongue flitting at the air.

"Samuel," he hissed.

The reptile's tail buzzed louder at the sound of his voice. Prophet glanced from the side of his eyes at Samuel. The boy had seen the snake, but Prophet could sense the fear and knew that he had frozen. Prophet had survived all his life by making quick decisions, and he immediately dismissed the boy as a possible solution.

Samuel gripped the rake hard, his eyes locked on the snake. It had whirled into a stiff ropelike coil a few inches away from the Negro's downturned face. Its savage head was angled away from him, and Samuel figured he could strike it with the rake, but he couldn't move. Not a muscle. He wanted to—but couldn't. Fear surged through his limbs, making them heavy and weak, and he shuddered and stared hopelessly at the scene in front of him.

Prophet was no longer thinking about Samuel. His thoughts were on the tiny man. Kishimoto was fast enough and skilled enough to save him. For the first time since they had met Prophet needed him, but he was sitting in his stiff-backed way, asleep, yards down the garden path. Prophet tried holding one arm behind him and snapping his fingers quietly to awaken the old man. But the little Japanese didn't move. A nerve kept firing in Prophet's head telling him time was running out, dangerously fast.

He tried pulling slowly away, even though he knew that once alarmed, a rattlesnake visually locked on its victim, freezing the picture in its mind. He also knew that if anything in that picture moved, even slightly, blammm! But it was still his best chance, his only chance.

The agitated buzzing of the reptile's tail rose to a frightening shrill, warning Prophet that the rattler's picture was dangerously close to changing. He froze. Sweat began to drip from the tip of his nose. Then he heard Zacharias calling his name from somewhere behind him. He tried frantically to wave the boy back with his hand, but it didn't work. Zacharias would be there any moment, certain to startle the snake into striking. The boy would also be in danger. Prophet determined that his and Zach's only chance was to make a desperate lunge, a lunge that he knew in his heart was hopeless. Trying to outjump this snake would be like trying to outjump a bullet fired into your face. Nevertheless, it was his last and only chance.

Zacharias was running fast down the row toward him now. Prophet determined to move on the count of three. One, he counted in his mind. Two—

Just as he was about to lunge, he saw a blurred movement from the edge of his eye, and the snake disappeared in an explosion of red. Prophet was numb for a second; then he hopped backward frantically. Mr. Kishimoto tripped the running boy with his foot.

Hercules had his one good wing out and his neck stretched forward, his hackles flared, defiantly facing off the coiled reptile. "No!" Prophet said, but it was too late. The old bird wasn't one just to face an enemy—even a rattlesnake—and he took a lunging leap at the reptile in the same instant that the snake spread its jaws wide and punched its massive head forward.

Then Prophet yanked Samuel's rake away, and it was over, the snake writhing headless on the ground. Hercules was standing and watching the creature coiling and twisting in death, ruffling his feathers as if to say, "That wasn't so tough." The old man was holding Zacharias back. Prophet knelt in front of the bird, and he raised his hackles menacingly; then he took a faltering step and fell. The massasauga had not missed. Zacharias was screaming and kicking at Mr. Kishimoto to get free.

Prophet sat down hard and gathered the bird into his lap. Hercules was shaking in rigid tremors. Prophet rested the rooster's head in the palm of his hand. The golden eyes were glazing fast. His hackles starting to rise, the bird seemed to focus on him for a moment. Then he went limp.

Zacharias took Hercules from Prophet, clutching him hard and sobbing. The tiny man was talking to the boy in Japanese, the words soothing and comforting, conveying a sympathy that transcended understanding.

Samuel wanted to hide. He dropped the rake that

the Negro had handed back to him and hurried from the garden. He was fighting back tears, conscious of the man's eyes on him as he stumbled down the rows. Once outside, the nausea overcame him, and he vomited.

He didn't hear the sound of the man's feet on the earth as he approached, but he knew he was there, and Samuel tried to stop crying.

"Sam," Prophet said.

He didn't answer.

"It happens to all of us at times. I froze as well. It doesn't mean anything."

He knew! Samuel started running for the house.

They dug Hercules's grave in a corner of the tiny enclosure where Matthew Eddy was buried. It was Zacharias's idea, but Pearl and the other boys agreed. Prophet spent the afternoon carving the words Zacharias wanted in a big wooden plank. He was faster at it this time.

HERCULES WAS MY FRIEND
ZACHARIAS EDDY

It was just before sundown, when the breezes stopped and the birds ceased their singing, that a peace that seemed right for a funeral came on the land. The sun was low in the sky and spraying golden rays over the garden. They all had come. Prophet figured Mrs. Eddy had ordered Samuel to be there. The boy avoided Prophet's glance, and the Negro did his best to try to act as if the boy weren't there. He felt sorry for him.

Mrs. Kishimoto and her three girls sprinkled pink and white flower blossoms over the small grave, and then each tied a little piece of white paper, which Eiko said were prayers, in the branches of an old lilac. The baby was asleep on Eiko's back. Pearl Eddy and her boys stood and watched, not saying or doing anything. Prophet guessed it was their way, but he didn't care much for it. Too quiet for his blood.

"Bless this bird. He had heart," he said.

No one moved or said anything after that until Pearl broke the silence. The sun was dropping behind the top of the barn. "Samuel and Fumiko, ye need to bring the pigs in."

Zacharias sat down next to the grave and put his hand on the freshly turned earth. Prophet squatted behind him, and the old man behind him. They didn't talk for a while. The garden was still in the thin shadows of late afternoon. The boy had quit crying, but every once in a while Prophet saw him draw a breath and shudder hard. "Thank thee for saying something about Hercules."

Prophet nodded.

"Where do chickens go when they die?"

Prophet scratched behind an ear. "Same place we do," he speculated.

Zacharias shook his head in a forlorn way. "Ma doesn't think so. She says that's just a people place."

Prophet rocked back on his heels and thought for a moment. "Your mother sometimes just talks like a mother."

"What's that mean?"

"Mothers want their boys to be logical-minded." He rubbed his chin. "So I think they tell them things like that, rather than tell them what's in their hearts."

"So thou thinkest chickens go to heaven?"

"Makes sense."

"Why?"

"I always heard heaven is just a better kind of earth, so things we love should be up there."

Zacharias twisted his mouth and thought about this for a while. Then he wiped a tear from his cheek and nodded. "Makes sense."

Prophet nodded in response.

"Then Hercules is with my pa?"

"I'd say so."

"Yes," the little boy said in a voice that seemed to float over the still gardens, drifting out into the wide expanse of prairie, sounding as if it might drift for a long time, a lifetime, if nothing stopped it.

The prairie was shading purple in the sunset by the time they found the pigs. Normally all the children except the baby tagged along with them on these excursions, and they turned the hunt for the hogs into a game. But not tonight. Hercules's death had cast a pall over things, and the smaller children were staying close to their mothers.

The shoats had rooted their way down the stream to the sandstone walls of the gully, a good half mile from the barn. They were bunched now around a prairie crab apple, searching the grasses for remnants of last year's crop. Samuel had walked ahead of Fumiko for most of the way, carrying a stick in case they found any more rattlesnakes. The thought made him cringe. He doubted that he could use the stick now, any more than he had that morning.

The memory of what he had not done was eating at him. Hercules was dead because of him, gone because he was a coward. He shuddered. He wished he could say something to Fumiko about it, but they had never spoken to each other.

He had a feeling that she might be angry at him for something. He wondered if that was it or if she just didn't like him. Whichever it was, she wasn't much comfort. Still, he felt better with her around. Something stirred inside him as he glanced back at her striding along in her confident way toward the grunting hogs.

Samuel stopped unexpectedly to avoid the prickly branches of a coyote thistle, and she accidentally bumped into him. She hopped quickly away and was off again. She hates me, he thought. She won't talk, can't stand me near her, and bristles when I accidentally touch her. He swallowed hard and started after the girl.

They were one pig short. Samuel had herded the animals into one of the blind turns of the gully and counted them twice. He tried to convince Fumiko to stay while he hunted for the missing pig. She would have none of it, tossing her head and striding off down the crumbling walls of the gully to search. Samuel didn't like it, but he stayed behind, knowing that if he let the shoats loose, they would never round them up in the dark.

Samuel sat in the sand and tried not to think about what he had failed to do, watching instead a blue kingfisher darting after minnows over the shallow water of the stream, trying to guess where the pig had gone. The pigs usually never wandered off. Fortunately, the animal was too big and tough for coyotes to bother with, and its arteries were encased in too much fat for rattlesnake venom to be a danger.

He shook again as his thoughts returned to Hercules. The brave old rooster had faced death without hesitation. Samuel quickly forced his musings away from the chicken to the lost pig. The only thing he could think was that it had fallen in a hole somewhere. There were a few dry wells around. Deerflies were pestering him now.

He brushed them away with his hat and went back

to watching the kingfisher again. Then he heard the shout. It could have been a hundred yards or a hundred miles away; it was hard to judge on the open plains. Still, any sound of humans out here in the lonely expanses of tallgrass caused a person to take notice. And he did so now, listening for a few more minutes but hearing only the evening wind moving through the stiff pencillike spikes of the blue vervain and leadplant lining the opposite ridge of the gully. But the voice had been real. He was certain of it. And it had come from the direction Fumiko had gone. Samuel stood for only a second longer; then he broke into a hard run.

They were holding her on the ground, hacking at her hair with sheep shears. Five boys struggled to keep her pinned, while a ring of men watched. Penny James was among the watchers, standing off to one side as if to make certain that things were done correctly, while his brother Hector did the clipping.

Fumiko was thrashing wildly, and it took them all to hold her down. Every once in a while she emitted a long scream, shrieking in pure anger, the reserve she had held in all this time now falling away. The pig squealed seemingly in sympathy and ran in circles around the trunk of a cottonwood where they had tied it.

Samuel was certain they had planned this thing. They must have watched the farm and known that it was Fumiko and his job to bring in the pigs at night. Samuel took a better grip on the stout stick he was holding and prepared to run down the hill from his hiding place in the grass. Then fear gripped him, and he froze. A nauseating wave of alarm splashed over him. There were too many of them. He couldn't hope to stop them. He needed help.

Samuel turned and started to run for the farm, his legs driving hard, groaning with the thought of leaving her. Then he stopped. He couldn't do it. His stomach churned. It didn't matter that he wouldn't be able to stop them or what they did to him. It only mattered that he try.

Hector was still hacking at Fumiko's hair when Samuel burst through the ring of men. Most of the boys jumped away at the sound of him, and Samuel grabbed Hector by the shoulders and threw him off. Then he pulled Fumiko up and helped her toward a sandstone wall that stood a few yards away. The boys followed at a distance behind, the men urging them on.

"Stop!" Samuel yelled, pointing a trembling finger at Hector as if it possessed some magical power to impede. "Ye have done enough wrong."

The men laughed, and Hector kept coming. He was in a crouch and cautiously eyeing the stick in Samuel's hand. Samuel pushed Fumiko behind him and took a step forward.

"I will not strike thee," he said, dropping the stick. "But, thou hast done enough," he said, his voice quivering.

Hector picked the stick up and flung it away; then he walked up close to Samuel. "I'm not done shearing." He brought a right hand hard into Samuel's face, and the boy staggered but didn't go down. The men were yelling encouragement.

"Put your hands up," Hector said tauntingly. Samuel didn't move, just stood with his arms hanging at his sides.

Hector hit him twice more before the boy sagged down onto his knees, blood spewing out his nose. Then Fumiko was clawing at Hector James.

Hector pretended to be hurt and squealed in fake

pain. But it wasn't all pretend. Long red scratches showed on his bare arms and on one side of his neck. After a hard rake of the girl's nails against the side of his face, Hector took a swing and knocked Fumiko onto the seat of her pants. Then Samuel struggled back up onto his feet and pushed her behind him. The girl was gasping for the breath that had been knocked out of her.

"He's going to fight. Hooolymaatheroffjesusss, the gawddamn sissy is going to fight," somebody said. The men hooted.

But Samuel was not going to fight. Again he stood in front of Hector, staring into the boy's eyes, with his arms down and taking blows to his face and chest until Fumiko couldn't stand it anymore. She bent and picked up a handful of sand, which she tossed into Hector's face, momentarily blinding him. Then she jumped forward and brought her foot up hard between his legs. Hector went down, clutching himself and gasping as if he had been gutted with a knife.

When he recovered, Fumiko was squatting and holding on to Samuel. Samuel was conscious but badly dazed; still, he struggled to control his body so that he could stand.

"Stay down! He kill you!" Fumiko screamed at him.

Samuel looked weakly into her face. She had finally spoken to him. He wasn't so groggy that he didn't know that, and hair or not, he thought she looked like an angel. Samuel tried to smile through the fog that clouded his brain and then shook her off, striving to stand once more. He half rose until his knees buckled, and then he sat down hard as he lost control of his legs. The men laughed.

"Get up and fight," Hector hollered.

"He doesn't fight because of his beliefs, but I don't believe in anything," Prophet said.

He was striding in his limping gait down the incline, smiling and nodding at the men, as if approaching a group of friends. The little sap was artfully hidden in the palm of one hand. Mr. Kishimoto trotted along behind, stick at the ready. It was the first time Prophet felt good about having the little man so close to him. He was chattering something that sounded like dried sticks being hit together. Prophet started to tell him to knock it off, that it was annoying, but he could see it was making the men nervous, so he let the old man continue.

The men backed away as the Negro and the Oriental moved through them. Prophet stooped casually to pick up Samuel's hat from the sand and then stopped in front of the boy and Fumiko. Kishimoto took up his wide stance facing the crowd while Prophet knelt and examined the boy and girl. Fumiko was shaking hard and holding Samuel's bleeding head, as if it might drop off into the sand if she let go. She looked a fright, her hair hacked off unevenly, a few odd strands sticking out around her head, a large bruise swelling on her left cheek.

"That one hurt him," she said, pointing at Hector.

Prophet recognized him as the ugly boy who had chased the Eddys home a few weeks back. "I told you to leave them alone."

Hector didn't respond; he just turned anxiously to his older brothers for support.

Fumiko's breath was coming in hard jerks, and she was fighting back tears. The old man came over and studied her, feeling her cheek in a tender way that surprised Prophet. Satisfied she wasn't badly injured, the tiny warrior looked into her face and said something that sounded comforting. The girl nodded in response and forced a little smile. Mr. Kishimoto bowed slightly to her, then turned back to the men.

Prophet propped Samuel against the sandstone wall. "Can you hear me, son? I need you awake."

The boy's eyes were rolling and showing too much white, and Prophet sensed he was barely conscious. "Never mind."

Though Samuel was having a hard time focusing his mind, he knew it was the Negro. Then he wondered if he was dreaming, but the spurts of pain in his head told him it was no dream. The Negro's words were lost in the roar inside his skull. He shook his head to clear it, until the pain slapped back hard and he stopped. Difficult as it was to believe, Jerome Prophet had waded into this fight. Samuel couldn't figure why, there didn't seem to be anything in it for him. Nevertheless, he was here. Then Samuel felt himself drifting away again. "Her" was all he managed to mumble.

"You'll both be fine," Prophet said, patting Samuel's hand. "Just rest." Prophet looked at Fumiko. "Can you carry him?"

She nodded. He wondered.

He looked at her shoulders and arms; they were thin but wiry. Maybe she could. Then he looked into her eyes and knew there was no doubt. "Good. When the fighting starts, you get him out of here, back to the farm. Understand?"

She shook her head no. "I fight beside my grandfather," she said resolutely.

The old man heard her and barked something over his shoulder in Japanese. She dropped her eyes and nodded obediently.

"Good," Prophet whispered. "Wait for the fight to start; then get to the farm. Follow the stream. When you tire, hide in the tallgrass. But keep going." He paused, looking at her eyes. She was staring at Samuel's face. "Do you understand?"

"Yes."

Prophet stood and faced the men. Mr. Kishimoto had moved a few feet in front of him and was staring without visible emotion at an empty piece of air, somewhere midway to the men, his legs spread wide. The little warrior was chattering up a storm now and tapping his stick rapidly on the ground in a wide half circle in front of them, as if inviting someone to try him. Prophet had the feeling that the tiny man had been in a fair number of these situations before, and he didn't look the least bit troubled by the odds in this one. Prophet wished the odds were better, but he liked the fact that the old man didn't really seem to care.

"I don't know what you did, gentlemen," Prophet said in an agitated voice, "but you got old Kish fired up, and that's bad. Some of you may make it out of this gully but not many."

Prophet made a show of staring at the chattering old warrior, then shaking his head. The men were watching the tiny man as well. "Seen him kill bullocks with that stick," he lied. "Not pretty.

"The way I figure it," Prophet continued, "you can back out now or take your chances with the little bastard. Your choice."

Prophet was a pretty good talker, and the men in the center of the line were actually looking at one another, uncertain what to do. Then Penny began moving in.

The men spread out, and it was tough to keep an eye on each of their positions. Suddenly one to Prophet's right made the mistake of trying a straight charge. He badly miscalculated Kishimoto's speed and range. The old man cut him down easily with a smashing blow to his neck that stunned him badly. Kishimoto was chattering now like a crazed monkey, high stepping, slapping

and twirling his stick like a baton tosser. The little bastard had style. Prophet had to admit that.

"Big mistake getting Kish agitated," he yelled,
trying to scare them into running one more time. It
didn't work.

The men were on them in a rush. Prophet caught
one of them with the sap alongside the skull, and the
man collapsed in the dirt. Then Prophet felt an arm
around his neck, and he ducked his chin and saved his
windpipe, just as somebody took a hard shot at his
ribs, then another. He went down, and the man
holding his neck went down with him. Prophet was
hurt but not badly. He moaned to let the pain out and
then drove his elbow hard into the temple of the man
who had been choking him.

Prophet lunged back up, knowing that the last place
he wanted to be was on the ground. He was trading
punches with a couple of men when he saw it coming
from the side of his eye and tried to dodge. He didn't
make it. The board bounced off his skull, and suddenly the sounds around him seemed to be moving
away at an incredible speed, until he felt as though he
were wrapped in silence deep underwater.

He could feel his legs giving way. Before he collapsed, he looked back to where he had left Fumiko
and Samuel. They were gone. She was tough. Then he
was falling and trying to hit somebody, but it was too
late. He saw the old Japanese go down swinging as
well. Then things went dark for him, and he was listening to Lacy telling him how beautiful the flowers
were. And somewhere in the distance he thought he
could hear Tyrone laughing.

The men were cursing and kicking at him, and
somebody spit in his face. Prophet felt his strength
ebbing and knew it was over. He looked up and saw
Penny James raising a heavy pipe to finish him. It was

a killing blow, intended as such. Prophet tried to roll desperately away but couldn't. The world seemed to be floating by, and he was in the best seat watching himself about to get his brains splattered.

The familiar sound reached Prophet somewhere deep inside some inner chamber of his mind: "Eiii!" Through the haze he saw his ally hop astride him, taking the downward blow of the pipe with his stick held high, but the pipe broke through and crashed into the old man. Then the world turned out its light.

Chapter Thirteen

Prophet woke with a start. He lay still and tried to figure out where he was and what had awakened him. He heard noise in the darkness, but he wasn't sure what it was and struggled to move. Pain bit into him like some feral beast, and he fought a pounding in his skull. He knew he was no longer lying in the dirt of the gully, but where? Had they taken him to a barn or somewhere else to hang him? Was that the old man chattering? His mind raced. He thought he could hear the boy Zacharias calling his name.

The blackness surrounding him was silent now, and he slipped back into his dreams, floating on a bed of harsh pain, in a world of nothingness, pain worse than any he had ever felt.

"Leave me alone," he screamed, the words clawing out of his throat, but barely audible even in the silence, the movement of his jaws causing his head to throb again. Then the darkness slowly began to spin around him, and he passed out once more, floating into black space, flipping head over heels, moving farther and farther away, searching in vain in this dark void for the old man.

He had no understanding of time, sensing only the cycles of light and dark in wherever he was. And in this manner the days passed. In the beginning he seemed to have no vision and grasped the fleeting thought that like Mrs. Eddy, he was now blind, but then slowly his eyes began to make shapes out of the darkness around him until he found himself lying in bed now, staring up at the ceiling, aware that a lamp was burning low. He tried to move his head and felt the searing pain shoot through his body. He could hear the old Japanese mumbling.

"Cut the gibberish!" Prophet muttered. Exasperated, he forced himself onto an elbow. His breath caught as his eyes, still blurred but able to see, moved slowly over the tiny form in the next bed. The voice told him it was the old man, but that was the only way he could tell. He couldn't see him through the bandages that covered the little Japanese. Then the fatigue was on him again, and he lay back and began once more to drift into oblivion.

He didn't know how long he had been unconscious before he heard the door to the room squeaking, but when he opened his eyes, the lamp was out, the room in darkness again. Then he heard steps nearby and thought for a moment that Lacy and Tyrone were finally coming for him. He always figured they would come to collect him when he died. And he felt dead now.

Samuel Eddy leaned weakly against the wall for physical support. His eyes were badly swollen, and he could only squint at the black man lying in the bed. He could see Prophet's face clearly in a strip of moonlight that came in through the window, but it didn't look like the man. The swelling and cuts distorted his features until Samuel finally just had to tell himself that it was the Negro.

In the five days since the attack the boy had regained much of his strength, though he occasionally felt faint. He cleared his throat and focused hard on

Prophet. He didn't understand why the man had risked himself, risked everything, why he had walked into a fight that he knew he was going to lose.

Samuel knew the old Japanese was just following the Negro, would have followed him anywhere. Plus the men were attacking his granddaughter. Therefore he had reasons for what he had done. But the Negro had nothing, nothing except to lose his life. That fact confused Samuel's mind. But it didn't matter.

Samuel went over to the still form. "Thank thee," he said quietly. The Negro didn't move or respond in any way, and for a moment Samuel thought he might be dead, but then he saw his shallow breathing.

"I misjudged thee—" He paused. "I wanted thee to know that in case thou art going to die."

The room's stillness was broken by a harsh sentence of Japanese uttered by the old man in his delirium. Samuel continued to study the broken black face. The boy drew in a long breath and held it. "I was scared again," he said.

Samuel jumped back. The man had motioned him with a slight crook of his finger. The boy watched him for a moment, then leaned forward. "Yes?"

"Not going to—" Prophet mumbled, the words scratching out of his throat.

"What?"

"Die."

Samuel nodded. "That is good."

The boy, supported by the wall, continued to watch him. Prophet was breathing hard as if the brief conversation had completely sapped his energy; then he crooked his finger again. The boy leaned back over him.

"Me too."

"Mr. Prophet?"

"Afraid."

Samuel looked as if he wanted to run out of the

room for a moment. Then he said, "I do not believe thee."

"Believe," Prophet said, straining to get the word out.

"But still thou fought. And Mr. Kishimoto fought."

Prophet thought about this for a while. "Practice. Old man and me—" He stopped talking and rested for a time, closing his eyes. When Samuel thought he had fainted, Prophet opened his eyes again and continued. "Lots of practice. Gets easier." What he had just said made him laugh, but the pained expression said it hurt too much, and he quit.

Prophet didn't say anything for a long while. Samuel just kept watching him as if he didn't want to leave.

Finally, Prophet said, "You aren't supposed—" He stopped and caught his breath. "Your mother—"

Samuel nodded at the man, but in his heart he knew it was more than just not having practice or obeying his mother. He was a coward.

"Samuel?" Pearl's voice came out of the room's darkness. She sounded groggy. "Is that thee?"

"Yes."

Neither Samuel nor Prophet had noticed her asleep in the chair in the shadowy corner of the bedroom. She tapped her thin cane over the floorboards until she was next to the bed.

"I will tell thee when Mr. Prophet awakens. Until then thou needest thy own rest."

"He is awake."

Her surprise was evident as she bent over him. "We've been worried about thee, Mr. Prophet." Dark circles underlined her weary eyes.

"Tell the old man to knock off his jabbering," Prophet said, straining to get the words out.

Pearl put a hand to his forehead to check for fever.

"Tell him," he insisted.

"Mr. Kishimoto wouldn't hear."

"Why?"

"He is still unconscious."

Something in the tone of her voice caught Prophet's attention, and he asked, "How bad?"

"I don't know."

Prophet remembered the pipe, the blow intended for him but taken by the little man. "What's the doctor say?"

"He hasn't come yet."

Prophet felt his head spinning and moved his body until the pain itself brought him back to full awareness. He repeated what she had said in his head, "He hasn't come yet." Prophet knew what that meant. It was over. The judge and the attorney had been right. The so-called respectable citizens of Zella were slowly, one by one, abandoning the Eddys to the town's rabble. He started to say so, then didn't. She had enough to worry about. He thought about the old Japanese again.

"He's just faking. He's lazy."

"No."

Pearl walked Samuel from the room. Prophet rolled over, ignoring the pain, and studied the bandaged head of the old man. Mr. Kishimoto's lips were moving through a hole in the material that covered his face, but no sound was coming out. As he studied the little form in the shadows, Prophet wondered things about him that he had never given much thought to before.

And he realized that he knew almost nothing about this man who had saved his life. Something seemed to be pressing hard against his chest. He knew only that the little man was a fighter, was like him in some ways. He rolled slowly back down onto the bed, pain shooting through his ribs, and stared at the ceiling for a long time. When he finally spoke, he had to clear his throat. "Serves you right, old man. You've been asking for trouble since you got here."

As if in response, Mr. Kishimoto rattled off another heated sentence.

"Be quiet, you old fool."

The little man suddenly stopped talking, and Prophet listened hard for his breathing. When he couldn't hear it, he rolled over quickly, ignoring the pain, and watched the small shape until he was certain he was still alive. "Damn fake," he muttered, easing himself back down. "You deserve what you got. Teach you to follow me everywhere like a damn dog."

Prophet heard the muffled sound of Pearl's voice in the hallway. "Zacharias, I'm not going to tell thee again. Thou must stop hanging around Mr. Prophet's doorway."

"He needs me," the boy protested.

Prophet smiled.

"No. He needs his rest. And thou has other things thou art supposed to be doing. Now run along."

Pearl entered quietly, tapping through the darkness of the bedroom to check Mr. Kishimoto; Prophet lay watching her, listening to the sounds the old man made.

"How's he look?"

"The same."

"He's faking."

"No," she said softly.

Prophet stared at her through the shadows. "You don't know how bad he is," he said.

"Only that he is in God's hands."

"God doesn't take things into His hands," Prophet snapped. Pearl ignored him and straightened Mr. Kishimoto's blankets.

A moment later he said, "You don't really believe that."

"Mr. Prophet?"

"That the old man is in God's hands."

"We are all in God's hands."

He shook his head. "If that's true, I've been dropped a lot by Him."

"Do not make fun of God, Mr. Prophet."

He didn't respond.

"I would have thought thou as a minister and I shared similar beliefs."

He looked uncomfortable and tried to change the subject. "The old man will be okay. He's a fighter."

"That is not a saving grace. It is in fact the problem."

He had finally had enough. "No," he said sharply. "We didn't start that fight."

"Thou started that fight, Mr. Prophet, when thou attacked Penny James in the street, then again in his house."

The wind had picked up and was banging a shutter against the side of the bedroom. Prophet listened to this for a while, trying to cool off. Then he said, "That's crazy. He attacked you in the street. And he was threatening to shoot the woman." He paused and rested. "And they were beating your boy." He was angry and breathing hard against the pain rising in his body. "Should we have let them, Mrs. Eddy?"

"Rest," she said.

"No. Should we?" he persisted.

"Thou must answer that for thyself."

"I have. That old man," he said, pointing at Mr. Kishimoto, "fought for the children. And was injured for the children. That's love, Mrs. Eddy."

"No, Mr. Prophet. That is ignorance."

He didn't say anything for a time, just lay looking up at her face, his frown intensifying. Finally, he said, "You aren't the keeper of the Holy Book."

"No. But I know that violence is wrong, that God would have saved the children."

Prophet stared at her with a shocked look on his face. "God would have saved them? Is that right?" he said sharply.

"Yes."

"When? Before or after your boy was beaten into snot?"

Pearl didn't say anything for a moment, then continued. "Mr. Prophet, thou wrongly confuse rescue with salvation. God would have saved the children in wondrous ways beyond mere physical deliverance from danger."

"Your religion makes you loony," Prophet mumbled slowly.

Then he drifted off again. In his delirium Pearl heard him calling for his children, telling them that he was coming. She brushed at the tears beginning to flow down her cheeks. Then she heard a noise and thought she heard Zacharias at the door again.

There were seven women sitting in her parlor. They had come in two carriages, and Pearl figured they were a delegation of sorts. Miss Belle Johnson and Mrs. Isabel Tutt were doing most of the group's talking.

Pearl considered the two women friends. They had worked long and hard on a number of causes over the years: raised money to stock the shelves of Zella's library and school, led a failed crusade against intemperance. And Belle and Isabel had joined Pearl in collecting blankets and warm clothing for the Indian Reservation Relief Fund when public anger had dried up desperately needed contributions after the Battle of the Little Bighorn in '76. They were good women, good friends. She knew the others in the room as well but was not as close to them as she was to Belle and Isabel.

Pearl leaned back into her chair and listened to their quiet breathing, the soft clicking of the cups and saucers, the fiddling of their parasols and knew they were uncomfortable.

"Pearl Eddy, how long have we known each other?" Belle asked.

"A long time, Belle," Pearl said softly, waiting for the real questions.

"That's correct. For a long time."

"We have too," Isabel interjected.

Pearl nodded and then folded her hands together in her lap.

"And, Pearl," Belle continued, "while we love Rose Sherman, we don't necessarily hold with all she says." There was a murmur of agreement. "I guess what I'm saying, Pearl, is that she doesn't run the women of Zella. At least not the younger women."

"I'm not certain I understand," Pearl said.

Belle cleared her throat. "Pearl, Rose is saying some hurtful things. That you're keeping time with a colored. That the Asians are selling opium." She paused. "And other things. She hasn't been doing much talking since Ernie's accident, but before that she had plenty to say."

"And thou?"

"That it's foolishness, Pearl," Belle said without hesitation. "We all know you. We're friends."

Pearl didn't say anything, just sat thinking.

"Pearl," Isabel said, "we want you to come to your senses."

"Meaning?" Pearl asked quietly.

"Talk in town is going against you, Pearl. People don't want these Chinese around. Philo Tucker at the hardware tells anyone who'll listen that they breed like rats. That today we've got six ... and tomorrow we'll have sixty. And, Pearl, more and more people are listening."

"They're Japanese."

"Pardon?" Isabel said.

"The Kishimotos are Japanese, not Chinese."

Belle Johnson pressed her lips together and shook her head. "Pearl, whatever race they are doesn't matter. They just aren't right for this town. They aren't right for your family." She paused. "We understand there was trouble out here a few days ago."

"Some men attacked Samuel and a Japanese girl, and an old Japanese man, and the Negro," Pearl said. "The old man is hurt badly."

"None of our husbands," Isabel said hurriedly. "But there are people willing to do almost anything to get rid of these people. And we're afraid for you."

Neither Pearl nor the women said anything for a while. Then Belle broke the silence.

"You've been a good neighbor and friend, Pearl Eddy. We don't want you and your boys hurt. We'll handle Rose. We'll also see to it that you get your seamstressing business back. We've come today with orders for twelve new dresses, and there will be more on a steady basis." There was a strong murmur of support.

Belle reached into her purse and pulled out an envelope. "And, Pearl, we've taken up a collection in town." She hesitated. "There's money here to take these people to either coast by train. And more to help them get settled someplace."

Pearl wasn't listening. She was thinking about Matthew and their Sunday dinners during the summer months. She had loved those. The laughter and the fun. The boys running and playing afterward in the yard while she and Matthew sat on the front porch and talked. That was all gone now. And worse, the bank was threatening to take what was left of her life. Tears were rolling down her cheeks. The women watched, and some of them began to cry as well.

Now her friends were offering her a way out, a way to save her boys and her home. Then her breath caught in her throat. Her mind seemed to drift. She tried to concentrate on Belle's words but couldn't. Couldn't stop the whirling thoughts in her head.

She seemed to see them all—the Eddys, the Kishimotos, and the Negro—sitting in a small boat in the middle of a dark ocean. Dying of thirst. The boat slowly sinking. Then suddenly her friends were there. Coming to rescue them. Smiling and bringing water. And she was crying and happy.

But when she tried to give the water to the little girls, to the old man, to the Negro, nothing came out but dust. The only people whose thirst she could quench were herself and her boys. Nothing for the others. Not the little girls. Not the baby. None of them. Then the little boat was beginning to swamp, and her friends were shouting at her to lighten the load by throwing the Kishimotos and the Negro into the dark waters. "My God! Do it for your boys," Belle Johnson was screaming.

Then the vision was gone, and she could hear Isabel saying what a wonderful place Zella was to raise children. She didn't disagree, but she couldn't think about that now. She could only think of the brutal choice they had brought her: Save thyself and thy boys. But no others. Cast them away. Cast them into darkness or hellfire or damnation . . . it didn't matter where. Just cast them away.

Pearl didn't move or speak for a long time. These women, her friends, wanted the foreigners and the Negro to disappear every bit as badly as the mob in

Main Street had. They just wanted it without unpleasantness. Pearl's stubbornness and wrath began to rise in her throat. A fly was buzzing in the room, and she listened to the sound. Then she stood up.

"No," she said flatly. "Thank thee. But no."

"Pearl, you are just being sill—" The word seemed to have been torn off at Belle Johnson's teeth. Then the room fell silent until Pearl heard Prophet behind her mumbling, "You stay away from me!"

"He's just delirious," she assured them.

But moments later screams and pandemonium broke out, and she could hear the women fleeing as if pursued by death itself. She couldn't figure it. Then she heard Eiko yelling in Japanese, then English, then back to Japanese.

"You go to bed!" she hollered. "Go to bed now! *Isogu! Isogu!*"

"Eiko?"

"Mr. Prophet. Ooooh," she moaned. "He break up the party."

"Yes. But why? These women have seen a Negro before."

"Not like this one," Eiko said. "Go bed! Beddo! Beddo!"

"Eiko?"

"No clothes. Big naked!"

Pearl sat stunned and still for a minute, listening to Eiko chasing Prophet back to his bed. Then she began to laugh. The laughter exploded through the house, so loud that Eiko quit chasing Prophet long enough to peek at her, then shook her head and went rushing back.

"Beddo! Now! No dance! Beddo!"

Pearl was doubled up with laughter. Then she heard Zacharias yelling. "Thou just fought a big battle. Thou needest thy rest. So thou canst fight again!"

She stopped laughing and folded her hands together in her lap. Then, slowly, she began to squeeze them, squeezed them until her knuckles were cream white from the strain.

Inside the Eddys' spare bedroom at the back of the house, in the soft warm air of June night that drifted through the open windows, after Prophet had slept through another day, he shifted between the sheets of his bed and felt the pain dig at his soul again. He opened his eyes and knew immediately that he and the old Japanese were not alone.

He tensed, the contraction causing pain to spurt in a hundred places over his injured body. He fought it and the feeling of faintness, rolling onto his shoulder toward the old man's bed.

Eiko was there, trying to give Mr. Kishimoto water. Unconscious, the tiny man was nevertheless still cursing at her. Prophet watched them for a while, then gruffly asked, "How is the little faker?"

"He sick. *Byoki* no." Then Eiko grinned at him. "You big party breaker."

He didn't understand the last part of what she had said. But then he often didn't understand her; that was probably the way she wanted it, he thought. He focused on the old man. "He'll be fine," he said firmly. "As long as he thinks he can pester me, he'll hang around."

When she was done with the old man, Eiko came over and looked down at Prophet's busted face and said, "You not so strong. No *tsuyoi*." She was smiling.

And he smiled back at her for the first time. "Stronger than that old man."

She looked suddenly serious. "Now. Maybe yes. Once. Maybe no."

They didn't speak for a while. Eiko had returned to

the old man's bed and was sitting in a chair, leaning toward him as if she wanted to tell him something.

"Who is he?"

"Shincho Kishimoto," she said, as if the name would mean something grand to him.

"I know that. But why the stick? And why does he follow me like a dog?"

She stiffened, ready to defend the old man on this quiet night. "No dog. He follow like great warrior. Shincho Kishimoto. Great soldier."

The old man was hard as scrap metal, but Prophet had trouble swallowing that Kishimoto, at something like four feet eight inches and maybe ninety-five pounds with his hair wet, was some famous Nipponese gladiator. But then he remembered he had been a gladiator against those brutes, had saved his life. Prophet willed for him to recover.

Eiko turned the kerosene lamp down until it cast only a dull smudge of yellow light over the bedroom. Prophet watched a mouse scurry across the wooden floor. They hadn't spoken for a few minutes, the stillness broken only by the old man's shallow breathing. Eiko returned to Mr. Kishimoto. Prophet watched.

"He once chief retainer for second daimyo of Naga Prefecture," she said with obvious pride in her voice. "*Okii samurai.*" The words were crisp-sounding as they came off her tongue. "Big samurai."

Prophet didn't know much about samurai but knew that they were mean and powerful. But that was then for Mr. Kishimoto.

"He's no longer whatever he used to be, so why's he always looking for trouble?"

She touched the old man's forehead through the bandages with the tips of her fingers in a reverent way. "*Itsu mo.* Always samurai."

Eiko spent the next few minutes straightening the

old man's bed. Then she turned and looked at Prophet across the shadowy light of the room. "He fight because samurai fight. Their way is *shi*. Death."

"What the hell does that mean?"

"Samurai live like already dead. *Iie osore*. No fear. Only loyalty to master."

Prophet shook his head. "And he thinks I'm his master?"

Eiko ignored him. "He try to commit *junshi*," she said, drawing her fist hard across her stomach in a movement of disembowelment that needed no translation. "To accompany master when he died." She shrugged her shoulders. "But *junshi* forbidden by shogunate."

The room grew silent. Eiko was whispering prayers. Prophet studied the strange old samurai, wondering at his willingness to die for other people. It was crazy. Prophet was almost a complete stranger. The only thing he had ever done for the old man was beat the crap out of him and then yell at him every day. Things that hardly seemed worth dying for. Prophet promised himself he would never die for anyone else. It was hard enough to do it for yourself.

Eiko stood and smiled down at Prophet. "You new master. *Shiawase na*. Happy."

"You tell him I'm not *shiawase* whatever. I'm not his master. And I don't want him following me."

"You tell him. He no listen to me." She paused. "Anyhow, he may die. Anyhow."

"Don't sound too sad about it."

She nodded vigorously and smiled. "Not sad. He dead already. Anyhow, that is what he like. Die for master. So why I be sad?"

"Very touching," Prophet mumbled, feeling suddenly weak.

* * *

Pearl Eddy waited awhile after she heard Eiko leave the sickroom before she tapped quietly inside. Zacharias was sitting by the door, and she scolded him and sent him off, his presence steeling her resolve that she was doing the right thing. She stopped next to Prophet's bedside. Neither of them spoke for a while. He could tell she had something on her mind and figured it was best to wait and let her roll it out. After a moment he yawned.

Outside the bedroom window the hogs were fighting over the remains of a yellow gopher snake they had killed in the fields, squealing and snorting as if it were a choice tidbit. With the curtains open, the room had pools of soft moonlight on the floor.

Pearl cleared her throat. "How dost thou feel, Mr. Prophet?"

"Fine."

"Good," she said quietly. There was something in her tone that caused him to listen closely. She let the squealing of the hogs die down, then continued. "Thou remember what I said about Zacharias?"

"About?"

"How he looks up to thee."

"Yes."

Pearl had reached up and put a hand on the wall as if she needed support. It seemed an odd thing to him.

"Dost thou also remember thy promise about violence?"

Prophet rolled his eyes, then said, "I didn't start anything with Penny James, Mrs. Eddy. He started it. Both times. And I sure didn't start things at the river."

She looked suddenly exhausted. "It doesn't matter, Mr. Prophet," she said quietly. "I asked thee to control thy violence, not to expose my children to it. But thou hast not."

"Mrs. Eddy, only lesson I ever learned in this life was that weakness invites trouble."

Her face seemed to tighten, as if what he was saying were making her uneasy.

He pressed his advantage. "You ought to think on that, ma'am."

Pearl could hear him speaking, but she was no longer listening to him, her mind flying back over the years to a painful memory. Matthew had once told her almost exactly the same thing. She shivered.

It happened in the first year of their marriage. Matthew was not yet living as a Quaker, had not begun his moral metamorphosis. She bit her lower lip hard, wishing now he had never tried, the thought tearing at her heart. They had been traveling west to Kansas when he had gotten into a fight with a drunk in the dining car of the train, the man having made improper remarks to her. Matthew had a quick temper and hit the man hard enough to knock him unconscious. Pearl exhaled with the painful memory.

"You okay, ma'am?"

"Yes." She wrapped her arms around her body, as if trying to hold herself, remembering that she had gotten angry and refused to talk the entire rest of the trip. For a thousand miles she had sat in silence. It was the first time Matthew had ever witnessed stubbornness coming out of the Quaker creed. She winced as if struck. Her awful wrath.

After that episode Matthew vowed to her that he would live as a Quaker, adopting the clothing, the speech, the beliefs. The nonviolence. Her breath snagged in her throat. He had sacrificed everything to believe like her. She knew that he had done it because he loved her and realized that they could never live together unless he did. She was fighting back tears now, turning and walking to the window so Prophet wouldn't see. And it had killed him. She had killed him.

Prophet watched her warily. He knew that when she was in one of her moods, she was tough to handle. A horned owl was sounding in the elm near the well, hunting mice along the barn wall, Prophet figured. He let his mind drift, wondering how owls saw something that small in the dark. He knew they could spot a mouse in grass at a hundred yards.

Pearl leaned against the wall by the window, her thoughts still on Matthew. About a year after the train incident, on a lovely summer evening, as they were sitting on the front porch watching the fireflies and listening to the sounds of the prairie, he had turned to her and said: "The passiveness, Pearl. It causes violence." Pearl shuddered hard. For years her way had been right. Then, eighteen months ago, the truth of Matthew's words had destroyed a large part of her life.

At the trial she heard that Matthew had been jumped by a group of men in front of the saloon. They claimed they were only having fun with a Quaker, grabbing his hat, then his coat and shoving him into a water trough, trying to get him to fight back. But he hadn't. She clamped her eyes closed tightly as if to try to shut out the vision in her mind. He had lived up to his beliefs. No, she shook her head. She would not lie to herself. He had lived up to her beliefs.

The men had followed him to his horse, and when he started to mount, they had spooked the animal, and his foot had caught in the stirrup. Pearl was crying without sound now. The horse had galloped the three miles home. It had been winter, and the roads were frozen hard, and when Pearl freed the horribly twisted leg from the saddle and touched his face, she had not recognized him, not recognized him until he had said her name. She was gasping for breath now.

"Mrs. Eddy?"

"I am fine, Mr. Prophet."

It seemed unbearably hot in the bedroom, and she wiped the back of her hand across her forehead. Yes. He had died because of her beliefs, her wrath. She would have to live with this knowledge for the rest of her life. She would never escape it.

But Matthew had also died doing the will of God. She pulled herself up straighter and squared her small shoulders. And she would not allow his sacrifice to be cheapened by this man teaching his sons violence, leading them to damnation. She could not. It was no more complicated in her mind than that. She saw it very clearly.

She stood and listened to the wind and the owl for a while, then returned to his bedside and said, "There is a saying in Proverbs, Mr. Prophet. I'm certain thou art familiar with it: 'A wrathful man stirreth up strife.' "

He didn't respond. Just looked at her face. What he saw there he found hard to believe. Maybe he just didn't want to believe it.

"Thou must leave, Mr. Prophet."

After all the time he had spent telling himself that he was wasting his time here, that he had to get on the road, he was surprised how torn he felt.

He watched her face for a long time. "I was going anyway," he said, "soon as I can get around."

She nodded but said nothing.

"I got things I've been putting off."

She turned away slowly and left the room. Somewhere in the hallway he could hear her crying. He fought the tremors around his mouth.

* * *

It was early morning, before full light, before the birds cut loose with their endless singing for the day, the room cool and dimly lit, and Fumiko was standing and frowning at the rumpled mass of blankets that covered Samuel Eddy's bed. She had entered the room moments before and stood staring down at him. Samuel was too embarrassed to say anything. He studiously avoided her eyes, studying instead her closely clipped hair. His mother's work for certain. She had turned Hector's ragged cuts into a smooth trim, shaped nicely to Fumiko's handsome head, a single lock of long hair draped stylishly down ponytail-fashion on one side, caught up in a pink silk ribbon.

Only his mother would have thought of this touch. Almost everyone else would have just clipped off the piece, leaving the girl to look like a prisoner rather than a beautiful young woman with an exotic hair-style. Even with the dark bruise on her cheek, she looked pretty. She moved closer.

He didn't know what to do, what to say. She was busy straightening his covers, and he was trying desperately to act natural. He cleared his throat. "Thank thee."

She stepped back and smiled, her beautiful white teeth seemingly breaking her handsome face in two, her eyes crinkling at the corners with a young woman's joy that had been hidden before. She bowed slightly. The bow was not cowed or obedient, just polite, as though simply acknowledging him. He raised his head off the pillow and bowed awkwardly back.

This seemed to embarrass her slightly, and she began to move around the room, opening windows, adjusting curtains and, in general, making the place ready for the coming day. She stopped and looked back at his bruised face, as if she didn't know what to do next. Then she bowed slightly once more, and said, "Thank you."

It was the second time that she had ever spoken to him. And it was wonderful.

"For?"

"Fusegu me," she said in her strongly accented voice, pointing vigorously at herself as if he might not be able to understand her words. "Protect me."

He thought her voice the loveliest sound in the world, deep and full, like a cat's purring. Then the familiar feeling of shame returned. She didn't look as if she were making fun of him. But he wasn't certain. She saw the darkness in his expression.

"I said wrong?"

"No."

"What is the"—she struggled for the word— "matter?"

"Nothing." He looked out the window at the back-yard. Jack was in his corral, looking toward the house. Samuel stared at the horse.

"Something."

He looked back and held his breath. "You did the fighting," he said finally. "I just stood."

She was nodding vigorously, and he wondered if she understood what he was saying. "You stand," she said, continuing to nod and holding her two hands in front of her, palms toward each other as if she might be measuring a very small fish, "like this. Face—face." Then she burst into a smile that he thought had the power to burn a hole in his heart. "For me. Fumiko." She paused, and the smile left her face. "No one ever do that for me or my family. Never," she said softly. "Like we not really ningen. People."

He watched her face, knowing what it was like to be treated that way. He didn't want to hurt her more by letting her believe he had done something he had not. He cleared his throat. "I didn't fight."

"You did this," she said, putting her hands up again. She stared at him as if he were a modern Lancelot. It made him squirm. Still, it was wonderful.

Chapter Fourteen

By the end of the week Prophet was complaining. "We
need to get out of this room. It isn't healthy. The old
man needs sun. I need sun." Pearl and Eiko were
standing in the doorway, as Prophet, in his pajamas,
tried to climb out of bed. But he was swaying.

"Mr. Prophet, if thou feelest well enough, fine. But
Mr. Kishimoto is in no condition—"

"I've been watching him. He isn't going to get any
better in here. Old man," Prophet called toward the
bed, "old man. We're going outside. You for it?"
Prophet pulled his pants over his pajamas.

Mr. Kishimoto had been awake for the past week,
but he had not spoken. His words seemed to have
stopped coming when he returned to consciousness.
Now he was moving his lips, but nothing came out.

"He just said he's for it," he mumbled, tugging on
his boots. Prophet felt stronger now. He bent and
picked up the man, surprised at how light he felt.

"Mr. Prophet," Pearl protested, "Mr. Kishimoto is
not well. And thou wilt not endanger him in this
manner."

"You're a worrier, Mrs. Eddy," Prophet said as he
moved through the house toward the back porch,
Shincho Kishimoto in his arms. Prophet's legs were

wobbling, and there was a moment when he almost lost his balance, but he steadied himself and continued forward, Pearl tapping along behind.

"If thou must do this, thou wilt do it only for a little while, Mr. Prophet," Pearl insisted.

"Sure, Mrs. Eddy."

She listened to Prophet straining to bear the old man in his arms down the porch steps and then across the yard, talking steadily to Mr. Kishimoto as he went, and got a funny feeling deep inside her. She had been right. God saved in mysterious ways. Then she heard Zacharias running down the steps after him and knew that she had also been right about the man's having to leave.

The rays of the midafternoon sun felt just as wonderful as Prophet had imagined they would. The day wasn't hot, just flooded with brilliant light. He selected a place near the old stone well house, and Eiko and Pearl spread blankets on the ground for them.

Prophet leaned back against the cool, smooth stones soaking in the sunlight, while Mr. Kishimoto sat in his familiar stiff-backed, cross-legged posture, still wrapped in his bandages and covered with blankets and looking like the dearly departed at a picnic. The old man still did not speak. But he was salivating, and Prophet kept drying his mouth with a rag.

"Kish," he said, dabbing the side of the man's mouth one more time, "you got to get a grip on yourself. You can't sit around, spitting up like a baby." He paused. "They'll kick you out of the samurais."

At the sound of the word the old man seemed to stir slightly.

Prophet turned his head slowly—he still had some pain when he moved—and took a close look around at the farmyard, the gardens, the barn, the watering sluice, the old house. His eyes moved carefully over details that he had missed before. He wanted to remember everything. He felt he would never see a place like this again.

It seemed he had lived here all his life. His chest began to tighten, and he shut his eyes and tipped his face up into the sunlight. "Waste of time," he muttered to himself.

Zacharias was sitting cross-legged on the ground in front of them, his freckled face covered by the shade of his large hat, holding the little wooden horse in his hands. "When thou art feeling better, we can go fishing." Zacharias scratched his ankle. "Thou ever been?"

Prophet's eyes were closed, and he was leaning back on his arms, taking the sun and ignoring the boy.

"Thou ever been fishing?"

"Yes."

"My pa used to take me. I'll show thee how to catch catfish. I'll bet thou dost not know how. Would thou like that?"

Prophet squinted at the boy and then said, "Sure. If we've got time."

Zacharias grinned. "We got lots of time."

Prophet sat up looking agitated. "Don't talk like that," he snapped. "Time runs out for a person. Understand?"

Zacharias looked hurt. "Yes, sir."

"Good."

"Zacharias," Pearl called from the porch.

"We don't have to go fishing."

"I want to go fishing. Now get before your mother comes storming down here after us both."

"I don't want to now," Zacharias said, turning and trotting toward the porch.

"Fine."

Prophet looked at Mr. Kishimoto. "You know I was right," he said. "And you know time's running out for us, old man." He stopped talking again, gathering his thoughts. "We got to come to an understanding."

The red shawl of the old Japanese had slipped to the ground, and Prophet put it back over his shoulders. Then he looked through the holes in the bandages into the small eyes. They seemed to peer through him as if the little man were staring at a distant memory. Prophet sat back down and let him alone for a while. He figured the old man didn't have much time left for remembering.

Finally, he said, "You listen. I am not your master. And you can't spend whatever little time you got following me. I got things to do. And you can't come."

Prophet closed his eyes. He thought that he had just daydreamed for a short while about Lacy and Tyrone, but when he awoke, the sun was going down and someone had covered them with additional blankets. The sound of children laughing drifted across the yard from the kitchen.

He cleared his throat. "You awake?" The old man didn't move, but Prophet could see that he was breathing.

"You just can't come where I'm heading," Prophet said. For some reason, it bothered him to say this. He turned and studied the side of the bandaged face. He cleared his throat. "You understand?" Prophet leaned over and dabbed at the side of the old man's mouth again. "Quit your damn slobbering."

Then the old man's lips were moving, and Prophet leaned closer. "Master" was all the old man said.

"No! You aren't some slave, and I'm not some boss." Prophet stared in frustration at the tiny man. "If you got to call me something, call me friend."

Prophet heard a noise, and he looked toward the barn. He could see three horses with their reins dropped near the big door. Two men and three horses. He wasn't great at arithmetic, but he knew what it meant.

They came over toward the invalids. "Well, that's what we are," Prophet said to himself. They were big men, rough-looking. If he had been well, he could have handled them. But he wasn't. He leaned back weakly against the well and just stared up at them.

"Let's go, Negro." The man who spoke had a bushy white beard like Santa Claus. But Prophet knew he wasn't. He glanced at Mr. Kishimoto; then he leaned over and pulled a blanket up to the old man's chin.

"We don't like this any better than you do. But we been paid to do it. So let's get."

Prophet was struggling to get to his feet when he heard her. Clutching a broom that she had been sweeping the back porch with, Pearl was stumbling hurriedly across the yard toward where she had heard the men's voices. Prophet looked at her. She was dressed in a long black skirt and wearing a simple long-sleeve white blouse, an apron tied to her middle. Her hair was done up in a neat bun, and her eyes were flashing that particular righteous fire of hers.

"What art thou doing?"

His heart sank. He didn't want her involved in this mess.

"You just stay out of this, ma'am. Our business is with the colored. Not you. Not the Chinaman. Not your place. We got no interest in any of that."

"Then leave," Pearl said firmly.

"Leave!" Zacharias shouted. He had come running from the house.

"Zacharias, thou art to go back." Her voice had an

edge to it that neither Prophet nor the boy had ever heard before, and Zacharias turned and started off in the darkness. Then he stopped and looked back at the Negro.

"Mr. Prophet?" His voice was shaking.

"Go on inside, son," Prophet said. "Everything will be fine."

The boy stared at him for a long time, his upper lip trembling. Then Zacharias broke at a run for the house. Prophet could hear him sobbing. Pearl was still holding on to the broom. He could see her shaking hard in the darkening air of the evening.

"I asked thee a question. What dost thou want with Mr. Prophet?"

"We don't want anything, lady. We've just been paid to collect him and bring him in. If you've got an argument, it's with those who paid us."

"Who paid thee, and why do they want Mr. Prophet?"

He could hear her voice changing.

"Lady, don't ask questions. Okay? Just get back into the house, and let us get this done."

"They're right," Prophet said.

Pearl ignored him and squared her body to the place where she had last heard the sound of the bearded man's voice.

"Thou art being used by Satan. Thou cannot participate in just part of this sin. Thou art involved in all of it."

Prophet didn't want to look at her. He wanted her to turn and go back inside the kitchen, to make dinner, to sew, to have her boys read to her. Just to do the things she did. And to let these men get on with it. They were going to do it anyway. No matter what she said. This wasn't a time for her talk.

"Lady, get out of here," the man warned.

"I will not." She paused. "I will be here while thou dost this thing. Thou will not have the comfort of the night to hide thy acts."

"I don't give a damn, lady. We're taking this Negro to the people who paid us. What they do with him is their business. Not ours."

Prophet had started to get to his feet, knowing they weren't leaving without him and not wanting trouble for her or the others, when, suddenly, he saw her swing. He didn't believe it. But when he turned his head, he saw the broom catch the man full in the face and pitch him backward onto the seat of his pants. Then Pearl Eddy was standing over him and screaming and striking wildly with the broom as if she were indeed fighting off Satan. Prophet couldn't move.

The second man was laughing hard while rushing to the aid of his friend, so that he didn't see the shape moving in the shadows toward him. Didn't see Eiko swing. The iron skillet hit him on the side of the head, and Prophet knew from the way he collapsed, he wouldn't be getting up for a while.

As quickly as she had begun the attack, Pearl broke it off. But she was still screaming as if she had witnessed something awful. The bearded man was bleeding from his nose, and he scrambled to his feet and just stared at her; then he bent and picked up his friend and stumbled toward the horses.

"And no come back!" Eiko yelled.

Prophet couldn't take his eyes off Pearl Eddy. She just stood holding the broom in both her hands, shaking as he had never seen her shake before; it was as if she had killed a man instead of just hit him with an old broom. Eiko stood quietly beside her, skillet in her hand, an arm around Pearl's waist as if she were afraid the woman might fall down.

Then, from behind them, came another voice: "Gosh!" Zacharias and his brothers stood staring at their mother dumbfounded. Prophet wanted to laugh but knew he shouldn't.

Eiko was squinting hard at the boys now; then she pointed a finger at the house. The gesture was clear. They turned and started off, talking with surprise and wonder about their mother's performance. Mr. Kishimoto was chattering about nothing from where he lay on the ground.

Eiko said something to Pearl that Prophet couldn't hear. She shook her head. Then the little Oriental woman reached out and put her hand on the broom, and Pearl let go of it as if it were a viper. She started walking slowly toward the corral; she seemed to be in a daze. Eiko started to follow, then stopped and returned to the house.

Prophet settled slowly back down onto the ground, watching the little woman through the gathering dusk, her slight frame dwarfed by the huge barn. He would never have believed her capable of doing what she had just done. And from the look of her, he guessed she had never believed it either. She had always looked so young and vulnerable to him, small and delicate. But he knew she had a backbone of steel and a willpower that she drew on from the depth of her soul. He wanted to talk to her, to tell her things that he felt he should. But the time wasn't right. He stared off at the gardens for a while, thinking about catching the late train. He could just about make the tracks in time.

Prophet saw it when he turned and looked back toward the dark shape of the barn. At first he thought it was the last of the setting sun, a pink tinge of light running across the sky above the barn. Then, with a start, he realized that he was facing north, the western horizon to his left. Hurriedly he stopped, picked up the small man, and started to run for the corral.

"Mrs. Eddy," he yelled.

She turned slowly.

"Mrs. Eddy," Prophet said, breathing hard, "get the old man inside."

"What's wrong, Mr. Prophet?"

"They're burning us out."

It didn't take long for Prophet to realize that fires in tallgrass prairie don't burn, they rage, and by the time he made it around to the back of the barn, this one was storming in a blizzard of flame toward the farm.

It was burning in the thickest grass. The wind was blowing so that it would drive the flames over them. Then, once on the other side of the farm, the fire would burn out in the sandhills, sparing the town. Yes. It had been set. The two men taking their revenge.

He studied the bright orange glow, choking in the smoky wind, watching in amazement as sheets of flame exploded thirty and forty feet into the air. But the fire was a good two miles off. There was still time. He ran in a hobbling gait for the barn, forgetting the pain and soreness in his body. Samuel had gotten there ahead of him and was hurriedly harnessing Jack.

"Where's the plow?" Prophet yelled.

"Under that tarp!" Samuel pointed to a darkened corner of the barn.

"This animal ever plowed before?" Prophet indicated the shivering horse.

"Just the gardens."

Then the women and children were inside the barn, eyes tearing and coughing in the thickening smoke. Prophet glanced at Pearl. Whatever shock she had felt after the broom attack was gone, and she was moving and giving orders like the fighter she was.

"Get the chickens into the crates and up near the house," she called over the building noise of the fire and the frightened animals and children. "And, Eiko, let's pen the pigs up there as well."

Then Prophet felt someone tugging on his leg, and he looked down into Zacharias's frightened face.

"I'm going with thee!" the boy yelled.

"No, you are not." Prophet knelt and pulled the boy closer. "You stick with your mother." He lowered his voice as if confiding in the boy. "She can't see, and there's a danger she'll walk into the fire. So you stay with her. Hear?"

The boy nodded. Then he said, "Mr. Prophet, thou wilt not die like my father, wilt thou?"

"No."

When they drove Jack to the back side of the barn, Prophet stopped and stood staring, unable to speak.

"What's wrong?" Samuel yelled.

"Fast!"

"Horse can't outrun them."

The flames had eaten up half a mile of grass in the time they had been inside the barn, and he figured that at best there was no more than fifteen or twenty minutes before it was on them. It looked like the fury of hell.

"Damn!" he muttered, climbing the corral fence and tying a wet blanket around Jack's head. The old horse fought him until Samuel clamped his nostrils down hard with his fingers.

The man nodded at him.

The boy nodded back, keeping his hand on Jack's nose and watching Prophet's face. He didn't like blindfolding the animal, but it was the only way to make certain he wouldn't panic and bolt into the flames. The only problem was that if he went down, the horse was lost. But there was no other way.

"I'll plow," Prophet said, grasping the handles and the reins. "You get water up on the barn and wet the roof down good. Then leave the barn and do the same with the house. Stay with the house to keep sparks off it. When I'm done plowing, I'll do the same with the barn."

"I'll stay with you," Samuel hollered.

"No. The house," Prophet insisted. The barn, he knew, would take the brunt of the firestorm, and Prophet didn't want the boy anywhere near it when the flames hit. But he didn't say this. "The house. Your mother and the others will be in it. Make certain the door and windows are shut, that they have water inside and wet blankets over every opening. Then get on top and beat out sparks. I'll join if I can."

Samuel started to say something else to the man, but Prophet cut him off. "Get going."

He turned and watched the flames fanned by new wind and roaring across the grassland, the air of the barnyard filling fast with drifting smoke, so thick that everything seemed to be disappearing in it. Not much time. He yelled at Jack and headed toward the tall-grasses, urging the nervous horse on with rocks and slaps from the reins. Then the wild animals came.

There seemed to be a living wall of them pouring through the grass, some on fire, all fleeing in mad desperation ahead of the flames. Coyotes and foxes were first, hunting along the front line of panic; then came deer, turkeys, and prairie chickens. These were followed by the rodents and the reptiles. Even insects came, the night sky filling with lacewings, digger bees, and midges; heavy-bodied grasshoppers zoomed low through the smoky air, crashing into the walls of the barn and house.

Soon the yard was crowded with thousands of creatures huddled in mixed groups, instinctively sensing that the clearing was their only chance to survive. Prophet and Jack were covered with frantically clinging robber flies, bees, and butterflies, the horse twitching his skin and swishing his tail but not able to dislodge the frightened insects.

But the birds were the worst. They came flying into the place in frantic waves and landed on the fences and the buildings until there was no more room, then covered the ground. They had been forced to abandon their young in the burning grasses, and their shrill cries were rending the air and making it hard to hear. Prophet cupped his mouth and yelled at Jack, driving the horse into the towering brush toward the on-rushing flames.

He plowed fifteen furrows in front of the barn at one hundred yards out, then whipped Jack hard to the north end of the gardens and started to do the same, in a desperate attempt to create a second firebreak. He had completed one two-hundred-yard run. Then he realized it was over. He stopped and turned and faced the oncoming holocaust of fire, stunned by its force.

Over a mile wide, the orange storm was still some five hundred yards from the barn, but when he faced it, he could feel the burning on his skin. He was having a hard time breathing in the smoke and heat, and he tied a handkerchief over his nose and mouth, then unhooked the plow and jumped up on Jack and kicked hard for the yard.

He checked the outer sheds to make certain all the animals had been turned loose; then he led the shying horse to the porch, where the women and children had huddled to watch the final assault of fire. Samuel and Fumiko were on the roof, their faces covered with wet cloths, their clothes wisely soaked. Hot showers of ash and sparks were beginning to drift down, starting small fires in the short-stemmed red clover that covered the yard. Zacharias ran across the porch and knelt and looked Prophet in the face.

"Are we going to burn up?"

"No," Prophet said, with more confidence than he felt. He had seen fires before, but never one like this, never one with this speed or intensity, a huge black cloud billowing out of the flames, drifting thickly across the land, obscuring the barn and other buildings in a dark and stinging fog.

"Can I help?" Zacharias asked.

The boy looked badly shaken.

"Yes. Get your mother and the others inside," Prophet said, stamping out a fire in the shortgrass near the steps. The wild creatures moved slowly away from him as he walked among them, seemingly afraid of nothing but the roaring inferno.

"The children?" Pearl called.

"Take the smaller ones in. But I need Samuel and the girl on the roof of the house."

Prophet pulled the harness and blanket off Jack and pointed the horse toward the sandhills and slapped him hard on the rump. Then Prophet turned and started to sprint toward the gardens, the wild animals again parting slowly in front of him. He soon disappeared in the dark haze, unable to see more than fifteen feet in any direction.

Zacharias tugged his mother toward the kitchen. "Thou must go inside," he ordered. Pearl nodded.

In the confusion and smoke-filled darkness, no one noticed Mr. Kishimoto sitting in the deep, smoky shadows of the porch. The old man's eyes were fixed on the Negro as he hurried toward the climbing roses; then Prophet disappeared in the drifting screen of smoke. The old man did not see him change direction and start for the barn.

Eiko caught Zacharias by the shoulder as he tried to slip back outside; then she shut the back door and nailed a wet blanket over the inside to stop the smoke.

"Let me go. I got to help Mr. Prophet. He needs me."

"You help no one," the woman said. "Go sit with other children."

Something he couldn't taste, feel, or hear told Prophet to stop. Whatever it was, it was triggering a nerve somewhere deep inside his brain. While he didn't know the origin of the sensation, he knew it was real. And he knew he was in danger. Physical danger. He just didn't know why. Or what.

Prophet turned and started back toward the house when the barn blew. It blew as surely as if it had been loaded with black powder and a match tossed into it, raining boards and farm implements over the yard, the roof sailing like some great ship of the night into the huge draft of the flames.

The concussion from the explosion hit hard like a board across Prophet's shoulders, knocking and tumbling him forward over the ground. He scrambled to safety behind the well, fighting hard against the sensation that he was passing out. He lay still for a time, his face pressed against the stones, trying to clear his head, the scorching flames searing the air around the edges of the well and illuminating the yard, house, and gardens in a harsh, wavering light.

For a fleeting moment he thought he saw a shadowy shape trotting toward the gardens; then it disappeared in the smoke. It must have been a trick of the mind. The heat was too great. And Samuel and Fumiko were up on the roof and had promised they wouldn't get down. Fortunately they were far enough away that the firestorm of the barn hadn't reached them. Everyone else was inside the house. "Had to be my imagination," he told himself. Five minutes later he tested the air above the well with his hand; then he began to pull back toward the house.

Prophet awoke on the floor of the kitchen, where Pearl and Eiko had carried him. He studied the ceiling and smiled. The boy and girl had saved it. Saved the old house. The room was dark. Prophet thought it must still be night; then he saw the crack of sunlight around the edge of the blanket. He was hurting badly. His face was burning, and he raised a hand, gingerly feeling the blisters and the peeled skin. It hurt like hell. But at least he was alive.

Slowly he pulled himself up, leaning back on his elbows, feeling dizzy and weak. Pearl was sitting at the kitchen table, holding Zacharias in her lap. The black dust had blown in through the cracks around the door and windows, and Pearl and the boy were covered with it, only the skin around their eyes white. The boy was watching him closely, a scared look across his freckled face. Pearl was listening.

"Art thou okay, Mr. Prophet?" Zacharias asked in a worried voice.

"Yes," he said through a throat full of ashes. Zacharias smiled and held the little wooden horse up in one hand.

"How dost thou feel?" Pearl asked.

"Like a baked potato."

"I salved thy face," Pearl said.

"Thanks. Samuel and Fumiko?"

"In the parlor resting."

He nodded, looking around the kitchen again. "They saved it." Then he smiled at her. "They saved it."

"Yes. I have thanked God," she said as if to remind him of the watchful eye of Providence.

They didn't say anything for a time. Then Pearl spoke. "Zacharias, go to the bedroom with thy brothers. Thou hast been up all night."

Zacharias turned and looked at Prophet and grinned again, then made the little wooden horse buck in the air. Prophet laughed at him.

She waited until the boy was gone, then said, "Mr. Prophet, I didn't want to ask Zacharias."

"What's that, Mrs. Eddy?"

"What it looks like, what survived." She paused. "Mrs. Kishimoto could not tell last night in the smoke."

Prophet struggled to his feet and pulled the blanket down off the window. It took him a while before he could say anything. And when he finally could, he didn't want to. He cleared his throat a couple of times.

"Mr. Prophet?"

"Nothing."

She stiffened with the word.

Maybe with another woman Prophet might have lied or softened the truth, but not with Pearl Eddy. "Everything is gone. The barns and sheds. The fences. The well house. The hens." He stopped and studied the black desolation of the yard. "The hogs panicked and stacked up on one another. They're gone." He paused. "Everything, Mrs. Eddy."

"The gardens?" She paused. "The berries?"

He didn't speak for a few moments; he was staring at two thin lines of gray smoke rising like ropes into the still morning air from the charred remains of Matthew Eddy's cross and the sign. When he finally spoke, Prophet said, "It's all gone."

It didn't seem possible. Even the green plants were gone, the blaze so hot that it had melted the iron pump handle near the well into a slumping mass of metal and desiccated every living thing, sucking the moisture from each fiber, before consuming it in flames.

She stood and turned toward the sink. "Coffee, Mr. Prophet?"

"There's nothing outside," he said quietly, not certain she understood the totality of the loss. "Nothing, Mrs. Eddy."

"Yes."

"No," he said, speaking his words carefully in order to make certain she heard him and didn't smooth it over the way she did some things. "Absolutely nothing."

"I heard thee. We will just have to figure some way to start over."

"No," he snapped, frustrated by her stubbornness. "It's over. Don't you understand. Nothing survived."

"Coffee, Mr. Prophet?" she asked again.

He ignored her as well. "You've got to leave. There's nothing here for you."

She didn't say anything, but he sensed that leaving wasn't something she planned on doing. Prophet whirled toward her, ready to tell her again, and again, if necessary; then he stopped and watched a shaft of sunlight pouring through the window, staring at the floating dust motes that looked like galaxies in the light. He knew she wasn't going to listen.

Then he remembered. "Where's the old man?"

She stopped moving and straightened up, holding on to the edge of the sink.

"Gone, Mr. Prophet."

He felt as if he had been sledgehammered.

"What do you mean? Where did he go?"

"Outside somehow."

Prophet didn't move. It hadn't been his imagination. It was the old man he had seen heading for the gardens. He knew why. He just didn't want to tell himself. He stepped closer to the window and studied the devastation again.

"Perhaps he made it to the sandhills," she said. But there was no force to her words.

"No."

"How canst thou know?"

"Because he was an old fool," he snapped.

"Not a fool."

"He looked it to me."

"He just believed in thee so much it made him look foolish."

"Poppycock," he said sharply. "Don't rope me into your crazy ideas. He was a lunatic. That's all."

Pearl didn't say anything more. Nor did Prophet.

He sat and thought about the old man awhile. In a funny way he didn't feel as if he were gone. He had shadowed him so much over the past months that Prophet felt all he had to do was throw open the back door and he would see him sitting cross-legged and scowling at the bottom of the steps. But no, he was gone.

A few minutes later Prophet saw the horse walk by the window and then stop, looking at the rubble of the barn. Old Jack had made it to the sandhills. He whinnied now for his breakfast.

Pearl turned toward the door and smiled. "Jack survived." Prophet sat down hard in the nearby chair, exhausted by the effort to stand, his thoughts on his old comrade. His eyes were staring blankly at Pearl. He watched her take the blanket down from the door, but he was still not focused on what she was doing. He began to feel a nagging somewhere inside him that he didn't like. Something felt wrong. But it hadn't registered in his brain, and he ignored it.

Slowly, churning deep in his gut, the nagging turned into a twinge, its urgency increasing now. Pearl had set the folded blanket aside, opened the door, and was stepping out onto the porch when Prophet finally realized what was bothering him and yelled, "No!"

It was too late. The massasaugas had been driven from their dens by the heat and had sought cover from the barren, smoldering earth and the sun in the shade of the back porch. There was a slithering mass of them, and Pearl was struck three or four times before Prophet yanked her back inside and slammed the door shut.

He stood holding her by her shoulders for a moment, not wanting to move or say anything, holding her still as if he might be able to keep anything bad from happening if she didn't move or speak again. Then she stepped away and began walking toward the hallway that led to her bedroom.

"Please wake Mrs. Kishimoto. I am going to need her assistance." She said the words as if she were about to clean rugs. Prophet watched her.

"Mr. Prophet," she said calmly.

He didn't move.

"Mr. Prophet," she said again.

"Yes."

"It's best to attend these matters quickly."

"Yes."

Something had snapped inside Prophet's head and overpowered his fear of snakes. He was standing on the back porch striking hard at the slithering mounds of rattlers with a garden hoe. Twenty minutes later he had killed the last of them, but still he continued to strike out at the bloody remains of writhing flesh, not in fear, simply to release an anger that threatened to explode inside him. Zacharias had come outside and was standing on a chair, crying and clutching at the little wooden horse.

"Is my mother going to die?" he sobbed.

"No. She's too tough."

"My pa was tough."

"Yes."

"He died," the boy said.

Prophet didn't have an answer for that. He bent and started to push the bloody mounds of flesh off the side of the porch with the back of the hoe.

"My pa died," Zacharias said again.

"Well, your mother isn't going to."

"Promise?"

"Promise."

Zacharias studied his face for a long time, then forced a sad smile through his tears. "Thanks," the boy said, as if convinced that Prophet had control over such things as life and death.

Prophet nodded, squirming inside.

Samuel had been gone a long time. Prophet had sent him to get the doctor, while he searched for Mr. Kishimoto. He couldn't find the tiny man's body anywhere around the debris of the gardens or the sheds or far out on the burn itself, so he had gone back to hunting snakes. Maybe she had been right; maybe he had wandered off into the sandhills or down the river and escaped the fire. He would look for him again when the boy got back.

He was poking with the rake handle under the back steps where he had killed a good-size snake a little while ago, wondering if the doctor would come to help Pearl, when he heard the noise. It was an odd sound, like the breaking of dried bread.

He stopped and listened.

Then he turned toward it and couldn't move again for a while. It looked as if the garden scarecrow had come alive and were walking slowly toward the house. He shut his eyes and just listened to the awful sound, hoping it would go away. When he opened them, Mr. Kishimoto was sitting down hard on the blackened ground, and Prophet was running for him.

For the past hour he had been sitting in the sunlight holding the charred body of the old man in his arms. He knew the little man was still alive beneath the brittle flesh, and he wished he would just die. The lips moved in the horribly seared face, then an arm, and Prophet heard the dry bread breaking again, the charred skin around his elbow snapping open as he moved. But the old man would not stop struggling.

"Stay still," Prophet said. "You won." Prophet paused. "Those men—they couldn't beat you. The fire couldn't. You won." Prophet blinked his eyes a couple of times to clear them, then bit down on his tongue to keep from crying out.

"When I said you couldn't come with me, that I had places to go where you couldn't—" He stopped and bit his tongue again until he could go on. "That was a joke. You can come. I'd like that. Anywhere I go." He paused. "You can teach me a few tricks. Maybe be my trainer. All you got to do is give me a little room when I walk. That's all."

Eiko and Fumiko tried to take the old man from

him, but Prophet shook his head hard and held him closer. He was dying because he had wanted to be with him, and Prophet wasn't going to let him go now, not before he was gone.

The women squatted in the dirt and mouthed prayers. Then Eiko stood and put her fingers over her mouth and stared at the old man for a long time. He could tell she wanted to say something, farewell, he guessed, but she didn't. She just looked at him. Then, she said, "It not matter. Remember?" She was crying softly. "He is samurai. He already dead." Then she turned and trotted back to the house and Pearl.

"Why?" Prophet moaned, whispering the word into the old man's ear. "Why?" Then he saw the tiny lips moving again, struggling to say something. He leaned close.

"*Tomodachi*," was all the little man said. "Friend."

They buried him that evening in the sand of the gully, in a place covered by calico aster and faced toward the river. Prophet figured he would have liked it: buried where he had fought his last battle.

Samuel and Fumiko offered to help dig the grave, but Prophet wouldn't let them. The two teenagers stood by the body for a while; then Samuel remembered something and reached into his pocket and pulled out a small yellow envelope.

"The telegraph operator, Peter Hermes, said this was for you," Samuel said, handing him the envelope.

Prophet looked at it a moment, then stuffed it into his shirt pocket, figuring it was some fight promoter in these parts who had heard he was living out at the Eddy place. He was done fighting.

Prophet waited until everyone had said good-bye to the old man and gone back to the house; then he dug the grave. He shoveled it deep, talking quietly to the still form as he worked. He talked about things he thought the little man would want to hear. The prairie night was chilly. Prophet shivered. The surrounding silence, the immense quiet of this vast, flat grass world, bothered him for a moment. He wondered if he had been right to choose this lonely place to bury the old man. Then he realized that in the time he had known him, the little Japanese had not spoken more than a dozen sentences to anyone. He listened to the soft sound of the night breeze moving across this empty land and smiled. It was the right place for Shincho Kishimoto.

He stayed at the grave until the moon was rising. Then he reached and put a hand on the mound of sand and said: *"Tomodachi."*

Prophet had talked to the boys for about an hour. They sat quietly in the living room as he talked about their mother and what they should do for her when she recovered. Like him, none of them could believe that Pearl Eddy might actually die. They also talked about their father, and Prophet promised to build a new cross and grave marker as soon as they got materials. He dodged Zacharias's questions about whether he was going to stay. Samuel seemed to have guessed, but he didn't ask. And Prophet told them nothing. Nor had he told them what he expected was going to happen next.

When he was finished talking with the boys, he went and stood in the corner in the weak shadows of Pearl's bedroom, thinking about all that had come to pass, while Eiko worked over Mrs. Eddy in the bed. Samuel and Fumiko were keeping the children occupied in the kitchen. He moved forward and looked down at her. The beautiful face was white; her lips were blue. He was so used to seeing her with her purposeful gaze, thinking hard about something, lecturing, or moving around like a steam piston, it scared him to see her this way, looking as if she were already dead.

Things had turned out as he had suspected: Nothing good had come of any of it. Pearl Eddy had been wrong: Right causes weren't any different from any other kind. The old man was dead. The farm gone. Her chances were lost. And maybe her life. He sat down hard in a chair, then stood up and paced the room. Eiko was talking quietly to Pearl as if she were awake.

He had seen a fair amount of death, but he had never been close to any of those people. So it hadn't mattered much. It did now. It had mattered with the old man. And it mattered with this woman. He let his eyes drift across the shadows to the bed, realizing that, next to losing Lacy and Tyrone, seeing this tiny woman near death was the hardest blow of his life.

He guessed it was because he had begun to think of Pearl Eddy as if she were his mother. He knew that was crazy. She was white and close to twenty years younger then he was. But she had done things for him, things, he figured, that only a mother would do for a son. Believed in him when nobody else did. Fought for him against bad odds. He smiled. Even made him behave. Prophet had never had any of that before in this life—before this woman—and it meant more to him than anything else in the world, except the love of his own children.

He took a deep breath and held it. If she died, the boys would be shipped off to places. He didn't mind her telling him to leave, he just didn't like the thought of her leaving. He felt as if somebody had reached into his chest and grabbed his heart.

He watched Eiko mopping moisture from Pearl Eddy's face. Nobody was going to help them. They would have to do it all, everything by themselves. Earlier Samuel had brought back snakebite instructions from the doctor, but Trotter hadn't come. He had given the boy two shotguns and shells and told Samuel to give them to him. Prophet knew what that meant.

He had watched people on horseback and in buggies come out all day long to see the burn. They stopped on the road away from the house—as if the place were quarantined—and looked. Just looked. None had come to offer help. He had learned over the years not to expect much more out of people. But Pearl Eddy deserved more. They couldn't save her from the venom. But they could have asked to help. That would have been something. But they were what they were. Nothing would change them. That was the thing she didn't understand: humans. They couldn't be changed. They had been that way since the world began.

He watched Eiko applying something to the bites. From what he knew, nothing much would alter the course of things. Whatever little there was to be done, the Japanese woman seemed convinced she knew. She had read the doctor's instructions, sucking hard on her teeth, and then snorted and crumpled the paper up. Then she had set about trying to save Pearl Eddy her way, mixing bowls of dried things she carried in her little bags.

Watching her working now, he felt something he had never believed possible: He was fond of her. He believed in her. He had never had much truck for Orientals. He did now. The old man and this tough little woman had changed all his feelings. He watched her moving in her quick, no-nonsense way and felt better, remembering how he had enjoyed her silly faces, her corny jokes. Beneath all her teasing there was common sense and intelligence and something of the same will that Mrs. Eddy possessed.

She had cut X's over each of the bites on Pearl's lower legs and sucked on them for more than an hour to get the poison out. Finally she sprinkled the wounds with powder from a small leather bag. After that she had had him split open three of the dead hogs to remove their livers, and these she pressed against the bites to draw more blood and poison. For the past couple of hours she had been carefully binding and unbinding the legs, then raising and lowering them to keep the blood circulating. She looked exhausted. But he knew, knew for certain she would never quit.

The chills and sweats had hit Mrs. Eddy first. Then came the dark, ugly puffing of her small legs as the poison began breaking down her blood system, swelling her legs so greatly that he thought her skin must burst from it. Pearl had remained conscious for a number of hours, and she had talked quietly to the children about things. About their schooling, about their father, about God, and about what they were going to do to get the farm going again. Samuel had glanced at Prophet, and he knew that the boy understood that it was over here, that there was no future for the Eddys in Zella. But he knew she would never believe that, would never believe that the people in the town could abandon her and her boys. It was her one great weakness.

She had talked to her boys through the pain as if their tomorrows were going to be brighter than ever. After Eiko had ushered the children out, she had lectured him about fighting and lying. He had listened without objecting, just happy to be hearing her voice. An hour later she had slipped into delirium. Prophet knew enough about rattlesnake bites to know that she would suffer a great deal, drift in and out of consciousness, go through periods of trying to stand and walk. These lucid moments might last for twenty or thirty minutes at a time, dragging out over days, but all the while the venom would be slowly eating away at her flesh, her veins and arteries. Until she either lived or died.

At one point he asked Eiko if Mrs. Eddy would make it. But the little woman only grunted. "*Hai!* Not difficult. Not difficult." He knew that wasn't the truth. But he also knew that this woman, her family rescued by this little Quaker, wasn't about to consider letting her die.

It seemed to him that death was in the room with them already and this brave Japanese woman was just whistling loudly so she wouldn't be scared. He looked at Pearl's face. She was covered with beads of sweat and talking quietly in her delirium. Yes, death was here somewhere. He could feel it.

The thing was, though a rattlesnake bite rarely killed a full-grown adult, Pearl Eddy wasn't much bigger than a kid. And she had been struck by three large snakes.

He felt he could barely breathe. He stood and walked to the window and looked out at the night. The scorched earth was as black as the vault of moonless sky above, making it impossible to tell where the earth stopped and the firmament began. Prophet shivered with the feeling that the old house was floating through empty darkness, drifting somehow toward hell.

He swallowed hard against the feelings rising in his throat. Eiko left the room to start the evening meal, giving him strict instructions to watch the woman until she returned. He sat down quietly in a chair next to the bed.

Pearl was breathing rapidly. He took a towel and gently wiped the sweat off her face, studying the features. He had never looked at her this carefully before. It was an angelic face. Maybe in some ways she was an angel. He knew she would scoff at that. Still, she possessed some of the magic things that angels have. Mostly she could do good for others. And until now nothing had seemed able to stop her, slow her but not stop her. Not the loss of her businesses, not blindness, not the town. It was strange, he thought, how she could do battle with the best of them . . . and never raise a finger. He tipped forward, clasping the towel tight in his hands, his elbows on his knees, staring blindly at the floor between his shoes.

"Mrs. Eddy," he said, stopping to clear his throat, looking directly at her, "there are some things I want to tell you."

He waited to see if she might respond. She didn't.

"I think you know some of it, but I've got to say it." He waited awhile, then said, "I stole the money and the photograph."

She didn't move.

"'That's the way I been making my living since I haven't been able to fight much like I used to. I steal whenever I can. That's how this mess got started. I tried to steal a man's wallet in the saloon." He paused. "We weren't arguing about church money like I told you." He tipped his face up toward the ceiling for a while; then he looked back down at her. "That was a lie," he mumbled.

"I lie about a lot of things, Mrs. Eddy. Like when I told you that I sewed robes for the monks and clothes for poor people." He hesitated. "Those were all just lies too.

"And I talk big, bragging about how I'm going to get my shot as a fighter. I'm not, Mrs. Eddy. I missed it. Whenever it was, I don't know. But I couldn't fight anybody good now. So now I lie about that too."

He waited a long time before he spoke again, clearing his throat hard so he could get it out. "And that stuff about getting religion in jail and becoming a minister." He stopped and looked off into the shadows as if he would rather be saying anything but this. He knew what it meant to her. "Those were lies too. I've got no religion. Never did."

He jumped when she opened her eyes. Her stare was fixed and remote.

"You awake?"

She didn't answer, but he could tell she was.

"You heard?"

"Thou lied." She sighed against the pain.

He felt the blood rushing to his face, trying to remember the things he had just said.

"Minister," she murmured.

He shook his head. "I'm no minister."

Pearl waited until she had caught her breath and then whispered, "Thou saved Zacharias and Mr. Kishimoto." Her face tightened, and she lay still struggling against the pain for a moment. Then she slowly collected herself. "Thou softened Samuel." She stopped again and lay panting for breath, sweat pouring over her face.

There she was again, believing grand things about him that weren't true. He squirmed. "I'm no minister. I don't belong to any church." He stopped and looked into her eyes. "I've never been inside one. I was never baptized." He studied the boards between his feet again, ashamed about so much of his life.

She lay without moving or speaking for a long time; then she smiled weakly. "Yes."

"No," he said quietly.

Then the bedroom door was opening, and Samuel came in with a worried look, carrying a pitcher of water, studying his mother's face.

"Hello," he said to her softly.

Pearl only smiled.

Samuel stood beside the Negro next to the bed, looking down at her for a long time. He didn't want to leave. "You want me to read that telegram?" he asked Prophet.

Prophet, his eyes still on the woman's face, reached for his shirt pocket. "Sure. It's some local promoter who heard I'm staying out here. But go ahead."

Samuel ran a finger underneath the edge of the envelope. Prophet continued to watch Pearl. She stared up at the ceiling of the bedroom, dealing with her pain. When Samuel didn't start reading, Prophet turned and looked at him. The boy was staring down at the words on the page with a stunned expression on his pale face.

"What is it, boy?"

Pearl swung her gaze so that she was looking at Samuel as well.

"Sam," Prophet said.

The boy held the telegram out to him.

"I can't read."

The boy took the paper back and scanned the words with his eyes as if he couldn't have possibly read it correctly the first time.

"Sam," Prophet said, "read it."

Samuel's voice broke badly when he started the first time and he stopped and cleared his throat and began again. "JEROME PROPHET. REGRET TO INFORM: WIFE JENNY, CHILDREN—LACY AND TYRONE—DIED FIRE KINGSPORT, TENNESSEE, TWELVE YEARS AGO. BURIED

KINGSPORT COLORED CEMETERY. NO REWARD RE-
QUESTED. REVEREND JAMES LEONARD."

Prophet was sitting on the steps of the front porch
staring out at the empty void of blackened earth and
sky, the night silent like he had never heard it. It was
as if everything had disappeared with the children.
Nothing remained. Nothing but the blackened silence
and his thoughts.

Lacy and Tyrone gone. Dead for twelve years. But
to him they had just died this night. Everything that
he had lived for had died this night. All that he had
dreamed—to hold them, to listen to them breathe, to
hear their voices—all gone. They would never speak
to him again, never call to him, never laugh with him,
never touch him, never wrestle or tease or cry. Only he
would cry. Only he would remember and call out to
them. Though they were gone from this earth, gone
from him forever, he knew that he would always track
the shadows of their lives for the rest of his. And never
would he find them.

He sat and thought about the times when they had
been together, plain times that now seemed so wonderful. He tried to remember their faces, their voices,
the feel of their skin. He remembered so little about
them. All he remembered was his love for them.

It was the only time in Jerome Prophet's life that he
had ever thought of killing himself. Everything that
he loved was dead or dying. His children, the old
man . . . Pearl Eddy. It seemed suddenly right for him
to die as well.

Three hours later he was still sitting on the steps
thinking about this and watching them. The flames of
the lamps looked like the lighted windows of a slow-
moving night train coming down the darkened road.
He had been staring at the procession for a long time

before he finally stood and went back into the house and Pearl Eddy's bedroom.

He walked over and stood looking down at her, not wanting to wake her, but knowing he had to. When his shadow fell across her face, she opened her eyes and stared up at him, and he could see her fighting the awful burning pain that was inching through her body, destroying the tissues of her legs.

"Mrs. Eddy, they're coming again."

"Thy children," was all she said.

He nodded, understanding. Then he repeated, "They're coming." He was holding the shotgun.

"They want me," he said.

She stared in the direction of his face for a long time. He could tell she was struggling to say something. He knelt by the side of the bed and leaned close to her.

"Leave." She winced at the pain. "I've been wrong. My stubbornness." She gasped for air. "But not violence."

He gazed down into her eyes for a long time, as if trying to see things in them, then said, "I'm sorry, Mrs. Eddy."

They were wearing Indian outfits and sitting on their horses in front of the house, their heads covered by painted masks. He guessed the masks were to hide their identity. But it wasn't hard to make out Simon James sitting on a big yellow gelding, his daughter behind him. There were maybe twenty of them. Most carried lanterns, the light casting an ominous wavering glow over the house.

Prophet was on the top step of the porch, breathing in the cool air and remembering things about the children, small things that didn't add up to much. Wondering if they were buried side by side, whether their graves were marked. Then his mouth began to twitch. He didn't try to hide it.

He watched a nighthawk flit across the moon and wished for a moment he could fly. But it didn't matter. There was nowhere he wanted to fly. Not in this world anyhow. The children were gone; Mrs. Eddy looked as if she were going. Everything that mattered was disappearing. He had no place and no one he belonged to, and that, he thought, was worse than being dead. So he might as well be.

For all her goodness, Mrs. Eddy couldn't make things around her good. He guessed that was what bothered him the most. Somewhere in his heart he had wanted to believe her. But this world wasn't good. She just saw it that way. But that didn't change anything. The world just remained full of hate and hurt and not much else but dying. And he was ready for that now.

Staring at the riders, at their masked faces, their ropes and guns, he was glad Pearl Eddy couldn't see them. People weren't good and holy things the way she wanted to believe. They never had been. They never would be. Not in ten thousand years. She was wrong about more than just violence. She was wrong about everything.

The sound of Zacharias crying in the house brought his thoughts back to the riders and what he faced. Eiko was keeping the children shut in one room with Pearl, away from the windows, keeping them there no matter what. She had promised him she would do it. The only time she was to let them out was if they fired the house. After she had agreed, the woman had pantomimed like a strongman one last time. But neither of them had laughed. He had shaken Samuel's hand. Whatever had been wrong between them seemed to be gone now. The boy had done a lot of growing. Prophet guessed he had as well. Samuel was wearing his new shoes, and that made Prophet feel good. Finally, he had held Zach until he had to go, telling him he was going out to fight a tiger, that Hercules and his pa were together. The boy had just watched him, clutching the wooden horse, watched him until he reached the back door. Then he said, "Don't go, Mr. Prophet."

But he had gone, and now he was wondering if what he had said about Hercules and Matthew Eddy was true: that they were together. And if it was, whether on this night he would be with Lacy and Tyrone again. He hoped so, but he didn't believe it. He didn't think things were any better after you died. Just more of the same probably.

He could still hear the muffled sounds of Zacharias's crying somewhere inside the house. He wished the woman would make him quit. It was harder when he couldn't concentrate.

He stood watching them and thinking about these things. Thinking that while she was wrong about things, she had still somehow made his death something valuable. He was going to kill Simon and Penny James and as many others as he could before they killed him, hoping that would take the fight out of the rest of them and they would leave Mrs. Eddy and the others alone.

"You the Negro they call the Prophet?" Simon James said.

He took a step down the stairs.

"The one that steals?"

Prophet took another step and watched one of the men take a long drink from a bottle, screwing up his courage to the sticking point with whiskey.

"The one intimate with the white woman Pearl Eddy?"

Prophet cocked the shotgun.

"Put it down," Simon James said in a soft voice. Chrissy was holding on to her father's middle with her thin arms and peering around at him.

"You the Prophet?" he asked again.

Prophet didn't respond.

"We've come to talk to you. No call for the gun."

Prophet stepped down on the ground, wanting to be as close as possible when he started it.

Simon watched him.

"The old man is dead. You burned him to death," Prophet said. "The house just has women and children in it."

Nobody moved or said anything.

"We don't want anybody in that house. We just want to talk to you." Simon swung a heavy leg and crooked it around his saddlehorn, so that he looked almost friendly. "Hell, I got a lot of men with guns here. You gonna kill them all?"

Prophet shook his head and took another step.

"Good." Simon smiled.

"Just you and one or two others."

The man was uncrooking his leg when Prophet heard the door open behind him, and he glanced quickly over his shoulder at Samuel coming down the stairs, carrying the second gun.

"Get back inside!" Prophet snapped.

The boy didn't respond. Prophet glanced quickly at the side of his face. "Get inside, Sam!"

Samuel didn't move.

Prophet turned back to Simon. "He isn't in this. Let me take him inside, and I'll come out without the shotgun."

"He's in it now."

"He's just a boy."

"Looks like a man with that scattergun. Anyhow,

you two aren't going to shoot." He paused. "There's no call for shooting."

Samuel cocked the hammer on the gun, the noise loud in the night air. Simon stopped talking.

"Sam," Prophet said.

"No," was all the boy said.

"You aren't going to shoot," Simon said again. And Prophet wondered whom he was trying to convince.

Prophet figured things had deteriorated to a dangerous stalemate when suddenly Eiko and Fumiko came out of the house holding a very sick-looking Pearl Eddy between them.

"Hell, we got the whole clan here, boys. You don't look so good, Mrs. Eddy," Simon said with a chortle.

"I told you to stay inside!" Prophet yelled.

"She make me break my promise," Eiko said. "You know how she get."

"Fine. So she broke your promise. Now get her back in the house."

But Pearl mumbled something, and they half carried her down the stairs. She looked near death, gray and wet with sweat, her eyes unfocused.

"Samuel?" she called as if he might be lost in the darkness.

He jumped. "Yes, Mother?"

She didn't say anything more, just sagged against Eiko.

Samuel shifted uncomfortably. "Thou told me that I would have to decide those things I believed," he said, not looking at her. "I've decided. They aren't burning anything else of ours. And they aren't taking Mr. Prophet."

"Mrs. Eddy," Prophet said, "you need to take your boy and the others and go back inside."

Pearl continued to stare in her fixed way. Eiko said something to Fumiko, and the girl darted back into the house, and returned with a chair for Pearl. Then Eiko was busy wrapping and unwrapping the bandages again. Simon and the others were growing restless.

"All we want is to talk, Prophet." Simon tried again. "There's no reason to involve women and children."

Eiko rattled a sentence off in heated Japanese.

"Stay out of this, Chinawoman," Simon warned. He looked back at Prophet. "I'd have thought you'd have avoided that."

Prophet knew this couldn't go on much longer. Some of these men were going to pull back into the shadows and drop him and the boy with rifles. They would probably finish Eiko as well. And maybe Mrs. Eddy.

"I'll make you a deal," he said. "You leave these people alone. I'll go with you."

Pearl said it first. "No."

Then Mrs. Kishimoto, Samuel, and Fumiko repeated it.

Prophet was just starting to respond when Pearl passed out, slumped in the seat and then sliding to the ground, looking to all the world as if she were finally dead.

"Is it a deal?" he hollered at Simon.

"Deal."

"No," Samuel repeated. "I'm not putting this gun down."

"Sam, I've never told you to do anything. I am now." He paused. "You take your mother and the women and get inside."

"No."

"Sam. Listen to me. They're going to put men with rifles out there in the dark. And they're going to kill me. You. Your mother. And the Kishimotos." He paused. "Is that what you want? Zach and Josh and Luke and the rest of the children walking out and seeing that? They'll have nobody. Sam. You've got to go in. You've got to take your mother in. For her sake. For your brothers."

"Smart, Mr. Prophet," Simon said.

"Shut up!" Prophet yelled.

Samuel didn't move.

"Sam."

The boy looked at his face for a long time; then he bent and laid the gun down on the ground. He was crying.

"Mr. Prophet," he said in a quiet voice.

"Yes?"

"I love thee."

Prophet felt as if he'd been kicked in the back by a horse, trying hard to get air but not getting any. He thought of Lacy and Tyrone. He cleared his throat hard. "Love you. Your mother and brothers too." He hesitated. "You tell them."

"Yes."

When Prophet fought his way out of his thoughts, Samuel, Fumiko, and Pearl were gone. But Eiko was still there beside him. "Get," Prophet said to her.

She shook her head. "They no scare me."

Prophet glanced at the little woman's determined face. He was certain they didn't. "Just go inside."

"I stay. You strongman," she said, making a small, tight smile.

Then four of the men were around them, one giving Prophet a hard lick to his head with a blackjack. He was badly dazed, but he was used to being dazed, and he stayed on his feet while they yanked the shotgun from him. Then Penny had a small gun pressed against his ribs. The others grabbed hold of Eiko.

"Let her go!" Prophet hollered. "We had a deal."

"Not where she's concerned," Simon snapped.

Prophet was calculating whether he could get a fist into Penny James and the pistol away and into

Simon's face fast enough when someone stepped out of the night and into the lantern light.

"What the hell are you doing here?" Simon barked. "You had your chance."

Prophet was as surprised as he had been that night on the river road when he had watched Hank Meyers staring after the buggy in his shocked way. Then he had figured the man's sudden conversion had simply been for convenience to save his hide. But that wasn't the case this night. Here he was unarmed and standing like a dumbstruck fool between Prophet and Eiko and a hanging.

"What the hell are you doing?" Simon bellowed again.

The man didn't seem able to answer for a moment. Then he said, "I'm a friend of Mrs. Eddy's."

Simon didn't wait for any explanations. "Then you can hang for her!"

Prophet couldn't figure it. He just stared into Hank Meyers's eyes as they grabbed him and tied his hands behind him. He didn't resist. As if just being here, silently standing up for the woman were enough. It made no sense. The man was staring at Prophet the way he had that night on the road when Pearl Eddy had set him free and told him to repay God. There was no figuring it. The man was a fool.

As he was thinking this, Prophet heard two new sounds. One he had half expected. The other surprised him like nothing else in his life. The first was the sound of Pearl Eddy stumbling once again out the front door and back down the stairs, supported by Samuel. Fumiko grabbed Zacharias and pulled him back inside and shut the door.

"Damn it!" he yelled, but they kept coming, hobbling off to the right, then she sat down hard on the ground, falling back weakly into Samuel's arms. Prophet looked at her. She was a fighter. And on this night, in this hopeless situation, when nobody involved on the Eddy side expected anything but to be lynched, her boy looked like one too.

Prophet was concentrating on the second sound now. At first he had thought it was another of Simon's riders, but then he saw the man dismount and start toward them through the shadows of the yard. He was tall and lean and disheveled-looking.

Simon turned and looked at him, surprised as well.

"Evening, Mr. Johnson," Simon said. "Come to join the Redmen?"

Johnson stopped and felt Pearl's pulse, then stood and looked at Prophet and the woman and the men holding them.

"What are you doing?" he asked, directing the question to Simon.

"What you should have done, Mr. County Attorney. Running these people out of town. That nigger robbed me and assaulted my boys. That woman is a whore and seller of opium. The other one is just a bum."

Edward Johnson adjusted his glasses on his nose. "No, you're not. You're not going to run these people out of town. You're going to shoot them, then dump them someplace where nobody will find them." The man was shaking with anger. "Let's be honest. That's what you're going to do. And that's murder."

Simon just sat on his horse. Chrissy was making funny sounds and reaching a hand out toward Pearl's still form.

"Well, you're not going to!"

Prophet couldn't believe it. Never would believe it. Not if he lived to be a hundred. A white country attorney, up for election, facing off a crowd over a Negro, a misfit, and an Oriental.

But it was over. The same man who had given

Prophet the whack gave Edward a shot just behind his ear, dropping him like a sack of oats. Whatever small glimmer of hope had been ignited inside Prophet went out with that blow, as Penny James and the others shoved him and the woman toward the horses.

Then out of the prairie darkness, coming from the direction of the road, Prophet heard a team and a carriage and a loud voice. "Jessssussspriest, Rose! Can't you make these damn horses behave?"

Followed by the haughty voice of the woman who had tried to get him put in jail for stealing her pillbox: "Judge Wilkins, if you don't care for the way I drive, you can just walk."

"I'll consider it next time, Rose."

Soon the old man was cursing at the horses and trudging across the yard in his raccoon coat, muttering and looking greatly agitated and ready to fight. He stopped and looked down at Edward Johnson, who had just managed to sit up and was trying to get his broken glasses back on his nose.

Slowly the old man turned and looked around at everyone. At the horsemen. At Prophet and the woman and the men holding them. At Pearl. Then back at Edward, who sat trying to clear his head.

"Who hit Mr. Johnson?" he barked in the stillness. "Who was it?"

The men began to look uncomfortable.

"Get up, Edward. You look silly sitting down there. Try to remember that you are an officer of my court. Act like it." Then he turned on the men again. "Who hit Mr. Johnson?"

Nobody answered.

Back in the darker shadows Prophet could see a crowd forming. Spectators come to see a hanging, he figured. They were on horses, in buggies and on

foot, standing silent as the breeze blowing in off the
sandhills.

The judge had moved on and stood looking down at
Pearl. He shook his head. She was awake and staring
up blindly at the old man.

"Lassie, you look a mess."

She smiled weakly at him.

"Judge, you and Mr. Johnson ought to take care of
Mrs. Eddy. She's been snakebit." Simon paused.
"We'll just take these folks and drop them off—
outside the town limits."

"When I want your advice, Simon James, I'll ask for
it," the judge snapped.

Prophet started to take a step backward, figuring
things had changed now and he would make a fight
for it, when Penny jammed a pistol hard into his side.
No chance.

"Penny James," Rose called, waving her heavy hand
in the air, "you leave that man alone. He designs
dresses for me, and if you harm him in any way, I'll
have you up on charges, young man." Mother Sherman was walking in her huffy way toward them,
dressed in her evening finest, her grandson, Ernie, beside her. She stopped and looked down at Pearl,
smiled, and said, "I'll be back in a moment, dear,"
then went on.

Prophet's head was swimming, his blood pounding
in his ears like hammers against stone. None of it
made sense. None of it fit inside his brain right. The
crowd on the road was growing larger, and it was
beginning to look like a religious revival of sorts,
people just drifting out of the darkness toward the
house as if they had just been touched by the Lord.
Maybe they had. He saw the two old barbers and a
homely-looking girl in a red dress. There were men
and women of all ages, some who looked too weak to

do much resisting of anything, but they came all the same. Prophet shook his head. He would never have believed it.

"Let's go," Penny hissed to him, cocking the pistol.

From the line of horsemen Prophet heard a shout: "Gawddamn it, grab her!" He looked up to see Chrissy James scurrying across the ground toward Pearl, with Hector and Mike James in pursuit. They didn't reach her before she had crawled onto Pearl, patting the woman's face and crying in a funny, pleading way.

"Bring her back here," Simon shouted.

Hector turned and looked at his father. "No, Pa."

Mike James stood by his little brother, nodding in agreement.

"Get going or I'll shoot this bitch!" Penny hissed, putting the gun into Eiko's back.

"Let her go and I'll go."

"No," Eiko said, rattling off something in Japanese that sounded right for the situation.

"Everything will be all right now," Prophet said.

"No," Eiko repeated.

Penny released her and was shoving Prophet forward when Rose Sherman suddenly appeared before them.

"Penny James, did you hear me? This man works for me," she said in her best high-pitched voice, as if even talking to Penny were something she found distasteful.

Prophet felt the man shift nervously and waited for the blast. He figured Penny wanted him badly enough to do it.

"He works for me too," Judge Wilkins barked. He had taken a place next to Rose, standing between Penny and Prophet and the horsemen. "The woman," he said, indicating Eiko, "does as well." The old man was squinting hard at Penny's face. "Aren't you on parole in Mason County for assault, young man?"

Rose cleared her throat. "Judge," she interrupted, in her haughty way, "the woman works for me on Mondays and Fridays. She can work for you any other day."

"Fine, Rose. But that's hardly the point," the old man said, continuing to stare at Penny James.

Slowly the man released his grip on Prophet and put the pistol away. The judge and Rose were squabbling again, but Prophet wasn't hearing them anymore. He just saw men turning their horses away and leaving Simon James sitting there alone. Then he saw the sheriff and his deputies grab Simon and Penny off their horses. Rose was debating who got Eiko on the weekends now. And the tall attorney was standing and looking at his broken glasses, a dazed expression on his face. Alfred Snipes stepped up alongside him.

"Don't start talking foreclosure, Snipes," Johnson warned, softly rubbing the side of his skull.

The little man grinned. "No need. Woman's lucky she has me as a banker. Too lucky for words."

Johnson looked at him and tried to focus his eyes. "Why?"

Snipes gazed around at the burned-out yard. "This fire."

"You got a strange idea of luck."

"Nope. Not at all. Before I loaned her late husband money for that equipment, I made him take out a policy against fire." Snipes puffed his chest out. "So I wouldn't be stuck with a bunch of worthless land. Damn lucky I did. For me and her." Snipes was beaming now.

Johnson shook his head to clear it. "How much insurance?"

Snipes was staring admiringly at the blackened

farm, as if it were some masterpiece that he had somehow created.

"How much?" Johnson repeated.

The little man looked back at the attorney. "Well, I guess since you're the Eddys' lawyer. Twelve hundred dollars. Subtracting what she still owes on the equipment leaves nine hundred fifty dollars. Tidy little sum."

Eiko was standing next to the banker listening wide-eyed. Suddenly she grabbed him by his thin shoulders and planted an enormous kiss on his cheek. From the shocked look on his little ratlike face, it could well have been his first.

"You *rikō na* man. Smart man." She was jabbing her finger convincingly into the side of her head and squinting hard at Snipes's blushing face. "I like that. I like smart man."

Snipes pulled himself up a little straighter and said, "I try to calculate risk and avoid it. Keeps the bank out of trouble. That's my job—"

Eiko was listening attentively. "*Rikō na* man. You married man?"

Snipes blushed. "I'm not. Been too busy protecting the bank's interests," he said, looking suddenly very important. He took a closer look at Eiko. "My name is—"

"Alfred Snipes," Eiko said, finishing the sentence for him.

Snipes was surprised and flattered. "And your name, ma'am?"

"Eiko Kishimoto. I'm not married either."

"There was a time last year when a couple of speculators—" Eiko nodded enthusiastically and stepped closer to hear the man's story. Johnson turned and walked off to tell Pearl the good news.

William Smith and Hank Fegan, the barbers, worked their way through the crowd until they were standing and looking down into Pearl's face. "Mrs. Eddy," William said, studying her features.

"She ain't awake, Will," Hank said.

"Yes," she whispered.

"We just wanted to say that fire don't kill asparagus. You'll have a new crop finer than ever. And Hank and me want to put our order in early."

"Deal," she smiled weakly.

Prophet stood off by himself, trying to collect his thoughts. Wondering how he could have lived so long and been so wrong about something like this, something so important. It didn't matter. It had happened. He had been wrong; Pearl Eddy had been right. And this realization made him feel better about things. He knew he wouldn't kill himself. He just had to figure out what he was going to do next. Mrs. Eddy didn't want him here, and he didn't blame her.

People were crowding in around her, and he figured this was a good time for him to get going. He didn't know where. Just somewhere. He saw Zacharias on Samuel's shoulders. They both were laughing. He would leave them that way. It looked nice. It was a good way to remember them.

When he finally got his legs to move again, he made his way through the crowd and stood staring down at her. She looked bad, but something told him she would pull through. Eiko was working on the bandages now, Alfred Snipes standing and watching her. Some other women had covered Pearl with a shawl. Then her eyes opened.

"You okay, ma'am?"

"Mr. Prophet," she murmured at the sound of his voice.

"I figured I'd be on my way." He paused. "Just wanted to say good-bye."

"Mr. Prophet," she repeated quietly.

"Yes, ma'am."

"I'm not pleased about those guns."

"Yes, ma'am."

She waited a moment, then said, "If thou art staying, we shall have to have a talk."

Prophet had the feeling that Lacy and Tyrone were floating above the yard, looking down on him. Smiling. He looked back down at the little woman.

"Yes, Mrs. Eddy."

THE DAWN OF FURY
BY RALPH COMPTON

Nathan Stone had experienced the horror of Civil War battlefields. But the worst lay ahead. When he returned to Virginia, to the ruins of what had been his home, his father had been butchered and his mother and sister stripped, ravished, and slain. The seven renegades who had done it had ridden away into the West. Half-starved and afoot, Nathan Stone took their trail. Nathan Stone's deadly oath—blood for blood—would cost him seven long years, as he rode the lawless trails of an untamed frontier. His skill with a Colt would match him equally with the likes of the James and Youngers, Wild Bill Hickok, John Wesley Hardin, and Ben Thompson. Nathan Stone became the greatest gunfighter of them all, shooting his way along the most relentless vengeance trail a man ever rode to the savage end ... and this is how it all began.

from SIGNET

Prices slightly higher in Canada.   (0-451-18631-1—$5.99)